The boar's eyes burst as horror pushed through its pupils

The thumb-thick worms in its eye sockets waved like feelers and stiffened like pointers at Doc. The boar's head swiveled in response, its tusks rasping against each other as its mouth fell open and its tongue lolled out, accompanied by an orgy of wiggling filth.

"By my stars and garters!" Doc exclaimed.

Ryan fired three 9 mm rounds through the dead boar's head. Its skull broke apart, spewing broken lengths of black worm. The porcine behemoth staggered, but didn't fall. Fresh worms waved forth from the shattered head and snout as if tasting the air. The corpse tottered toward the humans.

The entire fifty-strong herd of giant, newly dead mutie wild boars began to roll over and rise up

"Fireblas

D0881997

**Other titles in the
Deathlands saga:**

JAMES AXLER

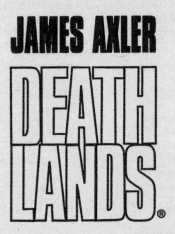

DEATH LANDS®

Hell Road Warriors

A GOLD EAGLE BOOK FROM

WORLDWIDE®

TORONTO • NEW YORK • LONDON
AMSTERDAM • PARIS • SYDNEY • HAMBURG
STOCKHOLM • ATHENS • TOKYO • MILAN
MADRID • WARSAW • BUDAPEST • AUCKLAND

HUDSON BRANCH

Recycling programs
for this product may
not exist in your area.

First edition March 2012

ISBN-13: 978-0-373-62613-7

HELL ROAD WARRIORS

The capacity for hope is the most significant fact of life. It provides human beings with a sense of destination and the energy to get started.

—Norman Cousins
1915–1990

THE DEATHLANDS SAGA

This world is their legacy, a world born in the violent nuclear spasm of 2001 that was the bitter outcome of a struggle for global dominance.

There is no real escape from this shockscape where life always hangs in the balance, vulnerable to newly demonic nature, barbarism, lawlessness.

But they are the warrior survivalists, and they endure—in the way of the lion, the hawk and the tiger, true to nature's heart despite its ruination.

Ryan Cawdor: The privileged son of an East Coast baron. Acquainted with betrayal from a tender age, he is a master of the hard realities.

Krysty Wroth: Harmony ville's own Titian-haired beauty, a woman with the strength of tempered steel. Her premonitions and Gaia powers have been fostered by her Mother Sonja.

J. B. Dix, the Armorer: Weapons master and Ryan's close ally, he, too, honed his skills traversing the Deathlands with the legendary Trader.

Doctor Theophilus Tanner: Torn from his family and a gentler life in 1896, Doc has been thrown into a future he couldn't have imagined.

Dr. Mildred Wyeth: Her father was killed by the Ku Klux Klan, but her fate is not much lighter. Restored from predark cryogenic suspension, she brings twentieth-century healing skills to a nightmare.

Jak Lauren: A true child of the wastelands, reared on adversity, loss and danger, the albino teenager is a fierce fighter and loyal friend.

Dean Cawdor: Ryan's young son by Sharona accepts the only world he knows, and yet he is the seedling bearing the promise of tomorrow.

In a world where all was lost, they are humanity's last hope....

Chapter One

Ryan shouldered his Steyr SSG-70 longblaster and put his hand on the lever to open the mat-trans chamber. His companions had cleaned themselves up from the jump, and everyone was geared up and ready to go except Doc, who was coming down from his postjump shudders. The one-eyed man waited while Doc pulled himself together. The walls of the mat-trans chamber were an amber color densely veined with black. Ryan had never seen one colored like that and it made him uneasy. He didn't know where they were, but it had to be better than the swamps, and Haven. "Ready, Doc?"

Doc took the hand off the wall he was using to steady himself. He drew his huge Civil War-replica model LeMat revolver and set the hammer to fire the shotgun barrel. "Bright-eyed and bushy-tailed!"

Doc looked like a stiff breeze would knock him over. His mind and body were damaged by being torn through time from the nineteenth century and into the twentieth century by the whitecoats of Operation Chronos. Proving to be a difficult subject, after a period of time they shot him via mat-trans into the future that was the Deathlands. Having his matter transferred from point A to point B never did him any favors.

Being discombobulated was something no one ever got used to, but looking around, Jak, J.B. and Mildred were postregurgitation and ready to go. Ryan's eye came to rest on the love of his life. Krysty raised one eyebrow. "Lover, if you don't pull that lever soon I'm going to pull yours."

A grin ghosted across Ryan's face. "Okay, everyone. Triple red." His companions spread out and leveled their weapons at the door as he pulled the lever. The door hissed open. Ryan's eye narrowed. The lights were on, and he could hear the hum of a generator. One glance told him this redoubt was unusual. Most were built to a pattern. The architecture here was all wrong. Ryan looked back at the mat-trans and then into the odd little redoubt. His instincts told him the mat-trans they had just stepped out of had been a last-minute addition. The party moved into a long, low room filled with workstations.

Mildred put her fists on her hips and stared around herself indignantly. "Okay, have we traveled back in time or something?"

Jak shook his head warily. "Hope not."

Doc's voice was very quiet. "I dearly hope so."

"What are you talking about, Mildred?" Ryan asked.

"Look at this place!" Mildred threw up her hands. "I mean, look at it!"

Ryan looked at it. The ceiling was low and supported by squat pillars. Everything seemed wrong. The floor was an odd checkerboard of green and white. "And?"

Mildred sighed. "You see the floors? That's linoleum. Have you checked the puke-green walls? The workstations are top-notch, but check the watercooler and the other stuff."

Mildred had been cryogenically frozen over a century earlier and, like Doc, was an unwilling citizen of the postapocalyptic Deathlands. Ryan knew she was on to something. "What about them?"

"This place? It's kitsch."

Ryan, Krysty, J.B., Jak and Doc stared at Mildred blankly. When she went predark in her speech, no one knew what she was talking about. Mildred gazed heavenward for strength. "It's totally retro." Mildred was rewarded with more tolerant looks. She plowed on anyway. "I'm saying this place was built in the 1960s. During the cold war. It's some kind of bomb shelter, and it's like it got refurbished fast and dirty at the last second."

Ryan nodded. He'd read old books about the cold war in his youth. Having a library of books was just one perk of being the son of an East Coast baron when he was growing up. Mildred was confirming his suspicions.

"Reactivated," he said. "Probably added that mat-trans at the last minute."

Jak shrugged. None of that meant much to the young man from the bayous of Louisiana. He had more immediate questions. "Where?"

Everyone turned at the sound of Doc tapping his cane on the wall. He tapped a painted flag over the door to the mat-trans chamber. It had two red stripes, one on each side and a white center. A stylized red maple leaf dominated the middle. A second smaller flag was painted beneath it. Ryan recognized the Union Jack in one corner of the flag and some shield off to the side.

Doc cocked his head. "I am confused."

That was news to nobody.

Mildred shook her head. "We're in the Great White North."

"A Mari Usque Ad Mare." Everyone stared at Doc. When it came down to being predark obscure, he had Mildred beat hands down. Doc sighed in defeat and translated from the Latin. "From Sea to Sea."

"So where are we?" Ryan asked.

"Canada," Doc concluded.

Ryan grimaced. He had been north of the Deathlands a few times, usually against his will and mostly in what had once been Alaska or Siberia. What little he knew about Canada was that it was vast and bastard cold.

"Where?" Jak repeated.

Doc tapped the smaller flag painted beneath the maple leaf. "That is what confuses me. At first glance the flag below is the Canadian Red Ensign, but upon consideration I believe the coat of arms is incorrect."

"It's the flag of Ontario," Mildred said. This garnered her more uncomprehending stares. The physician shrugged. "I dated a radiologist from Toronto once."

Ryan and his friends walked through the redoubt, clearing it room by room. They found a dormitory, an infirmary and a lavatory all in order. They looted supplies from every room. Mildred found a treasure trove of medical supplies, but it was the sight of toilet paper still in its packaging that nearly made her burst into tears.

Jak raised his head and sniffed the air. "Food."

"Damn!" Mildred swore. "No freakin' way! I smell pizza!" Blaster out in front of her, she made a beeline toward the smell of pepperoni and cheese. Ryan didn't know what pizza was, but he found himself salivating at the scent.

"Triple alert, people!" He kicked open a set of double doors. His longblaster pointed at an empty kitchen. Beyond it lay an equally empty cafeteria.

"Just missed whoever was here," J.B. observed. "We better take a look around here. Bastards might creep up and attack."

A recce of the immediate area revealed nothing. The companions went back to the kitchen.

"We just missed pizza!" Mildred was agitated at the loss. Ryan took in several receptacles stuffed to the gills with plastic packaging. A sea of plastic eating utensils lay in the sink. Whoever they had just missed, there were a lot of them. Other people were using this place.

Mildred scoured the kitchen. "Look at this!" Ryan looked. It was a freezer unit. A wall full of them, and walk-in size. It was more than a freezer. It was literally a kitchen cryogenic unit. Mildred picked up a white binder with the Canadian flag on it and began flipping through it. "Jeez! This thing is more sophisticated than the unit I came out of." She scanned pages of inventory. "Look at this, hams, venison, sides of beef, vegetables, fruit juice concentrate... Man, they even managed to freeze wine and beer!" Mildred closed the binder. "Someone went to one whole hell of a lot of trouble to stock this place, and not just with those crappy MRE packs in the redoubts, but with real food that would be as tasty as the day as it was frozen, even if that was a hundred years ago."

"Just like you?" J.B. observed.

Mildred's lips quirked. J.B. was a man of few words but every once in a while he said something sweet. "Something like that."

Ryan looked at the food vaults and then Mildred. "Can you unfreeze something?"

The physician tapped the binder. "The thawing process seems to take four-to-six hours, depending on the foodstuff, and that's not counting actual cooking time."

Ryan wasn't sure they had four-to-six hours. No one would leave a treasure trove like this unguarded for long. He was starting to get an itchy feeling. "See if they got ration packs or anything quicker."

Doc opened a regular refrigerator and pulled out four, fourteen-inch-diameter disks shrink-wrapped in military olive-drab packaging. "These seem merely cold. Mayhap like dear Dr. Wyeth, they are thawed and ready for the oven of this brave new world."

Mildred lunged. Her eyes lit up at what Doc found. "Damn, Doc." She shuffled the pizza pies. "Pepperoni and cheese...pepperoni and cheese...veggie... Oooh! Yeah! Hawaiian!"

Jak peered at the Canadian military pizza packages. "What Hawaiian?"

"Canadian bacon and pineapple." Mildred scanned the

control panel on one of the large ovens and punched buttons. Instantly heating coils blazed orange. "It says just five minutes to brown the cheese ..." Mildred slid in the pies on their packaged plates and set the timer. "What else have we got in there, Doc?"

Doc pulled out two six-packs of olive-drab cans emblazoned with maple leafs. He peered at the fine print. "Lager."

Jak's chin lifted. "Beer?"

Beer was at premium in the Deathlands. Only the most prosperous villes could devote any arable land or grain to produce it. Most just distilled shine out of whatever agricultural scraps were left over. Doc looked at the cans suspiciously. "One-hundred-year-old-resuscitated lager—it is hard to lend it credence. Perhaps one of us should test it first and—"

Jak snatched a can. The tab cracked with a decisive pop and hiss and suds spilled over his fingers. He blew off the froth and his ruby-red eyes closed as he tilted the can back. Everyone watched Jak's snowy white Adam's apple move up and down as he poured back about half the can. His eyebrows pulled down in consideration as he regarded the can. Jak let forth a belch longer than most sentences he uttered. "Good," he proclaimed.

"A most potent eructation," Doc declared. "And a good portent that the lager has lost none of its luster." He passed out cans to the rest of his friends. He fumbled with the tab for a moment but it cracked and he held up his foaming can. "To good friends!"

"To good friends." They clicked the cans together and raised their beers to their lips.

Ryan's shoulders relaxed and his eye nearly closed as he drank. Jak was right. It was good. It was real good.

Mildred sighed and squinted at the fine print on the can. "Diefenbunker? Hey, wait."

No one waited. Mildred ran back to the inventory binder

and pulled up a pizza wrapping from the trash. "Everything around here says Diefenbunker."

"'Facturer?" Jak suggested.

"No, the places with the mat-trans are called redoubts, but in my day, a place like this was called a bunker or a bomb shelter." Mildred began flipping through the kitchen inventory binder. "Allotments, Central Diefenbunker." Mildred stabbed her finger onto the page. "Borden, Borden, Ontario! There was a map on the wall back in the last room!"

Mildred ran off. The team followed clutching their beers and blasters. The woman stood in front of a wall-size map of Canada. Her finger traced a line up from Lake Ontario. "Borden! We're right here! About, oh, an hour's drive north of Toronto!"

Ryan scanned the map. There was little red star just east of someplace called Angus. Mildred's fingers began leaping from province to province locating little red stars. "Look, Nanaimo, British Columbia. Penhold, Alberta. Shilo, Manitoba. Valcartier and Val-d'Or, Quebec. Debert, Nova Scotia. Bunkers, all out in the sticks, but not far from each provincial capital."

Ryan nodded. "Good work, Mildred."

Mildred beamed. Ryan didn't hand out praise often. She went to the nearest computer and hit the space bar. The Canadian flag popped up, but other than that the computer responded to nothing she tried. "Without a password I think we're locked out."

Out in the kitchen the oven pinged.

The map was forgotten as they filed back into the kitchen.

"If Toronto's the capital," J.B. mused, "then it probably got hit."

J.B. was probably right, Mildred thought.

They sat around the kitchen counter as she found a pizza cutter in a drawer. She cut slices and doled out fresh beers all around. Krysty took one bite of the pepperoni and cheese slice and closed her eyes. "Gaia..."

Conversation ceased as the friends attacked the hot food and cold beer. It wasn't often that they got to eat their fill of anything. Much less something that good. Ryan spent some time savoring the flavors. "You pulled your weight today, Mildred."

"Yeah, well, it isn't Domino's." Mildred spoke through cheeks bulging like a squirrel gathering nuts for winter. "But damn, it's been a long time."

"Indeed." Doc finished his first slice and nodded. "I was always rather partial to Poppa John's, myself."

Mildred stared over her fourth piece. "When did you get Poppa John's?"

"During the time of my unfortunate captivity. Perhaps it was in the Chicago lab... I was particularly enamored of their anchovy and onion pies." Doc's eyes grew faraway as he reviewed pain and indignities inflicted upon him over a hundred years earlier. "That is, when the scientists saw fit to share any with me. I fear after my last escape attempt my rations were rather severely reduced in diversity, quality and quantity."

Mildred felt her eyes sting. Whenever she felt like she couldn't take living in this hellish future another second, she reminded herself that Doc's suffering dwarfed hers. Mildred pushed the plate over. "Have another slice, Doc."

"I believe I will try the Hawaiian, thank you, my good Doctor."

The pizzas disappeared to the last crumb. Krysty and Mildred weren't above licking their plates clean. The cans of lager were shaken, turned upside down and sucked for the last bit of foam. Ryan wiped his mouth with the back of his fist. "Someone's been here. A lot of them. And they're going to be back. We'll recce the rest of the redoubt and hopefully avoid a confrontation."

Doc sighed. "A shame to have feasted so well, only to regurgitate our repast in some mat-trans only the Fates know where."

Ryan admitted it was one bastard sad thought indeed, but there just wasn't going to be much time for digestion. "Let's do it."

They scouted out the rest of the redoubt. More of the rooms upstairs had been raided. In the second dormitory the beds had been stripped down to the frames. A tool room and a machine shop were bare bones. They came to another room, and J.B. rocked on his heels. "Dark…night."

Jak whistled.

Dark night was right. Ryan shook his head. The barrel-shaped vault looked like another add-on, quick and dirty as Mildred had said. It was an armory. Many of the racks were empty, but a shocking amount of weaponry was still in place. Ryan counted more than a dozen military blasters, the only difference being their plastic furniture was a dark green rather than the usual Deathlands black. Spare mags, bandoliers and crates of ammo were stacked along the walls.

"Nuke me!" J.B. ran to a rack. "Ryan! Ryan!"

The one-eyed man ran his hands over the racks of weapons as he walked over to where J.B. stood transfixed. Ryan looked at a little bolt-action rifle with a funny little scope that was set too far forward.

"Know what that is?" J.B. asked.

Ryan frowned. The Armorer wasn't normally the gushing type. But his old friend was a gunsmith of the first order, and the weapon in front of them had detonated his passion. "A blaster?"

J.B. gave Ryan an offended look. "That is a Steyr Scout longblaster, Tactical version."

"Yeah?"

"It was designed to be the ultimate do-it-all rifle—7.62 mm, big enough for a good shot to take any game in North America. But look at it!" J.B. handled the rifle with almost erotic enthusiasm. "Unlike most bolts, this detachable mag has a ten rounder." J.B. flipped the rifle over. "See here? It carries a spare mag in the stock. Here?" He pushed a button. "Cleaning kit in the butt. Here, sidesaddle on the stock holds five ready rounds in these clips. And here?" The fore end of the little rifle split and deployed forward like a praying mantis's wings. "Bipod." J.B. snapped the bipod back in place and handed the rifle to Ryan.

It was light, not much more than six pounds. Ryan eyed the short fluted barrel. "Going to kick some."

"Recoil reducing stock," J.B. said smugly. "And check the sling. Three swivel positions and two straps. One for carrying and one for wrapping your arm through to steady you."

Ryan looked at the little scope. "Not much magnification."

"It's 2.5 power." J.B. nodded. "It's not a sniper rifle. It's the weapon of a rifleman, of a scout."

Ryan shook his head. The scope was completely forward of the action. "Scope's too far forward."

"It's supposed to be. Shoulder it."

Ryan shouldered the longblaster and instinctively wrapped his arm through the sling. He peered through the scope. It was about a foot from his face, but the image within was crystal clear, and he could still see everything else in front of him.

J.B. knew Ryan saw it. "You see! That's what they call long eye relief. It allows you to see your target in the scope, but at the same time you can still see what is going on around you. When you shoot a Scout, you want to keep both eyes open, and that allows you to…" The Armorer trailed off as Ryan turned his single blue eye on him in vague amusement.

J.B. cleared his throat. "And if the scope ever breaks?" He reached over and flipped up front and rear iron sights. "Back in the day it they said it was one of the fastest, handiest rifles ever designed. Experienced men could bust clay pigeons out of the air with one."

Ryan wasn't sure what a clay pigeon was, but taking a bird in flight with a longblaster was something. He was a keep it simple kind of man. He had to admit everything about the little longblaster made absolute sense, and it felt absolutely right in his hands.

"One more thing." J.B. was grinning uncharacteristically. "Look at the muzzle."

Ryan looked. It was threaded.

J.B. reached into the rack and pulled out a factory-fresh black sound-suppressor tube. "I'll work up some subsonic rounds for you. Keep them in the side carrier. Between that and the tube you got a silent shot whenever you want it."

"Sold." There were three Scouts in the rack. Whoever had been here had probably looked at them and dismissed them at first glance like Ryan had. "I want ten mags on a bandolier. Take the other suppressor tubes. Cannibalize the other scopes and any parts you can think of for spares."

"Right. You'll probably want a slightly longer length of pull. I'll take a spacer from one of the spares and lengthen it for you."

"Just grab it all. You can smith it after the next jump."

J.B. festooned himself with rifles and gear.

They left the armory and followed the corridor, which opened up into a very large room. It was clearly another crude, last-second expansion. Ryan stopped short, and J.B. nearly dropped his load as he bumped into him.

Huge blast doors dominated the far wall. The most important thing was the vehicle bay off to the side. There were three bays, and two were empty. Ryan could smell gas and see fresh grease in the bays. The last bay was occupied by a Light Armored Vehicle. Ryan took in the 25 mm cannon and the eight giant road wheels.

The armored vehicle was painted a dark military green and looked like it had just rolled off the factory floor. "You remember, Ryan? When we wagged it up to Seattle in one?"

Ryan remembered. "LAV 25."

"Nah, this is a LAV III."

Ryan didn't see much difference other than the red maple leaf painted on the prow.

J.B. was shaking his head, only he wasn't smiling any more. "Ryan?"

Ryan was shaking his head, too.

It was too much. No one would leave this kind of wealth behind. There were only three explanations. One, it was a grotesquely well-baited trap. Two, something horrible was lurking in this Canadian redoubt that they just hadn't run into yet. Three, and most likely, there was simply too much loot here for whoever had been visiting to carry or wag away, and they would be back. Though that did beg the question, why didn't they leave anyone to guard it?

"Ryan?" J.B.'s eyes glittered behind his glasses in pure avarice. "Tell me we're taking that wag."

Jak looked around the Diefenbunker meaningfully and said what everyone was thinking. "Stuff it full," Jak voted. "Run south."

Ryan knew Doc's vote but he asked anyway. "Doc?"

Doc sagged with visible relief at the idea of not having to go through the mat-trans. "I believe a cross-country jaunt across Canada might be edifying to both mind and body."

"Mildred?"

"Doc's right. We're all tired of jumping. Last few things we jumped into were bad. In a vehicle at least we can see what's coming. Plus I'm thinking Canada couldn't have got hit anywhere near as hard as the States. Maybe clean air, clean water." Mildred's eyes got faraway like Doc's sometimes did when he thought of the past. "I remember Ontario being beautiful."

Ryan looked to Krysty. "Lover?"

"I'm going whichever way you're going, jump or drive." Krysty ran her eyes up and down Ryan's long, hard, scarred frame and then smiled at the Canadian Land Force LAV III behind him. "But I'll tell you something. That wag looks good on you."

One of Ryan's rare smiles crossed his face. The vote was unanimous.

"J.B., you and me load it and check it. Cannon, coax, top blaster, gren launchers, spare fuel everything. Full war load. Everyone else, food, trade goods and supplies. Blasters, ammo, ration packs." Ryan nodded at the external cleats and equipment cages. "Load it to the gills. I want to wag out of here within the hour."

Chapter Two

"Clear!" Krysty called. She tracked the security periscope. All the computers were locked down, including those controlling the sec cameras. The Diefenbunker did have several periscopes strategically placed around the facility. "Got some daylight left!" She let go of the periscope's handles.

Ryan stood in the commander's hatch of the LAV behind the pintle-mounted Minimi Squad Automatic Weapon. "Mildred!"

The physician hit a big red button and the blast doors began grinding open. The two women ran and jumped in the back hatch.

"Jak! Button her up and take us out!" The LAV's rear ramp whined up while red light spilled into the vault of the Diefenbunker's entry bay from the outside. Gears ground as Jak sent the LAV rumbling out into Ontario. The sun wasn't quite setting yet, but it was a low red ball in the sky. The sky pulsed with sheets of red and green light as if it were on fire. Ryan had seen the Northern Lights before, but not often while the sun was still shining. In the lurid light Ryan saw a plain of low rolling hills broken up by stands of pines. Ryan also saw a war going on about a mile away.

"Jak! Hold up! J.B., up top!"

The gunner hatch clanged open and J.B. stood from behind the cannon. Ryan pointed. The Armorer took up his binoculars. Almost a mile ahead the land dropped into a shallow depression. Within it a sizable convoy was pulled up into a defensive circle. Outriders besieged it on every side. Ryan ran his Navy longeye over the encircled wags. He counted about a dozen vehicles of all different descriptions with men firing out of, from underneath and between them. Diefenbunker gear and supplies were strapped to the outsides of the vehicles. Most interesting were the convoy's two LAVs. It explained the empty bays in the bunker. One was like the one Ryan and his companions were in, and it was burning out of control.

"Attackers." J.B. grimaced. "They got some kind of tank buster."

Ryan scanned the other LAV. "That one doesn't have a turret."

The Armorer's eyes went wide. "That, is an engineering-recovery vehicle. Check the crane folded down on the back, the dozer blade and the winch." J.B. sighed. "How many times could we have used one of those when we were with Trader?"

More times than Ryan could count. In the Deathlands a vehicle like that was worth its weight in anything, including human life. Ryan noticed it wasn't attracting much in the way of fire despite the fact a man in the top hatch was firing a machine blaster like the one Ryan stood behind. The one-eyed man scanned the enemy ringing the convoy. Most of them had off-road bikes, but they had laid their bikes down and were firing prone from behind rocks and folds in the earth. Some of the pits were clearly man-made. They had chosen their ambush site well. They had probably blown the LAV before the convoy knew what was happening. The convoy had been surrounded in plain sight of the sanctuary of the Diefenbunker and cut off. Ryan picked out some 4x4 pickup wags pulled far back from the fight. The attackers were numerous, heavily armed and equipped for cross-country speed. Most had painted their faces with skulls, abstract designs or swathes of color. It wasn't camouflage. It was war paint and designed to terrorize.

They were coldhearts.

J.B. pointed. "Watch there."

A coldheart rose up with broad length of pipe over his shoulder. A man behind him touched a flame to the fuse in the back and ducked. A rocket hissed out of the pipe and shot out of the tube. The object arced and twisted in flight and exploded into the ground in a blast of orange fire and gray smoke a dozen yards from one of the caravan's flatbeds.

J.B. snorted derisively. "Home made. Black powder. Not even spin stabilized. Real close you could take out a wag, even a big one, but nothing like what we're sitting in. They still got a tank-killer we haven't seen."

The driver's hatch clanged open. Jak's head popped up. His eyes were the same color as the sinking sun as he surveyed the scene. "Pickin' sides?"

Ryan was about the closest thing to a decent human being that could survive in the Deathlands. He could see there were women in the convoy, and the attackers looked like they were doing what they liked to do best. Nightcreeping and ambushing.

"Not our fight, and they got something down there that can kill us all." Ryan shook his head wearily. It was a scene he had seen far too many times in his life. He was reluctant to walk away, but his friends came first. "We're out of here and— Fireblast!"

Ryan's hand crushed the top of J.B.'s fedora as he shoved him back into the turret. Three men had crept up out of a fold in the terrain and a rocket hissed straight at the LAV. Jak slammed the driver's hatch shut. Ryan dropped down the commander's hatch as a thunderclap backhanded the LAV. Mildred yipped as the armored war wag rocked violently on its chassis. The brimstone stench of black powder filled the air from the open hatches. The coldhearts howled with blood-lust outside. "Die! Die! Die!"

"Jak," Ryan snarled, "we just picked sides!"

Jak answered by stomping on the gas. The LAV lurched forward. Bullets whanged and spalled off the hull. Ryan rose out of the hatch and leaned into the light machine gun's stock. He rattled off a 5-round burst into a shrieking, painted face. Dust flew from the chest of a second coldheart as Ryan hammered him down. The last man dropped his rocket tube and turned to run screaming. He was still screaming as he went down beneath the LAV's wheels.

Ryan knew he was a bullet magnet standing in the turret, but buttoned up it was very hard to see the enemy coming. "Jak, take us about a thousand yards out! Western side. Get us in range of those pickups!" Jak put a low hill between the LAV and the battle and began sneaking west.

"J.B.?"

The Armorer sat in the gunner's chair. He'd pushed his fedora firmly on his head and tapped his finger against a small comp screen. "Fire control comp is locked, like inside. Going to have to shoot manual. Jak, get me within three hundred yards!"

The LAV rolled across the terrain at speed. Jak suddenly drove up a low gradient and parked on the crest of a low hill looking down on the battle. It would be a matter of seconds before they were spotted.

Ryan called down into the cabin. "Krysty, Mildred, Doc! Out, and keep an eye on our six!"

The back door lowered and they spilled out, blasters at the ready.

The turret whined and the seven-foot, fluted cannon barrel dipped as J.B. picked a target. Sitting in the gunner's seat and looking through the manual aiming optical gradients, he was calculating more than aiming.

The muzzle of the cannon thudded and spit smoke.

Five coldhearts surrounding a pickup three hundred yards distant just about crapped their homespun coveralls as the high-explosive round detonated uncomfortably close. "Ten wide! Thirty short!" Ryan called. The turret turned a hairbreadth. The barrel tilted up an even tinier increment. The cannon spit. The coldheart pickup's hood flew up into the air and the windshield shattered. The man behind the wheel disappeared in a haze of blood and smoke.

Coldhearts scattered.

Ryan kept his eye on the big picture as J.B. traversed for targets of opportunity. A coldheart had leaped up from his firing position and was jumping onto his bike. The 25 mm blaster thumped and man and motorcycle burst apart in a cloud of flesh and metal. Ryan nodded as he continued to scan the surroundings. "Nice shot, J.B."

A pleased noise drifted up from inside the turret.

"J.B.!" Jak pointed excitedly at another pickup. Ryan whipped up his Navy longeye for a moment and smiled. The back of the wag contained a pallet of the homemade rockets.

"Oh yeah!" J.B. enthused.

Ryan thought he might be enjoying this a little too much. "I make it four hundred yards, J.B.!"

"Right!" The turret turned. The muzzle of the cannon elevated a few inches then. The blaster thudded and earth flew up in a geyser.

"Dead on but thirty short!" Ryan called.

The men around the wag didn't need a second shot. They knew what they were carrying and they ran for their lives. The cannon hammered again and more earth flew.

"Dead on! Ten short!"

The smoking muzzle of the cannon rose almost imperceptibly and thudded.

The wag and its load blew sky-high. Jak whooped. The

grass around it rippled and flattened out in a thirty-yard wave. A column of black smoke rose into the bloody sunset. The remaining pickups tore up turf in their haste to escape. Motorcycles fled the scene of the ambush and coalesced into a herd stampeding northward into the low hills. Ryan was interested to notice they took the time to take their dead with them. The pickups streaked after them.

"Moving targets!" J.B. called up. "Hard to hit on manual!"

"Hold fire," Ryan ordered.

Krysty looked up at Ryan in his perch. "We going down?"

"No. Let them come to us. J.B., stay on station, keep the cannon pointed at anything that comes."

Ryan watched the convoy. They stayed in defensive formation. A lot of heads stayed turned their way, but the people took care of their dead and wounded and transferred loads from ruined vehicles. A Volkswagen Iltis broke away from the defensive circle and drove slowly toward Ryan's band. A man stood in the back holding a white flag. Ryan filled his hand with his new Scout longblaster and clambered down from the turret. Jak hopped down after him. The muzzle of J.B.'s cannon watched them like the cold eye of death, making slight adjustments as the wag closed. The 4x4 stopped about twenty yards away. The driver was a gray-hair wrinklie in homespun, and he stayed behind the wheel. The man sitting shotgun and the man in back jumped out. The man in front was clearly in command, but Ryan kept his eye on the other one.

He was black, half a head taller than Ryan and looked to be about half again as heavy, all of it muscle. His head was shaved, and he wore a sheepskin coat someone had tailored to his massive frame. The stainless-steel lever action blaster he carried looked like a toy in his hand. He was obviously a sec man and a damned impressive one.

The leader was a plain-looking man and he stepped

straight up to Ryan. He was neither tall nor short. His brown hair was clipped short as was his mustache and beard. The most notable thing about him was his green eyes. They literally twinkled as he smiled at Ryan, and the man radiated a busy, competent sort of energy. His predark parka, cargo pants and boots looked as though they had only recently been put into use. A shiny knew Diefenbunker SIG-Sauer blaster was tucked under his belt. He raised an open right hand in friendship and spent long moments saying something to Ryan that sounded mostly like vowels. It kind of sounded like language Ryan had heard in Cajun country. He looked at Jak. The young man's snowy brows were bunching mightily. His head cocked slightly as he tried to digest what he had just heard.

Doc took a step forward and made a graceful bow. *"Parlez-vous anglais?"*

The convoy leader grinned. "But of course." He nodded at Ryan again. "Hello!"

Ryan nodded noncommittally. "Hi."

"I am Yoann Toulalan, son of Baron Luc Toulalan, baron of the ville of Val-d'Or."

Krysty shot Ryan a look, who had caught it, too. Val-d'Or was one of the Diefenbunker locations in Quebec. He nodded at the baron's son again. "Ryan."

"Uh…" Toulalan seemed nonplussed at Ryan's taciturn part in the exchange. He threw up his hands and grinned again. "Well! You are our savior!"

"Glad to help."

The big man's face split into a smile as he loomed over Jak. His voice was incredibly deep. "This one is mutant."

Krysty's lips tightened but she kept her mouth shut. For the moment.

Ryan's voice went quiet and cold. "Albino, it's a condition."

"Ah." Toulalan nodded. "We know of such things."

The big man turned to Ryan and tilted his chin at the LAV and the supplies strapped to the sides. "You stole from us."

Toulalan made a tsking noise.

Ryan spoke quietly. "You left it. Headed west. With no one to look after it." The one-eyed man lifted his chin toward the smoking ruins of the coldheart wags. "Except mebbe them."

The big man slowly straightened in outrage. For a heart-beat Ryan thought it was going to be a fight. Mildred had been in the LAV with J.B. She stepped out angrily. "Why don't you back off, brother-man!"

The man's rage fell away. He was clearly startled at the sight of Mildred. His mouth opened and closed again.

Toulalan took the opportunity to step in. "Monsieur Ryan, may I introduce my head security man, Vincent Six. Forgive him. We have taken losses, lost friends. We're all upset."

Six tore his eyes off Mildred for a moment. He looked like he didn't give a spent shell whether Ryan forgave him, but the big man grunted and nodded. Ryan nodded back. Six went back to openly eyeballing Mildred, who put her fists on her hips and glared back.

Toulalan gestured back at his wag. "And allow me to introduce my dear friend Florian Medard, he's our, how would you say…scholar?"

Florian nodded and touched a pair of fingers to his head in greeting. His eyes ran over each member of the companions and seemed to be cataloging them.

Ryan shrugged. "What do you want?"

Toulalan blinked in surprise. "I believe the question is, what do *you* want? You have driven off our enemies. For that we are deeply in your debt, but by the same token, you could easily decimate our convoy with your autocannon. I merely ask, what are your intentions?"

"I don't know." Ryan shrugged. "Head south mebbe."

"Well, would you care to join us in our evening meal? Six shot a wild boar just this morning."

"We just had pizza."

"We had pizza for lunch!"

"We noticed."

Toulalan gave Ryan a very shrewd look. "We have more beer."

One corner of Ryan's mouth quirked against his will. "Bastard."

Toulalan threw back his head and laughed. "Florian, go tell Cyrielle we have guests for dinner tonight."

Chapter Three

Ryan gnawed contentedly on a rib of barbecued wild boar. Little more than reconstituted Diefenbunker olive oil, salt and fresh-picked herbs had worked glory over the fire spit. The convoy had broken out predark folding picnic tables, lit fires, candles and storm lanterns, and it was a full-on feast. A woman played a mandolin, accompanied by flute, and several people were dancing. Toulalan's sister pressed a fresh can of Diefenbunker beer into Ryan's hand. She was nothing like her brother. She was small and dark with black hair, olive skin and huge dark eyes. However the twinkle in her eyes, the penchant for smiling and similar mannerisms made their kinship unmistakable. Ryan chewed the arc of bone more out of habit and for pleasure than anything else. In the Deathlands one often never knew where the next meal was coming from. Gorging was a reflex. The pig had been accompanied by green beans and something called potatoes au gratin that had sent Mildred to sighing with joy. The convoy had spent several days resuscitating large quantities of the Diefenbunker's cryo-frozen fresh food. Six's pig had also been accompanied by beer.

The convoy was celebrating survival. They celebrated Ryan and his friends as conquering heroes. They had moved the convoy to a little hill surrounded by flat plain. The convoy formed a loose defensive ring around the hill. Sentries had been sent out, and Ryan's LAV sat on crest with a 360° view of the landscape, ready to rain doom on anyone who approached. Jak was taking the first watch in the turret.

Krysty leaned her head against Ryan's shoulder. "You think they're fattening us up for the kill?"

Ryan spoke quietly into her titian tresses. "No, they lost their fighting LAV because they barely know how to operate it. If we hadn't shown up, they'd be dead. They're laying out the spread because they want us to join up."

"And?"

"I haven't made up my mind," Ryan whispered. "And Toulalan looks like he's about to get down to recruiting."

Yoann Toulalan raised an ancient piece of plastic picnic stemware full of wine in Ryan's direction. *"Salut, mon ami!"*

Ryan raised his can along with everyone else at the table and sipped the brew.

"So," Toulalan began, "you've been in the bunker, no?"

Ryan looked up at the LAV on the hill and back at Toulalan.

The man shrugged sheepishly. "Yes, but of course. But we have access codes. May I ask how you gained entrance?"

"You can ask," the one-eyed man replied.

The irony wasn't lost on the Canadian. "Yes, I see."

"Let me ask you a question," Ryan said.

"Anything," Toulalan replied.

"That bunker is still loaded with food, blasters and goods, and you're driving away from it." Ryan lifted his chin and pointed. "Quebec is that way. Why aren't you loaded to capacity and running for home?"

Toulalan shrugged. Ryan was beginning to believe the man's shoulders, hands and eyebrows were connected to his mouth. "Well, my friend, there's more to life than bullets and beans."

That struck a sympathetic chord with Ryan. "And so?"

"I'm an explorer." He shot Ryan a very shrewd look. "Like yourself."

Ryan kept his poker face. More times than he could count he and his friends had found places as decent as the Deathlands got to settle down in. But in the end Ryan always kept moving on, always exploring. He was more than an explorer, knew in his heart he was a searcher. Many people, even some of his companions had accused him of searching for something he would never find; and that he really didn't even know what he was searching for anymore. Nevertheless, his friends followed him, willingly.

Toulalan pursed his lips in thought. "Would you care to hear some Canadian history?"

There was nothing at the moment Ryan wanted to hear more. He took a sip of beer and idly considered the can. "If you want to tell it."

"Well, skydark came. This we all know. But Canada, we had no nukes and far fewer—how do you say…high-value targets? Oh, we got hit, but for the most part surgically. Capitals, military bases. It wasn't like the horrific exchange that created the Deathlands. We have been south. We know. Few earth-shaker bombs, tailored viruses or, as we say, orgy weapons like the United States and its prime enemies flung at one another." Toulalan sipped wine. "Nevertheless, the weather changed, the Earth changed. Tailored viruses will spread, and fallout and chem storms, well, they know no boundaries. When the big freeze happened, well…" Toulalan shrugged. "This is Canada."

"And?"

"And so. In the Deathlands, people left the cities because they were radioactive. In Canada, the cities were abandoned because in the nuclear winter they were freezing and there was nothing to eat. You have thousands of ruins. We have thousands of ghost towns. Winters were always long in the north and summers short. Now the winters are longer and the summers shorter. Spring and fall? Beautiful respites, but I warn you, do not blink. They are ephemeral. And come Father Snow, we have, what we call, the hard freeze. You can literally see it come toward you, like an avalanche across the horizon. Pray you never see it, except from behind thick stone walls with a roaring fire at your back."

"Speaking of that, isn't it getting a little late in the season," Ryan questioned, "to wag it cross country?"

"Indeed." Toulalan leaned forward. "We're behind schedule. We must push hard."

"Where are you headed?"

"West."

Ryan ran his eye over the collection of wags. "I noticed you don't have a tanker. You got tanks and cans loaded on every wag, but not enough fuel to cross country." Ryan crushed the empty can in his hand. "You're going from bunker to bunker."

Toulalan tossed off a postapocalyptic French-Canadian shrug and considered the one-hundred-year-old wine in his glass by candlelight. "Will you tell me how you got into the bunker?"

Ryan was starting to believe that Yoann Toulalan had no idea what the mat-trans chamber was. "Codes can be broken."

"The computers are locked."

"Trade secret."

"Ah."

Ryan threw his cards on the table. It might be for an ephemeral moment, but Ontario was green. His rad counter told him this was the cleanest land in North America he'd seen in a while. His friends didn't want to jump again, and despite his every effort he found himself liking Yoann Toulalan. "What are you proposing?"

"You and your friends can drive and fight a LAV. That's

worth its weight in gold." Toulalan set his glass on the table. "I'm tempted to offer you a place here in the convoy."

"But?"

"But I beg of you, tell me something of you and your friends."

Ryan kept it short and to the point. "I've led convoys, guarded convoys and drove convoys. I can drive any wag you got, and I can wrench a little."

"Very useful." Toulalan looked up toward the LAV guarding the convoy. "And your pale friend?"

"Jak's the best fighter I know, and he's a tracker."

"Excellent." Toulalan looked over at J.B. The Armorer was getting deep into his beer. "And your cannoneer?"

"Armorer. He can fix any blaster you got."

"Excellent." Toulalan looked at Mildred. "And her?"

"She's a healer, and you tell Six 'hands off.'"

"Understood." Toulalan ran an appreciative eye over Krysty. "And her."

Ryan smiled. "She's mine."

"Ah."

"She's a crack shot," Ryan said.

"Better and better."

Toulalan looked askance at Doc. "And him?"

Doc was well into his wine and speaking French to a good-looking young woman wearing a coverall and a tool belt. Ryan had to admit the old man was something of a sight wherever they showed up.

The one-eyed man smiled. "Doc's our…resident scholar."

"Ah!" Toulalan laughed. "Very good!"

Ryan watched Six walk by. He never stopped walking the perimeter, but each time he passed the feast he cast long looks at Mildred.

"Your man Six doesn't like muties."

Toulalan made noise. "Who does?"

Krysty's body went rigid against Ryan. He kept his tone neutral. "You don't tolerate them?"

"In the Deathlands, do you?" the man countered.

"Some villes do. Some don't."

"Ah. Well, in Val-d'Or those born mutant are culled." Toulalan shrugged again. He seemed to consider the matter to be of little consequence. "Life is hard enough without nurturing horrors."

Krysty's hand clenched Ryan's knee.

Ryan kept his voice neutral. "What're you proposing?"

"Accompany us west. As far as you like. My convoy will be far stronger with you among us. As for you, there's safety in numbers. Alone, even a wag as powerful as a LAV is vulnerable."

Everything Toulalan said was true. Ryan took another beer. "Authority?"

Toulalan shrugged again. "I'm the leader of this convoy. You're the leader of your people. If I wish something of any of your people, I'll ask you. You'll accept my authority over the convoy and obey my orders until the day you find you can't. On that day you and I'll shake hands and part as friends." Toulalan held up his glass again. "If you join us, the only thing I'll promise you is food like you have never known until that food runs out. That will be your—how do you say it in Deathlands, jack? And when the bounty of the Diefenbunker runs out..." Toulalan shrugged again. "Well, you have tasted Six's pig."

It was a damn tempting offer. "I'll have to talk with my people."

"But of course. Take your time. You may give me your answer in the morning, and whatever that answer should be, I insist you and your friends stay for breakfast."

"Mighty kind, and I'll think on your offer." Ryan rose and took Krysty's hand. He looked over at the mandolin

player and the flautist. A young man playing a hand drum
had joined them. "Right now I'm gonna dance with Krysty."
The redheaded beauty grinned in delight and stood to join
him.

RYAN SIGHED as Krysty collapsed forward onto his chest. He
pulled the top blanket back over them both. He handed her
the canteen without being asked, and Krysty gulped water
thirstily. She gasped and tilted the spout to Ryan's lips. He
drank deeply and relaxed back, staring up into the Northern
Lights. "What do you think?"

Krysty sighed. "It's greener here. The air is cleaner. Open
country. Just lying here I can feel Gaia more strongly."

"Toulalan said the good times don't last long."

"Neither does a man's orgasm, but I don't hear you com-
plaining much."

Ryan snorted and got back on topic. "And?"

"Lot of good food. Mildred isn't going to want to leave
until every last crumb is gone."

Ryan couldn't remember the last time he had seen Mildred so happy. "The sec man, Six, he's eyeballing her long
and hard."

Krysty chuckled. "Mildred said 'brother-man' probably
hasn't seen any chocolate good thing in a long time."

Ryan got the gist of it. "And?"

"And Doc could use a rest from jumping. Gaia knows
so could the rest of us. Besides, Toulalan said we can leave
whenever we like, and I think I believe him. He seems like
a decent man."

Ryan knew Krysty's moods all too well. Despite the wine,
the dancing and the lovemaking, he knew she had been simmering since supper. "You aren't happy."

"No." Krysty's voice grew cold. "I'm not."

Ryan had a real strong suspicion about what was bothering her. "And?"

"You heard him." Krysty clutched Ryan tightly. "He kills muties. And I'm one."

Bigotry was all too alive and well in the Deathlands, only now most often it was directed at the integrity of someone's DNA rather than any race, creed or color.

"If you want to go, we're gone. Right now."

Krysty rolled off Ryan and stared up into the night. "I didn't say that."

They were quiet for long moments as they stared into the shimmering veils of the light show above. Krysty was a mutie. It didn't show outwardly, unless her hair flexed around her head when she was in distress. Most places in the Deathlands tolerated muties if they weren't too deformed, or if their mutation proved useful somehow. A lot of places drove them out. All too many summarily executed muties upon discovery. It made Krysty sick to have to hide her own leap in evolution; but Ryan knew she would hide it, and take it, for the sake of the man she loved, and her friends.

"We're in this together, lover," Ryan told her. "I'll defend you to the death."

Krysty snuggled closer. "I know."

Chapter Four

Ryan awoke to the smell of real coffee. The Northern Lights shimmered in shifting golden sheets in the morning light. Mildred stood over Ryan and Krysty's bedroll grinning from ear to ear. She held two steaming sierra cups. "Wakey, wakey eggs and bakey!" Ryan sat up sniffing. The majority of the coffee he had drunk in his life was instant from one-hundred-year-old redoubt MRE packs, or old cans of coffee on redoubt shelves. Most people in the Deathlands drank chicory or a brew of herbs called coffee sub, and even that traded at a premium. The smell of what Mildred held set Ryan's mouth to salivating. He took the cup and drank deeply.

"French roast." Mildred sighed. "Who would have guessed?"

Ryan drained the mug and was grateful that Krysty had agreed that they stay with the convoy for another day or two and see how it went. Ryan rolled out of the blankets and shucked into his pants, drawn immediately to the smell coming from the mess wag. "Pancakes?"

"Oh yeah," Mildred enthused. "With syrup, sausages and mimosas."

"What's mimosa?"

"Champagne and orange juice."

Ryan's face showed that he thought that sounded like an excellent waste of two rather rare commodities. Mildred took a patient breath. "You'll like it. I promise you."

Ryan and Krysty sauntered over to the mess wag for

breakfast. He found that he did like mimosas. Krysty loved them. The friends sat at a table being waited on hand and foot. The redheaded beauty gave Ryan's leg a squeeze and whispered, "If we stay here much longer, Doc might just put on a pound or two."

Doc normally ate with relish, but maintained his spare frame. This morning he was enjoying a hearty breakfast, but he was smiling as he engaged one of the drivers in conversation. Canada was agreeing with him. It was agreeing with them all. If the pastoral beauty of the place was only going to last a few more weeks, then Ryan was tempted to wring every last second out of it. According to the map and Toulalan there were other Diefenbunkers ahead, and the one they'd exited contained one of the biggest stockpiles Ryan had ever encountered. He wanted to be there when Toulalan unlocked the next one.

Toulalan came over, smiling amiably. Six followed him, and with obvious effort managed an attitude short of open hostility. Toulalan gestured at the spread. "Breakfast agrees with you?"

"Yeah." Ryan nodded. "Thanks again."

"May I?"

Jak moved over and Toulalan took a seat. Six stood while Toulalan unfolded a map. Ryan raised an eyebrow at it. He had seen a fair chunk of what remained of Deathlands' West Coast. It didn't look anything like the map in front of him anymore. "That's an old map."

"The thing to notice is this." Toulalan ran his finger along a pair of red intersecting lines stretching from east to west. "The convoy follows the Trans-Canada Highway."

Ryan looked at the route dubiously. "It's still up?"

"I will admit time hasn't been kind to it. Many sections are out. But unlike much of your Deathlands, the basic path is still there. We have extensive maps of all the provinces.

Each time we've found an impassible stretch we have found smaller routes around it, and once more returned to the path. River traders tell us vast sections in the great central plains are whole. There we will make good time."

"River traders." Ryan poured more Diefenbunker syrup on his pancakes. "Why aren't they using it?"

"It is rumored there are dangers, plus fuel is scarce. A cross-continental trip?" Toulalan made a noise. "Few have the resources to attempt it. Besides, since time immemorial rivers have been the roads of Canada."

"But you have a map of the Diefenbunkers. Assuming they haven't been cracked, you got resupply depots in every province with all the fuel, food and supplies you can carry."

Toulalan nodded.

"You give away too much!" Six snarled.

Toulalan gave Ryan a poker player's smile. "I'm not telling our guests anything they haven't already surmised."

Six could no longer contain himself. "You'll give them a place among us?"

Toulalan sighed. "Vincent, my friend, you know I respect you. But you were here yesterday, no? Around sunset? During the battle?"

Six looked away. "I'll admit they were helpful."

Mildred mumbled into a mouthful of pancake and sausage. "Saved your Canadian bacon is what we did."

Six flinched.

Jak's fork froze midbite, and he snapped his head around. His eyes narrowed as he looked toward the thickets between the hills just a few hundred yards to the west. Ryan set down his mimosa and scooped up the Scout longblaster. He had seen that look on Jak's face before. "Something coming?"

The albino teen stepped away from the table and put hand to the ground. He crouched that way for long moments. "Herd."

"Oh?" Six frowned at the hills. "It's early for the caribou. They usually run south before the hard freeze, and that's weeks away." The big man's stainless-steel longblaster flashed like a drum major's baton as he twirled it through the rifleman's spin to cock the weapon and pushed on the safety to lock it. "Perhaps they migrate earlier here in Ontario."

Ryan, Jak and J.B. followed Six outside the perimeter. The Armorer began rapidly ejecting fléchette rounds out of his scattergun and swapping them for rifled slugs.

"Hunters!" Six called. "Go!"

A handful of Six's sec men gulped the last of their coffee and grabbed their blasters. The convoy was bristling with Diefenbunker assault rifles. These men came forward with predark bolt-action hunting weapons of .30-caliber or larger.

Ryan checked the loads in his Scout. "You say it's early for caribou?"

Six shrugged. The one-eyed man was starting to believe that everyone in the convoy's shoulders, hands and eyebrows were attached to their vocal cords. "I've never been this far west, though I've heard traders say the St. Lawrence lowlands have sizable herds of wild mustangs. Either way, meat is meat, no?"

Doc strode up to the hunting party. "A morning shoot?"

Ryan frowned at the tangled, impenetrable acres of scrub thorn between the hills. The sound was getting louder. "Thick cover for a migrating herd."

Six's brow furrowed. He was thinking the same thing. The thicket rippled with the passage of large animals and the sound of brush snapping sounded like the distant gunshots of an army starting a skirmish. Six pushed off his longblaster's safety. "In moments we'll know."

It didn't take moments. It took a heartbeat. The edge of the thicket exploded as the herd burst forth. They weren't caribou or wild mustangs. They were hogs. Boars, bigger than

Ryan had ever seen. They came out of the thicket between the hills in a wedge. He made the lead boar to be over nine feet long and four feet tall at the shoulder.

Its companions weren't much smaller.

"Good heavens," Doc opined.

Ryan didn't like what he was seeing. Wild boars were solitary animals. When you saw them in groups, it was usually a sounder consisting of a few sows and their offspring. Over half of the herd were adult males the size of wags. There were no piglets in sight. The fifty-strong herd arrowed straight for the convoy in a rumbling wave. Ryan dropped to a knee and shouldered the Scout. It was time to see what the new weapon could do.

Ryan wound his arm through the Scout's sling and dropped his elbow to his knee to form a solid firing platform. The scope was mounted well forward, and he could see the entire oncoming herd around it. At the same time the crosshairs of the heavy reticule were crystal clear as Ryan held them low beneath the gargantuan lead boar's shoulder. His finger slowly began putting pressure on the trigger as he watched the herd rumble into range.

Six watched Ryan with a dubious air. "Long range for a carbine. I would—"

The Scout bucked against Ryan's shoulder. It was a light rifle firing a high-power bullet. The muzzle-flash and report were impressive; the recoil was surprisingly mild. The huge hog's snout dug into the turf, and the momentum of its half-ton frame nearly made it summersault.

"Mon Dieu!" Six exclaimed.

The herd continued forward undeterred.

Ryan flicked the bolt on the Scout and trained the scope on his next target. The longblaster kicked and a supersize sow spun out as Ryan's bullet shattered its skull.

"Come here!" Six roared. "Come to papa!" Six's .45-70

sounded like a cannon going off. A boar dropped like it had been poleaxed. Longblasters began cracking and popping along the informal firing line. The shooters made hog calls and called out porcine insults in English and French as they shot. A slow smile crept across Ryan's face as he took his fifth pig. J.B. had been right. The Scout was like lightning. It qualified for the highest praise the Armorer could give a weapon. The Scout was as accurate as the man firing it.

Ryan was deadly accurate.

He took three more pigs with four more shots and quickly slapped in a fresh magazine. "They aren't stopping."

"No," Six agreed. He had stopped his hog calling. The giant beasts didn't seem to need much encouragement. Insults toward the oncoming pork and one another ceased among the sec men as they grimly fired as fast as they could work the actions of their longblasters. What was left of the herd was starting to get uncomfortably close. Members of the convoy came out and joined the firing line. Their assault rifles were too light for animals this big and only seemed to make them angry. Squealing screams rent the air as the wounded hogs bore down on the convoy in red-eyed, froth-spewing rage. At one hundred yards J.B.'s shotgun began slamming slugs. Jak carefully began pulling the trigger on .357 Colt Python in slow deliberate fire, and Mildred joined him. It was like some terrible shooting game where the prize was not to end up in a wild boar's belly. The boars didn't seem to care who won as long as they died going forward. Ryan's skin crawled as he aimed, shot and shot again.

The last half-ton hog fell to Ryan's longblaster only twenty yards from the firing line.

The entire convoy watched the plain shake with the convulsions and screams of the wounded and dying monster hogs in a picture of porcine hell. Ryan rose and drew his SIG-Sauer. He went forward to finish off the crippled and dying animals. Six drew his handblaster and nodded at two of his rattled sec men. "Sylvan, Alain with me." Six and his men joined Ryan in the mercy killings. There was plenty of ammo available, so why leave the animals to suffer?

Toulalan walked up beside Ryan as he put a bullet-riddled, trembling sow down. "I saw you shoot. You are incredible."

Ryan ignored the compliment. "Pigs like this normal up here?"

"I don't know about Ontario." Toulalan shrugged. "But in Quebec we don't allow our pigs the luxury of this kind of behavior."

Ryan had to admit Toulalan and his people had a certain sense of style. Right now Ryan wasn't laughing.

Doc pursed his lips at a specimen that had taken one of Ryan's bullets through the heart. "I am reminded of the wild boar of Argentine Andes. They were known for their size and aggression, and as famous for a carnivorous bent in their diet. Large males were known to break into chicken coups and sheep enclosures and wreak great slaughter. It was endlessly argued whether the boar were so large and aggressive because they ate meat, or they were naturally large and aggressive and it led to carnivorous behaviors. Nearly every village had a legend about someone's friend's, third uncle's grandmother who everyone knew had been eaten by one."

Six pushed fresh shells into his rifle. "Perhaps they were attracted by the smell of the pancakes, no?"

"No." Ryan knew that wasn't true. "They came for us."

Mildred's stomach got the better of her and she smiled at Six. "Pork chops for dinner?"

Six unveiled a mouthful of gold and silver teeth. "But of course. Whatever the lady wishes, the lady gets."

J.B. glowered.

Ryan shook his head at the slaughter. There was no way a herd of beasts behaving like that could be allowed to reach the convoy, but he hated wasting meat. Something between forty and fifty thousand pounds of pork was steaming in the morning light.

Six shrugged out of his sheepskins. Beneath them he wore a tomahawk and an enormous bowie knife. He drew his blade and cut into a boar's belly. The boar's flesh parted like butter beneath the razor-sharp steel. Six leaped back as squirming black horror spilled forth. *"Merde!"*

Mildred threw up.

Ryan raised his SIG-Sauer.

Doc peered at the ropey, viscous, black masses of foot-long worms as they tried to crawl back into the boar's carcass. "Surpassingly peculiar."

Mildred staggered away. "I'm never eating pork again."

Doc cocked his head as he watched the flesh of the dead boar ripple in waves. "Monsieur Six, with utmost caution, a few more cuts, if you do not mind?"

Six scowled but he stepped around the boar, his knife slashing a leg, making a cut along the spine and opening the head from jowl to ear. Ryan took note of his artistry with the blade. Six stepped away from the pulsating carcass and spit in disgust. "Parasites! Vileness! Val-d'Or is clean! We should never have left!" The sec man gave Ryan an accusing scowl. "You see! We're too close to the river! This is Deathlands filth!"

Ryan put a fresh clip into the Scout and reserved comment.

Doc leaned into the mess a little too closely for everyone's comfort. "No, Monsieur Six. These are not parasites. Parasites feed off their host, and to their host's detriment. When the host is dead, parasites flee if they are able, they do not crawl back within." Doc scratched his chin in thought. "Can they be commensals? Commensals receive benefit from their host but do no harm, and yet..."

Ryan gazed at the slices Six had inflicted in the pork.

The writhing black worms squirmed through the dead boar's muscles and squeezed around its bones and spine. Ryan had seen plenty of rotting corpses. Whatever was going on, the worms didn't appear to be feeding. There was almost some other kind of...

Ryan's single eyes narrowed.

Intention.

"Doc," Ryan warned, "step away."

"What? Oh, yes. Unknown infection, of course." Doc took several prudent steps back but continued his scientific musings. He pointed his swordstick at the writhing masses within the mutated hog. "Observe! No living creature could survive such a cataclysmic infestation, unless somehow it derived some sort of benefit from it in return. This is neither parasitism nor commensalism. This must be symbiosis of some sort. I believe it must somehow work to— Oh dear!" Doc leaped back adroitly as every visible worm in the dead boar's wounds contracted in unison.

The swine corpse rolled over and lurched to its feet.

The boar's eyes burst as horror pushed through its pupils. The thumb-thick worms in its eye sockets waved like feelers and stiffened like pointers at Doc. The boar's head swiveled in response, its tusks rasping against each other as its mouth fell open and its tongue lolled out, accompanied by an orgy of wriggling filth.

"By my stars and garters!" Doc exclaimed.

"Mon Dieu!" Toulalan cried out.

"Merde!" Six reiterated.

Mildred screamed.

Ryan fired three 9 mm hollowpoint rounds through the dead boar's head.

The boar's skull broke apart, spewing broken lengths of black worm. The porcine behemoth staggered but didn't fall. Fresh worms waved forth from the shattered cranium and snout as if tasting the air. The boar corpse tottered toward the humans. Ryan holstered his SIG-Sauer and spun the Scout off of his shoulder. He flicked the bolt as he backed up. "Fireblast..."

The entire fifty-strong herd of giant, newly dead, mutie wild boars began rolling over and rising up.

"J.B...." Ryan kept backing up. "Get to the LAV. Load HE. Jak, get behind the wheel."

It took a lot to shake up J.B. The Armorer's eyes were as wide as dinner plates behind his glasses as he backed up alongside Ryan. "Right."

"Run!" Ryan roared.

J.B. ran. Jak was already gone.

Six's guide gun thundered as he put a .45-70 shell into the hog's sagging skull. The pig kept coming. Ryan raised his rifle. "Forget the head!" The Scout bucked against the one-eyed man's shoulder, and the pig formed a porcine tripod as the bullet shattered its shoulder blade. He flicked the bolt and his next bullet crushed the hog's opposite collarbone. The undead pig went snout-first into the dirt. "Take their wheels!"

"*Oui,* Ryan!" Six flicked the lever of his rifle and blasted apart a corpulent, pulsating sow's femur. "Everyone! Back to the convoy! *Allez! Allez!*"

Humans ran.

The pigs shambled forward. There was no squealing. The only noise the dead animals made was the thud of their huge hooves in the soft soil and the sickening crackle of their muscles, joints and fascia as their corpses were manipulated from within. Mildred and Doc began shooting pig knees. Ryan flicked his bolt and fired with mechanical precision. "Yoann! Get your people in the wags! Button up!"

Toulalan shouted to his people in French and they scattered. Six and his men kept shooting. Ryan fired his clip dry and clawed for a fresh one. "J.B.!" A thousand-pound pig tottered toward Ryan, worms waving out of its eyes like flesh-detecting divining rods. "J.B.!"

The closest hog burst like a balloon as it took J.B.'s 25 mm high-explosive shell broadside. "Everyone! Up on wags! Go! Go! Go!" The firing line ran for the convoy as J.B. cut loose. The LAV's automatic cannon slammed in slow, aimed fire. Hogs exploded in sprays of blood, bone and black worms. Ryan leaped up into the bed of an ancient Toyota Tacoma jacked up on off-road wheels. He pulled Krysty up after him. The pickup had a MAG machine gun mounted on a post. Ryan got behind it and racked a round into the chamber.

Doc stood in front of the march of the monster hogs with his LeMat forgotten in his fist. He stared at the oncoming creatures quizzically and discoursed to no one in particular. "I have never seen nor heard of such coordinated effort among an invertebrate species. Well, bees, ants and some other social species, yes, but among annelids imbedded in a host animal? Truly this species is—"

"Doc, get out of there!" Ryan roared.

Doc suddenly seemed to notice a pair of pigs lurching toward him for the first time. "Ah! Yes! Right! Very good!" Doc turned as Ryan began putting bursts into the offending animals. Doc pulled up short as another pig tottered between him and Ryan. "Oh bother."

"Here!" Mildred shouted. She stood on the hood of an old police cruiser covered with hillbilly armor with Six twenty yards away. "Here!"

Doc hightailed it with his coat flapping behind him. Six grabbed him by his collar and heaved him to the roof. The pigs were among the convoy. It was too close for cannon work. Jak sent the LAV rolling forward and ground several hogs into hamburger under the LAV's eight massive road wheels.

"Six!" Toulalan shouted from the top of his camper wag and pointed at the engineering LAV. *"Le LAV! Le LAV!"*

Six shoved his rifle into Mildred's startled hands. She shook her head in horror. "No! Six! Don't—"

Six jumped from the hood and ran for the other LAV. He wove through the hulking, undead horrors like a fullback breaking tackles. He literally ran up the engineering vehicle's dozer blade and jammed down the driver's hatch. The engine roared into the life and the dozer blade rose with a whine. Six followed Jak's example of pitting 34,000 pounds of steel against half-ton worm-controlled meat puppets.

Steel won.

The people of the convoy huddled on the hoods and roofs of their wags and fired down into their attackers. A vast amount of the fire was doing little good.

"Toulalan!" Ryan bellowed over the sound of battle. "Get the wags rolling! Pull away and let the LAVs finish it!"

"Oui, Ryan!" Toulalan jumped from the top of his wag and slammed the driver's door closed seconds behind the snapping tusks of a sow.

He shouted to Cyrielle on top. "Hold on!" The air horn blared the signal to pull out.

Ryan was nearly knocked from his feet as the pickup beneath him lurched. A huge hog had lowered its head against the passenger door. The pickup slewed. The behemoth boar lowered its snout beneath the chassis. Worms extruding out of its ears pointed at Ryan and Krysty almost in accusation. The chassis creaked and lurched again.

The pig was going to roll the pickup.

Ryan tilted the machine gun down and dropped the hammer on the hog. Bones splintered and shattered. Metal-jacketed bullets pulverized the pig's shoulders into masticated meat. The creature fell forward, its legs shattered.

"Krysty! Drive!"

The woman limboed through the driver's window and slid behind the wheel. The engine roared and the pickup bucked as she rolled over the fallen hog's head with a crunch. Krysty drove the pickup a good fifty yards away from any carcass moving or not. The convoy pulled out of its defensive circle, leaving the remaining creatures suddenly milling around in a lost fashion. Only Doc and Mildred stayed on the roof of their wag. Neither seemed eager to jump down and start the car. But they were a lone island now rather than part of a confused melee.

Jak and Six descended like ironclad guardian angels. The two men seemed to be in race to see who could reduce the most pounds of pork flesh into mulch. J.B. stood in the turret watching the perimeter as the destruction derby wound down.

Ryan tapped the roof of the pickup. "Let's get Doc and Mildred."

Krysty rolled up to the old sec cruiser. The field around it was a butcher's morass. Ryan held out his hand. "Mildred, Doc, jump here in the back. I'll drive that one."

The two men handled Mildred across. Ryan held out his hand to Doc, who was looking at the strip of ground between the two vehicles. The broken worms seemed to have no life left in them but many were still whole. Ryan watched as those that were burrowed into the soft dirt.

"Ryan."

"Yeah, Doc?"

"I think we should only eat food from the Diefenbunkers, or dried goods."

"Right."

"We should boil any water we drink," Doc added.

"Right."

The two men watched as the last of the worms disap-

Chapter Five

"Did you see that!" Mildred was incensed. She was outraged and paced in circles, waving her arms. "Goddamn Night of the Pigging Dead!" No one got her reference, but everyone took her meaning. The convoy was almost half a mile away. They had left behind camp gear and equipment, a heartbreakingly sizable spread of food and a sea of spent brass. No one wanted to wade through the swathes of goop rotting in the sun or risk what might be squirming beneath in an attempt at salvage. Ryan and his friends were having a private palaver behind their LAV. "I'll take good old-fashioned American deserts, rads and stickies any day of the week!"

Ryan pulled the chain of his flexible cleaning rod through the Scout's barrel. The new longblaster had been baptized the hard way and seen him through. Ryan shook his head. He'd seen more horrors than he cared to think about in his travels. That last bit had been bad. "J.B.?"

The Armorer was on the same page. "That was bad."

"Doc?"

"The coordinated effort of the annelids, particularly once their porcine hosts were obviously postmortem, clearly bespoke some sort of collective intelligence," Doc enthused. "Really quite extraordinary. I would be curious as to—"

"Jak?" Ryan asked.

"Bad," Jak agreed.

Mildred had already spoken her mind. It wasn't something she ever had much problem with. Ryan looked at Krysty. She sat at the top of the LAV's ramp door and hugged her knees. Her good feelings for this land had been rocked like everyone else's. However her connection to the earth left her a little more sensitive to abominations.

Ryan wiped down his weapon, loaded it and put the cleaning kit back in the recess in the stock. "So, jump? Run south? Keep going?"

"Either of the later." Doc sighed. "But you know I will jump if it must be."

"I know." Ryan nodded. "Thanks."

J.B. finished running a rag over his M-4000 shotgun and began loading fléchette and slug rounds. "South."

"South?" Krysty sighed. "Alone? It's four hundred miles to anywhere we've been, much less heard of. Got coldhearts to the north. Those…things to the south. Mebbe there's safety in numbers. Mebbe the plains will be better. Mebbe we should head west with a convoy a bit more before we break and run south."

It was a lot of mebbes, but she had a point.

"Jak?"

"West," Jak replied.

Mildred's lips quirked. "Wouldn't have anything to do with a little grease monkey in coveralls?"

Everyone looked over at the engineer LAV. A short girl with curly brown hair covered by a bandanna was perched on top, half in and half out of the engine compartment wrenching away. She wasn't classically beautiful, but her big brown eyes, full lower lip and dimpled chin were something to look at. She currently had a smudge of grease on the tip of her nose. For the past twenty-four hours Jak's ruby-red gaze often strayed to whatever wag she was working on, and she seemed to work wags 24/7. He lifted his chin at the mechanic.

"Name's Seriah. Yeah." Jak nodded at Ryan again. "West."

"Mildred?"

"What the hell, west. The weather's nice. The food is good. The people seem friendly."

J.B. stared hard at Mildred. "Six seems real friendly."

Everyone stared at the Armorer's comment.

Mildred stared in wonder. "J. B. Dix, are you jealous?"

J.B. snatched up his shotgun and stomped away without another word.

Ryan looked around the circle. "We got five votes west. In a while I'll—"

"It's unanimous." The Armorer stomped back just as quickly. "West it is."

Mildred stepped toward him. "J.B.?"

"Doc?" J.B. reached into his pocket and held out what appeared to be six beige wine corks.

Doc took the objects and exposed his gleaming white teeth. "These are suspiciously of a 16-gauge conformation."

"They're high explosive. Those pigs got me thinking. Can't just shoot them full of holes. That's an ounce of HE. Should shatter some bones."

"Thank you, J.B. I shall refit myself this instant." Doc set about reloading his LeMat.

"J.B.?" Mildred questioned.

"Walk?" he asked.

Mildred slid her arm in his. "I'd love to." The two of them walked off in a circuit of the wag camp.

Ryan took Krysty's hand. "Let's sign up." They walked back to the circled wags. People were checking loads and prepping to go. Toulalan watched the proceedings. His sister Cyrielle and Six seemed to be doing most of the directing. Toulalan stood by his personal wag. It was a Chevy Silverado, lovingly maintained, with a camper mounted in the bed. Unlike a lot of the vehicles it was almost miraculously free of bullet strikes.

Ryan had taken an informal survey of the convoy's vehicles. They currently had twelve wags rolling and four motor-bikes. The big rig, the engineering LAV and Toulalan's home on wheels were the most spectacular. Ryan counted three armed wags—a pair of pickups and an El Camino, sheathed in sheet-iron chicken armor with post-mounted machine guns in the truck beds. An old ambulance was stuffed with Diefen-bunker med supplies. Six's jacked-up Crown Victoria was almost unrecognizable under the added-on plate. The rest of the vehicles had been repaired, rebuilt and remodified so many times the lines of their original pedigree had been lost. The convoy consisted of about seventy-seven souls at the moment, not counting Ryan and the companions.

"Impressive collection," Ryan said.

Toulalan smiled delightedly. "*Merci*. We're quite proud of it!"

"Is your next destination another bunker?"

"Indeed."

"So how come no one has cracked these Diefenbunkers before?" Ryan asked.

"Long before skydark, there was the cold war. You've heard of it, no?"

"Yeah."

"Yes, well, the Diefenbunkers were built for the cold war, but when she was won, they were deactivated. They became museums. After skydark, why go to a cold bare hole in the ground? The few who did, found the massive blast doors locked to them. The Diefenbunkers were placed out in the countryside. There was no time for historical expeditions when most were simply trying to live one more day."

"But you cracked one."

Toulalan smiled slyly. "My father did. Would you like to hear the story?"

Ryan nodded.

"Val-d'Or means 'Valley of Gold.' We were a mining

town, and in our valley far from the horror that fell. Of course, regardless, in the nuclear winter, many died, the ville contracted. But being a mining town we knew construction. The ville was also fortified. We dug a system of tunnels beneath the ville to survive the winter. Again, many died, but still many lived. Our forests were thick with timber and thick with game. Rivers and lakes abounded. Come the new hard freeze, huge herds of animals migrated south before it. There is always a great culling and smoking of meat. We survived on that, in some ways better than other villes farther south. We were far enough north not to take much radiation or be faced with the horrors it brought with it, but south enough that we could reap the benefit of the freeze without being hit by it, except only once every few years."

"But you cracked your bunker."

"My father found a cache of papers. They were—how do you say?—eyes only, for the mayor of Val-d'Or and few of the civic leaders. There was a flurry of activity at the Diefenbunker, construction, top secret, right before skydark, but the local people were never aware of it. That convinced my father there might be something down below the earth besides empty desks and concrete."

"How did you get in?"

Toulalan thumped his chest proudly. "The men of Val-d'Or have always been miners! My father figured the bunker must be like, oh…" He pointed at the LAV. "More heavily armored on the top than the bottom. A thick foundation, yes, but not hardened against the nukes like the top, no? He sank a shaft down and came up underneath. It took three years of effort, whenever that effort could be spared, but in the end my papa broke inside! I was with him!"

"What did you find?"

Toulalan kissed his fingertips and grinned. "Potatoes!"

Ryan blinked. "Potatoes?"

"Seed potatoes, actually, preserved for the future. There was a vast storehouse of them. The people weren't pleased. Oh, there were blasters and medical supplies, a machine shop and much that was useful, but the men of Val-d'Or had survived since skydark as miners, hunters and fisherman. We weren't farmers. Many said we couldn't afford the time to take up the plow. Our spring and summer were for catching as much meat and fish as possible and smoking it for the long winter." Toulalan smiled in happy memory. "My father joked that we lived half our lives underground like potatoes anyway. In the end he convinced them. We planted. There was trial and error, but that first season there was a crop. The seed potatoes had been modified, with the conditions of the new world in mind. They were hardy, resistant to the cold and matured quickly to take advantage of the brief warmth."

"And suddenly you had a surplus," Ryan surmised.

"Yes, no longer were we dependent upon hunting, fishing, trapping and the always uncertain migrations. We had a food staple, and we now had time for other things. We built more. Learned more. The seed bunkers also contained a number of other vegetables, and more importantly, hemp. It grew like, well, a weed in the short spring. We cleared forest and planted that, too. With that we had hemp seed oil and seeds to supplement our diet, textiles and paper. Hemp oil can be used directly to fuel diesel engines. We're very busy underground during the winter, spinning, pressing manufacturing. We still hunt and fish, but now we mine once again, as well. Val-d'Or has gold, silver, zinc and lead. Whoever stocked the Val-d'Or Diefenbunker had put a great deal of thought into local survival."

Ryan glanced back at the Borden Diefenbunker. "No seeds in that one."

"No, instead there were bays for armored wags, and equipment and spares to repair them. There were also many, many blasters." Toulalan shot Ryan another pointed look. "And a strange chamber of glass."

"We saw that." Ryan shrugged. "But it was the beer and pizza that grabbed our attention."

"Mmm." Toulalan nodded, but his eyes were seriously trying to read what Ryan was really thinking.

Better men had tried and failed. Ryan changed the subject. "So each of the bunkers seems to have been stocked differently."

"So it seems. We have used the radio at Val-d'Or and tried the Borden one, as well. No other bunker responds. The computer links between them fell long ago. We don't really know the disposition of the other bunkers. But whatever their function, they must be a treasure trove. We decided an expedition west would be the best course. We would head for Borden. If successful there—" Toulalan grinned again "—we would make an attempt for Shilo Diefenbunker in Manitoba."

Ryan did a little math with the maps he'd recently seen. "That's a long haul."

"Indeed." Toulalan didn't seem overly concerned.

Both men knew the other wasn't revealing all his cards. "And those coldhearts?"

"We have you to thank for bloodying their noses. I suspect they won't be back. Also, according to traders, the farther west you go, the flatter and more open the land becomes. Also, villes in the center are increasingly farther apart and increasingly more primitive. I believe we will be able to roll past them, using their awe at our trade goods and the offensive power and majesty of our convoy."

"And if this hard freeze of yours hits before you're back in Val-d'Or?"

"We have lost a bit of time, that is true, but once we hit the central plains it should be, how do you say, a straight shot."

"And if we get caught with winter coming on?"

"My friend, I have considered that. You have seen the inside of the Borden Diefenbunker. The one in Val-d'Or also had the same stocks of frozen food. I assume the one in Shilo does, as well. If we reach Shilo, we'll give the weather a hard appraisal. If we know we won't make it, we turn back. Either way, should worse comes to worst, we can winter in either bunker, warm, safe and fed until spring. Should you not wish to winter with us, as I say, you can always run south for your warmer Deathlands."

There were more than a few major "ifs" and question marks involved, but exploration was risk personified. In the end Ryan had to admit it wasn't a bad plan. He wanted to see more of this land that was new to him.

"And, so?" Toulalan inquired.

Krysty spoke first. Ryan knew her reservations and was glad she did. She stuck out her hand to Toulalan. "We're in."

Toulalan ignored the proffered hand, and Krysty's body stiffened in shock as Toulalan kissed her on both cheeks. Only the fact that he seemed so smiling and pleased, and Ryan had seen that the rest of convoy behaved this way, kept the one-eyed man from challenging the man. To Krysty's horror Toulalan started to lean in to give her lover the same treatment. Something in Ryan's single blue eye made Toulalan stop short at the last moment. He shoved out his hand awkwardly between them. "Well…good! Very good! I'll tell the others. They'll be most pleased to have you among us."

Ryan shook the man's hand, and he and Krysty walked back to tell their friends. Krysty's cheeks were flushed red and not because she was blushing. "If he does that again I'll kill him."

Ryan grinned. "Not if I get to him first."

THE CONVOY WAS READY to roll. Ryan's LAV would be positioned roughly in the middle. Except for the big rig it was high enough to shoot over all the other wags. The armored wag's huge, aggressive off-road tires would allow it to break formation to either side and rush forward or back if need be. The two off-road armed wags formed outriders on the sides. The ancient El Camino sheathed in chicken armor was on point, and the engineering LAV's armor and machine gun protected the rear.

Cyrielle Toulalan approached the LAV. "Ryan!"

The one-eyed man nodded from the turret. "Yeah?"

"A word, please."

Ryan hopped down. "Yeah?"

"You have driven a…" Cyrielle's English wasn't as good as her brother's. "Big rig?"

"Yeah?"

"Mmm." Cyrielle walked over to the semi and Ryan followed her. She pointed at a single bullet hole in the driver's side of the windshield.

"You lost your driver," Ryan surmised.

"Oui." She nodded.

Ryan sighed. Krysty walked over. "What's up, lover?"

"They need me to drive the semi."

Krysty's green eyes narrowed. "We need you in the war wag."

"We're part of this convoy now. Big wag like this takes know-how. I got it. Jak can drive the LAV and J.B. can fight it."

Krysty didn't blink. "I need you in the war wag. With me."

"The convoy needs someone who can drive this rig." Ryan gave Krysty an experimental smile. "And I need someone to ride shotgun with me."

"I don't have a shotgun."

"We'll find you something."

Krysty sighed and slid her hand into Ryan's. "Let's take a look at her."

Cyrielle clapped her hands.

Ryan examined his new ride. It was a Kenworth. It had
been extensively modified with giant off-road tires and a
new suspension. A hatch in the roof over the passenger seat
opened onto a ring-mounted machine blaster. Ryan suspected
it was a Diefenbunker special, and it was just about cherry,
save for the slightly ominous bullet hole in the driver's-side
windshield patched with a piece of scrap metal. Krysty's
hands slid out of his and they climbed into the cab through
opposite doors. There were some cracks in the plastic dash,
and whatever ancient leather had once upholstered the cab
had been replaced with deerskin. The driver's seat had dried
bloodstains on it. There was what looked like a functional
hot plate, chem toilet and a bunk in the back.

Krysty ran a finger over the laced leather of her armrest.
"Plush wag."

It had been a while since Ryan had been behind the wheel
of a major cargo wag. Toulalan walked up and waved. "You
like?"

Ryan hurled a shrug back at the Quebecer. "It's okay."

Toulalan kissed his fingertips, popped his lips and walked
away.

The biggest problem with wags in the Deathlands was the
lack of batteries. That usually meant cartridge or crank ignition. Seriah walked up and pulled the crank handle from the
rack above the bumper. She grinned and shoved the crank
spoke through the hole in the grille.

Ryan leaned out the driver's window. "Light it up!"

Seriah hurled her tiny frame against the crank handle and
spun it in a huge circle. Ryan tapped the gas pedal lightly at
the apogee of the crank. The turbine turned over, whined and
trembled on the first attempt. Seriah jumped up and down
and clapped her hands. *Très bien!*

Ryan pulled the horn chain and the Kenworth bellowed

like a twentieth-century dinosaur into the postapocalyptic Canadian sky. The people of the convoy hit their horns, leaned out of their windows and clapped and whistled in response. "Ryan! Ryan! Ryan!" they called. Their enthusiasm was infectious. Krysty's full lips twisted in a smile. "I'll go tell J.B. he's in command of the LAV."

Chapter Six

"Hey, Mace! Lars is wormy, eh!"

Baron Mace Henning glowered out of his hammock at his sec man. "Baron to you, Shorty."

Shorty lived up to his name. He made up for it with an almost artistic appreciation of violence. They had been partners as sec men until Mace had led a coup and made himself baron. Shorty had backed him. Sometimes when Shorty got excited he forgot protocol and flashed back to the old days. "Uh, sorry, Baron. Lars is like, definitely 'fected. Too bad, he'd just earned his loonie."

Henning rolled out of his sleeping sling and walked over to the campfire. Shorty heeled after him like a faithful dog.

Mace Henning was a huge, sagging bull of man. His short curly red hair and beard were shot through with gray. Green eyes peered out of a nearly permanent squint. Even in his youth no one had ever accused him of being handsome. A badly set broken nose and the dent in the ride side of his face from a fractured cheekbone hadn't helped matters. Scar tissue beneath his left eyebrow raised it up a tad higher than his right. It made it look like anyone or anything he laid his gaze upon was being weighed, measured and found wanting.

He or she usually was.

He had sixty-eight armed men in the saddle. He'd had seventy-five but the tide of yesterday's battle had turned into a costly and unpleasant surprise. His best men greeted him as they rolled up hammocks, wolfed their breakfast of jerky and pine tea or prepped their bikes, wags or weapons. A sizable crowd of his new-hire coldhearts was gathered in a circle beyond the campfire, morning maple-liquor ration in hand and watching the entertainment.

The circle parted for the baron. Mace turned his gaze on Lars. The buckskin-clad sec man was red-eyed and lunging at the chain tethering him to a motorcycle lying on its side. He'd shown worm-sign just before dark the night before. Sometimes other maladies could be mistaken for early worm symptom, so they had chained him and waited while he begged and pleaded and screamed he'd just eaten something bad.

Lars was definitely infected. His muscles rippled with Herculean effort and infestation. The man's fingers curled into claws as he lunged again. The motorcycle weighed around five hundred pounds. Each lunge dragged it a few inches along. The baron stood unconcernedly a bare meter out of range of the filthy clawing hands. In his hand Mace carried his badge of office and the source of his nickname. It was a blackthorn club about two feet long. The root ball at the end was as big around as a large apple, and he had drilled out its center and "hot-shotted" it by pouring in molten lead to give it killing end-weight.

"Hey, Baron?" Shorty asked.

Mace heaved a sigh. Shorty combined the traits of not being particularly bright but also being something of a ponderer. Mace didn't take his eyes off Lars and his carnivorous, worm-fested carryings-on. "What?"

"What do you think goes through a man's mind? I mean, you know, like, when the worms get to his brain and stuff?"

Some of the sec men muttered in amusement. Shorty's ponderings didn't exactly soar up into rarified intellectual heights. Mace moved with the sudden, stunning speed most of his opponents never expected. He whipped his club up and around like a tennis serve and sank it through Lars's skull.

The scout dropped to his knees and fell face-first into the dirt. The sec men gaped. The baron shrugged carelessly as he pulled his bludgeon free of Lars's brainpan. "Probably not much more than that."

The men roared.

The baron reached down and snapped a leather thong from around his former scout's neck. An old, predark, Canadian dollar coin—known as a loonie for the waterfowl on one side—hung from it. Mace closed his fist around the coin. Shorty was right. It was too bad, but Lars wasn't from around here, and it looked like he hadn't heeded the warnings. And even if you took every precaution, sometimes the worms found a way. Mace jerked his head at the corpse. Filth was already squirming into activity in the shattered skull. "Butch, Ledge."

Butch and Ledge were twins. The two lanky, ponytailed young men came forward unlimbering their clubs. Theirs weren't as fancy as Mace's. They were just well-turned, tapered lengths of hickory each with a gaff hook imbedded in it. Butch and Ledge were local boys. They knew what to do from long experience and weren't squeamish about it. They quickly broke Lars's knees and elbows. Lars started twitching as worms writhed beneath his dead flesh. Arms and legs were levers, and denied the fulcrum of the knees and elbows, the best the worms' contractions could manage was some awkward heaving and flopping. The two men expertly shattered Lars's jaw to keep him honest and his collarbones to keep him armless. They gaffed him through the armpits, and the other sec men shoved out of the way warily as the twin exterminators dragged Lars's twitching corpse over to the campfire and heaved him into the flames.

Mace went for a walk while his men oohed and aahed in fascination as Lars's carcass slowly twisted and burned and worms snaked out of his body in a panic only to wriggle, blister and burst in the flames. Mace jerked his head at a man in passing. "Tag."

Skin Tag rose and followed his baron. The mutie's name said it all. Skin tags a half-inch long covered every inch of his exposed body. They covered his head like hair. The only place he didn't visibly have them were on his eyelids and the palms of his hands. Mace had never cared to look, but it was rumored they covered the rest of Tag's body, including his dangle. Rumor was some women liked it, but even Shorty wasn't dumb enough to ponder it in Tag's face. Mutie or not, Tag was just about the most dangerous man Mace had ever encountered, and one of the smartest. But beyond his skill with blaster and blade or his ruthless cunning, it was something radiation and mutation had set inside his skull that made him a gold mine.

Tag could sense other muties, even ones that outwardly appeared perfectly normal.

When Mace had first met him, Tag was making a living out of it. He would appear at the gates of villes that were known to kill or drive out muties. What had been central Canada had taken the least of skydark's damage. Human muties were a lot rarer there and often more feared and reviled than in the Deathlands or what was left of Canada's coasts. Tag would appear at the villes on the plains and throw back his robe. Seconds before they shot him he would shout out that unclean as he was, he could detect the unclean among them. Mace had been a sec man in such a ville in Saskatchewan when Tag made an appearance. Mace's first instinct was to crush Tag's fleshy-headed mutant skull for the charlatan he was, but the baron was obsessed about keeping the gene pool clean and demanded a demonstration. Tag had walked straight toward a sec man named Voor. Mace had known Voor for years, but Tag pointed a melodramatic finger at Voor in judgment.

"Mutie."

At the baron's order Mace and the other sec men had grabbed Voor, howling and struggling, and had stripped him. The crowd had gasped at the pale baby fingers protruding from Voor's underarms. Mace didn't give a dark night one way or the other about muties, but he'd crushed Voor's skull instantly and without being asked, much to his baron's rabid approval. Tag found two more victims. Afterward he had been given food, jack, ammo for his blaster, and at his strange request, allowed to take any books of his choice from the ville if the ville had any of the rare items. The baron generously allowed Tag to sleep in the ville that night. In a bed.

That night the baron had decided to keep Tag around for the sake of the ville's genetic hygiene and ordered Mace to kneecap Tag and chain him. Mace had bigger plans. He found Tag in his room, and instead helped Tag to escape and proposed a partnership. It was simple. They went from ville to ville. Tag would go first and perform his act and receive his reward. However, if he found several mutants, he would allow one or two to escape undetected. The next day Mace would come to the ville posing as a trader. That night he would inform the undisclosed muties of their impending discovery and relieve them of everything of value that Mace could put in his pack.

It was a profitable racket and went on for several seasons. Finally they had come all the way east to Ontario. There they found a ville on the brink. Tag pulled his act but Mace stayed on. The ville was prosperous, but the baron was old, he had no sons and his sec men were already forming factions for the succession. Mace had joined up, ingratiated himself and become the baron's right-hand man. Mace recruited a small, very hard-core corps out of the various factions, starting with Shorty. Meanwhile, Tag lurked. It was something he was very good at.

One night Mace and his picked cadre silently slaughtered the baron and his family, but let his two daughters live. The ville had awakened to find Mace Henning enthroned, entrenched in the hall. Though well bruised and abused, the old baron's daughters acknowledged Mace as heir. It had almost turned into ville civil war until Mace pulled his ace card. Tag appeared out of nowhere. He pointed at Mace's main rival and said the dreaded word.

"Mutie."

It didn't matter that the man showed no sign. The people of the ville had seen Tag ferret mutants out earlier in the spring. The accused's own men turned on him. Strangely enough, over the course of the next few days, most dissenters or loyalists to the old regime found themselves declared mutie and found themselves summarily shot. Strangely enough, after the coup, Baron Mace Henning discovered a tolerance for human muties as long as they were useful and fell short of outright abominations, and they began flocking to him and his ville in a slow, steady and extremely loyal trickle.

Tag had been Mace's right-hand man ever since, and the only man he let call him Mace, though even then only in private.

Mace and Tag hadn't stopped at usurping a backwater ville. They had turned their former blackmail victims across Canada into a web of informants. Knowledge was power, and Mace had waxed strong. Half a dozen villes paid him yearly tribute, and word of what was going on in other villes he had yet to conquer or intimidate was nonetheless whispered in Mace's ear.

Mace had had his eye on Val-d'Or for some time.

The previous year Tag had pulled his act in Val-d'Or, and what he had discovered had been a game-changer in Mace's dreams of conquest, and his plans for the ville.

Tag followed the baron on a slow walk around the raiding camp. "Mace?"

"What do you think, Tag?"

"About the battle?"

"Yeah."

"Didn't like it."

Mace snorted and spit. Yesterday had hurt. "Pulling out that third armored wag, like an ace in hole. I didn't expect that out of Toulalan. Oh, he's smart, mind you. Too smart for his own good, a damned intellectual, but he ain't battle clever. Not like us. He's shown us that more than once. Him switching tactics like that stinks of something. Maybe he's finally started listening to Six." Mace's ugly face flushed angrily. Six had been a thorn in his side for years. "And why none of the boys can seem to put a bullet in that son of a bitch is beyond me."

Tag pushed back the hood of his robe. He preferred clothes of flowing homespun. Pants and tight clothes chaffed and tore at his affliction. Around his neck he wore a gleaming silver coin. "It's not a new tactic, and it's not Six. Six never wanted to leave Val-d'Or. He thinks the mission is foolish. That's part of his problem. It undermines his strategy."

"Oh?" Mace's face flushed redder. "We've been picking away at the bastards for weeks. I mean nuke it! We could have taken them the last time out if we'd pushed it. Yesterday we had them dead to rights. I was about to pull the men back and let the bastards lick their wounds for another week when that third war wag came out of nowhere and rained on us like a chem storm!"

"They weren't part of the convoy," Tag asserted.

Mace stopped walking. "Oh?"

"You saw. Toulalan's people can barely drive those iron wags, much less fight them. The people in the third came out of that bunker coldhearted and knowledgeable. Took out our scouts, flanked us and rained on us."

"So how'd they get into the bunker in the first place?"

"I don't know." Tag shook his head. "It's anomalous."

Mace raised his left eyebrow a hair higher than normal. "Don't give me the big words, Tag."

Tag smiled. Despite the mutated flesh studding his face, it was surprisingly charming. Beneath it he was undoubtedly a very handsome man. "Don't know. Don't like it." Tag leaned in conspiratorially. "Tell you this, though."

Mace leaned in. "What?"

"The newcomers got a mutie among them. I felt it."

There was nothing charming at all about Mace Henning's smile. "Interesting."

Chapter Seven

The convoy rolled north. Krysty was positively giddy behind the wheel of the big rig. It was a warm afternoon. The windows were open, and the wind of their passage ruffled her red hair. She was a beautiful woman. In the pink light of Canada's shimmering skies her beauty was heartbreaking. Krysty could drive a wag, but a big rig was something else entirely. Ryan was proud she was picking it up so quickly. He dragged his eye back to business. He stood in the machine-blaster hatch and scanned backward through his Navy longeye at the distance they had put behind him. There was nothing there, but Ryan's gut was speaking to him and he always listened to it. He saw Six standing in one of the outriding pickups. Ryan clicked on the radio. "Six, Ryan."

The big man sounded distracted over the static. "What?"

"I think we're being followed."

Six made a noise. "I guarantee it."

"Want to do something about it?"

Six considered this for several long seconds. "Why not?"

The iron-skinned pickup closed up with the convoy and pulled alongside the semi. Six scowled even more mightily than usual at the sight of Krysty grinning behind the wheel. He shouted over the cacophony of engine noise. "What do you propose?"

"Get us two of the bikes!"

Six got on the horn, and two of the motorcycle scouts headed back in.

Ryan slid down into the cab. "Keep her straight." The one-eyed man took up his rifle as the vehicle came alongside, and he jumped into the pickup bed. Six thumped his hand on the roof and the driver brought the pickup to a halt.

Six got back on the horn. "Seriah, Krysty is driving the truck. Why don't you ride with her for a while?"

The little wrench's voice came back. "You got it, Vinny!"

Six made another noise. Seriah's attitude seemed to be eternally sunny. The two bikers pulled up. "*Oui*, Six?"

"Ryan and I are going for a ride. Give us your bikes."

The two riders didn't look happy about having their rides usurped, but Ryan was quickly getting the impression that no one in the convoy other than Toulalan and perhaps Seriah ever gave Six any lip.

Ryan threw a leg over an ancient Honda Nighthawk that looked as though it had been rebuilt from stem to stern more than once. He gave the 'Hawk some gas and began tooling down the road the way the convoy had come. Six followed, and Ryan could feel the big man's eyes burning into his back. He ignored the sec man and thought like a coldheart. The land was low and rolling, and the road wound between the hills and stands of forest. There was no way for the convoy to hide its tracks.

The one-eyed man looked back, and the convoy's dust plume rose into the sky like a giant pointing finger. All of the convoy's vehicles had been modified. Beefed-up suspensions and offroad tires gave them the ability to traverse the raddled, broken and often overgrown Canadian roads, but they had few genuine offroad vehicles. The symbolism was obvious. The convoy was a herd. A dangerous herd, as it had horns, but like a migrating herd it stayed on its route. The coldhearts were a wolf pack, which could strike wherever and whenever it wanted. Chipping away, picking off stragglers, just the presence of a few of them in the distance would keep the convoy on the razor's edge, day after day, wearing them down.

Ryan was pretty sure they were close.

He pulled off the road and drove up a steep green hill-side, followed by Six. Ryan reached the top of the hill and stopped. On a hill opposite them to the east a coldheart stood dismounted and was watching the convoy's dust. He didn't seem particularly cautious.

Six's voice was bitter with frustration. "This isn't the first time they've done this."

"Oh?"

"Yes, my second in command, a man named Guy. He doubled back to find our trackers. The situation was much like this. He and his team gave pursuit."

Ryan thought he knew the answer. "And?"

"And we used to have six motorcycles," Six said bitterly. "Now we have two."

"They drew Guy into an ambush."

Six scowled across the rolling grassland separating him from someone he desperately wished to kill. "Guy was brave, and strong, but impulsive. I have since forbidden hot pursuit of the enemy."

"So they pick at you, waging a war of attrition."

"Yes." Six glowered. "Look, he has seen us."

"No doubt," Ryan agreed. Quicksilver flashed in the pink, late-afternoon light on top of the far hill. "They're signaling with mirrors. He's got more behind him."

"I can see that." Six turned his glare on Ryan. "Somehow I thought you had a plan."

"I do."

"Oh? I would very much like to hear it."

Ryan lifted his chin toward the other hill. "We kill that guy."

"Oh?"

Ryan looked at the laser range-finding binoculars Six wore around his neck. The one-eyed man almost never carried battery-operated devices himself, simply because in the Deathlands the rads, electromagnetic anomalies and the nearly universal lack of recharging facilities made them a dangerous crutch to become dependent on. However, since Six happened to be carrying one...

"Yeah, range me."

"Ah, your magic rifle," Six scoffed, but raised his optics to his eyes and pushed a button. The laser aligned with the glass gave him an exact distance. "The range is nine hundred and seventy-five meters," he reported dryly.

Ryan dropped prone and deployed the Scout's internal bipod. The blaster had proved to him it could unleash lightning during the boar attack. Now it was time to see if it could hurl the thunderbolt. Ryan tilted his cheek into the stock of his rifle. At 2.5 power, the magnification was low and at nearly a thousand yards the range was long. The man on the opposite hill was still doll-size in Ryan's scope. The Deathlands warrior considered his target very carefully and raised his aim until it barely occupied the lowest visible point of his crosshairs.

"You think you can hit a man at a thousand meters, in this light, with that—"

Ryan's fingertip gave the trigger a slow kiss and the Scout bucked against his shoulder. The man on the other hill jumped in alarm.

"A miss!" Six spit.

Ryan flicked the bolt and fired again.

"Miss! You are wasting your am—" Six suddenly shifted his binoculars. "No! Hit! Hit!"

"Six!" Ryan put a final round into the other man's bike. The coldheart didn't dare try to jump on as bullets kept cracking against it. "Get him!"

Six jumped onto his bike as the coldheart broke and ran. The big man popped a wheelie and tore across the grassland separating him and his prey. Ryan snapped his bipod shut, slung the Scout and got in the saddle. The Nighthawk snarled and spit blue smoke.

The Quebecer flew over the hill and disappeared. Ryan came to the crest and spun to a stop. The sec man quickly caught up with the coldheart. His longblaster flashed in his trademark big spin. The running man turned only in time to scream and take a big .45-70-caliber bullet through the sternum. Six swept past the fallen man and turf flew as he spun in tight circle.

Ryan unlimbered his longblaster once more as massed engines rumbled like thunder in the distance.

Six knelt over the man and drew his huge bowie knife. Despite the slug in his chest, the coldheart managed a thin scream as Six scalped him. Ryan looked at the coldheart's motorcycle. The tailpipe was torn, tufts of wool batting stuck out of the bullet hole in the buckskin seat. Ryan had hit the tank, and he could smell the home-stilled alcohol the coldheart had been burning for fuel. Ryan took a precious butane lighter out of his pocket, then pushed the stricken bike over with his boot. In the Deathlands you didn't mess with another person's ride. Most likely it was the same in Canada.

This was war.

He took a rag from a pocket, touched the flame of his butane lighter to one end, then tossed the rag onto the bike. Pale blue flame played across the engine block.

"Six!" Ryan shouted. The big man leaped onto his bike and rode back to the top of the hill and spun to a stop next to Ryan. From their vantage the one-eyed man saw a mob of motorcycles cresting the next row of hills to the east. He took out his Navy longeye and extended it, counting about a dozen. The two forces stood and regarded each other over the half mile between them. A thin plume of black smoke rose from the burning bike beside Ryan. Six slowly held aloft his grizzly trophy. The scalped man was a bloody rag lying between the contenders. Ryan waited for the cavalry charge and hoped for it. If the coldhearts were hot for revenge, they would roar down in a swarm, and Ryan and Six would drop prone and shoot the riders out of their saddles as they came on.

The coldhearts didn't take the bait.

Ryan was pretty sure they had taken note. Six had made his bloody mark, and the one-eyed man had made his point. Stalking the convoy had turned into a much rougher game. Unfortunately the enemy had made a point, as well.

For roving coldhearts they had a sense of discipline that Ryan didn't care for at all.

BARON MACE HENNING wasn't pleased. He sat on his camp tool with his cluboss his knees like a samurai warlord. "What's that you say, Shorty?"

Shorty scuffed the toe of his boot into the ground nervously. "Said Jimmy Pickering's been chilled."

"Oh yeah?" Jimmy had been one of Mace's better scouts. "How'd that happen?"

"Old Vinny scalped him." Shorty cleared his throat. "Burned his bike."

"You saw it?"

"Saw after. Old Vinny was up on the next rise. Wavin' Jimmy's scalp at us."

Mace's eyes went to slits. "So what'd you do about it, Shorty?"

Shorty started paying intense attention to his boots again. "Nothin'…"

"Nothing?"

"Vinny was up on that hill, like I said, 'bout a klick away

with that big shiny blaster of his and nothin' 'tween us and
it but a lot of real open ground. And there was another guy
with him. I saw him real good. Through my 'noculars. Guy
was one-eyed and had some kind of funky-lookin' carbine. I
don't think he's from around here, or Val-d'Or neither. Real
coldheart-lookin' prick. Lookin' like he might even give
old Vinny a hard time. 'Cept they was standin' side-by-side
and Vinny was smiling. We had 'em numbered, Baron, but
I didn't like it. I didn't like that stranger or his blaster, and I
sure didn't like the smile on Vinny's face."

Mace stared at Shorty. It was undoubtedly the most intelligent thing the sec man had ever said. Mace looked to Red,
who was one of his sons. He was nowhere near as big as his
father; indeed he took after his mother in being short and
thin. Mace neither denied Red nor acknowledged him, but
the red hair, green eyes and ugly features were absolutely unmistakable. When Red had first come to his father and asked
for a job as a sec man, he didn't bring up his blood. Mace
had told him to go to a rival ville and bring him three ears.
Red had come back with ten. He was unlikely to ever win a
stand-up club or tomahawk fight, but Red was a nightcreeper
extraordinaire, a decent shot with a blaster and could think
on his feet. The chunk of change he wore around his neck
was proof. "Red?"

"Like he said, Baron. Those two just stood there waitin',
and Jimmy all laid out on the killing ground between us with
the bedsheet pulled off his skull. No one sneaks up on Jimmy.
That means they picked him off at range, and that says some-
thin' right there. Some of the boys wanted to go straight in.
Shorty said no." Red met his father's eyes. "I backed him."

Mace had been working very hard the last few years to
instill some sense of tactics into his men. It had taken some
head cracking, but it was starting to pay off. Baron Henning

still wasn't ready to start handing out compliments. "Don't suppose anyone retrieved Jimmy's change?"

"No." Red flinched. "Vinny's got it. Added it to his collection."

Mace slowly rose. His club hung loose from his wrist by its thong. Tag rose behind him. His gaudy-house fancy auto-blaster wasn't quite pointing at anyone in particular, yet. The baron looked at the arc of men arrayed in front of him on the other side of the campfire; his eyebrow permanently cocked in judgment. The men stared back, mentally laying bets on whether Shorty, Red or both would get their skulls crushed and lose their change. Would Mace really put his club through his best friend's brain? Or his own redheaded bastard son?

Baron Mace Henning bellowed like a bull and shoved his club skyward. "Who wants to winter in Val-d'Or?"

Shorty shouted first. He'd seen Mace rally the troops before, and he was ecstatic his skull was still intact. "Fuckin'-ay, Mace!"

The baron let the lack of protocol go. "Who wants to winter down in that underground gaudy palace they got? Heard they got central heating!"

More men took up the chant. "Fuckin'-ay, Mace!"

"Who wants to winter sleeping on bearskins, smoking hemp and eating poutine? Heard they're growing taters in excess!"

The chant grew. "Fuckin'-ay, Mace!"

"Who wants his own blond French slut to chew his boots this winter, and slobber on anything else a man has a mind for?"

The chant grew to a roar.

Baron Mace Henning's riding skins creaked as he slowly sat and once more laid his club across his knees. "The way I figure it, Vinny owes me about fifty dollars now. Who's going to bring me back all that jack?" Mace leaned forward. "Who's going to bring me a black ear?"

Every man shoved a club, tomahawk or blaster toward the shimmering Northern Lights and shook it. They whooped and shoved one another, each man shouting out how he was the one who would take down Vincent Six.

"Boys?" A silver coin appeared in Mace's hand. He held it up to gleam in the firelight. "Who's going to earn himself a silver Voyager?"

The whooping stopped and the assembled sec men stared at the coin that only a few ever earned. "I want Vinny's ears. I want Yoann Toulalan alive and in condition to give me the codes to the bunkers and the keys to Val-d'Or. I want his sister Cyrielle bent over my bike."

Guffaws broke out around the assembly.

The baron grew serious again. "I don't care if everything else burns, but I want the big rig and I want that wrecker LAV, intact." Mace rose once more. "Each of you who ain't on picket duty tonight, you can draw one ration of maple hooch. Check your blasters, check your rides, make sure your blades are sharp and bright. I want them nicked and bloody tomorrow. We're gonna burn ahead of the convoy hard. They gotta head north to hit the Trans-Canada. We're gonna drop that overpass we marked right in their way. We don't let them circle up. We stop that convoy cold, and then we take it. No more messing around. Tag will give each of you your jobs tomorrow."

The men nodded and the circle began to break up.

"One more thing boys." The men gasped as a second silver coin appeared between Mace's fingers. "I want the other eye of that Cyclops son of a bitch."

Chapter Eight

"You see!" Six threw the scalp at Toulalan's feet. "I told you! It is Henning!"

"Henning?" Toulalan had stopped smiling. Ryan could tell this was an argument they'd had before. "I see a man's hair, Vincent. My father allows you these excesses, but you know I don't approve of you taking such trophies."

"I don't take scalps as trophies," Six rumbled. "I take scalps as a warning." Six reached into his sheepskins and pulled out a leather necklace with two coins dangling from it. He threw it on top of the scalp. "When I want a trophy, I take these!"

People around the council circle gasped. Seriah stood next to Ryan, and she looked very upset. He spoke quietly while French started flying fast and furious between Toulalan and Six. "What's that?"

"There's a baron up here named Henning. Mace Henning. He's bad news. They say his ville hardly produces anything anymore except sec men. Just about lives off tribute. He turned his eye on Val-d'Or a few years back. He's sent probes, scouts and last year a raiding party, but they keep running into Six and losing their hair."

"What's with the coins?"

"They're old money, jack to you guys, Canadian, predark. The goldy looking one is a loonie, 'cause of the bird on the back. It's our old dollar. They say you kill ten of Mace's enemies, or his enemy's people—man, woman, child, mutie, it doesn't matter—you get to wear one. The two-color one is a toonie, the old two dollar coin. You get one of them if you kill twenty."

Doc eyed the necklace glinting dully in the dirt unhappily. "So, a three-dollar man."

Six's head snapped around. "*Oui,* Doc. A three-dollar man." Six reached into his sheepskins and pulled out a thick leather wallet. He upended it, and over a dozen necklaces loaded with denominations fell to the ground. Some had up to four or five coins on them. "Across old Ontario, beware of a man who jingles, and should you meet a man with a silver coin? Unless you are with me, I suggest you run."

"Henning—" Toulalan stared at the coin necklace "—he is far from his territory."

"Yes, well?" Six spit in disgust as he snatched up the jingling pendants and shoved them back into his wallet. He left the scalp where it lay. "So are we."

"I don't see how he can be following us. I—"

"I told you he would find out! I told you he would use the opportunity to attack us or attack Val-d'Or! Now we know! He's after us! It was foolish! Foolish to mount this expedition during the raiding season! Filling your father's head with dreams! Going on a wild-goose chase when—"

"The Diefenbunkers are no wild-goose chase! They are real! You *know* what we seek, Six!"

"I know a bird in the hand is worth two in the bush! And we have a golden bird in our hand, Yoann! Our Val-d'Or!" Six sighed heavily. "We never should have left it."

"Henning and a few picked men! Their ranks swollen with motorcycle coldhearts!" Toulalan scoffed. "A rabble—"

"The rabble nearly took us two days ago!"

Doc spoke quietly but his voice carried. "They are not coldhearts. They are dragoons."

Everyone around the circle cocked their heads at Doc.

Doc continued. "These men are not simple motorcycle raiders like we have seen in the Deathlands. They are dragoons."

Six rolled his eyes.

Ryan hoped Doc wasn't going to go into some lecture about some general no one had ever heard of from a war no one remembered.

Toulalan gave Doc a tolerant look. "What is this...dragoon?"

Doc forged on. "Men who ride to battle like cavalry, using their mounts for speed, but then dismounting to fight on foot like infantry."

Ryan nodded. Everyone once in blue moon Doc made some sense. "Doc's right, bike raiders are easy if you don't break and run. They depend on terror. They ride into a ville and everyone scatters. A good man with a longblaster can shoot them out of the saddle before they ever get close enough to do anything from the back of their bike. Mace's men have some tactical sense."

Six began walking in circles and waving his arms in a remarkable imitation of Mildred. "So what do you suggest we do! I have only two motorcycles left! I can't fight them at their own game!"

"LAV them?" J.B. suggested.

Six did his looming routine over the little Armorer. "Don't think I haven't thought of it. But it is big, and loud, and we could never sneak it past Mace's pickets. Even if we managed it, they would scatter before the LAV in all directions, only to regroup later."

Toulalan threw up his hands. "And what do you suggest, Six?"

"We turn back. We achieved the Borden Diefenbunker. We can try for another next year."

"And then we have to fight them? All the way back to Val-d'Or?"

Six got that sudden dry, sarcastic look on his face. "We can fight them all the way to Manitoba, and then all the way back if you prefer."

"He will tire."

"Mace Henning never tires. He hates you, he hates your father! He hates me and he wants our ville! He wants it all. From the Lakes to the mouth of the St. Lawrence. Val-d'Or is the key to his dreams of empire!"

Ryan watched the two men argue. Yoann Toulalan was a man with a dream. Vincent Six was a sec man who wanted to be back home defending his ville. He saw both men's point, but both men were missing the bigger picture. "You're thinking defensively. Best defense is a good offense."

"Oh?" Six tried to give Ryan the looming routine and failed. He went back to sneering. "Please, I beg of you, show me your offense."

"This Mace. How far away's his ville?"

Toulalan's eyes narrowed. "He has a small confederation of villes that he rules, and still more that pay him tribute to avoid war." He shrugged. "Nonetheless the nearest is nearly three hundred kilometers northeast of our current position."

"So where is he getting his fuel?"

"Uh…" Toulalan grappled with the new question. "He trades for it."

Ryan gave the heir to Val-d'Or a dry look of his own. "You're the head of a ville or a settlement that stills its own fuel. Are you going to open your gates to Mace Henning at company strength, armed and in the saddle?"

It was Six who answered. "No."

"You figure he's been taking the time to conquer every settlement on the way while he's been following you?" Ryan continued.

"No," Six reiterated. "We have been wearing Mace Henning and his men, like buckskins, for days now."

"And?" Ryan nodded encouragingly. "So?"

Six gave one of his rare, metal-filled smiles. "And so Mace Henning has a tanker."

Ryan glanced at the scalp in the dirt. "I smelled his fuel when I burned his bike. You're burning Diefenbunker diesel. He's burning alcohol. Takes a long time to distill enough to fill a tanker wag. He's like you. Out of his range, with the good weather fading fast. Take his fuel supply, and he has to burn for home, and hope he makes it before he has a bunch of cold, hungry sec men on foot in unfriendly territory."

Toulalan calculated. "Or it could spur him to total desperation, and one last all-out attack."

"Yeah, and if that happens," Ryan countered, "this time you got a LAV with J.B. in the turret."

Toulalan nodded. He was well aware J.B. had saved his bacon. "So what do you propose?"

"Mace's coldhearts, the bikes, the 4x4s can run off-road, shadowing you from the bushes and hills. But with a tanker full of fuel there's only one way. Mace's tanker is paralleling you, the best it can, on smaller, backcountry routes."

"Mmm." Toulalan nodded. "And?"

"And so I go take that tanker."

Mildred's eyes went wide. "So you're just going to go off alone, sneak past a bunch of postapocalyptic Hells Angels and steal a fuel tanker?" She pointed a condemning finger at Ryan. "You know? I've seen this movie."

Ryan looked at Mildred with sudden interest. "It was in a vid?"

"Yeah, a pretty good one, actually. It was called *The Road W—*"

"Did it work?"

"Um, well, yeah...it did."

Ryan nodded. "I'm not going to steal the tanker. I'm just going blow it up, and I won't be going alone. Six is coming with me."

Six gave Ryan a look, but he didn't say no.

Toulalan wasn't happy. "You would leave the convoy without its best sec man! Your friends without their leader!"

Ryan walked over to Toulalan and pulled a looming routine of his own. The one-eyed man duly noted Six didn't get in the way. The scalp on the ground had whetted the big man's appetite to put some hurt on his opponents, and apparently he liked the way the outlander rolled. Ryan's blue eye bored into Toulalan. "I'm going to leave J.B. in charge of the convoy. Jak in charge of the perimeter. Then me and Six are going to nightcreep on Mace Henning, open their main fuel vein and bleed them dry of every last drop of spare fuel. Meantime you burn for the Trans-Canada. We'll catch up. Do you have a better idea?"

To his credit, Toulalan didn't flinch under Ryan's tombstone gaze. "What if I said I did? And it didn't involve sending our two best men on a suicide mission?"

"I'd be curious," Ryan admitted.

"Let me ask you a question."

Ryan's eye narrowed but he kept his tone neutral. "Shoot."

"Are Baron Henning's coldhearts amphibious?"

Six whirled on Toulalan. "No!"

Ryan shrugged. "No?"

"Not him!" Six snarled.

Ryan watched Six stomp away from the meeting in a fine rage. Ryan turned to Toulalan. "Who's him?"

The trap was set, and Baron Mace Henning was pleased. Six barrels of black powder were set in the groins of the crumbling overpass. It was the only decent path that would take them to the old Route 69, which was the only way for a convoy that big to regain the Trans-Canada. Mace had gotten good information on the convoy's formation from Jimmy Pickering before he got himself chilled. They would drop the span after the first two wags. Nolan was in a covered firing pit with the Carl Gustaf recoilless. He would put his rocket-propelled grenade into the fighting LAV like he'd done at the bunker, and take out the newcomers. This time the convoy would have no time to circle up. What they would have was a twelve-wag pileup against the rubble. His men would surge in from the bushes on both sides and dismount. They would discharge the home-rolled rockets into any wag trying to pull out of the pile, and then his every last man would assault the convoy.

It was a good plan.

Tag had had a good hand in it. They both accepted they would lose men, but the survivors would earn their change, and Mace would have Toulalan's knowledge to open the bunkers and his body to use as a hostage against his father. His sister would be leverage against both. The bunkers would open in front of him. Val-d'Or would open in front of him. In the end he would kill Baron Luc Toulalan and his son, Yoann, hard for defying him, but not before he had learned every last scrap of useful information they had. He would let Cyrielle Toulalan live and impregnate her. In any ville Mace conquered, he generally kept one female of breeding age from the baronial line alive and gave her one of his. It helped cement the new line of succession.

The sound of a bike at full throttle interrupted the baron's dreams of conquests of battle and the flesh. "Look alive, boys!" he bellowed. Mace checked the loads in his old C-1 submachine blaster. He thrust his club under his belt and loosened his long wickedly curved skinning knife in its sheath. It was a risk going in, but Mace had learned long ago that barons who hid in their villes and leaned on their sec men ended up being replaced by their sec men. Mace had been just such a sec man of ambition himself.

Leading from the front was one of the basic tenants of leadership. He was utterly ruthless with his men. He had only one punishment for transgression or failure. Every man knew Mace Henning would crush a skull just as soon as he would hand out a loonie. By the same token each man knew in his bones that Mace Henning doled out neither unless it was deserved, and each man knew in his bones Mace wouldn't send them anywhere he wouldn't go himself. His sec men lived off his largess, and they lived large when not on duty.

Mace unlaced the neck of his riding skins. Sec men who were close by nudged one another and began whispering up and down the line as Mace exposed the sun-bright Canadian gold maple leaf coin that lay against his chest. It was the other symbol of his rule. The only other person allowed to wear the golden coin was the son he had left behind in his base ville to rule while he was on the road. Mace readied himself for battle. If he fell, so be it. The favored son he had left behind would never be the man he was, but he was brave, and if he listened to Tag he might live long enough to see grandsons himself. Mace threw back his head and laughed.

Frankly, he was looking forward to this fight.

His men laughed with him. They were salty. They were ready to take Toulalan's wag convoy once and for all. Their baron was going in with them. Mace's eyes narrowed as a lone rider came into view. He lifted his field glasses. It was his bastard Red. The younger man's bike went airborne over every lump and fold in the ground. He was at full throttle and driving out in the open to make time.

This couldn't be good.

Mace stepped out of his blind. "Tag, Butch, Ledge. Everyone else stay in position."

Red caught sight of his father and sped over to him, jumping off his bike breathlessly. Mace took his own canteen and tossed it to the scout, who gulped water. Mace let him cut the dust for a few seconds and then growled. "What?"

Red lowered the canteen and gasped as he wiped his mouth.

"They aren't coming!"

"What do you mean, they aren't coming?" Mace demanded. "They have to come north on the 69 if they went to hit the Trans-Canada, and to do that they have to come through us."

"I know, Baron. I know." Red nodded vigorously. "But they broke north by northwest. They went straight up the 10 and didn't stop."

"North by northwest—" Mace pulled out his map and shook his head in disbelief. "They're heading up the Bruce."

Tag tapped a finger on the Bruce Peninsula. "Then we have him."

"Yeah, but why? Why is he paintin' himself into a corner? Yoann's smarter than that. Even if he isn't, Vinny is."

"The First Nations have a trading post." Tag's finger moved up the finger of land that split Georgian Bay from Lake Huron. "Here, at the tip, at Tobermory."

"What good is that going to do him? That's land end."

"Trading camp," Tag reminded him. "High summer, neutral ground."

"What's he going to do, winter there?" Mace scoffed. "They've got no facilities for a convoy like his. His wags will freeze up and be useless come the thaw. He isn't running scared. He's won our last two dust-ups."

"Only two explanations then," Tag agreed. "He's either laying some kind of trap we can't figure or he doesn't see the Bruce as a dead end."

"There ain't boats on the Lakes that can carry his convoy. Only the biggest barges can carry a wag, and he's got a semi and armor. He'd need every barge on the Lakes, and if he'd lined them up we'd know it."

Tag gave his baron a sidelong glance. "There's one."

Mace stopped short. "He hasn't been on Huron in years. Not since the Soo Lock Pirates broke the shipping treaty. Swore he'd never come back."

Tag shook his head unhappily beneath the hood of his robe. "Toulalan got inside the bunkers. He's got the kind of wealth that can buy almost anything. Once he's on the water, we can't track him. We don't know where his next destination is yet, and he can make landfall anywhere. He's going to get one hell of a jump on us."

"Can we get ahead of him? Drop the same ambush we got here?"

Tag looked up at the sun and calculated. "He's got a jump on us. We'd have to leave now. Go overland and ride hard as we can. We'd have to leave the wags behind, and we'd be far from resupply and most importantly, refueling. We'd be on fumes, and even then there's no guarantee we'd make it in time."

"You been to Tobermory, right?"

"Years ago."

"How are the roads?" Mace asked.

"That's to our advantage. The only decent route up the Bruce is the 6, and from what I hear it isn't in good shape. The Tobermory trading camp is on the tip of the Bruce. Almost everyone who goes there goes over the water."

"We're only fifteen klicks from the water ourselves. We get a boat, a good-size one. Red's been on the water. So have you. Butch and Ledge lived around here most their lives. Red will lead it, but you tell him what to do. You put a strong party on it, sail hard for the point and drop into Tobermory camp a good day before Yoann and his convoy, and be ready for him before he embarks."

Tag stared at his baron long and hard. "Red, Butch, Ledge. Take a walk."

Mace nodded and the three men went back to their positions in the bushes by the road. Tag took a deep breath. One didn't contradict Baron Mace Henning lightly, and never in public.

"Mace, no one raids fishing villages except mutie bands or the most desperate idiots. Half of the provinces live on smoked fish come the winter. You'll set a real dangerous precedent." Tag's voice grew cold and urgent. "No one, and I mean no one, raids a trading camp. That's holy ground. Word gets out Mace Henning makes war in the trading camps, and we'll be banished. Worse, we'll be at war with the First Nations, and we'll be in a permanent state of war with every ville on the Lakes. You attack shipping, then you're a pirate, as well, and the trifecta will be complete."

Mace Henning seemed remarkably unconcerned. "What's a trifecta?"

"It means you'll be pounding down the last three nails in your coffin, Mace—one, two, three."

The baron laughed. He shook his head at Tag's concern. "Tag, you're going to trade for that boat, generously, as a matter of fact. You're going to pay the captain to get you to Tobermory as fast as he can, and pay him handsomely. You're going to treat him like a prince."

"And Tobermory?"

"You're just going there to do some business, like everybody else."

"Business?" Tag asked. "It may not have reached the Lakes yet, but soon enough everyone is going to know that you've been trading punches with Toulalan and his convoy. If we nightcreep Toulalan or any of his people in camp, that's as bad as an open fight, worse actually."

"Tag, you're going to be downright respectful of camp

law, and if you see Toulalan, or even Six, you're going to be polite. Hell, buy them a spruce beer on me and tell them what noble opponents they've been."

Tag started to smile. "And if they're really going out on the water?"

"If you're right, and it's who we think it is, Toulalan and his people won't be his only passengers, and the convoy won't be the only cargo."

Tag's smile turned shrewd. "You want to put some cargo on the same boat with Toulalan?"

"I do."

"A bomb is risky, Mace. All we have is black powder. It's hard to fuse long term, and we have to expect to see our cargo inspected. Besides, if you sink them, we lose everything."

"I didn't say sink, Tag."

Everyone once in a while Tag had to remind himself that he wasn't smarter than Mace Henning, just better educated and well read. It galled Tag to admit he had no idea what Mace was planning. "What do you have in mind?"

Mace seemed quite pleased with himself. "Oh, a little disruption. A little something to slow them down, until we find out where Toulalan is really headed."

Tag gave up. "What do you want me to do?"

"Pick your men. Say, eight, besides Red and the twins. Pick veterans, and don't just pick them for the coins around their necks. Pick men who can keep their head in the trading camp. Men who will stay steady even if Vinny smiles at them across the gaudy-house bar and waves a scalp or Jimmy Pickering's change at them."

"So...not Shorty?" Tag inquired.

Mace snorted. "No, not Shorty."

"What's this cargo you want me to place, Mace?"

"Well, I've been thinking about what we've seen since we come south. I'm thinking you're going to need them spent ammo cylinders from Nolan's recoilless. I'd say maybe, oh, eight of them."

"Yes?"

"Then I think you're going to need maybe four buckets of blood. Just tell the men to line up and contribute."

Tag mulled this strange set of instructions over. "And…"

"And when you get to Tobermory—" Mace's grin was as ugly as Tag had ever seen it "—trade for some ice."

Chapter Nine

Ryan was back in the LAV. Krysty was behind the wheel of the big rig and she was taking to the semi like a duck to water. Seriah stood in the turret next to Ryan. The LAVs needed the least attention of any of the vehicles in the convoy, but the little wrench loved spending time around them when she had any to spare. She also seemed to like hanging around anyplace where Jak happened to be, and Jak was driving.

The convoy found itself inside the Bruce trading camp long before they got to the gates of Tobermory. The land around the trading camp was a camp itself. It was high summer. People from all corners of the Lakes and even farther afield were getting in their last bit of trading before they scrambled home to dig in and beat the freeze. Tents and lean-tos filled every available inch of open space. Looking upward, many of the larger trees sported temporary tree houses. Every eye turned to the convoy as it passed. Even in the Deathlands the Val-d'Or convoy would be something to see. Ryan stood in the commander's hatch of the LAV and knew that somewhere Trader was smiling.

The convoy stopped at the gate.

A twenty-foot-tall wooden palisade of thick tree trunks surrounded Tobermory trading camp proper. The gates were open. A guard tower crouched on either side of the gate, and a battered Browning .50-caliber machine blaster in each put anything approaching the gate in a cross fire. Gun teams manned each weapon. The men were wore their hair in black braids and wore homespun shirts, breechclouts, leggings and moccasins. The heavy machine blasters eyed the approaching road like the chilling eyes of death. The men behind them tried to look mean.

The sight of Ryan standing in the turret of the LAV with a 25 mm autocannon beneath him was clearly giving the gate guards pause. One guard reached up and began yanking on a bell rope. The bell clanked more than rang, but the effect was immediate. In the blink of an eye braided and buck-skinned sec men appeared on the walls of the palisade bearing blasters of every description. Toulalan stepped out of his camper wag and climbed up the ladder to the roof. Cyrielle joined him.

A whitehair appeared on the wall. Despite his advanced age, he was a towering figure of a man. He wore his hair in a single, grizzled braid that hung over his left shoulder. Though the late-afternoon was hot and humid, he wore a blanket wrapped around his shoulders. Toulalan called up to the wall. "Jon Hard-knife! Great sachem!"

The old man's voice was deep and carried. "I am Jon Hard-knife!"

"I am Yoann Toulalan, son of Baron Luc Toulalan! Baron of ville Val-d'Or across the Ottawa!"

"I have heard of the great Baron Luc Toulalan! I see his son has become a great leader, as well!"

"I wish to enter your camp to trade and then embark upon the water!"

Jon Hard-knife's hand extended from beneath his blanket. He pointed a stick hung with fetishes at the wags in the convoy. "All here obey camp law! All here are under my protection and the protection of the First Nations! Why do you come with so many men, and so much iron and fire? Many here will not accept it."

"I'm at war with Baron Mace Henning! Only in strength can I traverse Ontario."

"This is known to me." Jon Hard-knife shook his head. "You know camp law. Take your war away from here, and off the Bruce. The First Nations will not abide it."

Toulalan turned and nodded at Ryan. Toulalan had briefed them. Ryan spoke quietly down the commander's hatch. "J.B.?"

The turret whined. Ryan pivoted on the balls of his feet gracefully to stay facing forward as the turret turned to face back. The turret turned its back to the gate and the barrel of the 25 mm weapon lowered to its deepest declination. Every member of the convoy simultaneously lowered whatever blaster they had shouldered or were stationed behind.

Toulalan spread both hands. "My people will all dismount, all except for the drivers. They'll drive to the docks and then put every wag in your custody until we embark. I'll put myself and my sister beneath your knife while this takes place."

Toulalan took out a long belt of shell beads. Most were white, but lines of purplish ones made a pattern through the belt. It had been a while but Ryan knew wampum when he saw it.

"Stephane Toulalan, the first baron of Val-d'Or, married a woman of the First Nations!" Toulalan held the wampum belt high. "It was she who first recorded the history of Val-d'Or since skydark in the old way! It has recorded the days of my people ever since! This belt speaks my truth!"

Jon Hard-knife lowered his stick. "Many years has it been since the French have come to the Bruce. You are welcome here. Drive your wags to the docks, and keep them."

A First Nations warrior jumped into the back of the lead wag and the convoy rumbled through the gates. Very little of predark Tobermory remained. Most predark construction, even if it was well preserved, couldn't withstand the hard freeze without electricity. Nearly all of the original buildings had been stripped and torn down to their foundations to be replaced by heavy timber houses and cabins. The Bruce trading camp was booming. Booths and open tent warehouses filled every inch of open space.

People were everywhere and everywhere people were trading. Bales of dried and smoked fish were piled chin-high. Piles of skins and bolts of wool, hemp and cotton were everywhere. In one tent a man was hawking homemade blasters while in the one next to it a woman was selling predark ones. A blacksmith and his two apprentices next to them had set up shop to repair both. Ryan saw barrels of oil and blankets covered with ivory harvested from the narwhals of Hudson Bay. Bearskins, both grizz and polar, competed for attention. Piles of scrap metal and predark salvage lay everywhere. Tinkers abounded, specializing in mending or hybridizing almost anything predark. Painted women stood in front of gaudy brothel tents pedaling their wares.

Most of the shelters in the ville proper were obviously temporary, and Ryan suspected the population of the camp contracted severely in winter. Like mayflies spending their lives in a single day, Canada hummed in the ephemeral warmth. Sowing, reaping, raiding and trading all had to be done before the long cold came.

The convoy rumbled through the trading camp and came to the docks. Boats of every description filled the wooden piers, and the beach around it was a sea of canoes, kayaks and rowboats. Ryan stared out across the main channel. Its dark waters was dappled pink, red and gold by the low sun and sheeting Northern Lights. The convoy came to a halt on the concrete pier that had once serviced major lake-going vessels. Ryan clambered down and joined Toulalan on the dock. Their First Nations guide gave them the quick low-down.

"Camp is worm free, but you can't be too careful. Don't sleep on the ground. If you sleep in your wags, button up. You sleep in camp, buy a hammock if you don't got one. No stealing. We catch you stealing, you're banished. No fighting. If you brawl, you're banished. Your trades are your business. If you have a dispute, you come to us. If you don't want it mediated, you take it outside, and you take it all the way south till you're all the off the Bruce and the 6 ends."

Toulalan gave a short bow. "Be assured, we will observe all camp laws and protocols."

Jon Hard-knife turned and walked away without another word.

Toulalan clapped his hands happily. "Well, Ryan, *mon ami!* I'm going to take gifts to Jon Hard-knife and discuss the situation on the Lakes. I will also ask him about hiring guides for the journey ahead. We'll be spending the night here. I suspect most of my people will seek diversions and amusements. Were I you, I would avail myself of the opportunity to trade. I intend to beat the cold, but should we lose the race, you'll want winter gear."

It wasn't bad advice.

Ryan and his crew took some trade goods out of the LAV and then went shopping.

Most exchanges in the camp were barter of goods or services. The trading camp accepted ville jack but at a pretty steep exchange rate. Their own jack was a simple wooden token with "1" for First Nations carved and then branded upon it. It seemed like pretty easy jack to counterfeit, but rumor had it doing so was a death sentence and war with the entire First Nations Federation.

Ryan and his people had taken a great deal of disposable wealth out of the Borden Diefenbunker. Predark steel was always at a premium, and Ryan had taken the bayonets that came with the Diefenbunker blasters they had taken for trading. With them the one-eyed man acquired a Russkie-style ushanka and muff that nearly matched Krysty's bear-skin coat. Jak, J.B. and Mildred got hooded capote jackets. Mildred found Doc a surtout that was a blanket-cut version of the frock coat he normally wore and could wear over it. Krysty found Ryan his winter gear—a buffalo robe that had been cut while the animal had still been wearing his thick, shaggy, dark brown winter coat. Everyone acquired gloves, fur overboots and skin leggings with the fur on the inside.

Beyond that Ryan and his people didn't need much.

A handful of shells at the seamstress stall got Doc's long-serving frock coat once again patched and mended to a semblance of its former glory, and a bullet hole in J.B.'s fedora had been skillfully mended. Jak got his blades professionally sharpened by a bald, blind man pedaling a stone wheel. The sharpener nodded appreciatively as he ran his hands over Jak's knives. Sparks flew from the wheel as the man turned the edges of Jak's fighters and throwers shaving sharp. "Nice blades," he said.

"Thanks." Jak made his arsenal of steel disappear. Sometimes Ryan wondered how it was that Jak didn't clank when he walked.

Ryan had watched the man's work and let him put a new edge on his panga and slaughtering knife. A chorus of whoops and cheers suddenly erupted out of a tent down the lane. "What's that?" Ryan asked.

The cutlerist looked up and exposed his few remaining teeth in a smile. "Throwin' contest."

Krysty whirled instinctively. "Jak…"

Jak was already walking toward the action. Ryan paid the craftsman the agreed two .22 rounds for his services, then he and Krysty strode after Jak. The open tent was crowded with spectators and stank of sweat, spruce beer and maple-sap hooch. A thin-as-a-blade First Nations warrior stood shirtless in the middle of the tent while onlookers pounded him on the back. Someone shoved a stoop of spruce beer into his hand and foam ran down his chest and belly as he drank deeply in victory. A stocky ville man stomped out of the arena and dropped a pair of end-heavy, diamond-pointed throwers onto a blanket loaded with blades, jack and loot. He had obviously lost, and he cursed and was roundly cursed as he passed by onlookers who had bet on him and lost.

Jak stood in front of a six-foot First Nations woman who towered over him. A man's plaid shirt barely restrained her enormous breasts. It was pretty clear she wasn't wearing anything else underneath, and she was flashing perilous amounts of long thigh. She wasn't a beauty, but she was long, tall and gaudy hot with attitude as she stood straddling the blanket loaded with jack and loot. She tossed her braids and talked to Jak like he was a small child. "Costs to get in, kid."

Jak stiffened. Ryan almost stepped forward. If you wanted to start a fight with Jak Lauren, and that wasn't hard at all, a good way to cut to the chase was to call the young man "kid." The woman noted Jak's body language and grinned as she ran a tongue over her teeth. "Kid?" she rubbed in. "Costs even more to lose."

The man on the throwing field called out, "You got another sucker for me, Maddie?"

"Don't know, Tommy!" Maddie called back. "Even for a white guy, this kid's awfully pale." She looked Jak up and down from head to toe. "But for a little punk, he's awfully pretty!"

Ryan stepped forward as Jak reached under his jacket. The albino teen produced one of the P-226s they had taken from the Diefenbunker armory and tossed it on the blanket. "SIG-Sauer, 9 mm, loaded mag. In."

Several spectators gasped. A handblaster in such gleaming condition represented a small fortune. "Jak…" Krysty cautioned. "Those are for trade, not gambling."

Jak didn't grin often, but he was grinning now. "Friendly contest."

Maddie tossed back her head and laughed. It was like a bell ringing in the tent. "Tommy True-flight has another victim!"

The crowd roared.

Ryan leaned into Jak's ear. "These people are just like the First People back in the Deathlands. They don't give you a name unless you earned it. This guy's name is True-flight. He doesn't have wings."

Jak just kept grinning. "Bet against me," he suggested.

Maddie watched the exchange with a frown and put a bare foot on top of the SIG. "Blaster's on the blanket! Bet's on!"

The crowd roared again.

Tommy True-flight tossed back his beer and tossed the stoop back over his shoulder for one of his admirers to catch. "Come on, kid! Let's see how handy you are with the steel!"

Jak stood unmoving. "Wager?"

Tommy gave Jak a pitying look. "What ya got?"

Jak turned to Ryan. "SIG."

"Jak…"

Jak just stuck out his hand. Ryan sighed as he drew the spare, personal SIG he'd taken from the bunker and staked his friend. Jak tossed it on the blanket. "'Nother SIG."

Tommy True-flight looked on the weapon sourly. Jak's entry fee and his wager trumped all the jack on the blanket. "You come here and challenge me? Make a bet my blanket can't cover and think you make your rep that way? Tell you what, kid. Me and you can take a ride down the Bruce. Just off the 6. Play for blood if you like."

Several First Nations warriors wearing the red sashes of camp sec men stepped forward, blasters in hand to intercede.

The tent grew very quiet.

"Nah. Take the blanket." Jak looked up from the blanket of Tommy's winnings and grinned at Maddie. "And her. One hour."

The crowd roared.

Maddie looked at Jak in open speculation,

Tommy True-flight looked none too pleased.

An enormously fat man in homespun overalls who smelled suspiciously like a pig farmer slammed Jak on the back. "You're the man, kid!"

Jak's red albino eyes went dead as he turned them on the pig farmer. "What you call me, Fatty?"

Fatty recoiled. "You…I mean…I said…you the man! You the man!"

True-flight gave Jak the stone face. "You're on."

The crowd roared once more.

Maddie didn't seem totally displeased with the stakes.

Bets flew around the tent.

Tommy True-flight was heavily favored, but a vocal minority liked Jak's style and they were putting their jack where their mouths were. Ryan pulled out his pocket full of wooden First Nations jack. "Five to one on Jak!"

Krysty held her jack between her hands and shook it overhead so that it clicked and rattled. "Ten to one!"

Fatty raised a leather purse and swung it around overhead with renewed enthusiasm for his hero. "Ten to one on the man!"

The bets were covered instantly.

Tommy True-flight stepped up and used his height to look down his nose at Jak. "Coming up on noon. I want a beer, my woman and a nap in my hammock. Let's make this quick. Three throws. Most hits in the bull's-eye wins. If it's close or a tie, second, sudden death throw-off. Good?"

Jak looked at the target. It was a barrel-thick round of soft wood on a pair of sawhorses. The target was painted in three concentric circles. The outer circle was painted red with a pair of "2s" painted in black like three and nine o'clock on a chron. The next ring was painted white with similar black fives. The center was the size of a small plate, painted red with a black 10 dead center.

"Double?" Jak suggested.

Tommy True-flight's hands creaked into fists. "Double what?"

"Distance?"

The tent erupted. The distance had just gone from four yards to eight. Whatever bet they might have made, everyone in the crowd liked Jak's style. Tommy spread his arms and the crowd behind them parted like the sea. "Fine, Whitey. You go for it."

Jak shook his head. "No."

Tommy scowled again. "Challenger goes first."

Jak kept his ruby-red appraisal on Maddie and her best assets. "No. You."

"Well, fine! You just watch and weep, kid!" Tommy took three blades from the back of his breechclout and stalked to the line. His blades were short and wasp-waisted, and unlike Jak's they had no edge to be used like a real knife or any heft for penetration. Ryan recognized the soft steel construction so they would bend and be bent back into shape rather than snap on a bad impact. The blades had no practical purpose except to mark a target. They were sporting devices, and ones Tommy was obviously long practiced with. Tommy measured off four more yards with a professional stride and drew a line in the dirt floor of the tent with his toe. He stuck out his chin at Jak.

Jak nodded.

Tommy suddenly threw. "Lah!"

His lazy overhand throw was perfect, and his knife sank into the red of the 10-ring, three o'clock right of center.

"Lah!" His second knife stuck just below the one and the zero.

"Lah!" His third throw thunked in right next to his first.

The crowd roared in appreciation as Tommy stepped forward confident of his prowess and yanked his knives free of the target. Even Ryan was impressed. The crowd shouted in a cacophony of conflicting encouragement and jeers.

"Shut up!" Tommy boomed. "Let him throw!"

Ryan knew Jak didn't care. He was in his zone. The albino teen stepped to the line. One of his leaf-bladed throwing knives slid out of his sleeve into his palm. The silence in the tent was deafening as he raised his knife. Jak drew back his hand to throw and—

"Loser loses his blades," Tommy chided. "That's the rules."

Krysty was outraged. "Hey!"

Tommy shrugged innocently. "Just makin' sure the kid here knows the rules."

Jak ignored them both. "Two."

"Two ring?" Tommie shook his head. "We said the bull's-eye was—"

Jak threw. He didn't hit the two ring. He put his point into the curlicue of the numeral two. Jak made another knife appear in his left hand.

"Five." Jak sank his second blade into the curlicue on the bottom of the numeral five. The crowd gasped. Jak ignored them.

"Two!" Jak nailed the two on the opposite side. "Five!" Jak repeated his performance. Jak finally deigned to turn his bloodred gaze on Tommy.

"Ten, one-zero split," he declared.

Tommy True-flight's eyes rolled up toward the top of the tent. "Fuck me."

Maddie bounced up and down on her heels in anticipation.

The tent was absolutely silent.

Jak took a slow breath and threw.

His blade stuck right between the two painted numerals in the center.

Five knives bisected the target, piercing the scoring numbers on a nearly straight line.

The tent erupted into cheers.

Jak shrugged. Fatty shoved a sleeve of spruce beer into Jak's hands, and Jak let him. "The man! The man! The man!" he shouted. The tent took up the chorus. Tommy strode up and dropped his blades on the blanket. "You win."

"Call me kid, ever?" Jak stared at him frankly. "Kill you."

Tommy watched Fatty as the losers queued up to cross his palms with wooden jack. "The man!" he chortled as the jack sifted between his fingers. "The man!"

Tommy looked long and hard at Jak. "Guess I'll have to call you the man, then. And today—" Tommy smiled ruefully and shoved out a long-fingered hand "—the better man."

Jak shook Tommy's hand.

The crowd applauded the show of sportsmanship. J.B., Mildred and Doc pushed their way into the tent. "What's up?" Mildred asked.

Ryan nodded as Jak folded the four corners of his blanket of winnings together to make a sack. He handed Ryan back the spare SIG. "Friendly contest. Jak cleaned up."

A voice spoke over the hubbub of slowly dispersing sports enthusiasts and gamblers discussing the contest. "Is the bettin' over?"

All eyes turned to a redheaded, bearded man in buckskin riding leathers. He was even shorter than Jak.

Jak flipped his sack of winnings open. "No."

The crowd recoalesced in avid interest.

Vincent Six's laugh was never pleasant. Now it dripped with scorn as it boomed. *"Mon Dieu!"* Six threw back his head and laughed. "A *petit* Henning!"

The man smiled and took no umbrage. "Call me Red."

"You must be one of Mace's bastards," Six declared. "Though I thought they drowned runts here in Ontario." He gave Red a scathing look. "I would have."

A tall man in a hooded robe stepped into formation with Red. The crowd went quiet as he pushed back his hood to reveal a head studded with skin-tags the size of pencil erasers. They sucked in a breath as he opened the neck of his robe slightly to reveal a silver coin gleaming beneath his collarbone.

Everyone in the province knew what it meant.

Six's face became deadly serious. "Tag."

Tag ignored Six and regarded Jak with interest. "You are very skilled."

Jak nodded at the wisdom of the statement. "Thanks."

"A wager?" Tag suggested.

Jak toed the blaster on the blanket. "P-226 SIG, loaded."

"I admit form follows function," Tag remarked. "Yet, I find it crude-looking."

Jak just waited. "And?"

Tag extended a flesh-studded finger at the satin-finished .357 Colt Python Jak wore on his belt. "That's pretty."

Mildred was appalled. "Jak! No!"

Jak drew his blaster.

Ryan put a hand on Jak's shoulder. "Jak, I'm not going to tell you what to do. But he saw you throw, and still wants a piece of you. That blaster is—"

Jak dropped his cherished weapon onto the blanket.

Ryan removed his hand. "Fireblast…"

"Bet against me," Jak reiterated.

Tag's gleaming smile rivaled Doc's, and it was all the more disturbing coming out of the fleshy foliage covering his face. Tag's hands went to the engraved Browning blaster with the attached wooden holster stock that hung from the baldric over his shoulder. Jak shook his head. "No."

Tag cocked his studded head. "No?"

"Semiautos. Not trust. Jam."

"This blaster has never jammed." Tag tossed a careless hand. "Nevertheless, tell me, my friend from the south, what wager would please you?"

Jak pointed at the silver *voyageur* coin on Tag's chest. "Sure shiny."

Red gripped Tag's arm. "Tag! No!"

Jak's red eyes locked with Tag's startlingly pale gray gaze. Some kind of understanding bordering on respect passed between them. Tag nodded very slowly. "A gentleman's bet, then?"

"For blades?" Jak countered.

"Done."

Jak jerked his head at the line. "Two more yards."

The crowd gasped once more.

"Done." Tag nodded.

A thunderstorm of wagers broke across the tent. Ryan shoved all his tokens into Krysty's hands, and she just dropped the pile between her feet. "Ten to one on Jak!"

"The man!" Fatty howled. "Ten to one on the man!"

Tag paced off two more yards and drew a new throwing line. "Red?"

Red went to the target. He took a deck of pasteboard cards out of the purse on his belt and shuffled out the king of hearts. Red took out a horseshoe nail and hammered the card into the middle of the bull's-eye with the back of his tomahawk. "Tag?"

Tag nodded. "Jak?"

Jak nodded. "Three throws."

"Of course. But I am something of a stickler for the rules. As challenger, shall I go first?"

Jak spit on his hands and rubbed them together. "Sure."

Tag reached into his robe and pulled out his weapons. Both Ryan and Jak gave them a very hard look. They weren't so much knives as throwing spikes. There were three of them in a leather sheath. Each was fifteen inches long and an inch thick in the middle. From there the weapons tapered down to wicked needlepoints on both ends. They looked to be about two pounds of pig iron a piece. They would sink through flesh with brutal penetrating power, and even if they failed to stick a living target point-on, they would still impact with bone-breaking, sledgehammer force. Tag stepped to the line. His weapons rang grittily as he rolled them in his hand.

Tag threw.

The throw was almost lazy. The lob sent the dark iron revolving through the air in a high arc. The spike hit the target with an impressive thud point-on and sank six inches into the wood through the king of hearts' crotch. Despite his bet Fatty whistled. "Rad, thunder and fallout!"

Tag threw again.

It took deceptive strength to send two pounds of metal twelve yards. Ryan didn't want to think about what would happen if Tag wound up and threw with all his might. The torpedo of iron hit at a slight angle and clanged like a horseshoe at it hit its brother.

Tag's third throw obliterated the bottom right heart on the card.

Red walked up and yanked the iron torpedoes free with obvious effort. About two-thirds of the card came with them. Tag frowned slightly as Jak approached the line. "We know the dimensions of the card. I will accept any throw within them. Unless you demand a fresh target?"

"No." Jak palmed a blade. "I hit paper." Jak shrugged. "Or you win."

Jak's madness drew another gasp from the crowd.

Fatty was beside himself. "The man! The man!"

"Woo-hoo!" Mildred cheered.

"Get him, Jak!" Krysty cried.

"Show him what for!" Doc rallied.

Tommy True-flight agreed. "Show him!"

Tag's voice cut through the cheering and jeering. He held one of his spikes as if he were about ready to throw. "I want absolute silence."

Silence reigned in the tent. Jak raised his blade. Ryan leaned in. "Jak?"

"What?"

"No pressure."

Jak's ruby-red eyes narrowed. "Thanks."

"But Seriah's watching."

Jak turned his head. The little wrench was in the crowd. Her hands clasped the front of her coverall. Her eyes were wide and her cheeks flushed as she looked at Jak. She blew Jak a kiss, and he tilted his head so that the invisible affection would hit him on the cheek. Seriah stopped short of bursting into flames.

Jak threw his blade, and it slammed straight into the side of the king of hearts' head.

The crowd nearly went mad.

His second throw shaved off the king's ear.

Jak raised his third blade and took a long breath. The only sound in the tent was the crowd breathing in with him and then holding it.

Jak threw.

A single spark shot like a tiny meteor as his blade scraped between the first two. Nothing remained of the king of hearts' head but Jak's three-petal blossom of steel.

The crowd went berserk.

Jak's friends thumped him roundly. Krysty and Mildred dropped a kiss on both cheeks. Tag dropped his spikes on the blanket and bowed away gracefully. Jak was pelted with a hail of wooden tokens in tribute from the crowd. Seriah ignored the flying jack and hurled herself into Jak's arms. Maddie stood in front of him with her fists on her hips. She raised an eyebrow at Seriah. "And me?"

"Anything?" Jak inquired.

Maddie lifted her chin. "For one hour, I do anything you say, that was the deal."

Jak shrugged. "Make Fatty happy."

Maddie's jaw dropped.

Fatty waved his arms and shouted to the tent top. "The man! The man!"

Jak squeezed Seriah tighter. He had what he wanted.

Krysty slid her arm around Ryan's waist. "That was fun."

"Yeah, fun," Ryan said.

Mildred shook her head. "Dude, don't you ever relax? Jak won the wager, won the contest and got the girl."

Jak folded up his blanket of winnings and wandered off toward the docks with Seriah glued to his hip.

"Yeah," Ryan agreed.

"Ryan?" Mildred was starting to get steamed. "We won."

"Ryan is right," Doc said quietly. "We were the strangers in the iron wag. The wild card. Now our numbers have been marked and noted. Jak's skill has been measured and weighed."

"We didn't win." Ryan watched Red and Tag disappear into the crowd. "We just got recced."

Chapter Ten

The sky was purple, the Northern Lights red. Between them everything was bathed in pink light. Ryan smiled to himself. The camp had guitarists, flautists, bagpipers, drummers and even a hammered bongo player in attendance. The iron law of the First Nations camp was live and let live, or die, and with it came a relaxed sort of freedom. It had been a good night.

Ryan and Krysty were swaddled in bear and buffalo hides on top of the big rig.

"Mmm...lover," Krysty said.

"Yeah." Ryan sighed.

"Jak and Seriah?"

Ryan turned his head toward the LAV. Jak and Seriah had taken a skin of maple shine, raised the ramp and not been heard from since. "They're both short," Ryan stated. "They got that."

"They got more than that."

"She makes him smile," Ryan conceded. "Haven't seen that in a while."

"He makes her smile, and she's handy with a wrench."

"If he wants to steal her and carry her off—" Ryan stretched and yawned "—I won't stop him."

Krysty was quiet for long moments. "I didn't like Red. Six insulted him ugly and he just kept smiling."

Ryan grunted. The Henning runt was worrisome. If Red was any indication, then the big Henning was a genuine concern. "Camp law. Six tried goading him into breaking it, Red knew better."

"And Tag..." Krysty shivered. "He's a coldheart. Cold as ice. I could feel it."

"Chilling cold, with both hands," Ryan acknowledged. "Six was right. Mace doesn't hand out those silver coins for nothing. I don't like them being in camp. They didn't come here to trade or throw knives."

Krysty shook her head against Ryan's chest. "Well, they're under camp law. Just like us. Yoann and Six say no one dares break it."

"Yeah, well, they're doing it."

"How?"

Ryan shook his head as he looked up into the kaleidoscope in the clouds. "They're foxing us, Krysty. I don't know how yet, but they are."

Krysty buried her face into Ryan's chest. "Fox them back."

"I will. Don't know how yet, but I will."

Krysty sighed. "I want coffee."

"I want some loving."

"I want pancakes for breakfast."

"I want you for breakfast."

"Well..." Krysty rolled onto her back with a happy sigh and set the table. "You win."

RYAN FOLLOWED THE SMELL of Diefenbunker coffee to the convoy mess wag. A sizable crowd had gathered at the docks. Everyone seemed eager to see what might wash up with the tide. Toulalan was positively smug. Even Six seemed abnormally satisfied with the world. "You seem happy."

Ryan accepted a cup of coffee and sniffed the air. "Pancakes?"

"Last night I spoke long with Jon Hard-knife." Toulalan raised his mug. "With luck, we hire scouts today."

"With pancakes?"

"It rendered us your services, no?" Toulalan laughed. "I ask you, can a First Nations man resist them?"

Almost on cue three First Nations men approached the convoy council. Ryan recognized the man in the lead as the one who had stood next to Jon Hard-knife at the gate the day before. He stood in front of Toulalan. "My father tells me you're looking for scouts. These men are the two best scouts in camp. They were going to go home, but my father told them you're heading west. They have seen your convoy and are interested." He gestured at the two men flanking him. "This is Donnie Goosekiller and Boo Blacktree."

Donnie Goosekiller looked like a First Nations version of J. B. Dix, except that he was even shorter, even more wiry and had thicker glasses. The main difference between them besides their race was that Donnie wore a maroon tuque over his braids despite the heat and unlike J.B. he seemed to smile constantly. With its 36" barrel the bolt-action, 10-gauge scatter blaster he carried was nearly as tall as he was. He wore a bandolier of home-rolled, waxed-paper shells. Goosekiller leaned on the huge, ancient water-fowling piece like it was a spear. Ryan was pretty sure he knew how Goosekiller had earned his name.

Boo Blacktree was Donnie Goosekiller's polar opposite. The First Nations scout was in a race with Ryan and Six for most physically imposing man in camp. Ryan was tall and rangy with cables, ropes and cords of muscle pulled across his long bones like the physique of a gladiator.

He was simply a solid block of human, tall enough to look both Ryan and Six in the eye, and he was neck and neck with Six for sternest scowl. He carried a heavy, unstrung recurved bow in a case with several dozen arrows slung at his side. He'd thrust a big-bore, single-shot, break-open handblaster

through his belt and wore a brutal, paddle-shaped war-club
with the handle sticking up over his shoulder.

Six looked the two scouts up and down and seemed not to
totally disapprove of what he saw. "You have been to Manitoba?"

Donnie Goosekiller's smile went up a few watts. "Oh,
yeah! Me and Boo been all the way 'cross to the Porcupine
Hills in Saskatchewan, and all the way up Lake Winnipeg
to the Ross Island trading camp." Goosekiller's smile turned
shy. "Not like the back of our hands you know, but we can
get you 'cross it. Heck, Boo made it all the way up to Hudson
Bay once, in winter."

Blacktree grunted once in affirmation. "Yup."

Toulalan turned to Six and nodded. Six opened the bed
of one of the wags and unfolded two blankets full of Diefenbunker trade goods. "For each of you, a sleeping bag, ground
cloth, pad and two blankets each, predark. Two C-7 blasters,
with mag, six spare mags, all loaded, cleaning kits, plus web
gear, bayonet and canteen. Poncho-shelter half. You want to
sleep indoors, you sleep in the med wag, unless someone
wounded is in it. You eat at our table, our food, with us."

Ryan smiled. The mess wag had prepped for this inter-
view. They were cooking Diefenbunker pancakes and the
scent mixed with real coffee. The two scouts sniffed the air.

"Two more longblasters and accessories each," Six concluded, "if we come back alive."

Toulalan held up his wampum belt. "Whatever happens,
you will be rewarded."

Ryan watched the two First Nations scouts fondle the mer-
chandise. It represented a tidy fortune. The fresh out-of-the-
box blasters alone would trade for enough to live like kings
for a year. Goosekiller touched each trade item individually.
He liked what he saw. He turned to Toulalan. He was still

smiling, but his small dark eyes were hard behind the thick glasses. "Heard you got Mace Henning after you."

"I do."

Goosekiller eyed Ryan. "He isn't one of you. Who is he?"

"A friend, like you, who we met on the path."

Goosekiller tilted his head back to look Ryan in the eye. "He looks like a good friend to have if Mace Henning is after you."

"He is. Are you with us?"

Goosekiller turned to Blacktree. "Boo?"

The archer looked up from fondling the digital, camo-pattern Canadian armed forces poncho in the truck and nodded once in affirmation. "Yup."

"We're in!" Goosekiller grinned. "My name's Goosekiller, but you can call me Goose. Boo's name is Boo, but you best call him Blacktree until he tells you different." Goosekiller's nonstop smile grew even bigger. "He won't."

Toulalan made an expansive, French gesture. "Please, join us for breakfast."

Blacktree beelined for the pancakes. Ryan called to his diminutive partner. "Donnie Goosekiller. That's a good name."

Goosekiller waved a dismissive hand. "Aw, gee, no one calls me the whole thing unless it's a lodge meeting. We're in the same convoy. Call me Goose."

"The First People in the Deathlands call me One-Eye Chills."

Goose regarded Ryan soberly. "That's a good name, too."

Ryan stuck out his hand. "You call me Ryan."

"Aw, gee!" Goose blushed. "Good to meet you, Ryan."

"Good to meet you, Goose. I've been on a couple of convoys and caravans in my time. Led them, sec'ed them and scouted for them." Ryan allowed himself a small smile. "You've got to stay on the good side of your scouts."

Goose wagged a finger in agreement. "Now that's true.

You look like a scout. And I heard the Deathlands are wicked rough."

"Tell you the truth, Goose. Canada seemed all gaudy soft at first," Ryan countered. "Then I met some pigs that were all wormy, and met Mace Henning and his boys. Taught me different."

Goose nodded sagely. He dropped to his heels and began drawing a remarkable map of Ontario with a twig. He tapped the Lakes and the peninsula they bordered. "The big peninsula between the lakes, that's worm country. It's like what you might call a local phenomenon. Once we're off the Bruce, we leave the worms behind." Goose scratched his head and readjusted his tuque. "Baron Henning's like a nonlocal phenomenon, and sounds like he's on us like winter."

Ryan liked the way the little scout was already saying "us." Jon Hard-knife had sent them good men. "You were right. Me and my friends aren't part of the convoy. But we're with them for the duration. But just between you and me, you watch our asses and we'll watch yours."

"Us scouts gotta stick together!" Goose enthused.

"Got that right."

The shriek of steam whistles split the morning calm. The crowd on the docks exploded into whoops and cheers. Ryan and Goose rose and joined the mob. Ryan had to admit he had doubted, but Toulalan had done it. Leviathan bore down on the docks. Toulalan had really, really done it. A floating citadel steamed its way toward the point. Black smoke belched into the morning sky from the thick, central smokestack. The chug of her engines was reminiscent of a locomotive. Ryan's companions quickly found him. Though heavily modified the vessel was clearly predark.

"What do you make of it, Mildred?" Ryan asked.

"It's a RO-RO," Mildred said.

Jak squinted at the ship. "Not a row boat."

"No, not row-row-row your boat, Jak. RO-RO, it means roll-on, roll-off. It has a ramp front and back."

"Bow and stern," Doc corrected her.

Mildred made an impatient noise and forged on. "You just drive on to it and then drive off the other side when you get to your destination. It's easier than loading with a crane or an elevator or having to turn around. It's a ferry."

"*Queen of the Lakes!*" Goose pointed excitedly. "The old girl hasn't been seen around here in years!"

The vessel had seen some extensive modification. A heavy wooden catapult squatting on an iron lazy Susan dominated the forward observation deck. Sandbag revetments were roped into place against the guardrails. A pair of heavy ballistae flanked the catapult. The barrels of machine blasters poked out of the sandbags. Every window had iron shutters. Nearly every inch of the vessel was cratered with bullet strikes old and new. Dozens of canoes hung from her sides. Except for the ramps, the first six feet of hull above the line was strung with double-thick curtains of storm fencing. Ryan made her about three hundred feet from ramp to ramp. The steam whistles shrieked again and tuques flew into the air like a flock of birds in response.

"Goose," Ryan asked, "why hasn't the *Queen* been seen on the Huron?"

The man scooped up his tuque. "Boycott."

"Boycott?"

"Oh, there's pirates on the Lakes, and everyone agrees they need chillin' wherever and whenever you find them. Well, this one pirate, Thorpe, got himself a plan. He got a bunch of boys together and rebuilt the locks guarding the Soo Canal. Started demanding a toll from anyone who wanted to get on the Superior or leave it. McKenzie is the captain of the *Queen*. Biggest thing on the Lakes as far as I know. Well, he refused to pay and Thorpe nearly sank him. McKenzie said he would boycott the Huron until the Soo Lock pirates were cleared out. Been doing his hauling strictly on the Ontario and Erie every since."

"No one has cleared out the locks?"

"Lot of talk about it. Putting an army together. But it's hard to get two barons to agree to anything. Besides, any baron who takes the locks from Thorpe would probably just go into business himself." Goose sighed and leaned on his weapon. "First Nations had a bunch of powwows about it. There was talk of sending a fleet of war canoes, taking the locks and making them a trading camp. But Thorpe is dug in like a tick. People talk, but most people either pay or take a land route to the Superior."

"And now McKenzie is back on the Huron."

"Yeah," Goose said with a grin. "He sure is!"

The *Queen of the Lakes* reversed engines and slowed to a stop before the dock. Her original auto ramp had been replaced by timber sandwiched between sheets of iron. The hydraulics had been replaced by human muscle. Dozens of crewmen strained against the fore and aft capstans, and heavy chains rattled and clanked as they lowered the ramp to the dock like a drawbridge.

Captain Robert McKenzie stood in front of the crowd. To Mildred's twentieth-century eye he bore a startling resemblance to Popeye's old nemesis, Bluto, right down to the barrel chest and bushy black beard. The long red tuque spoiled the effect slightly. His badge of office appeared to be a sword of some sort. All of the gold plating was gone, and at somewhere along the line the blade had been broken. Someone had chiseled a new point on it, and the three-foot ceremonial sword had become a wicked two-foot-long stabbing knife. McKenzie waved the blade around like a willow wand, pointing at things that displeased him and bellowing orders at his crew.

Jon Hard-knife and a First Nations delegation stepped next to Toulalan. Goose shook his head in admiration. "Toulalan, he did it."

McKenzie stomped down the ramp and stood in front of Toulalan. He looked long at the big rig and even longer at the two armored LAVs. "Yoann, you really did it."

Six popped a bottle of Diefenbunker champagne on cue. Toulalan shrugged modestly and held out the foaming bottle. "Welcome back to the Huron, Captain."

Chapter Eleven

Ryan rolled the big rig into her birth for the trip. Engines rumbled and echoed on the vehicle deck as McKenzie's loadmasters scrambled and yelled and instinctively distributed vehicles and cargo to keep the *Queen of the Lakes* in sailing trim. The loadmaster was lanky, long-haired, potbellied and missing his front teeth. He waved his tuque for Ryan to come forward into his spot and then shoved out his palm to stop. He shot Ryan the thumbs-up and the Deathlands warrior cut the engine. The convoy wasn't the only cargo or the only passengers. There would be a trading stop at Manitoulin Island. Fatty was bringing a nonworm-infected herd of pigs to Manitoulin Island. Some whose trading was done for summer were paying for a birth on the *Queen* just for the thrill of her being back on the Huron. It was big news. The fact that she was going to run the Soo Locks for Lake Superior in direct defiance of Thorpe the pirate king was even bigger.

Canoes and small boats had already left the Bruce in swarms.

Ryan knew Thorpe would be waiting.

He climbed down out of the cab. Work was going on everywhere, but Ryan he could tell McKenzie had far more crewmen than he needed. They all seemed like sailing men, but a lot of them had nothing better to do than clean their blasters and comment on the state of the passengers and cargo. McKenzie was overcrewed and the extra men were sec. He was spoiling for a fight. Twenty-five of Hard-knife's men had volunteered for the battle on the locks, and Toula-lan had paid each with a new longblaster.

There was a ruckus shaping up on the ramp. Ryan took his Scout longblaster in hand and went to see what was up. Six, Sylvan and Alain stood at the top of the loading ramp. Red, Tag and a half dozen of Mace Henning's buckskinned sec men stood at the bottom surrounding a pallet of trade goods. Captain McKenzie was bellowing like a bull between them. "There'll be no fighting on my ship!"

"No fighting," Red acknowledged. "Just trade."

"Trade?" McKenzie spit into the water. "I know your father is at war with Val-d'Or, Red! What're you trying to pull? Are you saying you want to go to Manitoulin and stay with the Haw eaters until I get back? You ain't coming with me to the locks! Not this trip!"

"That's it exactly. Baron Mace Henning wishes to extend his hand to Baron Poncet on Manitoulin. I bring him gifts, and on your return trip I hope to bring back his goodwill, as well as hawberry wine and other goods for trade."

Six's blaster was in his hand, but he kept it lowered. "He's a snake, McKenzie! Don't trust him!"

McKenzie purpled. "That's Captain McKenzie to you, you black frog!"

Sylvan and Alain paled. Ryan expected Six to explode. Six's sudden icy calm was even more dangerous. "What is his cargo, I wonder?"

Red lifted his chin in challenge. "Baron Henning's business."

McKenzie gave Red an ugly look. "And if it goes on my ship, it's my business! Last I heard the only thing Mace Henning's villes make is sec men!"

Red nodded at his men. Eight, yard-long, green-painted metal cylinders were strapped to the pallet and packed in ice. One of his men went to the one on top, pulled open the hinged lid and pulled out a frozen black chunk of meat and handed it to Red.

"Baron Henning's got three things in abundance, Captain. Sec men, blasters and, come summer, bison." Red held out the meat. "We got livers and tongues. On ice, for as long as it lasts. Figured Baron Poncet might be tired of eating lampreys and hawberries on that island of his."

McKenzie regarded the liver grudgingly. "Best part."

Red nodded. "I'm only takin' two men with me as a delegation. You can confiscate our blasters if you want. The rest of my men'll stay here on the Bruce under camp law until I return."

"Ain't necessary." McKenzie snatched the organ out of Red's hand. "Ship law is like camp law. You start anything, you swim. You endanger my ship, you walk the plank with your pockets full of rocks." McKenzie tossed the liver to his third mate. "Mr. Niall! Take this to Skillet! Tell him I want it fried in onions for supper."

"Yes, Captain!" Niall ran through the passengers and crew thronging the lower deck. "Make a hole! Captain's dinner coming through!"

"Loadmaster!" McKenzie bellowed. The man stepped forward. McKenzie pointed at Mace Henning's cargo. "Find a place for Baron Henning's trade! And try not to put it in the sun!"

"Yes, Captain."

McKenzie turned and looked at the convoy delegation. "Six, Ryan, you have state rooms upstairs. Get settled in. I have a meeting in an hour with Yoann. Your attendance is required."

IT WAS A COUNCIL of war. Ryan, Jak and J.B. sat with Toulalan, Six, McKenzie and his first mate, Mr. Smythe. Goose and Blacktree had been through the lock a dozen times and sat in, as well. A man named Loud Elk represented Hard-knife's contribution. Doc was in the room because although at times he was known to ramble, he was an intelligent and thoughtful man. Doc was currently peering intently out the porthole at something as the *Queen of the Lakes* chugged across the main channel toward Manitoulin Island doing a sedate eight knots. The sun was low. Loading the convoy had taken a long time, and the captain had been forced to meet with endless delegations at the Bruce Point camp. They wouldn't make Manitoulin before dark.

"How many are we expecting?" Ryan asked.

Toulalan looked at the captain. McKenzie shook his head. "Too many. Last time I faced him he had over two hundred pirates under arms. He'll have more now. He's had the Superior corked up like a bottle for years. He just keeps getting fatter and stronger."

"How's it fortified?"

McKenzie laid out a crude but serviceable map of the Soo Lock. "It's like two forts, one either side of the canal. Then two smaller ones on the islands in the middle. Built up on rammed earth and each topped with a wooden palisade. The lock is draped like a curtain between them, but our first obstacle is about half a dozen timber chains roped together across the canal. Getting through those will stop any head of steam we can get up. Then there's the lock itself. Double timbered. Takes two dozen oxen on either side to open it. Even with a running start and at full steam I couldn't ram it without sinking the ship."

Goose looked at the map admiringly. "Captain's got it about right. Me and Boo been through the lock just last year. We'd better expect at least three hundred, maybe four hundred pirates. And they live off the tolls. That lock is their sausage and syrup. They'll defend it, and defend it hard."

"Yup," Blacktree agreed.

"Anything else we should know about?" Ryan asked.

"There's a lesser gate in the lock itself on the northern side. It lifts up. They open that for canoes and small boats."

Ryan filed that away. "So what's your plan?"

Toulalan shrugged. "Simple. We deploy men in canoes to cut the timber chains. Meanwhile the catapults bombard the lock and break it. The LAVs will cover these activities respectively."

Ryan stared at the picture. "That's your plan?"

"As a matter of fact—" Toulalan nodded "—yes. Why?"

Ryan looked at Six. "This is your plan?"

Six made a derisive noise. "My plan was to stay in Val-d'Or, wrap my woman in furs of mink and sable, and make love all winter."

"Not a bad plan," Ryan admitted.

"Yes, well, now I'm here." Six looked at Ryan challengingly. "You have a better plan?"

"I've seen your catapults. You're going to have to get real close to use them, and the *Queen* will take a thousand blaster hits while you try, and your crews will be exposed. You don't just have to break the locks, you need to punch a hole big enough to sail through, and do it without the wreckage bogging you down. If you don't get that done by dark, you're going to have a hundred boats trying to board you by night, and if Goose is right, we're outnumbered by more than three to one."

Toulalan's smile was forced. He didn't like his plan being dissected. "We have the LAVs."

"You lost your fighting LAV back in Borden. You know they're vulnerable. They're as slow as ducks paddling in water, and the turret can only point in one direction at a time. If the pirates are as determined as Goose says, they can swarm them with canoes, get enough men on top they can tip them and sink them before they reach land. The

25 mm on mine is small. I could waste every last shell I got and still not make that hole you need. Your LAV is an engineering vehicle. All it's got is a machine blaster."

"You pick my plan apart well, Ryan," Toulalan said begrudgingly. "But perhaps that is why I invited you to this council. As Six asked, tell me you have a good plan."

"I don't have a good plan." Ryan smiled bleakly. "Just a better one."

Everyone at the table leaned forward.

"We took some high explosives from the Diefenbunker. Did you?"

"Yes!" Toulalan nodded. "The catapults! We build bombs!"

Ryan looked at McKenzie. "Are you good with those catapults?"

"It is a new skill…" He sighed. "Better with the ballistas."

Ryan nodded. "We aren't going to build bombs. J.B.'s going to make demo charges, and someone is going to have to go set them."

The brutal lines of Six's face twisted in question. "A land assault?"

"Tactical assault," Ryan corrected him. "Covered by what was called naval gunnery in predark times."

"Naval gunnery…" McKenzie almost smiled. "I like that."

Ryan flipped the map over and drew a remarkably accurate sketch of the *Queen*. "We switch out the catapult and put my LAV on the forward observation deck." Everyone except J.B met this with shocked looks. Ryan continued. "With the LAV on the prow we can engage the entire lock from fort to fort and all the way across. Sweeping anything that needs it with the cannon, the coax and the machine blaster on top. Its main job will be covering fire."

Toulalan sighed. "My catapults…"

"My catapults," McKenzie stated.

"Aren't going do us much good on the loading ramp," Ryan

said. "Even if we didn't need it closed to steam forward, the crews would be cut to pieces."

Doc suddenly stepped away from the porthole and tapped the stern of the *Queen* in Ryan's picture. "Place the catapults here and here. On the rear observation deck, but facing forward, one with a line of fire to port and one to starboard."

Ryan smiled.

McKenzie threw up his hands. "I spent weeks making the traversing plates! How are we to turn them?"

Doc blinked uncomprehendingly for several moments. For a while Ryan thought Doc might have lost it again. It turned out Doc wasn't uncomprehending, he was just incredulous. "My good Captain, your men are sailors, are they not?"

McKenzie regarded Doc very dryly. "Last I heard."

"Well then, I gather they have had some experience hauling on a rope and heaving enormously heavy objects?"

McKenzie turned his bemused gaze on his first mate. "Mr. Smythe, you and the lads ever hauled on a rope before? Maybe pushed something heavy?"

A slow smile spread across the first mate's face. He flexed forearms big as bowling pins. "Once or twice in our careers, Captain."

A few welcome laughs broke the tension in the room.

"Yes, good, very well then." Doc flipped the map and began pointing all over the place. "Once within range, the catapults will engage the forts on either side, and anything else that begs to have a very large rock flung at it, and, firing from the back deck, the catapults and their crews shall have a measure of protection from returning fire."

Ryan looked at Doc steadily. "What about accuracy?"

McKenzie drummed his fingers on the tabletop. "Again, not what it could be, and we practiced firing from the bow, head-on. Now it sounds like we're firing from the stern."

Doc waved a dismissing hand. "Well, unlike your auto-

cannon or the ballistae, which fire line-of-sight, the catapults hurl their missiles at a steep arc. So, in a sense, it does
not really matter where the catapults are positioned. I realize
your projectiles are most likely not completely uniform, but,
given observation of a few flings, one could make a reasonable assessment of the standard range and trajectory. From
there, given the known speed of the *Queen*'s forward progress, a pocket watch, the grace of God and some Kentucky
windage, a man with a reasonable knowledge of mathematics
should be able to make an educated guess as to the catapult
projectile's projected line of fall. Should we require direct
fire we can calculate—"

"Doc," Ryan said.

Doc blinked. "Yes, Ryan?"

"You just became Captain of Catapults."

Doc suddenly blushed. "Oh, well then. Capital. Glad to be
of service."

Six looked between the picture of the *Queen* and the picture of the Soo Locks. "So, I gather the men who deploy to
set the charges will go in the engineering LAV off the back
ramp?"

Ryan nodded. "That's the way I figure it. If for any reason
the charges don't quite get the job done, the LAV's got a
winch and a crane. We can do the rest of the demolition the
hard way if we have to."

Six leaned back in his chair, his eyes narrowing in suspicion. "And who is going in the LAV to deploy these plas-ex
charges?"

Ryan smiled. "You."

"Ah."

"Me," he continued, "and Jak. I'll drive it. If I get chilled,
Six, you bring it home. LAV holds three crew and seven-plus
gear in the cabin. I'll need seven volunteers. Starting with
Goose and Blacktree."

"But, Ryan!" Toulalan objected. "They're our scouts!"

"If we don't make it through the locks, we won't be needing scouts. Besides, they're the only ones who have already been through the locks. They know it better than anybody here."

"Goose?" Ryan said, looking at the scout.

Goose gazed wonderingly at the sketches. "Jeez, busting the Soo Locks. Sure would be something. People be talking in the lodges about that for years. Talk about the men who did it forever." He shook his head again. "Count some wicked good coup on that."

Blacktree nodded once. "Yup."

You could feel the momentum building in the room. Ryan laid out the rest of his plan. "Our group has experience with explosives. Jake and I will lead the demo team. Six, I want you to stay with the LAV to defend it and in case we need the crane or the winch, and I need a man who can give us covering fire with the machine blaster on top."

Six nodded. "Sylvan and édouard."

Toulalan watched the plan come together. "You're still short by three."

McKenzie turned to his first mate. "Mr. Smythe, you're volunteering."

Mr. Smythe didn't seem to mind much. "Yes, Captain."

"Pick two people you like for the job and volunteer them, as well. Someone who'd enjoy helping Mr. Six with the winch and the crane, and someone wicked with a blaster to help with the covering fire."

"Yes, Captain. I bet Loadmaster's Mate Timms and Miss Tamara will be real glad to hear they been volunteered."

"Very good, Mr. Smythe."

Ryan recapped the plan. "J.B. fights the LAV on the forward deck. Doc fights the catapults on the back. The captain fights the ship and his crewmen cut the timber chains. Six,

Jak and I take the lock. Captain, I'd like at least two canoes with fighting crews ready to deploy off the back ramp just in case something unexpected comes up."

"I have two whaleboats," the captain suggested.

"Even better. Loud Elk, I'd like to put you and yours in one of them."

The First Nations warrior liked it. "Good."

"The most dangerous part will be crashing into the lock. We're going to be slowed to a crawl, in a picture-perfect cross fire, and they're going to be firing down into us. Yoann, I want you to dismount the machine blasters from the wags and put their crews wherever the captain wants them. We're going to need every crew and convoy man without a job to do on the rails firing back. We'll clear a space in the middle of the cargo hold. That's where Mildred and Krysty will set up the aid station. Captain, you got a healer?"

"We got a saw doc who ain't half bad when he's sober."

"One other thing, Captain. If it looks like the locks aren't going to fall, don't worry about us. Get your ship out of there."

McKenzie leaned forward and put his finger on the map of Canada. "You don't need to worry about that, but if it happens, take your iron wag. Head for the Trans-Canada if you can. There's a fishing ville about seventy-five klicks east of the locks called Thessalon. I'll wait for you there, two days, and your people will have my protection for as long as they want it. You have my word." The captain stared back down at the map and the sketches. You could hear the wheels turning in his mind as he contemplated a thousand contingencies, but it was clear he liked what he was hearing.

"Best plan I heard all day," he concluded. "Best thing I heard since Thorpe and his rad-pest pirate sons of bitches closed the canal."

Toulalan sighed. "So, Six, are you happy with the plan now?"

All eyes turned on Vincent Six.

"I was happier with Venus in furs back in Val-d'Or." Six gave Ryan another grudging look of admiration. "But I'll admit this plan has gotten better."

Captain McKenzie rose. "Mr. Smythe, it's going to be hard as the hobs of hell to get that iron wag up on the promenade, and we may need beams to brace it. I want that done at port on Manitoulin."

"Yes, Captain."

McKenzie gazed toward the porthole and the sinking sun. "We'll weigh anchor here and stay in open water tonight. Give Dr. Tanner his catapult demonstration while we're at it. Tonight we rest. Tomorrow we make every arrangement except raising the LAV and sail into Manitoulin looking mean. There won't be no shore leave on the island. We're running drills until every man knows his job. Yoann, I need you to do the same."

"But of course, Captain."

"Mr. Smythe, I want everything done and to weigh anchor at Manitoulin by noon."

"Yes, Captain."

"Everyone else, get drunk, get laid, do whatever you're going to do. It's all drilling after Manitoulin and then its gonna be a fight."

The captain rose and the meeting broke up. J.B. paused at the door. Boo Blacktree stood by the table staring down at the maps and plans. The big scout's fingers unconsciously tapped at the bow that hung by his side.

J.B. stared at the antiquated weapon. "Bow, huh?"

Blacktree slowly raised his head. He spent long moments considering this observation. "Yup."

"Bows," J.B. conceded, "never jam."

Blacktree chewed that over. "Nope."

J.B. was a man of few words, except when it came to discussing weapons. Then he became downright chatty. Boo Blacktree's monosyllabic answers were giving even J.B. a run for his money. "Don't trust blasters much?"

"Nope."

"Failed you before?"

"Yup."

J.B. nodded at the Thompson Center, single-shot blaster in Blacktree's belt. "So why that?"

Blacktree stared, stone-faced at the Armorer, who almost thought he wasn't going to answer until he suddenly spoke. "Worm insurance."

J.B. blinked. "Yeah?"

"Yup." Blacktree ran an affectionate finger over the wood of his bow. "Man or beast, worm-alive, you can take them with this, first time. But if you ain't quick, then they get up their second time. Worm dead."

J.B. remembered the porkers he'd killed outside Borden rising up like thousand-pound puppets all too well. Blacktree drew his blaster and broke open the action. He pulled out a single, cast-lead .44 Magnum round. The face of the bullet was as flat as a hammer, and someone had carved a very deep cross into the lead with a knife. "The worm dead, then you gotta bust up."

"I like running them over with armored wags," J.B. stated.

Blacktree slowly nodded. "That'd work, too."

"What's with the worms?"

Blacktree rolled his mighty shoulders. "Forget 'em. We left the Bruce. We left them behind."

Chapter Twelve

Ryan awoke to screams and blasterfire. He rolled out of bed with his SIG-Sauer in one hand and his panga in the other. Krysty sat up. "Lover...what—"

"Gear up." Ryan heard Krysty's blaster clear leather. "Stay behind me." More gunshots and screams rang out below where the convoy, cargo and the majority of the passengers were berthed. Ryan heard a slamming noise in the corridor outside. He swiftly and silently opened the door of their stateroom. The corridor of the passenger suites was dimly lit with smoky, fish-oil lamps. A man was slamming his shoulder into Doc's stateroom door.

Ryan spoke low. "Hey."

The man whirled. Ryan recognized him as one of the passengers taking birth to Manitoulin Island. A wordless scream tore from this throat as he charged Ryan. Foam flew from his mouth and his fingers curled into claws. Ryan burned half a mag of hollowpoint rounds into him before the intruder fell twisting to the metal floor, spraying blood at his feet. Krysty leaned out into the corridor with her blaster in both hands, covering her lover's back. "Ryan..."

"Ship's under attack."

Doc stuck his head out of the door, blinking in the lamplight. "Did I hear someone knock?"

Ryan shook his head. "Doc..."

Doc cocked his head. "Is that gunfire and screaming? By my stars and garters I swear most days I wake up to it. One could almost set one's watch by the…" He trailed off at the look on Ryan's face and what the man was looking down at. "Oh dear."

"Fire blast…"

Ryan had put eight rounds into his attacker, all center body mass. The man was getting back up. Worms pushed through his pupils as he got his feet under him. Ryan's panga flashed. He lopped off the left-reaching arm at the elbow, then sheared off the right at the shoulder. The worm-dead leaned toward Ryan. Its jaw dropped open, and a clutch of worms stretched toward Ryan like a questing hand. His panga hissed through the air.

The passenger's head came off in a fountain of blood and waving worms.

The dead thing staggered drunkenly as the worms sticking up out of his neck realigned themselves toward a target. Ryan's panga sliced beneath the passenger's patella and the former human fell twitching and spilling symbiotes. A foot-long length of filth squirmed across the deck toward Ryan. He crushed it beneath the heel of his boot. "The ship isn't under attack. It's infested. Doc, get Krysty to the bridge. It the highest place on the ship and the safest. McKenzie and his officers will gather there and start fighting their way down deck by deck."

"Of course my friend, but you—"

"Jak is down on the wag deck with Seriah in the LAV. J.B. and Mildred are in the big rig's cab. I'm going to go get them."

Below them screams, gunshots and the bloodthirsty roars of the infected melded with the squeals of Fatty's herd of pigs under attack in a chorus of horror. Toulalan, Six and Seriah came out of their rooms almost simultaneously, blasters in hand.

"Yoann! You, your sister!" Ryan stared at Seriah. "Seriah! Get to the bridge!"

"No!" Toulalan objected. "My people are down below!"

"Fine! You're with me! Doc, take Krysty, Cyrielle and Seriah! Go now!"

"Yes! Of course!"

Ryan ran down the corridor, Toulalan and Six falling in behind him. Doc bowed to Krysty, Cyrielle and Seriah. "Ladies, if you will kindly—"

"Come on, Doc!" Krysty pushed past him. The Canadians followed her.

"Oh, well, of course, ladies first…" Doc hurried after the women. Krysty ran down the corridor. Shots were echoing in what had once been the cafeteria and gift shop. She threw open the door. Skillet, the *Queen*'s cook, lay on the floor feebly twitching and mewling as a bare-chested, blood-covered crewman held him down and bit huge bloody chunks out of him. The crewman leaped up and turned on Krysty. The whites of his eyes were solid red and his muscles strained against his bones. His veins stood out in crazy striations of strength. Bloody froth spewed from his lips as he lunged at Krysty. She shot him five times in the chest, and he faltered as her blaster clicked.

Cyrielle shoved Krysty out of the way. "Stand aside!" Her Diefenbunker C-7 made a sound like tearing canvas as she blasted an entire mag into the worm-infected crewman. He jerked and shuddered beneath the bullet storm and fell face-first to the deck. Cyrielle slammed a fresh mag into her blaster. *"Merde!"*

"No, Cyrielle." Krysty put a hand on her shoulder. "He isn't—"

The bullet-riddled crewman lurched to his knees. Worms pushed forth from every bullet hole and orifice in the corpse, straining toward the living bodies in front of them. Seriah raised her blaster.

"Ladies…" Doc stepped forward. "Stand aside." He cocked and leveled his LeMat revolver. The worm puppet that had once been a man shambled forward. Doc flicked the lever on his hammer for the shotgun barrel and fired.

The 16-gauge roared and its payload hit the thing right above the heart. The crewman's head, left shoulder and arm blasted away from the body and flopped to the deck in a shower of gore. The remaining arm and torso flailed backward from the shock of the explosion and fell. Doc's sword flicked out from its sheath. He took a cue from Ryan and slashed his point beneath both kneecaps.

Worms began exiting the body en masse.

Cyrielle threw up. Seriah clutched Krysty.

Skillet had a huge stockpot of water boiling on the stove. Doc began piercing fleeing worms and deftly flicked them into the scalding caldron where they turned white, coiled into parboiled fists and died. Doc methodically pierced and flicked. "Ladies, I dare say, please bar the door."

"SERIAH!" JAK SHOUTED. "Seriah!"

The vehicle deck was under siege. Bedlam reigned. The worm-infected charged, bit and ate their shipmates in mindless bloodlust. The chilled worm-dead rose up, their lifeless bodies manipulated as the infestations within looked for living flesh to infect. A worm-shambler shuffled toward Jak along the rail. It was Toulalan's old scholar, Florian Medard. There was nothing scholarly about the worms waving out of his dead face. Jak drew the three throwing spikes he'd won from Tag. He'd practiced with them out on the promenade until a mate had told him to stop deflating the sandbag revetments.

Jak took half a second to gauge his throw and aimed to hit

side-on rather than point first. He threw. The steel shaft hit the worm-shambler in the chest with a sternum-cracking thud and knocked it back three steps. The albino teen took three steps forward to maintain his throwing distance and threw again. The thing stumbled back against the stern guardrail with the impact. When Jak's third throw cracked its skull, its head rubbernecked with the impact and the momentum toppled it over the rail into the lake.

"Jak!" Mildred was at the top of the landing shooting and screaming. Jak's ruby eyes narrowed. Fatty was heaving his way brokenly up the stairs toward her. His rolls of flesh shook like milk with the horror that moved beneath them. Someone had taken off the top of his head with a scattergun, and worms waved out of his broken melon like Krysty having a bad hair day. Fatty barely jerked as Mildred's .38 punched precision holes in his torso. "Jak!"

The albino youth drew a throwing blade and sent the steel spinning into the back of what used to be his number-one fan's left knee. The limb buckled and three hundred pounds of worm-infested corpulence collapsed and tumbled down the stairs. Jak's favorite fighting knife filled his hand and he swiftly hamstrung Fatty's other leg. He slashed the tendons in its elbows and wrists and ripped his knife beneath each armpit. Jak leaped back as the puppet masters within began wriggling forth from their now stringless marionette of flesh. "Mildred!" Jak shouted. "J.B.! Where?"

"I don't know, we got separated and— Jak! Jak!" Mildred warned.

The albino teen spun to find Sylvan and two of Fatty's prized pink porkers stumbling forward in a phalanx, cratered with bullet holes. The worms in their eyes pointed straight at him. Jak drew his Magnum blaster. Ryan's voice echoed in the cargo hold like thunder. "Jak! Don't move!"

Jak froze.

He felt the supersonic whip cracks of blasterfire flying all around him. He recognized the bark of Ryan's new rifle, and the thunder of Six's .45-70, and the snarl of half a dozen Diefenbunker blasters on full-auto. Sylvan was shredded beneath the barrage, and the pigs puddled into collapsing piles of chewed flesh as the fusillade of rifle fire grew.

"Form on me!" Ryan's voice boomed above the sound of battle.

Embattled convoy and crew desperately coalesced to Ryan's call. He hit the foot of the stairs with Six, Toulalan, Captain McKenzie and more than a dozen armed crewmen. Two worm-alive convoy men charged screaming, followed by one of Fatty's squealing pigs. Their bodies rippled and shuddered as combined firepower of Ryan's formation passed through them like a killing wind of lead. "Torches!" Ryan shouted. "Torches and gaffs!"

McKenzie echoed the sentiment. "Queensmen! Crewmen! Convoymen! Torches and gaffs! Burn the worms and get the bodies over the side, rad-blast it!"

"Form on me or get on top of the wags!" Ryan ordered. His formation wound like a mutually supporting snake through the parked wags and cargo pallets, blasting the worm-alive and the worm-dead alike with massed blasterfire. Crew and convoy trapped on top of the wags shot down into the infested. Men high-stepped as they raised their boots and crushed squirming worms beneath their heels. Behind them convoy and crew alike jumped down and began applying torches to wrigglers twisting on the deck plates and gaffing shot-to-pieces abominations to be dragged and dropped off the side.

Toulalan shouted as his moccasin slid on a spill of blood and he fell onto the deck and almost went underneath the big rig. Six grabbed him and the baron's son came up screaming.

He clutched his wrist, howling, as a worm flailed between his fingers and burrowed its way into his palm.

Ryan's panga flashed.

Toulalan gasped as his hand came off at the wrist, and he collapsed back to the deck. The mouthparts and two inches of worm continued to push in between his exposed ulna and radius bones. Ryan stepped on Yoann's stump and pinned it to the deck. Six bellowed in indignation. "Ryan!"

The one-eyed man ignored him.

Ryan's blade scythed through tendon and bone with a butcher's skill and took off Toulalan's infested arm at the elbow. The man fainted. Six looked torn between seeing to the heir of Val-d'Or and chilling Ryan.

The one-eyed man had no time for recriminations. "Get him upstairs!" he ordered. "Get him to Mildred!" Six swore in French as he scooped Toulalan into his arms like a baby. He wrapped one huge hand around the man's mutilated arm and squeezed his thumb against the brachial artery, then swept him away up the stairs. Ryan picked up the severed limb and hurled it into the lake.

Almost at the same moment silence suddenly fell across the cargo deck. The screaming and blasterfire had stopped. "Everyone stay where you are!" Ryan commanded. "We'll come to you!"

Ryan's head snapped up at the distinctive sound of J.B.'s mini-Uzi firing. The shots almost seemed haphazard. One shot here, one shot there. That wasn't J.B. at all, and Ryan feared the worst for his friend. "Fireblast it, J.B.! You're alive!" Ryan called. "Where are you?"

J.B.'s voice responded raggedly. "Here..."

Ryan charged around the fighting LAV. J.B. sat against a bulkhead bare-headed, his glasses askew and bleeding copiously from his left leg. Ten feet away lay a pig he had almost blasted into its component parts with his scattergun. Worms were wriggling across the deck from the corpse toward him with hostile, hungry intent. He burst each one with a 9 mm hollowpoint round when it got within three feet of his boots. Ryan steeled himself and hesitated. "J.B., tell me you aren't infested!"

"I'm bit," J.B. said wearily. "But it was berzerko when it gave me the tusks. I killed it. The worms came after."

Ryan hurdled the pig carcass. He hauled J.B. up and threw him into a fireman's carry. "Mildred'll patch you up fine."

"Mildred…" J.B. sighed and passed out.

"Yeah." Ryan nodded beneath J.B.'s weight. "Mildred." He adjusted the Armorer across his shoulders.

"Captain, I'd get everyone—and I mean everyone, on top. In the morning, clean every inch of deck space, top to bottom, stem to stern."

"You don't have to tell me that!" McKenzie stormed.

Ryan nodded tiredly. "I know. I got to see to my people."

McKenzie's shoulders sagged. "Okay. See to your people. I just don't get how this happened. Infection is immediate. No one was worm-alive when they boarded. Not even the pigs or chickens."

"I'll tell you in the morning." Ryan turned and began trudging upstairs with J.B.. "But you aren't going to like it."

"SONS OF MUTIE WHORES!" The sun rose; so did Captain McKenzie's voice. Ryan had gone below with two score of armed men and shown the captain what he knew he would find. Red and Tag's pallet of metal cylinders were all opened and surrounded by a wide puddle of melted ice.

"Goose tells me the worms are dormant during the freeze, and come up out of the ground when the ice melts." Ryan had seen savagery he didn't like to think about in the Deathlands. Baron Mace Henning putting a worm bomb in the belly of the *Queen of the Lakes* was trying real hard to top the list. At

Ryan's suggestion they had sent six-man teams, three with blasters, two with gaffs and one with a torch into every cabin, cubby and hold in the ship. All the teams had reported back. The ship was clean. The good baronial bastard Red!"

"Done a head count." The loadmaster was covered head to toe with blood and filth. "Him and his two sec men are gone."

"Well, does anyone remember blasting them?" McKenzie stormed. "Maybe shoving their worm-'fested carcasses over the side?"

Passengers and crew clutched their blasters and stared at one another.

Mr. Smythe called from the starboard bow. "Captain! We're missing canoe number seven!"

"Rad-blasted sons a pesthole gaudy..." McKenzie broke into a fine stream of profanity. He finally regained his composure. "Are we clean, Mr. Smythe? You assuring me?"

"Everywhere except the bilge, Captain." It was the first time Ryan had seen Mr. Smythe balk at anything. "But after what I saw last night, I won't order a man to crawl down into that space."

"Oh, you won't, eh?" McKenzie's anger detonated. "Well, I'll scuttle this bitch with every passenger and hand aboard before I have her bringing worms to every port of call on the Lakes!"

This met with a disgruntled silence.

It was Doc who spoke. "Good Captain?"

"What!"

Doc flinched. He was utterly exhausted, but sometimes that was when he was most lucid. "Disconnect the screws. Bring the boilers to full. Vent steam into the bilge. Scald it clean. I once read that was how riverboats dealt with vermin in their bellies."

McKenzie whirled on his engineer. "Rad-blast it, Mr. Hicks! You heard the man! Get it done!"

Engineer Hicks just about jumped out of his homespun boiler suit. "Yes, Captain!"

Ryan knew he was speaking out of turn, but the Canadians were out of their normal freeze-thaw-plant-fight-harvest-and-store-their-nuts-for-winter cycle. The French of Val-d'Or had jumped the Ottawa, Captain McKenzie was back on the Huron, and Baron Mace Henning was willing to break every law of the north to stop them. Something had changed. Ryan knew he and his were in the middle, and no one was telling him the whole story.

"Captain McKenzie?"

"What now?"

Ryan's blue eye burned into McKenzie unblinkingly. "What the fireblast is going on?"

McKenzie's hand eased toward his blaster. "What do you mean?"

"Why are you willing to risk your ship? Why is Mace Henning willing to risk total war with the First Nations and all the villes around the Lakes?" Ryan glared at Six. "Why didn't Mace finish the convoy when you were sucking like a landed fish and he had the chance?"

The captain loomed, ugly. "Tell you what, Ryan. We'll drop you off on Manitoulin. That LAV of yours is amphibious, but for fording rivers and streams, not for sailing out of sight of land. I got the only ship on the Lakes that can move that wag and you know it, but I bet Baron Poncet would love to have it. You can trade it for a canoe, maybe some pemmican, paddle your way all the way to Michigan. Then you and your friends can walk your asses all the way back to your pest-infested Deathlands."

Ryan's gaze was glacial. "Drop the ramp. We'll leave now. Good luck with the locks."

McKenzie swelled up for another detonation. Ryan felt Jak and Doc behind him getting ready for the fight to come. It was Cyrielle who spoke from the stairs. "I will tell him, Captain. If you won't."

The tension drained from the deck. All eyes turned to Cyrielle except Ryan's. He kept his eye on the captain. No matter what happened, he died first. "Tell me."

"Lady Cyrielle!" Six protested. "No!"

Cyrielle's shift was spattered from breast to knee with her brother's blood. She pulled Ryan aside to the ramp. Six stepped up behind them. Cyrielle spoke very low. "We seek the prize, Ryan."

"Yeah, well, sure as shit, that prize is a lot more than Diefenbunker beer, blasters and champagne."

Cyrielle cocked her head. "You know what a nuclear reactor is?"

Ryan kept his eye on Six. "I do."

"Have you ever heard of a 'cartridge' nuclear reactor power unit?"

Ryan had heard of compact nuke units in the Deathlands, but had never come across one. "Yeah."

"Well, the Diefenbunker we seek has four of them. In as pristine condition as the Diefenbunker beer, blasters and vehicles."

Ryan contemplated that. "That's why you need the big rig."

"Each reactor can generate 70 megawatts of heat energy. In Captain McKenzie's world, that is 27 megawatts of electricity from a steam turbine. The reactors are simple. Add water, pull the rods and the lights go on. Do you know what that means?"

Ryan had an inkling. "Tell me."

"That is enough electricity to power twenty thousand predark homes for five years. Enough to power all Val-d'Or for a decade. In that time, we fire up the machine shops. We lay electricity throughout the ville. We run power lines to our neighbors and allies."

Ryan was pretty sure he knew the answer, but he asked anyway. "And when the rods die?"

"We fire up the second. With what we have already built, we will use that power to build a coal-fire reactor and reactivate the mines. Then Val-d'Or is no longer a ville, but city, and one that exports power."

"And you give one to McKenzie."

"Correct, he will pick a ville on the Ottawa, take his reactor and become a baron. With electricity, a ship and Val-d'Or as his ally he will become a major power, and the second coal-fire reactor we build will be his. We will be able to do more than survive winter. We will beat it. That will be the beginning of a new Canada, and a new world."

"And I want to help you because…?" Ryan asked.

"Because I will give you the fourth reactor."

"My lady!" Six was practically bursting. "You cannot!"

Cyrielle ignored her sec man. "The reactor is small enough to strap into a trailer in back of your LAV. Ryan, you told my brother that, like him, you are the son of a baron. Take the reactor back to your Deathlands. Take it back to the ville of your birth. Fill it with electricity, heat and light and prosper. All the while knowing you have powerful allies in the North."

Ryan rubbed his chin. It was one hell of an offer, but he had no desire to become a baron. If he had, he could have ruled Front Royal.

"With your help we have left Mace Henning behind us. However, the Diefenbunker we seek is on the other side of the Soo Locks. I fear we cannot prevail on either path without your help."

Mildred appeared at the top of the stairs. She was even more exhausted and blood-spattered than Cyrielle. "How's J.B.?"

"That pig gored him pretty deep, but it missed the femoral artery and the bone isn't broken."

"Will he be able to fight from the LAV?"

Mildred smiled wearily. "Oh hell, if that pig had taken his leg off at the hip he'd still fight from the LAV."

"How's Yoann?"

Mildred's face fell. "Not good. He lost a lot of blood, and he's showing signs of infection."

McKenzie and his crew's hands moved toward their blasters.

The physician rolled her eyes. "Oh for God's sake! I said infection, not infestation!"

No one seemed reassured.

"The wound is clean, but he's got a fever and it's rising. I think it must be something in his blood. Doc thinks the worms must secrete something into their host to help them survive such a massive infestation and keep them charging around looking for meat. Maybe it has something to do with being attacked, but without symbiosis being achieved. I don't know. I have no experience with something like this." She looked at McKenzie. "Do you?"

McKenzie shook his head. "Never heard of a man worm-bit but not infested."

"You think it laid eggs in him?" Ryan asked.

The group grew very quiet.

Mildred looked back toward her makeshift infirmary. "I can't imagine it had time. Doc seems to think that infesting a large mammal is just one part of the worms' life cycle. They don't seem to eat their host, but they make it run around and eat like a rabid wolverine. Doc suggested maybe they're getting something they need to breed from the glands, maybe hormones or something."

"Is he safe?"

"I can't imagine whatever he has is catching. Right now

he's unconscious, and just to be on the safe side I have him in restraints, and the sailors around here tie good knots. I'll keep monitoring him. Krysty's watching him now. Any change and I'll let you know."

Cyrielle's eyes were bright with unshed tears. The rest of her face was hard. "Thank you, Mildred."

"Think nothing of it." Mildred went back to her charges. She had more than a dozen of them.

Cyrielle turned to the assembly on the cargo deck. "I'm taking command of the convoy."

Six spoke deferentially, but he loomed over her. "No, my lady. I think it's best if I take command. I'll run all decisions by you."

"No," Ryan said flatly. "I'm taking command."

The dark, beautiful, smiling young woman instantly turned into a baron's daughter. "You will not."

Six very slowly rolled his shoulders. His sheepskins fell away, and his hands opened by his sides. One hovered over his blaster and one over his tomahawk. All sneering and scowling was gone. His face was the blank mask of a cipher. Like most of truly dangerous people Ryan had met, the worse things got, the more he relaxed. Six was a stone chiller of men, and he was silently daring Ryan to go for his blaster, panga or both. The strategic part of Ryan's mind noticed that McKenzie wasn't raising any objections. The tactical part of Ryan's mind was utterly focused on Six.

Ryan spoke quietly. "I'm not going to fight you, Six."

Six's hands stayed exactly where they were. There wasn't a tremble or tic to them. They just eerily hung in space over his weapons. "I'm very glad to hear that, Ryan."

"I'm taking my people. I'm leaving."

"Mildred stays."

Ryan was getting very tired of being threatened this morning. "I'm taking her with me."

"I'll kill you."

"I've seen you, Six," Ryan stated. "I'm faster."

"I'll still take you with me."

Ryan's burning gaze went dead. "You'll try."

Doc sighed heavily. "We are all on the same side. We have mutual enemies. Cannot there be some form of compromise?"

"I'm not compromising Mildred," Ryan stated.

"No," Jak agreed.

"Then let us come to an agreement," Doc suggested.

Cyrielle's voice was tight. "Six doesn't demand Mildred for himself, but for my brother's life."

"I know that," Ryan acknowledged. "That doesn't change anything. I'll make it simple. You want to run the locks, I'm in command. You want your convoy to make it to those reactors, I'm in command. I've been in fights on the water, on the land, in the air and below the ground. I've led convoys. Six, you're tough, and you're smart, and I'll give it to you. The day I try to nightcreep Val-d'Or, there's a good chance you'll take my hair. But that's just it. You've been thinking defensively the entire time. We're going on the offense. Lady Cyrielle, you take charge of your people, but all military decisions are mine.

"Captain, you've fought pirates in canoes. I've fought ship to ship. You run your crew, but all naval decisions are mine. No discussion. If you don't like it, me and mine leave. If you don't like that, we kill each other now."

Goose and Boo seemed to appear out of nowhere. They fell into formation behind Ryan. Goose looked around sincerely. "I'll tell you something. Not all First Nations tribes agree or get along. But in bad times—I'm not saying we give up our rights or laws or nothing—we elect a war chief. Give him command to get us through. Me and Boo are First Nations. Lady Cyrielle, you and yours are French. Captain McKenzie and his are Canucks and sailors. Ryan's people are Deathlanders. I'm not saying anyone gives up anything, but I nominate Ryan war chief on the water and war chief on the land until we get what we came for, and part ways. Laden with profit."

McKenzie spoke with gravity. "I'm captain of the *Queen*. You want to be captain? It's easy. Kill me. Then you're captain. If the crew'll have you. But as long as I'm captain, I'll accept Ryan as war chief upon the waters."

Cyrielle took a deep breath.

Six shook his head. "My lady! I beg of you! For your brother's—"

"Ryan is convoy commander."

Ryan's eyes never left Six. As far as he had seen, the huge sec man had never expressed any emotion other than rage or scornful bemusement. He wore his heart on his sleeve now, and it was breaking apart. His hands dropped limply to his sides as he turned away. His mighty shoulders sagged as if the weight of the entire nuked planet was pushing them down.

His voice was a ghostly rasp of its normal boom. "As you wish…"

The big man walked away, and Cyrielle followed, speaking in rapid French. Six wasn't listening. He waved her away.

Ryan shook his head. "This isn't good."

Krysty gave his hand a squeeze. "Tell you something else that isn't good."

"What?"

"Six is in love with Cyrielle."

Chapter Thirteen

"Heave!" McKenzie hollered from the promenade. "Heave, you scurvy, rad-blasted bastards!"

Crew and convoy heaved and groaned on the docks; timbers heaved and groaned on the beach; the capstans groaned; ropes groaned; the cranes groaned and bent dangerously. A LAV 3 swung perilously in the air. It was a madly dangerous operation. The *Queen*'s two cranes worked in conjunction with a newly hewed tripod-winch of mast-size timbers. Between them the LAV slowly oscillated over the loading ramp like a seventeen-ton pendulum. The capstans ratcheted another notch and stopped. The men on the capstan spars moaned with frustrated effort. The men on the tripod ropes bit through their lips as they strained to the utmost. Immense weight met human will and hung in the balance by mere ounces of effort.

The LAV would go no farther.

The native population of Manitoulin Island thronged the docks and watched with the fascination of people waiting for something absolutely terrible to happen. The capstans were jammed three men per spar. There was no more room. Only coils of tripod rope remained. As Ryan shrugged out of his coat, Krysty put a hand on his shoulder. "Lover, someone's going to get herniated, and it had better not be you."

Ryan stripped off his shirt and spit on his hands as he strode up the line to the end coils of the winch rope.

McKenzie hollered once more. "Heave! Heave, you bastards! Heave till your hearts break! Heave till your balls burst! But heave, you bastards! Heave!"

Ryan wrapped his callused hands around the rope and roared in response. "Heave!"

The men hurled themselves against the horrible, inexorable, dead, iron-clad weight of the LAV as their new war chief joined the line. They shouted with renewed effort. "Heave!"

Ryan heard his joints pop and crackle with strain. The LAV jerked up another foot.

"Heave!" McKenzie thundered.

Ryan and the pullers shouted back and pulled. "Heave!"

The LAV jerked up another foot.

Momentum began to gather.

Blacktree walked up pulling off his doeskin shirt and took anchor behind Ryan.

"Heave!" the captain called.

Boo Blacktree's strength stopped just short of being inhuman. Ryan felt him taking up slack and heaved to meet it. "Heave!"

Hearts hammered. Blood pulsed in men's temples. Backs threatened to give way. Flesh threatened to fail. But suddenly every man knew this thing might be done.

McKenzie hurled his voice to the heavens. "Heave!"

"Heave!" the call came back.

Six strode shirtless up to the rope line. His torso was an ebony tree trunk of power. He stepped in behind Blacktree and took rope into his mighty hands. "Men of Val-d'Or!" he challenged. "Show these Canucks what Québécois can do!"

"Heave!" McKenzie shouted.

Even in quiet conversation Six's voice sounded like distant thunder. Now the storm broke out in French. *"Tirez!"*

Every Quebecer convoy man roared and pulled with smooth and sudden power. *"Tirez! Tirez fort!"*

The LAV lurched upward.

"Heave!"

The Quebecers roared in a storm of strength. *"Tirez!"*

"Heave!"

Everyone man took up the call and response as blood, sweat and sinew worked as a unit against unforgiving iron. Ryan felt the power of massed humanity in motion, and he bellowed from the pit of his belly as he heaved.

The loadmaster screamed at his men up top. "Pull it in! Pull it in! Pull it in!"

The loadmaster's crewmen pulled on the guy ropes and brought the LAV teetering over the promenade. "On the plate! On the plate! On the plate! Now! Lower! Lower! Lower! Lower easy, you bastards! I said—"

The men on the capstans and Ryan's crew on the winch rope made horrible noises of effort as they reversed course and tried to lower the LAV without dropping it through the promenade, the vehicle deck, the bilge and into the dark water below.

The loadmaster screamed with consternation and excitement. "Easy! Easy! Easy! Easy I said—" Men fell forward as the LAV settled onto the deck and the heartbreaking weight disappeared. More crewmen rushed to chalk it in place. For just a moment there was no sound other than the gasps of the crowd on the dock and the rasping breaths of the capstan and linesmen shuddering with suspended effort.

The loadmaster's voice was the first thing everyone heard, and even he was awed by what had been wrought. "Well, fuck me running with a pitchfork…"

Tuques sailed skyward.

The docks erupted into cheers.

Ryan rose from where he had fallen from the sudden slack. Boo Blacktree wrapped his hands around Ryan's biceps and heaved him skyward, laughing, shaking him and whooping war cries.

Ryan restrained himself. "That'll do, Boo."

Boo dropped him.

"Get drunk tonight, boys!" McKenzie bawled. "'Cause when the *Queen* sails tomorrow she sails as a ship of war!"

The dock burst into genuine bedlam.

Ryan found himself being pounded on the back by Six. "*Sacre bleu,* Ryan! We will win this! We will win the locks!"

Ryan wasn't quite willing to claim victory yet. But they had left Henning behind, beaten his worm bomb, and a LAV 3 sat on the promenade like an avenging angel of death. They had done it. The *Queen of the Lakes* was a ship of war. The one-eyed man knew victory begat victory, and momentum was a flame that needed to be fanned. Their palms popped as he slammed his hand into Six's. "Fireblast it, Six! Me and you! We'll go right down their throats and see if they got the stomach for it!"

Six scooped Ryan in his arms, lifted him off his feet and kissed him on both cheeks. Convoy and crew surged around Ryan roaring and cheering. Sailors pounded his shoulders on all sides with bone-rattling force. More French Canadians than Ryan wanted to think about slobbered on his face. He found himself elevated onto the men's shoulders and being paraded around the docks to the cheers of all Manitoulin and a shower of tuques.

Ryan endured it all gracefully.

"Canadians," Doc observed. "I believe they are as cute as buttons."

"A worm bomb?" Baron Oliver Poncet was an enormously fat man. His chair creaked beneath him. Hawberry wine and lamprey pie seemed to agree with him a little too much. He was clearly part First Nations, and between his braids and his burgeoning belly he might have almost seemed ridiculous. There was nothing ridiculous about the fear and deference his people showed him. He wasn't pleased at all with what he was hearing. "That's coldhearted. And you say he was sending it my way?"

Ryan sat at the baron's table along with J.B., McKenzie, Mr. Smythe and Six. Cyrielle had stayed by her brother's side aboard ship. "It was meant for us," Ryan said.

Poncet wasn't having it. He stabbed a fat finger at McKenzie. "First time the *Queen*'s been on the Huron in years! Gonna finally give Thorpe and his pirates their due, and about rad-blasted time if you ask me, and Henning goes and sticks that broken beak of his in it! Nearly fucks up the whole thing!" Poncet's vast bulk sagged back in his chair. "Mace Henning…" he mused. "I knew him when he was just a wandering sec man with nothing but his war club to his name. Now he calls himself a baron." Poncet shook his head. "About time someone had a real up close and personal chat with that boy."

"Henning will be dealt with. Our current priority is Thorpe and his pirates."

"Thorpe," Poncet said, "used to be one of ours. Manitoulin man. Bastard son of a gaudy slut, and not a particularly good one. Didn't impress anyone enough to make sec man, and with no family or connection he scraped by picking berries, mending nets and hauling in other people's catch. I remember giving him hell a few times."

"Why?" Ryan asked.

Poncet grunted. "Probably because he was breathing and had a pulse. I was meaner when I was skinnier. Anyway, one day Thorpe upped and stole a blaster and a canoe and paddled west. They say he paddled all the way to the Michigan, then all the way down it. That's where most Lake pirates like to winter it. Chicago? Waukee? Green Bay, they get hit hard, still some bad rads down there and decent folk stay clear."

"And came back a baron," Ryan said.

"Calls himself a king, actually." Poncet suddenly sighed. "That was something this morning. Seeing that iron wag raised. I swear I wanted to waddle my fat ass down and haul on that rope, but my wives wouldn't let me." Poncet craned his head around at three buxom young women quilting at a side table. "Would you!"

The clearly dominant of the trio gave her baron the glad eye. "We need your fat ass here, Ollie. We need you rested. You need more sons." The other two giggled.

Baron Poncet shook his head in disgust. "I used to be a warrior. Now look at me!" He jigged his vast belly. "Soft! Every part of me! Every part except one." He craned around to give his wives another sour look. "And they lead me around by it."

The baron's wives smirked and continued sewing.

"I wish I was going with you. Give Thorpe and his crew a good chilling. But who needs a beached Beluga in a blaster fight?" Poncet muttered into his wine. "That is for anything except cover."

Ryan suppressed a smile and cut himself another wedge of lamprey and mustard pie. "The captain tells me you were the wrestling champion of the Huron back in your day. I still wouldn't want to tangle with you."

Poncet flushed with pleasure and tried to cover it with a scowl. "Now you're greasing me, Ryan. Not that I don't like it. Tell me. How many'd you lose to the worms?"

"Fifteen dead," McKenzie said. "Mostly sec men and sailors, about a dozen more bit up bad, including the baron's son."

"You'll be wanting to recruit men, then."

McKenzie nodded to his mate. "Mr. Smythe?"

Smythe unfolded a blanket. A gleaming Diefenbunker C-7 blaster lay on it as well as a SIG.

Ryan took the ball. "We'll give you ten of each for the

right to recruit on your island. Each man who volunteers gets a blaster just like it, with seven full mags, belts, mag pouches and bayonet, plus a handblaster with an extra mag and ammo."

Poncet eyed the predark blasters. "I'll give you thirty men. Can't spare no more. Plenty of work around here still needs seeing to before winter. And any man who lives through the fight—if you win—gets a hundred in First Nations jack as bonus."

Ryan looked at McKenzie. The captain nodded. "Done."

Six leaned forward. "If we break through, I want them to stay and help sec the convoy. Are you agreeable?"

Poncet frowned. "The Soo Locks? They need cleaning. If I order my men to do it, they'll do it. But sec'ing your convoy west of the Superior this close to winter? That they get the choice of volunteering for."

"Fair enough," Six agreed. "Convoy duty will pay a second rifle and another hundred in First Nations jack."

"Sounds fair." Baron Poncet raised a finger. "But I'm sending one of my sons along, to get some experience."

"Three barons' sons on one boat." McKenzie grunted. "Normally I'd say that's a recipe to get someone chilled."

"Hunk!" the baron called. "Get over here!"

Hunk Poncet lumbered over to the table. He was huge, blond and blue-eyed, almost all arms and legs in his long shirt, breechclout and leggings, and very earnest-looking. All eyes turned incredulously on the baron.

Poncet shook his head. "I know, I know. He doesn't look nothing like me. Sired him off one of those Minnesota Viking-cult bitches I took in a raid years ago." Poncet's eyes grew far away in memory. "Dagmar. Rad blast it, I miss that woman. She had sand." Poncet shook his head and returned to the present.

"Hunk, you're going to take thirty men and go with our guests to clean out Thorpe and the locks."

Hunk nodded eagerly. "Yes, sir."

"I'll pick the men for you."

"Yes, sir."

"No, you pick them. Time you learned."

"Yes, sir."

Poncet nodded at Ryan, McKenzie and Six. "You do whatever these men say."

"Yes, sir."

"Fight hard. Don't shame the island."

"Yes, sir."

"Take some of the dogs, three of them. Assuming you get past the locks, you're going to sec for the convoy. If you go, I think the rest of the men will, too, and the dogs might come in handy once you get dirt under your moccasins."

"Yes, sir."

"Oh, and try to get back before the freeze."

"Yes, sir."

"And try to bring some of the men back alive."

"Yes, sir."

Baron Poncet reached beneath his garment and pulled out a blaster. Ryan recognized it as a Glock. The slide was pitted and missing most of its finish from hard use. Its plastic grips and frame had failed in the intervening century, and a blacksmith had forged a new grip and lower receiver out of iron. The baron tossed the weapon to his son casually. "Here, take this. It was my first blaster. Now it's yours."

Hunk caught the weapon. He looked at his father and his lower lip started to tremble. Poncet swallowed the frog in his own throat and snarled over his own emotion.

"And eat something before you go, would you? Look at you, you got a frame like an oak, but I swear when you turn sideways you don't cast a shadow."

Hunk flushed red. "Yes, sir."

Poncet's sec men pounded the table in approval of Hunk's elevation in status. J.B. waited for the applause to die down. "Been thinking."

"Dangerous occupation," Poncet opined. "Or so I'm told."

"Thorpe's going to see the *Queen* coming long ways off. It might make some sense to insert some men by canoe, under cover of dark. Swim under the lock with the charges and—"

Poncet, McKenzie and every Canadian in the hall burst out laughing. J.B. bristled. "What?"

"So—" Poncet leaned forward waggling his eyebrows in humorous question "—you like the pie?"

More men laughed.

J.B. waited for the rub. "Like it just fine."

"I'll admit you're a little on the small side, J.B., but I tell you what. If you go take that moonlight swim, the lampreys are going to like you just fine, too. With or without mustard."

Men roared with laughter and pounded the tables at this new height in Lake Huron humor. McKenzie wiped tears from his eyes. "No one swims the Lakes, J.B., least no one north of the Saint Clair."

J.B. took a big deliberate bite of lamprey pie and chewed it and swallowed. "Fine." He washed it down with more hawberry wine and raised his stein. "Like Ryan said, then. Naval gunnery."

Pewter steins rose and clacked together around the table. "Naval gunnery!"

Chapter Fourteen

"Kagan! Kosha! Quinn!" Hunk called. The Manitoulin Island platoon had arrived on the *Queen*. The islanders trooped up the ramp proudly. Each bore a new Diefenbunker C-7 blaster over his shoulder and a SIG-Sauer at his hip. A new bayonet was mounted on every muzzle, and each man carried his own favorite mix of tomahawks, knives and war clubs. The men of Manitoulin all wore a red tuque with a crude, five-petaled white hawberry blossom stitched on the front and a matching sash.

First Mate Smythe shook his head. "Haweaters..."

Mildred eyed the massive dogs. The three animals were cream-colored, silver and black respectively. "Those are some mighty-looking poodles you got there, Hunk," Mildred observed. They were huge. Their poodle lines were unmistakable, but they were built on some kind of postapocalyptic Great Dane–size frame. Mildred was pretty sure there was something in them besides standard poodle, but it was hard to tell under the thick, curly coats covering every inch of their massive bodies. There was definitely something a little wolfy around the eyes, and their jaws were just too damned big.

Hunk nodded. "Poodles will do anything dog. Gun dog, guard dog, water dog, lamprey retrieving—"

"What!" Mildred was appalled. "What kind of inbred sicko throws his poodles to giant, man-eating sea lampreys?"

Hunk looked shocked. "Lampreys don't eat people. They got no jaws. They suck people, and they don't give you the tongue and start suckin' less their mouth gets a good seal." Hunk dropped to a knee beside Kagan and ran a hand over her dense cream coat. Kagan stood imperiously wagging her tail. She was clearly the alpha bitch of the trio of dogs. "Try to latch on to a poodle," Hunk continued, "and all the lampreys get is a mouth full of fur. Those thorny little teeth? They just get lost in the curls. Now, when a poodle bites a lamprey back?" Hunk smiled mischievously. "Pie for dinner."

"That's just wrong," Mildred said.

Hunk scratched Kagan behind the ears and gave the woman a reproachful look. "If you ever fall in the water, these dogs are gonna be just right."

"Don't worry about it. I'm never swimming again. I'm never eating pork again, and I'm never going to take another a nap in a refrigerator again, ever." Mildred walked away waving her hands. "I have to check on my patients."

Hunk watched Mildred walk away. He looked up to find Ryan in front of him and Hunk leaped to his feet. "Ryan!"

"I see you got your men squared away."

"Even my pa the baron says they're salty!"

A smile hinted at the corners of Ryan's mouth. "You know the plan?"

"Your friend, J.B. told me everything. Everything except our part in it. I guess we're blasting from the rails and repelling borders."

"No, I got plenty of Quebecers doing that. You're an island man, sailing man, right?"

Hunk thumped his chest. "Got that right."

"Listen, the *Queen* carries a pair of whale boats. I want two detachments of sailors I can send to any trouble spots. I'm going to put a machine blaster on the prow of each one. I got one filled with a bunch of Jon Hard-knife's men, and I want to give the other to you."

Hunk swelled with pride. "I won't let you down!"

"I know."

Mr. Smythe stepped forward with his volunteers. "The *Queen*'s contribution to your raiding party, Ryan. Captain's compliments. This is Loadmaster's Mate Timms."

Canada seemed to be dripping in giant humans. Loadmaster's Mate Timms wasn't gladiator-built like Ryan, or in a strongman frame like Six, or a monoblock of man like Boo Blacktree or sumo-wrestler-vast like Baron Poncet. Mr. Timms was simply built on a separate scale. Timms was impossibly tall, impossibly broad and best described as a full-blown human. Man-mountain came to mind. Ryan wondered how they would fit him in the LAV and if he would sink it.

Timms shoved out a hand with fingers like a bunch of bananas. "Nice to meet you, Mr. Ryan."

"Just Ryan, Mr. Timms."

"Hear we're tearing down the locks."

"Looks like you could do it all by your lonesome."

"More fun to do it with friends."

The first mate gestured at the woman. "Armorer's Mate Tamara."

Tamara had long dark hair, broad shoulders, large breasts, a flat behind, and slightly canted eyes that bespoke some interesting Canadian hybridization. First Nations tattooing banded her right biceps. What Ryan noted most was her early model, ancient Armalite AR-15 and the equally ancient but apparently serviceable Colt 4 x 20 scope mounted on the carry handle. He remembered McKenzie telling Smythe to pick someone "wicked good" with a blaster. Ryan liked what seemed to be a permanent smirk. Tamara didn't miss his appraisal. "I'm your guardian angel, Ryan, and you're Deathlands ass belongs to me. Captain's orders."

"Glad to hear it."

"Don't worry about your flame-headed girlfriend. What happens in the iron wag stays in the iron wag," Tamara said with a smirk. "You keep it in your pants, Ryan, and I'll see about keeping your head on your shoulders when the shooting starts tomorrow."

"WHO'S TAMARA?" Krysty asked dryly.

Ryan turned his face from the sinking sun, lowered his sleeve of spruce beer. And looked Krysty dead in the face. "She's my guardian angel. My Deathlands ass belongs to her. Captain's orders."

Krysty's eyebrows drew down dangerously.

Ryan tried his hand at a Gallic shrug. "But if I keep it in my pants, she's going to see about keeping my head on my shoulders when the shooting starts tomorrow."

Krysty was vaguely mollified. "Oh." She took the wooden stoop from Ryan's hand and took a swallow. She wiped her mouth with the back of her hand. "You know something, lover? I like drinking beer with you out here on the—"

"Loose!" Doc's voice boomed all the way from the rear promenade.

Ropes snapped like gunshots and spar-size timbers slammed together. Ryan and Krysty looked up as an enormous chunk of stone tumbled through space off the starboard bow. It hit an outcropping out on the water with an enormous rock-on-rock gunshot sound. The missile skipped off the outcropping and hit the water to skip twice, throwing enormous ripples.

Onlookers out on the decks cheered.

Krysty shook her head and smiled. "Boys and their toys…"

Ryan's eye narrowed. "What does that mean?"

Krysty returned Ryan's shrug. "Something Mildred says."

"He's doing all right since the jump."

"Canada agrees with him." Krysty slid her free hand into his. "And you gave him something to do."

Giving Doc something to do was one of the best ways to

control his condition. Ryan knew that all too often the man from the nineteenth century felt helpless. It was worse when he felt useless. Then he retreated into his memories, and Ryan knew from long experience that ville was haunted. At the moment Doc was excited about his catapults. He'd asked for quicklime and Greek Fire among other obscure items, and had almost got himself fired as Captain of Catapults. Then he'd asked for barrels of pitch mixed with the local bison fat soap. J.B. had sat up and taken notice at that. The Armorer had reviewed the local soap and pitch and insisted on an infusion of diesel fuel.

Doc had asked for caldrons, barrow loads of sand and the mess wag's twin portable ovens, and despite Captain McKenzie's misgivings about open flames on his deck, Doc had gotten those, too. Doc also had what he called single, double and triple weight rocks for various ranges. The old man had marked arcs of fire for both catapults like giant chrons in chalk on the stern promenade deck. Ryan didn't know about the sand and the pitch, but in practice, Doc was dropping huge rocks like you could set your chron to it.

Ryan was really hoping the coming fight just might be one of Doc's mad-genius moments. "You want to go for a walk?"

"Someplace where we won't get hit in the head with a bastard huge rock?" Krysty suggested.

"Someplace where there's some Diefenbunker rations," Ryan countered. He slid his arm around Krysty's waist. The decks were festooned with a double watch of convoy and crew, but most were relaxing, blasters ready as they sipped beer and waited to be relieved. Ryan and Krysty went inside. Three-quarters of the benches that had served the forward passenger deck had been ripped out and replaced with poles to hang hammocks from. The Deathlanders moved through the ranks of Canadians to nods of greeting. Ryan and Krysty reached the cafeteria-pub and the smell set Ryan to salivating. Cyrielle Toulalan had left her brother's side temporarily to distribute rations among convoy and crew. Ryan and Krysty were hailed by one and all and ushered to the front of the chow line. Ryan stared at long, Diefenbunker-marked tin pans of what appeared to be ruptured stickie and mystery meat. Ryan stopped short of wiping drool from his chin.

"What is that stuff?"

Mildred let out a belch from the end of the closest table and looked just about ready to roll onto the floor and stick all four legs up in the air like a dog drunk on slaughterhouse blood. "That on the left? That's lasagna with Italian sausage. And that?" Mildred sighed and put a hand on her stomach. "That's macaroni and cheese. And that? Those are ham slices with pineapple."

"Thought you gave up pig, Mildred."

"A girl's got to keep up her strength, Ryan, and I got a bad feeling I'm sewing tomorrow, like all day."

Ryan lifted a trencher board toward the cook's assistant. "For the lady and me. All three." Ryan saw the board piled high and he and Krysty took a seat with Mildred. "Where's J.B.?"

Mildred made a noise. "Shining his cannon. At first I thought it was a Freudian thing, but now I'm beginning to believe this just might be true love, and I starting to wonder if I should be jealous."

"Ah yes, Sigmund and his phallic symbols." Doc took a seat at the table. His cheeks were flushed from his work with his catapults. He tucked into a small plate of mac and cheese with unusual gusto. "However by the same token he always insisted that a fear of weapons was a sure sign of a retarded sexuality."

Mildred rolled her eyes. "Sigmund Freud was one seriously messed up sexual retard."

Doc cocked his head. "I never found him so in any of our conversations."

Mildred's face went flat. "You knew Sigmund Freud."

"As an American studying in England, there was no practical hope of spending ones holidays at home, so my fellow Yankee school chums and I often took our holidays upon the Continent. One summer some of us who fancied ourselves fencers decided we would go take on the Heidelberg boys for the glory of Oxford, and then travel to Vienna. I shared coffee and cordials with Sigmund several times after faculty symposiums. Fascinating man. I remember once when he was talking about his principles of dream interpretation..." Doc slowly trailed off and stared into the middle distance.

Ryan recognized the look. He rapped his knuckles once on the table. "Doc."

"What?" Doc blinked. "Yes?"

Ryan nodded at the food. "Big fight tomorrow. Need you tossing rocks. Eat."

Doc cringed with embarrassment and began picking at his food. "Ah yes, indeed, of course."

"Where's Jak?" Ryan asked.

Mildred smirked.

Jak was getting downright domestic with the mechanic. Ryan looked around the crowded tables and decided to review the troops. He got up and walked among convoy, crew and mercenary deputations. Ryan stopped at the island contingent's table. "How you haweaters doing?"

The Manitoulin men laughed. Hunk grinned through a massive mouthful of lasagna. "Well, it isn't lamprey pie, but Lord, Thunder and Fallout! If you'd said the chow was this good, you coulda got the whole island to volunteer!" Hunk's men shouted in agreement.

Ryan clapped Hunk on the shoulder. "Listen, I know you boys don't like being held back as a reserve." This was met with a round of good-natured cursing in the affirmative. "So I'm giving you a job. I want you and your men cutting the log chains tomorrow. It's going to be rough. You'll be out in the middle of the canal, no cover, and Thorpe and his pirates are going to rain on you."

Hunk jabbed his thumb into his chest. "Haweaters aren't afraid of a little rain, are we, boys?" The islanders shouted and pounded their beer mugs on the table. "Besides, we'll be sitting in the shade, the shade of J.B. and that big iron wag he got parked on the promenade."

Ryan grunted in amusement. Hunk was irrepressible. "You'll have that." Ryan went over to the First Nations table. Loud Elk and his crew were a little more taciturn than the island boys but they were just as eager for the fight. Ryan pulled the First Nations warrior aside.

"I know you and your men aren't happy about being the marine reserve."

"Someone's gotta do it," Loud Elk said. "And no matter what the island boys say, no one can oar a whaleboat faster than us. If the attack has any holes, we'll plug 'em."

"One other thing I want."

Loud Elk gave Ryan the stone-face. "What?"

"If we get through, nothing's going to stop Thorpe from coming back and trying again unless he's dead. If he is, there's nothing to stop some other baron coming in, rebuilding the lock and replacing him."

Loud Elk's eyes narrowed. "You're saying that if you get through, you want me and the boys to row hard, back for the Bruce. Have Hard-knife call a tribal gathering with as many Sachems as we can reach before the hard freeze. Declare the Soo Locks a trading camp and subject to camp law."

"Only sure way I can see making this worth the effort," Ryan said.

Loud Elk gazed at Ryan very steadily. "We will do this, and all will know these were your words."

Ryan and Loud Elk shook hands, and the First Nations warrior returned to his men. The one-eyed man looked out across the dining hall. Spirits were high. He put a hand on the wall and felt the vibration of the boilers chugging like a giant mechanical heartbeat. The plan was insane, but it was as good as it was going to get. Everyone knew his or her job, and Ryan had some bastard-tough sons of bitches on his side. Every resource they had was allocated and they had even come up with some new ones. He considered himself and knew he was more rested and fit than he'd been in a long time. His blasters were clean, his mags were full and so was his belly. His blades were razor-keen. There wasn't much more he could do about this battle except fight it, and to do that he was going to sail an iron wag across open water and blow up a pirate-infested wall, outnumbered five to one, with the enemy behind fortifications. The plan was insane.

Ryan allowed himself a small smile.

But it wasn't bad.

The only remaining thing he could do was get a good night's sleep. Getting shut-eye on the eve of battle was hard, but he knew something that might relax him. Ryan looked over at Krysty. She was laughing at something that was passing between Mildred and Doc. She almost instantly turned her head and favored him with a long slow smile across the mess hall. Krysty always knew when he was looking at her, and always seemed to know what was on his mind when he was. Ryan turned without a word and headed toward their stateroom.

He reminded himself to make sure both canteens of water were full.

Chapter Fifteen

Ryan stood on the bridge and watched the lake bottleneck down into the last stretch of river that would take them to the locks. The dawn was overcast. The top of the St. Mary's River formed a question mark girded by islands. They were about to hit the apex of that question mark. There was no question in Ryan's mind as the *Queen* approached the narrows. This was the gauntlet, and there was a solid wall dripping with pirates waiting at the end of it. Ryan looked at McKenzie. The captain nodded and began bellowing through his brass speaking trumpet. "All hands! Battle stations!" Boatswain's whistles shrieked on both decks. The *Queen of the Lakes* reverberated with the pounding of feet as her passengers and crew made ready for war. Every inch of rail had been sandbagged and began dripping with men and blasters.

"Loadmaster!" the captain called. "Raise nets!"

Capstans clanked as crewmen pushed against the spars on all four cranes. Heavy fishing nets brought from Manitoulin crawled up the sides of the *Queen* port and starboard to impede boarders. Both Ryan and the captain looked at the roof above them as a tremor and groan creaked through the ancient ferry as the weight of the heavy sodden strands rose. The *Queen* was a very shallow draft vessel to begin with. Raising the LAV to front promenade and putting both catapults and their loads of missiles on the back had raised the *Queen*'s center of gravity several perilous degrees. The men crowding every inch of rail space and now the netting was only exacerbating things. Captain McKenzie and his Load-master had rearranged the vehicles and cargo on the bottom deck to try to compensate but only so much could be done.

The *Queen of the Lakes* was dangerously out of trim.

Outfitted as she was for war, the *Queen* could probably fight off hordes of war canoes until the next nukestorm came, but when and if the locks came down and heavy wreckage filled the river, or the if the enemy had anything heavier than a war canoe or an oar-driven whaleboat, Ryan and the captain both knew it would take just one heavy blow or ramming attack to tip the *Queen* and sink her, and then they would all be swimming with the lampreys.

They still had a few advantages.

Again, Ryan was averse to becoming dependent on bat-tery-operated devices, but they had them at the moment and in abundance. Yoann had been hording much of the Diefen-bunker equipment and tech the convoy had taken; but this would be the battle that decided the convoy's quest. With Six's help Ryan had convinced Cyrielle to spread out the tactical radios. Ryan tapped the one attached to his jacket. "Captain, you want to run a last check?"

McKenzie grimaced at unfamiliar tactical. "Show me again?"

"The radio in J.B.'s LAV is the central synchronization system. We're all on the same channel. All you do is press the button." Ryan clicked. "J.B.?"

"Forward promenade, ready," J.B. replied.

"Doc?"

"The stern fighting deck is fighting fit! Sand is hot! Pitch is ready!"

Ryan raised an eyebrow. Doc was sounding awfully salty. "Rear loading ramp!" Ryan called. "Sound off!"

Six immediately came back. "The LAV is trimmed for

sail. All equipment and crew assembled, except you and Mr. Smythe."

"Right! Hunk?"

"Whaleboat and men of Manitoulin ready!"

"Loud Elk?"

Jon Hard-knife's contribution to the festivities came back. "First Nations whaleboat ready."

Mr. Smythe trotted in. "All machine blasters manned. All nonessential crew manning the rails. Pikes issued on the cargo deck. Miss Mildred, Saw-Doc and Miss Krysty are ready at the aid station."

"Very good, Mr. Smythe." McKenzie took a long, deep breath. The die was cast. There would be very little for him to do now other than to steer his ship. "Well, Ryan. My navigator tells me that assuming we don't meet too much resistance on the way we should round on the Soo Locks in ninety minutes. You're welcome to stay on the bridge or wait for deployment down in the hold with your assault crew."

"Think I'll stay topside, mebbe go down on the forward promenade with J.B. Mebbe check on Doc."

"As you wish." McKenzie's concentration was already laser focused on the approaching river. Ryan took the bridge stairs down to the passenger deck and stepped out onto the promenade. J.B. stood in the LAV turret scanning the water ahead with a pair of Diefenbunker binos. Ryan rapped his knuckles on the iron wag's armor. "J.B."

The Armorer kept his gaze on the gauntlet of the river channel ahead. "Yeah, Ryan?"

"I need you to conserve ammo."

"Know that."

"I mean, we may need every last round of 25 mm to punch through the locks."

"Know that, too."

"Just saying, let Doc, the machine blasters, and the sec men and sailors take out the canoes."

"And give thunder only as needed."

"You knew that."

J.B. shrugged. "Doesn't hurt to hear it."

"Good luck."

J.B. turned his head. He was grinning. "Dark night, Ryan. This is going to be something. You put that LAV in the water—" J.B. leaned over and slapped the fluted barrel of his 25 mm "—I got your back."

Ryan nodded. "I'm depending on it."

The *Queen* chugged into the final, curving stretch of the St. Marys River. The hull throbbed as her boilers pushed her against the current. What once been Canada and the United States girded the border river north and south. The fallen, overgrown shells of ancient and abandoned towns peaked out of the trees on the northern side. The southern bank was windswept rock. The symbolism wasn't lost on Ryan.

McKenzie's voiced boomed over the passenger decks. "Watch for snipers!"

Ryan unlimbered his rifle. It would come soon.

J.B. spoke up right on cue across the tactical. "Smoke."

Ryan didn't need an optic to see it. Around the bend in the river a plume of smoke rose up from behind the landform. It was quickly joined by a second and a third. "Smoke, Captain."

"I see it, rad-blast it!" McKenzie blustered back.

Jak, Six and Tamara appeared at Ryan's elbow. Six gave his big-thunder rifle its trademark spin. "We figured we would lend a hand until it was time to go."

"If you get chilled," Ryan cautioned, "I don't have time to press new volunteers."

"And you get yourself chilled, *mon ami?* That makes me

war chief upon the water." Six raised one brutal eyebrow. "Should I go back down?"

Ryan found himself liking the man more and more despite the animosity between them. "Welcome to the forward fighting deck, Mr. Six."

Tamara strode to the forward rail, clambered up on the sandbags and shoved her rifle skyward in challenge. "Gimme something to shoot at, you pirate sons of gaudy sluts! I'll jolly your every last roger right now!"

Crew and convoy whooped at the sharpshooter's bravado. Doc was right. The *Queen of the Lakes* was salty and ready for the fight. McKenzie's voice reverberated across the decks like an angry god, except for the fact he didn't sound entirely displeased. "All hands! Shooting stations! That means you Tamara, you blaster whore!"

Tamara flopped across some sandbags and took a bead on the river ahead. She purred back at Ryan without taking her eye off her optic. "Got a sandbag that could use a man's hand next to me, Ryan." He wound his arm through his shooting sling and dropped to a knee beside Tamara.

The man in the crow's nest called the warning. "Fire ship!"

It was a wooden ship, the size of small fishing boat, running about fifty feet and well ablaze from stem to stern. The pirates release had been nearly perfect. The arc of the river and the current took the fire ship slowly but unerringly into the *Queen*'s path. The *Queen of the Lakes* was a ship of steel and configured as she was, there was little about her to set ablaze. Then again she was dangerously out of trim, and a collision could well prove fatal. She had never been agile, and now with her offset loads Ryan knew McKenzie was probably as equally afraid of hard maneuvering as he was of the fire ship. "Pikes to port!" the Captain called. "Pole off!"

Two dozen, twelve-foot boarding pikes slid through the cargo netting on the port vehicle deck. Their iron, leaf-shaped blades were painted red against rust. The fire ship came in with the current, billowing black smoke in her flaming death throes, seemingly intent on taking the *Queen* with her. Ryan winced at the heat washing off the burning vessel as the captain bawled out orders. "Reverse port engine! Prepare to fend off!"

Men on the upper decks hunched behind their fortifications as heat and smoke poured across the *Queen*. The pikemen below snarled and swore as they took the brunt of the ovenlike heat. The vessel slowly turned around the incoming fire ship in a slow dance. The pikes thunked into the burning hulk's side and prevented contact.

"Both engines forward!" The *Queen* left her burning partner behind her as the second fiery suitor joined the dance. "Rad-blast it! Pikes starboard! Reverse starboard engine!" Pikes thudded into burning hull and the *Queen* danced another slow S-curve with disaster.

Ryan squinted against the heat. "McKenzie's good."

Tamara glowed with the heat and exultant pride. "This ship is the *Queen* of the Lakes, Ryan, and Captain Robert Douglas McKenzie is the king."

The current and the curve of the river brought the third fire ship toward them straight-on. Gray smoke roiled from her deck in ugly waves. McKenzie hesitated as he tried to choose the best path to avoid playing chicken with a death ship. "Back engines! Do it slow! All pikes forward!" Men cursed and wood clattered as the pikemen manhandled their unwieldy weapons across the cluttered cargo deck. "Advance pikes on either side of the ramp! I want to have—"

"Hell burner!" Doc roared. The old man spent a lot of time mumbling, but with proper motivation he had an opera-quality voice that had probably reached the men in the boiler room. "Hell burner!"

Ryan clicked his com. "Doc! What are you talking about?"

The one-eyed man shook his head as Doc came charging down the port rail with his frock coat flapping like a cape and waving his arms like a maniac. "Hell burner! Hell burner!"

The captain roared through his speaking trumpet. "Dr. Tanner! Get back to the catapults!"

Doc skidded onto the forward fighting deck. "Hell burner!"

"Rad-blast you, Tanner!" McKenzie thundered. "Get back to your post!"

Ryan leaped up with a snarl. "Fireblast, Doc! Get on station!"

"She's not a fire ship!" Doc waved his arms frantically and pointed at the fire ship. "She's a hell burner!"

"Doc, you had better—"

"The Dutch!" Doc gasped. "They used them against the Spanish in the siege of Antwerp! They—"

Ryan suddenly had a real bad feeling. He grabbed Doc by the shoulders and shook him. "Doc! Talk sense!"

"Look at the smoke! It's gray! Not black! The ship isn't burning! There is simply a fire set on top of it! It is a ruse!"

"What kind of ruse!"

"They saw us pole off the fire ships rather than sink them!" Doc cried. "They want this one to get that close once more! It's a bomb! Probably full of black powder, incendiary material and shrapnel! We must—"

Ryan dropped Doc and hurled his voice to the sky. "Everybody down! Down! Down! J.B.! AP incendiary! Now! Now! Now—"

The LAV's autocannon slammed off three rounds in quick succession. The predark, armor-piercing incendiary ammunition had been designed to punch through the rolled steel skins of armored wags back in the day. The wooden side of the fire-hulk proved no obstacle at all.

The hell burner went sky-high.

Half of the explosion shot into the sky in a geyser of black powder smoke and fire, and the other half shot straight at the *Queen* in shaped, malicious intent. Ryan's eyebrows singed as the heat wash hit him like a tidal roller and slapped him off his feet. Men howled and fell twisting as they were raked by the rocks and iron shards the pirates had laden in the hell burner's belly to act as shrapnel. Pikemen on either side of the raised forward loading ramp screamed as they were burned alive by the dragon's tongue of superheated gas and fire. The blast effect pushed the *Queen* violently off course, and she dipped to starboard sickeningly as her top weight tried to tip her. "Back engines! Back engines!" McKenzie bawled. The *Queen*'s boilers howled, screamed and chugged as McKenzie's engineers desperately tried to compensate with full reverse power to both screws.

Ryan looked at Doc, who sat on the deck yawning and blinking. The Deathlands warrior could barely hear his own voice as he shouted past ringing ears. "You all right?"

"Hell burners..." Doc mumbled, "from the Dutch *hellebranders*. *Brander* is Dutch for 'fire ship,' you know. They used them at the Siege of Antwerp to break the—"

"Nice work, Doc." Ryan hauled the old man to his feet.

"Oh, well, thank you very much indeed. You could tell by the smoke that the ship was not truly on fire, it was really—"

Ryan took Doc firmly by the shoulder and pointed out onto the waters. An armada of war canoes was furiously paddling their way. "Doc, I need you back on the catapults."

"Oh, yes, indeed. I admit I do go on sometimes. But I now feel that it is—"

"Now, Doc," Ryan urged.

"Right! Indeed! Yes!" Doc raced back to his siege engines.

The war canoes came through the smoke. Each had a man in the prow firing his blaster as they came into range. Ryan counted nearly two dozen. McKenzie was in a fine fury. His voice boomed down from the bridge. "Mr. Dix! Would now be appropriate?"

J.B. slid down into the turret and into the gunner's chair. He flipped the dual feed switch on the 25 mm to feed HE rather than AP incendiary. He silently yearned to unleash his own little 25 mm nukecaust on the approaching pirates, but he remembered Ryan's words. Cannon shells were at a premium, and this was only the opening round in the hostilities. J.B. flipped off the safety on the coaxial machine gun. He leaned forward to look through the optical sight. One hand slid around the firing grip and the other on the turret traverse. The turret whined and the 25 mm gun and the coax lowered in tandem. "Ready."

J.B. laid the coax optical sight-aiming gradients on the closest canoe. The men aboard paddled furiously to close the gap and take the battle hand to hand. The pirates favored shaved heads with scalp locks and drooping mustaches. Most were bare-chested and they were covered in blue tattooing. J.B. squeezed his trigger and walked a burst right up the line of rowers. Paddles fell from dead and wounded hands, and pirates flopped forward or back as the bullets struck them. J.B. goosed the traverse and laid another line of fire up another canoe. Men shattered under the onslaught. The pirates were in open canoes and in open water. There was no cover and nowhere to run. No one jumped overboard and tried to swim for it in the confusion, and J.B. had a pretty good idea why. The only recourse was to keep paddling forward and close.

Right down the muzzle of J.B.'s smoking autoblaster.

The Armorer's machine gun was a merciless scythe, and he reaped pirate lives like wheat. Half a dozen canoes floated adrift in the current as the coaxial blaster racked open on empty. J.B. reached into the rack beside him for another hundred-round belt of ammo and clicked his com. "Forward fighting deck. Chill them all."

McKenzie relayed the order through his trumpet. "Forward deck! Commence to blasting! Fire at will!"

"About time!" Tamara whooped. Ryan was already shooting. The Scout bucked against his shoulder, and the pirate firing from the prow of the new lead canoe buckled and fell into the water. His body wriggled twice oddly and suddenly jerked beneath the water and disappeared. Ryan filed that away as he worked his bolt. He killed the first paddler, the second and the third, and went right down the line. He didn't stop until nothing moved in the canoe. Ryan reached for another mag. Blasterfire crackled and popped along the arc of the promenade. The hell burner had failed, and pirates in the follow-on assault wave were sitting ducks.

Tamara whooped with each shot she fired. "Yeah! Oh yeah! Eat this!" With every shot a pirate slumped dead from his paddling bench. Tamara popped her spent mag howling like a banshee. "You want the *Queen,* you rad-blasted sons of gaudy sluts?" She slammed in a fresh mag and her blaster "clatched" as she hit the bolt release and chambered a fresh round. "Bring it!"

Ryan was glad Tamara was on his side. All along the promenade men aimed and fired in the shooting-gallery slaughter.

J.B. was suddenly standing in the turret once more. "Fighting deck! Cease blasting!"

A few overexcited souls popped off another round or two but the shooting ceased. Ryan gazed through the fog of war. Clouds of smoke hazed the already overcast day. War canoes slowly drifted toward the *Queen.* The dead and dying didn't paddle. The canoes just drifted with the current, riding lower and ever more sluggishly as the bullet-riddled hulls of hide

took on water. "Pikemen!" the captain ordered. "Prepare to
fend off! Look sharp! Some might be playing possum!"

Ryan craned over his sandbag revetment with his longblaster ready, but there was little to see. Red-painted pikes
stretched out from the sides to keep the canoes off the *Queen*.
Dying men moaned for water, their mothers or mercy. They
screamed as men of the *Queen* speared them and sped them
on their way to hell. A few blasters fired sporadically from
the top decks giving equally harsh mercy to any living pirates out of reach of the pikes.

"Mr. Smythe! Damage report!" McKenzie shouted. "Miss
Mildred! Casualties!"

Mildred's voice spoke across the link with cold precision.
"I've got ten dead. Four more with third-degree burns that
are going to be dead within the hour. Seventeen noneffec-
tives. Thirty walking wounded."

"Quartermaster!" McKenzie called. "Rations! Pemmican
and a pint of spruce beer to all hands! Navigator says we got
thirty minutes to the locks! Wet your tongue and fill your
belly! Look sharp!"

Ryan slid down the sandbags and took a moment to rest.
Shooting was thirsty work. The First Nations and Manitoulin marines had nothing to do until they hit the log chains
and they ran rations to the shooters on the promenade. Hunk
Poncet rushed to be the man to shove a stoop of spruce beer
and a pemmican cake into Ryan's hand. Loud Elk literally
vaulted up the prow of the LAV to give J.B. his due. Ryan bit
into his elk meat, bison fat and hawberry ration. Right now
it was neck and neck with Diefenbunker pizza for one of the
best things Ryan had ever eaten. He washed it down with
several long, cool swallows of spruce beer.

Tamara watched Ryan rip into his ration. "Yo, lover, you
gonna—"

Ryan nearly sprayed beer out his nose.

Tamara cocked her head. "What?"

"Call me that at your risk."

"Right, your flame-head girlfriend."

"Right," Ryan agreed.

Tamara frowned. "You don't think I can take her?"

Ryan smiled as he ate and drank. "Give her a full mag, at a hundred yards, and then run like hell."

"Oh?" Tamara challenged.

"Yeah." Ryan sighed as he thought about Krysty. "Because then she's gonna be mad."

"Well, you want to go downstairs to the med station and claim blue-balls fatigue for twenty minutes, I won't tell." Tamara gave Ryan another appraising look. "You want me to take care of it for you right here, I won't tell neither."

"You want to watch over me while I shut my eye for twenty minutes? You can have my pemmican and beer."

"Done!"

Ryan leaned back into the sandbags and closed his eye. He power napped and waited for the worst that was yet to come.

Chapter Sixteen

Ryan awoke to a scream on the deck and the report of the blaster in the distance.

"Sniper!" someone called.

Tamara pushed the safety off her blaster. "Rise and shine, Ryan!" A crewman lay dead on the deck with his head blown off. The one-eyed man rolled up but stayed low behind cover. He beheld the Soo Locks. They looked a lot more like the ancient 1798 version than what had once been twentieth-century marvels of engineering for the Great Lakes freighters to pass through. It was no longer a true lock at all but a barrier, a place to demand a toll. A long double-timber palisade fortified the canal stretching from shore to shore with two built-up island towers in the middle and forts on either side. Catwalks and rope bridges stretched across the sections of palisade and they were dripping with pirates. Before they could reach the gates, the log chains stretched from one end of the canal to the other, barring their way.

Bullets began striking the *Queen* on three sides.

"Mr. Dix!" the captain called. "At your pleasure!"

J.B. slid into the gunner's chair and put on his headset. He flipped the arming switch on the LAV's quadruple smoke dischargers on both sides of the turret and pushed the red button. "Countermeasures away!" The quad dischargers popped and arced M-90 smoke grens in a random pattern port and starboard. J.B. shouted to the third mate. "Mr. Niall! Irritant!"

J.B. heard Niall's boots on the hull and the click-clack of

the rounds locking into the clusters of stubby mortar barrels. He watched his first salvo through his optical sight. Each gren deployed three individual bomblets with a separation puff of smoke. The grens hit the shore and red phosphorus and butyl rubber began burning together to form clouds of screening smoke on both banks.

Niall shouted down the hatch. "Reloaded, Mr. Dix!" He jumped down on and slapped the side of the hull. "Clear!"

J.B. pumped the red firing button a second time. The smoke dischargers popped and clouds of military-strength tear gas joined the mix of choking, obscuring fun on the banks of the canal. The smoke and gas only helped illuminate the flash of blasterfire and the crew and passengers of the *Queen* started homing in with deadly precision. Blasterfire from the shores immediately began tapering off. A sweet thrill ran up J.B.'s arm as he flipped the switch to arm the 25 mm blaster. He had loaded her up with M-792 High Explosive Incendiary Tracer with Self Destruct. J.B. had read the LAV's manual of munitions. It said the HEI-T-SD round was ideal for "destroying unarmored vehicles and helicopters and suppressing antitank missile positions and enemy squads out to 3,000 meters."

Seemed like a good round to clear the top of a wooden palisade.

J.B. put his sighting gradient just below the western end of the lock. He flipped his selector to Low Rate Fully Automatic to give himself one hundred rounds per minute and slid his finger around the trigger. "Firing on the lock!"

J.B. squeezed his trigger and began traversing. The 25 mm automatic cannon began slamming off rounds almost in time with J.B.'s heartbeat, which, given the size of the hardware the Armorer had his hands around, was beating somewhat faster than normal. The tracers drew smoking lines through the air that impacted into the top of the palisade. It was almost like the palisade was a giant string of firecrackers. Each impact sent smoking wedges of wood and bloody pieces of pirate flying. J.B maintained his slow traverse and walked his fire across the canal from shore to shore. He traversed back, firing bursts from the coax at anything stupid enough to be returning fire from the shattered wall top. Smoke oozed from shore to shore. It looked bad but it was far from enough. The lock was double thick, and J.B. couldn't blast it down. All he had done was give it a haircut. It was time to go tactical.

J.B. spoke into his radio. "Lower the stern ramp. Send out the LAV. Send out the chain-breakers."

"Go!" RYAN HOLLERED. The capstan men sagged against their spars as the rear ramp hit water. Hunk and his crew ran out the whaleboat and leaped onto their rowing benches, and their three giant dogs went with them. Ryan glanced up at Six where he stood behind the engineering LAV's single machine blaster. Six nodded. The LAV was prepped. "We are in amphibious trim, Ryan!"

That was an ambitious statement. LAV's were not particularly good swimmers. The crane and dozer blade made this version even worse. It had a max water speed of about six miles per hour. Ryan clambered up the side of the hull and slid down the driver's hatch. He slipped on his headset and the diesel spit blue smoke into the cargo hold as Ryan stepped on the gas. His hatch came down with a clang. "Button up!" Six dropped down from the gunner's position and closed his hatch. Ryan checked his driver's periscopes and the wake of the *Queen* lay ahead of him like white water. Ryan eased the LAV down the ramp. Water splashed off the bow as the LAV met river. "Here we go!"

The LAV lurched grotesquely as it suddenly went buoyant in the churning water like a 25,000-pound steel cork. Actually it was more accurate to say the LAV wallowed like a 25,000-pound hog. Ryan punched the button on the selective water drive and hit his throttle. The twin propellers in back hummed through the hull and the LAV took on purpose as Ryan flipped the toggle on his four rudders and turned the LAV out of the *Queen*'s wake. Ryan spoke into his radio. "LAV away."

McKenzie's voice came back. "We see you!"

Ryan shoved his throttles forward and took the LAV toward the southern shore. Bullets began rattling off the armored hull but not in any concentration that Ryan had expected. Between the smoke, the gas, the blastermen lining the *Queen*'s rails and, most importantly, J.B. in the turret of a LAV III, the *Queen* was giving a lot better than what she was getting. Ryan's own LAV crept through the water like a sloth going for a swim. He checked his starboard periscope. By comparison Hunk and his men were slicing across the water like an arrow. The whaleboat thumped against the first log chain, and Hunk and one of his men leaped out barefoot onto the massive timber. Double bitted axes began chopping in a ferocious one-two rhythm as they hacked at the arm-thick rope strands holding the log chain together.

In that, they'd caught some luck. The current coming down the canal was heavy going for the out-of-trim *Queen,* but by the same token they only needed to break one link in each log chain and the current would then sweep each chain open like a door. Ryan kept his prow aimed at the shore and his own task. Bullets began peppering the hull in earnest as the enemy became more and more aware of the behemoth crawling toward them.

Hunk shouted breathlessly over the link. "First chain open!"

A huge black hand slammed across Ryan's shoulder. "I'm going up!" Six said.

"Go!" Ryan kept his eye on the shore as he armed one of the quad smoke dischargers. "Popping smoke!"

The commander's hatch flung open as the grenade dispensers popped. The smoke grens soared to the shore and bloomed. In the renewed smoke screen the enemy fire turned into bright orange and yellow flashes. Six began rattling off short bursts. The LAV lurched as one of its road wheels hit something solid. Six shouted down the hatch. "Shallow water, Ryan!"

Hunk called across the link. "Second chain open!"

The LAV had full-time four-wheel drive to the four rear wheels. Ryan shoved a lever in his gearbox and engaged the optional eight-wheel drive. The LAV rocked on its chassis as its road wheels hit rock and mud. He shoved the 6V53T Detroit diesel engine into low gear and the aggressive cross-country tread of the giant wheels bit into the riverbed. They weren't sailing anymore. The LAV was driving. The vehicle hauled itself ashore like some primordial river beast that had decided to look for prey on land. Its prey was the southern tower fort of the lock. The lock fort had other ideas.

The LAV began attracting bullets like a magnet.

The fort was more a fortified operating tower for opening and closing the lock than a genuine fortress, but its rammed-earth walls were supported by heavy timber. It looked to be three stories tall. The top floor had firing slits cut into its face, and the embrasures were sheathed in stone. It would be impossible to burn down, and it would take a howitzer to pound it into rubble. They would have to take it by storm. Ryan hit his second smoke discharger. The radio crackled. "Third chain open!"

The LAV lumbered toward the squat tower. The pirates had dug ditches and put up heavy stakes to impede any enemy advance. They hadn't planned on armor. Stakes snapped and the LAV bounced violently over the ditches. It was heavy going. Six shouted from up top. "Look out!" The big man dropped down and slammed his hatch. A hailstorm of hits walked up, down and across the hull. The enemy had machine blasters, and more than one.

"J.B.! I'm taking heavy fire! Machine blasters!"

"Engaging!" J.B. reported. "Dark...night!"

At this range Ryan's periscopes gave him no view of the top floor. It sounded as though a horde of hornets was trying to smash its way into the roof of the LAV. Her armor was rated against .30-caliber blasterfire, but the armor on top was the thinnest. Ryan's eye slit in anger. J.B.'s cannon shots burst and sent stone chips and shards of wood flying, but he wasn't knocking anything out. Six shouted what Ryan was thinking from the commander's chair. "The autocannon is ineffective! The stone and earth are too thick!"

J.B.'s voice rose with urgency. "Ryan! I can't cut through the embrasures, and I can only engage one at a time! It's like smashing gophers!"

Ryan could tell. Enemy fire wasn't being suppressed. He flinched as green paint spalled from the hull over his head and stung his cheek. "J.B.!" Ryan roared. "I need something and I need it now!"

The sad fact was that there was no better bullet stop than three feet of dirt, and the enemy wasn't just sand-bagged in. They had three feet of dirt between heavy timbers and dressed stone. J.B. could empty an entire belt of 25 mm rounds trying to break through, and the enemy could simply move to the next firing position within.

"Doc! Give me something!"

Hunk shouted breathlessly across the line. "Fourth chain open!"

The tactical clicked and popped while Doc fumbled with his radio. "Ryan! I see your dilemma and believe I have the remedy!"

Ryan grimaced as he watched the roof of the LAV's cabin began to dimple with the unceasing hail of .30-caliber impacts. In seconds the hull would start spalling lethal steel fragments from within. After that it would tear, and all bets would be off. "Remedy it now or not at all, Doc!"

Doc's voice soared over the radio as he called out orders. "Loadmaster! Ten more degrees to port! Load carcass! Captain! Speed!"

"Half a knot!" McKenzie bawled back.

"Duly noted!" Doc announced. "Wait for it, Ryan!"

"Fuck waiting, Doc!"

Doc was in his own little world of relative speed and arc of trajectory.

"Wait…"

A fragment of roof ripped across Ryan's forearm in a bloody line. "We're about to get chilled, Doc!"

"Wait… Three, two, one…" Doc paused another heartbeat. "Loose!"

Ryan looked back through his rear periscope at the *Queen* and saw what looked like an airborne, beige tombstone come revolving into his view. It was a bison skin, stuffed like a large sofa cushion, and it was smoldering. It was Doc's burning sand. The missile hit a firing embrasure dead-on and burst apart in an explosion of sand. The forward momentum of the flight and the shape of the embrasure funneled most of the sand straight within. Anyone who had ever been to a beach knew that sand got inside everything, your clothes, your eyes, your mouth and any other available crevice. The sand mass hit and dispersed inside with the force of a catapult throw. Doc had heated his sand in red-hot iron cooking caldrons on the rear promenade.

Iron glowed red-hot at 900° F.

Ryan thought he could hear the screams of the burning damned within. The machine blasters instantly ceased. The tower had no visible gate, which meant it was on the other side. The LAV bucked and rocked as Ryan guided it around the tower.

McKenzie called across the link. "Ryan! We've lost sight of you!"

"Fifth chain down!" Hunk was getting excited.

Ryan pulled around the tower and sighted the gate. More pirates than he could count on the other side of the lock sighted him. "Six!" The bigger man slammed open his hatch and got to blasting. Ryan frowned through his periscope. The door to the tower was an iron grill too narrow for the LAV to ram and they couldn't afford to waste a demo charge on it. "Team! Get ready to deploy! Mr. Timms! Six! Winch!" Ryan pulled right up to the iron gate. Bullets began smacking the roof again.

"Goose! Tamara! Alain! Covering fire!" The hull rang as someone up top dropped something very large on top of the LAV. Ryan hit the button and the rear ramp of the vehicle lowered and his team spilled out, keeping the hull between themselves and the slew of pirates on the lock. Édouard replaced Six on the machine blaster, sending several bursts through the tower gate. Timms snaked winch cable and hooked the iron bars while Six worked the motor. Mr. Smythe, Tamara, Alain and Goose drilled covering fire toward the top of the tower. Jak and Blacktree stayed in the LAV with the demo charges. Ryan watched as Timms circled his hand and Six engaged the winch. The LAV leaned slightly with the traction but held firm. The winch was made to pull another LAV that was damaged, rolled or bogged down and was rated for 30,000 pounds dynamic.

Iron screamed and sparked as the lock tower gate ripped off its hinges. Six shouted across the link. "Ryan! *Allez!*"

Ryan slid out of the driver's seat and grabbed his long-blaster.

"Look out!"

Édouard flailed and screamed as he was engulfed in a boiling gray froth that cascaded through the commander's hatch into the turret of the LAV. Ryan flinched backward as the hissing, scalding soap and steam splattered his clothes and slopped around the crew cabin. Édouard flopped down the hatch, twisting and clawing at his face. The boiling soap clung and continued to sear. Blacktree grabbed the man by his boots and dragged him out of the bubbling puddle. Ryan grabbed a cargo cleat and swung himself over the mess and dropped to a knee beside Édouard. The smell of boiling soap and parboiled flesh was sickening. Blacktree was holding Édouard down. The man's eyes were scalded out of his head. He had to have looked up when Tamara screamed. Foam and blood oozed past his parboiled lips out of his boiled throat.

Blacktree looked at Ryan, who nodded. He drew his single-shot blaster, pressed it between Édouard's heat-erased eyebrows and sent him on his way. Then he snapped open his blaster and slid in a fresh round from his belt.

Ryan grabbed a demolition charge and slung it. "You ready?"

Blacktree filled his hands with four more. "Yup."

The radio crackled with Hunk's voice. "Sixth chain down!"

Jak had a charge over his shoulder and was already waiting on the ramp, Colt Python drawn. Everyone else was outside shooting.

Ryan shouted to Alain. "Stay with the LAV! Try to get that machine blaster going! Draw some diesel to cut the soap!"

"Oui, Ryan!" Alain ducked into the LAV and instantly started cursing in French.

Ryan shot a glance at the other side of the lock. A rat warren of low blockhouses and cabins formed a small ville on both banks. The one on this side was about three hundred yards away, and they were taking fire from it. There were still pirates behind them in the no-man's land along the bank. It was only a matter of time before a pack of pirates tried to rush them. "Mr. Smythe! Stay here with Six! Fight the LAV! Call in Loud Elk and his men and tell them to bring a couple of machine blasters from the *Queen* with them! We don't lose this wag, and no pirate gets up in this tower behind me and my team!"

Smythe slapped a fresh mag into his blaster. "At once!"

"If Loud Elk doesn't get here in time, pull out. Load the LAV, button up, run over anyone who gets in your way and swim for the *Queen*."

"You just drop that big fence of theirs, Ryan," Smythe said. "We'll be here."

Ryan slung his Scout and gripped two handblasters. "Let's go!"

He went through the door. The bottom floor was a windowless murk barely illuminated by the light of fish-oil lamps. It was mostly storage filled with barrels, coils of rope and other oddments. Ryan glanced up at a heavy wooden trapdoor in the ceiling and the scratches on the floor where the ladder had been. He looked at the heavy iron handles of the hatch ten feet above. "Timms! Winch!" Ryan nodded at his team. "Blacktree, Jak."

Blacktree stepped beneath the hatch and the albino teen scrambled up onto the big man's shoulders. Timms charged in and handed up the hook. Jak looped it through the two handles and locked it. He hopped off Blacktree and both men stood back. "Winch away!"

Six hit the lever and the cable went taut. Everyone stood back as the wood of the hatch flexed and creaked. One handle popped its nails and came off like a gunshot. The second creaked and held. The hatch suddenly broke in two.

Blasterfire streamed down from the hatch. Ryan reached

into his coat and pulled out a gren, a 76 mm from the LAV's quad dischargers. They were mostly used for sending out obscuring smoke and tear gas. The planners at the Diefenbunkers had obviously worried about hordes of hungry citizens and also added loads of M-99 Blunt Trauma rounds. At 66 mm in size and over one-and-one-half pounds, the gren was too heavy and awkward to throw any safe distance, and nothing was designed to shoot it but the quad launchers of an armored vehicle. That hadn't stopped J.B. from removing its propulsion charge and reducing its pyrotechnic fuse from 4.5 seconds to two; and it wasn't too heavy and awkward for Ryan to lob up into someone's attic. "Step back!"

The one-eyed man dropped to a knee and slammed the base of the gren into the floor to arm it, feeling it hiss and vibrate in his hand with ignition. Ryan rolled the gren off his fingers in an underhand pitch right up through the hatch. They heard a shout of alarm upstairs. "Gren! Gren! Gre—"

The deadly orbs detonated.

The audio stimuli clapped with a thunderous 170-decibel bang and the visual stimuli was a several 1000-candle power flash of lightning. Within the blinding and deafening display 140 .32-caliber PVC balls expanded outward in a body hammering blunt-trauma cloud. "Timms! Blacktree!"

The loadmaster's mate took station beneath the hatch and even he grunted as Blacktree climbed him. Jak scrambled up the human ladder and Ryan followed with the rest of the team. Ten pirates lay stunned and blinded on the floor. Tamara and Goose finished them off with their knives while Ryan and Jak hauled Blacktree's huge frame up the hatch. "Pay out more cable!" Ryan called.

The ladder to the third story was still down, and Ryan was pretty sure he knew why. He clambered up and put his shoulder to the hatch. Grimacing, Ryan shut his eye as sand that was still steaming hot sifted down on him. He slammed the hatch back. A dozen men lay smoldering and steaming on the floor. A few were still twitching. The bare-chested, bald men looked like they had been rolled in sugar and then cooked alive. The three machine blasters that had hammered the LAV hung in their firing slits unattended. Ryan stared at the hatch to the roof. The ladder was still down. The men above had heard the screaming below and had wanted no part of it.

Hunk's voice soared with victory over the radio. "Seventh chain down! We're through!"

Ryan climbed the ladder and hooked the winch cable through the handles. He readied a second gren. It wouldn't be as effective this time. The open top of the tower would dissipate a great deal of the thunder, and daylight would have a similar effect on the flash. Ryan stepped away. "Winch!"

"Winch away!" Timms bellowed from the bottom of the tower.

The cable took up slack and tore the hatch right out of its frame. Everyone jumped back as a waterfall of boiling soap sheeted down into the second story.

"Sons of bitches!" Tamara cursed.

"Yup," Boo agreed.

Ryan slammed the gren on the floor and tossed it up the dripping hatch. He clicked his tactical communicator. "Hold fire on tower top! We're hitting it!"

"Holding fire!" McKenzie called. "Loud Elk is on the shore!"

The M-99 detonated and men above screamed as the .32-caliber rubber balls beat them. Ryan surged up the ladder, but his free hand and his boots slipped and skidded on the soap-scalded rungs. "Fireblast!"

A huge hand slammed into the seat of Ryan's pants, and with a bellow of effort Boo Blacktree just about shot-putted the one-eyed man up through the hatch. A bullet whined and cracked an inch from Ryan's head. He returned the favor and put three rounds in the offending pirate's chest. The range up on the tower top was spitting distance. The blunt trauma round had taken the pirates down, but they were not out. Most of the pirates were armed with muzzle-loaders or single-shot blasters. Scalping knives, war clubs and tomahawks slid free. Jak popped up through the hatch borne on Boo Blacktree's brute force. He shot a pirate in the face with his Colt Python and gave another a sliver of steel with a left-handed throw. The beating, sound and light made the pirates a step too slow, and even at short range clumsy and inaccurate.

Ryan emptied his SIG into three pirates who were crowding into one another and pistol-whipped a fourth screaming over the edge of the tower. Donnie Goosekiller showed he knew something about slaughtering men as well as waterfowl as he hamstrung one pirate and slit the throat of another. Tamara's ancient C-7 rifle had an equally ancient bayonet, and somewhere along the line she had learned to hang it on the end of her blaster and use it. A pirate screamed as she buried the bayonet in his bladder. The man behind him lived just long enough to gasp as Ryan's panga slid up beneath his sternum to chill his heart.

The tower top was taken by the time Blacktree carefully and laboriously got his bulk up the soapy ladder. Tamara's left arm was swelling like a balloon from a glancing club blow. Goosekiller had two black eyes but insisted he could shoot. Ryan contacted the captain and reloaded. "We own the tower. Taking the lock. Give me covering fire."

"Right!" McKenzie kept insisting on shouting over the link. "Dr. Tanner! Covering fire!"

Large objects began tumbling in huge arcs from the stern of the *Queen*. Ryan crouched and checked his demo charge.

Now came the hard part.

Chapter Seventeen

Doc's stentorian voice challenged the heavens. "Starboard catapult! Loose pitch!"

The loadmaster yanked the trigger rope and the arm of the mangonel slammed up against the padded stop. The entire catapult bucked like a mule and jumped its chalks with the expended energy. The crew pulled it back onto the smeared chalk lines. The stern promenade was a perilous clutter of red-hot caldrons, burning pitch, piles of huge stones and wooden engines that could crush bones and tear the limbs off the unwary. Doc stalked to the port rail and shaded his eyes as the cask of pitch sailed over the southernmost of the two midcanal, island lock towers.

"Hmm..." Doc thumbed his tactical radio. "Captain, would you be so kind as to turn the boat three degrees to port?"

McKenzie broke into a fit of profanity. The *Queen* was trying to hold position against the current and now Doc was telling him to the give the current more of the vessel to push against. Nonetheless he roared orders. The *Queen*'s boilers chugged, and the smokestack belched black ash as the firemen gave her more coal.

"Excellent." Doc looked at his watch. "Loadmaster! Port catapult! Load pitch!" Sailors groaned and heaved and cursed as the boiling hot keg seared through the rags wrapping their hands as they put the cask in place. "Light fuse!" Doc stalked to the rail and lifted a pair of Diefenbunker laser range-finding binoculars as the punk was applied. Doc pressed the button and the binoculars told him the range was 107 meters. "Oh, now that really shines!"

The loadmaster called with some urgency. "Fuse lit!"

"Port catapult!" Doc cut the air with his swordstick decisively. "Loose!"

The mangonel's arm thudded against the frame and J.B.'s witches brew of pitch, soap and diesel catapulted through space. Doc lowered his binoculars and leaned over the rail to watch its progress. A bullet whip-cracked past his head, but he was oblivious as he mentally compared his math to the actual arc of flight. His mind was utterly absorbed by the geometry of siege craft. The canal had two islands. The southern island formed one-half of the big gate. The keg of pitch hit the southern tower top and sluiced across it in a puddle of fire.

"A hit!" Doc crowed. "A most palpable hit!"

The catapult crews cheered.

Burning men hurled themselves from the tower top. Most hit the ground of the island and bounced like bundles of burning rags. A few hit the water and none of them resurfaced. Doc's cheek ticked as he became aware of what his calculations had wrought. "Oh dear."

McKenzie's voice boomed across the link. "Rad-fire, Doc! Good shooting!"

Doc gave the black smoke billowing up from the tower top a leery look. "Yes...well..."

The LAV on the forward promenade fired occasional bursts of cannon and coax fire at pockets of resistance or against the firing ports of the towers to keep them honest.

"The log-chains are down!" McKenzie was eager. "If I advance the *Queen,* can you still give fire?"

Doc shook his head as ugly shivers shook him. He clutched at his sanity. "No, Captain! The catapults will overshoot beyond this range with everything except the heaviest stones!

I recommend we hold position! The catapults will engage in suppressive bombardment of the northern island and the northern shore fort while J.B. and the ballistae give Ryan's team covering fire along the southern gate!"

"Very good! Maintaining position! Fire at will!"

"Oh, well, very kind of you, Captain…." Doc gazed between the two mangonels. They were his instruments of destruction. He gazed at the burning tower top and the burning men who had stopped moving atop it.

"Doc?" the loadmaster called.

Pangs of guilt and horror began nudging Doc's damaged psyche. His swordstick shook in his hand. He opened his mouth and closed it. He could feel "it" coming on.

"Doc?" The loadmaster gave him a desperate look, "Doc!"

The old man tamped down his guilt and fear.

His friends needed him.

Doc shouted with a certainty he didn't feel. "Starboard catapult! Turn sixty degrees! Burning sand! Port catapult! Pitch! Keep your eye on the southern canal tower! On my signal!" Doc raised his binoculars and checked the range again. Without a shadow of a doubt, Ryan Cawdor was a dear friend. It was his show now. The *Queen* would break the Soo Lock or be sunk by the success or failure of Ryan's efforts. Doc flung friendship, honor and duty into the face of madness.

He would give Ryan a fighting chance. "Loose!"

RYAN WATCHED THE SECOND CASK of burning pitch shatter and sluice across the south island tower. It would be worth any pirate's life to open the hatch and step out into the inferno. Doc called across the radio. "Now, Ryan! While the fire is still hot!"

Ryan unslung his Scout and leaped to the catwalk. It took dozens of oxen to open the gate but only the current to hold it shut against all comers. Beneath the tower squatted a blockhouse encasing a capstan the size of a windmill without any sails. Half of the curtain of palisade was fixed into the river bottom, and it was fixed on the island side. The swinging gate overlapped the fixed one with six cut-out sections like the teeth of an old-fashioned key. Ryan had to shatter the six overlaps and the current would do the rest. Doc had smeared the southern island tower top with fire, but the catwalks, rope bridges and island shacks behind the gates were still pirate infested.

Tamara's longblaster began cracking on rapid semiauto. "Go, Ryan!"

Ryan charged across the top of the lock catwalk that J.B. had busted and blackened with the LAV's autocannon. Blood, limbs and burned timber were everywhere. Jak and Blacktree were right on his heels. McKenzie's voice came across the link. "We see you, Ryan!"

A half dozen pirates burst out of the top of the tower ahead and braved the burning pitch to bring down Ryan and his team.

J.B.'s voice spoke wisdom across the link. "Down!"

Tamara joined the save-the-demo-men crusade. "Down!"

Blasterfire raked the top of the tower. The pirates never made it ten steps toward the catwalk. They fell wounded or dead into the puddles of fire.

Ryan's link echoed with J.B.'s urgency. "Go!"

Tamara's guardian angel voice rang from behind. "Run, Ryan! Run!"

Ryan ran for it. A pirate swung up from the rope bridge below, and the one-eyed man shoved out the Scout and fired it point-blank into the pirate's screaming face. Another pirate swung himself up into Ryan's path with club and blade in hand, screaming. Goosekiller's swarm of buckshot smeared away the pirate's head and sent him toppling into the canal below. Ryan slung his rifle. Jak uncoiled a knotted rope and made it fast to the top of the wall.

Tamara shouted over the sound of her own longblaster. "Make it fast, Ryan! You're attracting attention!"

Ryan pulled on elk-skin gloves, filled his mouth with nails and went down the rope. He stopped just as his boots hit water and put his boots on one of the knots. A bullet smote splinters a foot away from his arm. The one-eyed man ignored the bullets seeking his life and pulled a hammer from his belt. He leaned his weight against J.B.'s satchel charge and hammered the explosive pack into the wet wood of the gate. Ryan yanked the cord holding the satchel closed on top and reached in to arm the detonator pin. He looked down as something nudged his right foot.

A huge, goofy-looking, almost eellike fish was awkwardly nuzzling at his boot. Its blue eyes looked up soulfully at Ryan. It rolled over as it pushed up out of the water to try to reach Ryan's calf and revealed a round, jawless maw like a giant, inflamed, thorn-filled rectum.

Ryan snapped the toe of his boot into the lamprey's teeth and it fell back in the water. "Haul up!"

Blacktree hauled him up to the next gate overlap. "Charge!" Jak dropped down a charge and Ryan caught it. He hammered it into place and armed it. "Haul up!" Blacktree hauled him up another increment and Ryan pounded in another charge.

"Ryan!" Jak shouted.

Tamara shouted in warning. "Ryan! Get out of there!"

The one-eyed man looked to his left. The top of the tower still burned, but the men on the floors below were very much alive. They didn't have any firing slits facing the inside of the great gate, but someone had tattled on Ryan and what he was doing. Pirates flooded out of the bottom of the tower faster than Tamara and Goosekiller could knock them down. Ryan hung midgate like a very exposed spider—a spider several dozen pirates intended to squash once and for all.

Jak fired his Colt Python as fast as he could pull the trigger.

Blacktree hauled on the rope and waited for Ryan's order.

The one-eyed man hammered in the charge and shouted into his radio. "Six!"

Six's voice was a welcome boom across the link. "I see you! We have you!"

Ryan risked a glance to his right. The LAV splashed to the edge of the water right next to the great gate capstan. Mr. Smythe was perched behind the machine blaster, and it ripped into life. A dozen of Loud Elk's men clustered around it, firing their blasters into the pirates. A dozen more spilled onto the top of the southern gate tower and began firing with Tamara.

"Haul up!" Ryan called. "Charge!"

Jak dropped Ryan another charge and he nailed another satchel into the string of explosive. "Haul up!"

Ryan repeated the process twice more as an occasional bullet smacked wood nearby.

He hung six feet from the top over the last overlap with the last charge. "Get out of here!"

"Ryan!" Jak protested.

There was nothing left for Jak or Blacktree to do except to stand on the catwalk and get shot at. "Go and cover me!"

Jak and Blacktree ran for the cover of the shore tower. Ryan hammered in the last charge. He snarled and kicked away from the timbers as a hand reached out for his face from beneath the catwalk.

Ryan examined his opponent for the heartbeats he had while he swung out into space. It was fish-belly white like a stickie but more robustly built. It was also wearing a pirate vest and breechclout. Unlike a stickie it had hair that had been shaved into scalp braids. The sharklike black eyes, the needle teeth and the suckers on its outstretched fingers and palm bespoke some grotesque and undoubtedly nonconsensual crossbreeding. It clung to the bottom of the catwalk with one hand and its bare feet.

Ryan swung back in and gave the hybrid both boot heels in the teeth. The stickie flopped vertical, held to the bottom of the catwalk only by its suckered feet. Ryan cracked it between the eyes with his hammer and its feet released. The stickie fell to the dark water of the St. Marys River. Lampreys began churning around it.

About half a dozen of the hybrids were crawling along the bottom of the catwalk from both sides of the shore. Where they had been hiding was a moot point. Ryan had a problem. He hauled himself up the rope to the catwalk as the muties scrabble-sucked themselves toward him in their all-too-fast upside-down progress. Ryan pulled the detonator from his coat.

A hand wrapped around his ankle and yanked him flat.

The detonator clattered to the catwalk.

A voice cackled out of the smoke from the burning, mid-canal tower top. "You know who I am, boy?" Ryan slid as the suckered hand began dragging him back down. Ryan drew his SIG-Sauer and three hollowpoint rounds separated the sucking hand at the wrist. The voice bellowed. "I'm Thorpe! The pirate king! You come here to break my locks, boy?"

Ryan shoved his blaster toward the tower top, but Thorpe had ducked down behind the crenellations. A suckered hand shot out from beneath the catwalk and vised around the one-eyed man's forearm. The spatulate hand contracted like a noose and the blaster fell free. Ryan slipped his panga from its sheath and returned the favor across the veins and nerves of the mutie's inner wrist. Ryan ripped his hand free and drew his second SIG.

Thorpe shouted gleefully. "How you like my stickie men, boy?"

A stickie pirate rolled up onto the catwalk, and Ryan shot it three times in the face. The Deathlands warrior rolled over and shot the one behind him with a double-tap to the forehead. Four more rolled up on the catwalk in front and behind him. Covering fire tapered off as Ryan's friends were afraid to shoot into the melee. A dozen voices on the link and on the tower shouted out.

"Ryan!"

Ryan snapped off four rounds into the stickie man in front of him and fired a double tap into the one behind.

Thorpe cackled with glee. "Bred my stickie men special to climb up the side of a ship or over the walls of a ville! I tell you it's hard to get a stickie to do anything! Tie a woman down for them and half the time they don't know whether to kill her or poke her!"

A stickie man rolled up from under the catwalk right next to Ryan. He slapped it between the eyes with the slide of his SIG-Sauer and fired his blaster dry into the next one coming down the catwalk.

Thorpe roared with mirth from behind his cover. "But once I got my half-breeds, these boys are crackerjack creepers!"

Ryan dropped his spent blaster. There was no time to reload. There was no time to unlimber the Scout. He heard the slap of stickie feet behind him and saw three running toward him. Ryan scooped up his detonator, flipped off the plastic shield of the arming button, pushed it and flipped the switch. He took what might be his last second on Earth to cover his eyes with his palms, shove his thumbs into his ears and curl into a ball.

The gate braces blew in a string.

Ryan's world turned into orange light and thunder. The

stickie men behind him went up with it. The catwalk he lay
upon took most of the wooden shrapnel. The swinging section
of the great gate groaned as everything that braced it suddenly blew apart and it swung with the current. The section
of catwalk Ryan clung to sagged with damage and his boots
scrabbled over the edge. He heard the *Queen*'s steam whistles shrieking in victory and people on the far tower shouting his name desperately. Thorpe roared with rage from his
own tower top. "You're dead, boy! You're cut off! I'm gonna
throw you in the lamprey pit, and when I eat my pie tonight
I'm going to taste your blood! I'm gonna watch them suck
you dry, boy! I'm gonna—"

Ryan rose, shoved his slaughtering knife between his teeth
and dived for the *Queen*.

It was a long plunge, but the canal was deep and Ryan hit
the turbulent water like a knife. The cold hit him like a fist
to the heart, and Ryan instantly kicked upward. He breached
the surface and saw the *Queen* steaming toward him. The
LAV, convoy and crew spewed blaster flame in all directions
as the mighty ship headed for the gap. Ryan hurled his arms
ahead of him and his hands slashed like axes into the water
in an all-out sprint. He turned his head, sucked air with every
other stroke. As he turned his head, Ryan looked down and
saw the lampreys rising from the river bottom for him in a
swarm.

He knew he wasn't going to make it.

The first lamprey arrived, seven feet long and staring at
him dopily with its blank blue eyes. There was nothing dopey
about the rubbery, inverted cone mouth filled with teeth. It
wasn't the first time he had faced off against this type of
creature.

Ryan took his slaughtering knife from between his teeth
and stabbed it straight down the lamprey's throat. The creature spasmed into a paroxysm of wriggling and sank down-

ward. He stroked ahead, but faltered as he felt a cone of thorns close around his calf and a rasplike tongue begin boring into the hardened muscle. Ryan turned turtle in the water and pulled his knees into his chest. His blade sheered the offending lamprey's mouth off at the gill line. Ryan lurched as he felt the horrible, thorny kiss against his right buttock. He twisted and stabbed through a gill hole. A thorn-filled maw twisted against his knife arm, trying to find suction. Ryan stabbed the lamprey just beneath its head and ripped down its belly, opening it like a letter.

The battle had taken him six feet below the surface and his lungs burned. He stroked and kicked for the surface.

Ryan flinched as a horrid lipless mouth gained the seal between his shoulder blades. He gasped as the rasplike tongue scraped his spine. White fire shot down his back and down his left leg. His lungs and throat reflexively filling with water, Ryan clawed toward the surface. A lamprey latched on to his bleeding right buttock, and another hit his inner left thigh. They wriggled and yanked against him to drag him back down. A lamprey hit him in the stomach, and its tongue tried to bore past the hard plates of his abdominal wall. He ignored them and clawed for the surface. Only there would there be surcease or any kind of rescue.

Ryan broached the water like a drowning man rising for the third and last time.

He saw the Manitoulin whaleboat a dozen yards away, but it was trying to oar past huge chunks of lock debris.

"Ryan! Ryan!" Everyone was shouting his name. Hunk Poncet's voice called out in clear command from the Manitoulin whaleboat. "Kagan! Kosha! Quinn! Man in the water! Lamprey!"

Ryan sagged beneath the water for the last time as the lampreys dragged him down. The monster poodles hit the water in an answering wedge. Ryan's struggles weakened with blood loss and the weight of the fish sucking him dry. The dogs beelined for him. Lampreys boiled around the giant dogs in the water, nuzzling and twisting and trying to attach themselves, but the water-shedding, corkscrew coats of the poodles confounded their jawless efforts. The giant poodles ignored the lampreys attacking them and instead took a dim view of those latching on to Ryan. Kagan's jaws clamped on the lamprey boring into Ryan's back, and she began savaging the parasite like an old slipper. The lamprey spasmed and released as its cartilaginous spine crushed beneath Kagan's teeth. Kosha and Quinn joined the fray, ripping savaging and releasing. Kagan's teeth closed around the sling of Ryan's Scout, and she began pulling him along like a canine outboard motor. Kosha and Quinn rode like convoy guards, snapping at any fish trying to latch on to their charge. The prow of the whaleboat appeared in front of Ryan's face. Hunk and his men hauled him out of the river.

"Ryan! You did it! You really did it!"

The Manitoulin men pulled the poodles aboard. Kosha still had a lamprey in her jaws. Hunk's big earnest face loomed into Ryan's. "Talk to me!"

Ryan coughed and threw up water for a long time. He finally sagged back and wiped his chin wearily. "Get on the radio. Tell Krysty I'm all right." He lay back between the benches, watching as Kosha savagely yanked her head back and forth to cease her lamprey's struggles. She dropped her prize at Ryan's feet. "Put that in a pie for me."

He nodded at Kosha. "Good dog."

Kosha wagged her tail happily.

She liked Ryan.

Chapter Eighteen

Lake Superior

All eyes turned in the *Queen*'s makeshift main sick bay as Krysty walked in. She raised an eyebrow at the sight of Ryan lying naked on a cot with his rear end propped up in the air by three rolled blankets like a man over a barrel. Mildred worked at dressing the grotesque lamprey wounds. She was currently working on Ryan's right buttock. The man stoically stared into the middle distance without flinching.

Krysty smirked. "Lover? You look like you got gang-banged by stickies."

"Feel like it," Ryan grunted. He thought back to the last seconds of the fight on the great gate and Thorpe's hybrid pirates. "Almost did."

Krysty looked to Mildred. "How is he?"

Mildred swabbed the tongue wound in the middle of the bite perforating Ryan's posterior. "The wounds are disgusting to look at, but for the most part they seem clean and nearly ninety percent superficial. Only the tongues went anything near deep. He half drowned in the river and the lampreys left him a couple of pints short. Rest and food will take care of what ails him."

"Then let me provide the initial repast!" Doc walked in jauntily carrying a trencher board with a stoop of spruce beer and a steaming lamprey pie. "Ryan, may I present you with your antagonist, courtesy of noble canines Kagan, Kosha and Quinn!"

"Doc!" Mildred stared disbelievingly. "Get that out of here!"

Ryan lifted his head and sniffed the air. "Nah, Doc, bring that here."

The old man brought over the platter and set it at the foot of the cot. Ryan scooped up a spoonful of lamprey, mustard and onion pie. He shoved it in his mouth and chewed. Maybe everything tasted better after beating death, maybe it was the sweet taste of victory, or it might just be that Ryan's blood was the secret ingredient that every lamprey pie called out for. Whatever the reason, to the one-eyed man it was damn fine pie.

He mumbled though a full mouth. "Those dogs get steak tonight."

Mildred watched Ryan wolf his food. "Well, he's hungry, always a good sign."

Ryan took a healthy slug of spruce beer. "Thanks, Doc. So, how are things?"

"Well, my friend! Did we not all see you sail forth in your iron wag! All saw you take the tower and run forth across the great gate! All saw you shatter the gate at the risk of your own life and your mighty dive into the river! You are the hero of the hour! Even Mr. Six speaks of you in only the most glowing of regards!"

"I had help." Ryan nodded up at the man from the past. "Including you, Doc. You and your catapults. You did real well."

Doc was visibly moved by Ryan's rare praise. "Thank you, my friend."

"Jak and Six brought the LAV back?"

"Yes, the main pirate ville is on the north bank of the canal, so he drove up along the southern shore until they reached the calmer waters of Whitefish Bay, where upon sighting us they sailed to meet us."

"Did we get Thorpe?"

Doc sighed. "Alas not, while you rested the rogue retreated into his island tower. With time the mangonels could have battered it open, but it was time we did not have. J.B. and the captain debated sending in a landing party to take it by storm, but again all feared the time and casualties it would cost. But I believe the hammer blow has been struck. The gate has been shattered, and with catapult fire I leveled his capstan house and severely damaged the gate frame. He cannot rebuild before the freeze.

"Loud Elk and his men are already sailing posthaste for the Bruce. Before the ice comes, Loud Elk said that Thorpe will receive a First Nations delegation. He will be allowed to vacate the premises and save himself and his men's lives. Should he fail to reason he shall find himself at war with the First Nations and every ville on the Lakes that wishes free passage. J.B. estimates his casualties were nearly fifty percent. His power is broken. Should he return to a life of piracy upon the Lakes, I suspect his future will be short and grim."

Ryan didn't like leaving an enemy behind but there was little to be done about it now. "What about the pirate ville?"

Doc shifted uncomfortably. "Captain McKenzie wished me to bombard it with pitch. I refused to, on the grounds that it was a civilian encampment undoubtedly filled with women, children and noncombatants. The captain was quite put out by this. Some of the catapult crew were close to rebelling against me. However, J.B., bless his heart, backed me. In the spirit of compromise I agreed to set their pier afire and sink any ship in dock larger than a canoe. We left it burning. Thorpe now has almost nothing in the way of naval force projection."

Ryan craned his head around at Mildred. "What about our casualties?"

Mildred sighed. She had been very busy during the battle. "Captain McKenzie eased seven sewn up into their hammocks over the side. I got three who are going to be dead by nightfall and another four critical. Another ten were hit badly but are going to make it. The ship's healer is a lush, but he does seem to have a lot of experience patching bullet holes."

Ryan nodded and ate. The *Queen of the Lakes* had started the journey overcrewed, now she was short-handed. Convoy men would have to take up the slack. "How's Yoann?"

Mildred paused in her ministrations. "Bad. I've done all I can. The amputation site is clean. There's been no blossoming of parasites anywhere that I can tell, though I've still got him under restraints. I'm sticking with my prognosis that whatever is ailing him is a blood infection. His fever will break on its own or it'll kill him. Right now he's roasting alive. So for the foreseeable future it looks like you're still Grand Marshall of the Host. Not that anyone has a problem with that, except maybe Six, and even he's pretty damned impressed with you right about now." Mildred leaned back and gave her work a critical eye. "You're done."

Ryan pushed away his empty platter. "I'm fit to leave?"

"You took a beating and you lost blood." Mildred shook her head. She knew that unless this particular patient was missing a limb her advice would probably be ignored. "I've seen you worse. I've been told it will be a few days of sailing on the Superior to get where we're going. If I were you, I'd take advantage of it and rest."

Ryan rolled over gingerly and perched his left buttock on the edge of the cot and looked at the bandages swathing him. His impressive collection of sucking flesh wounds made him loathe to put on his clothes. He gingerly stood and draped a blanket around himself to mostly avoid his dressings. "I'm going to go talk to the captain. C'mon, Doc," Ryan said.

He slung his Scout and limped out of the sick bay. Everywhere he went convoy, crew and islander hailed him. Many pressed forward to clap him on the back. Doc warded off Ryan's admirers with just short slashes of his cane. "Captain's business! Make way!"

Ryan eased himself up the stairs to the bridge. McKenzie, Mr. Smythe and Six stood in the wheelhouse looking quite pleased with themselves and the world. "Ryan!"

They clustered around him. Ryan winced as his wounded back and shoulders took a good-natured pounding and he accepted a wooden teacup full of something. He winced again and tears nearly came to his eyes. As near as he could tell he was drinking diesel fuel with a vague hawberry tang to it. The hooch blossomed into warmth in his stomach. "Thanks."

Doc gasped at the Manitoulin firewater and its effect. "A most potent...potation."

"To the victor—" Six grinned and slugged back his cup "—the spoils."

Ryan shook his head at a second cup and Mr. Smythe filled it again anyway. "We haven't won yet."

McKenzie grunted over his cup. "I hear you. We got a hundred more battles and a thousand klicks before we're all back home and bedded down for winter." The first genuine smile Ryan had seen on the captain split the man's black mustache and beard. "But we did something today, Ryan, and rad-blast you, I want you to admit it! We were something to see!"

A rare, genuine smile crossed Ryan's face. He quoted Donnie Goosekiller. "We counted some wicked good coup. They're going to talk about it for years." Ryan raised his cup. "They'll talk about the men who did it forever."

Hawberry brandy sloshed as the cups clashed together. Ryan gazed down at McKenzie's charts of the Great Lakes. "Where're we headed?"

"The last place they'll expect." McKenzie's finger stabbed down onto the northwest edge of Lake Superior. "Thunder Bay."

THORPE, KING OF THE PIRATES, stood on the northern shore of the canal and watched his kingdom smolder and sag in the aftermath. The great gate was shattered at the seam. It looked as if some leviathan had taken giant bites out of it like a sandwich. On the southern tower frame three of the six great leather hinges had snapped when the current had slammed the gate's enormous weight against the shore. The frame was split, and the great gate hung at a horrible angle like the sail of a sinking ship with its hull beneath the water. The gate slowly swung in the current and made horrible, creaking death groans of strain. Thorpe's master builder stood beside him and wept like a man watching his firstborn son go into the grave before him. The lock had been his idea, his masterpiece, and Thorpe's fortune. The old man's scalp locks were gray, and among the pirate tattoos covering his body he bore the mark of the mason's on his chest.

"She'll snap," he said, "rip free by nightfall. Best we cut her loose before she takes the tower frame with her."

"We'll rebuild," Thorpe said.

"Yes…" the mason whispered.

The pirate king and his mason both knew it was a dream that would shatter with the oncoming winter.

An entire new gate would have to be cut. The capstan house was rubble. Even under ideal circumstances it would take all of spring and summer to rebuild, and now Thorpe's forces were at half strength. He had no ships, barges or piers and he was out of time. He had little enough time just to prepare for winter. He shook his head. There was little to prepare. His people lived off the toll. Without it he would have to buy or trade for supplies to get through the long cold months.

Many villes might refuse him, and he wasn't sure he had men enough to force the issue.

He'd have to slaughter and smoke the capstan cattle to keep his people alive. He'd have to slaughter his stickie men, as well. They couldn't be trusted not to nightcreep their own if things got lean. Word would already be spreading. Canoes would be crisscrossing every stretch of water with the news that Captain McKenzie was back on the Lakes and the *Queen* had run the locks. Even if he could erect some semblance of a barrier, Thorpe knew many would refuse to pay. He would have to go back to pirating on the waters and make more enemies. Come the spring, half the Lakes would be blasting for him. And before that, there was the *Queen*'s return run to contemplate.

It was enough to make a man go back to picking berries.

"Do it." Thorpe sighed bitterly. "Cut her free."

"Yes, Captain." Thorpe called himself king, but his own people still called him "Captain."

"Captain!" Thorpe turned at the call of his highest-ranking surviving pirate, Grizz. Grizz was an aptly named bear of a man with long braided hair and long braided beard. Grizz was running toward him, bearskins and braids flapping, waving his arms hysterically. "Captain!"

"I got concerns, Grizz!"

"Coldhearts, Captain!" He pointed south. "Coldhearts!"

Thorpe looked south. Dust was rising off the old Trans-Canada. Thorpe closed his eyes. So it was to be a one-two blow. The *Queen* had knocked him to his knees, and now came the land attack to slit his throat. Thorpe opened his eyes and checked the loads in his scatterblasters. He had a long, over-and-under trap gun for when things got social, and a side-by-side that had been sawed down into a handblaster for when things got intimate. "Grizz, gather every man who can walk and point a blaster on this side of the canal. We make our stand at the North tower."

"Yes, Captain." Grizz ran off to rally the men.

Thorpe watched as motorcycles and war wags began to fill the horizon. He watched with some surprise as three broke from the formation in a wedge. One of them bore a white flag. Thorpe stood his ground as bison horns called behind him and his men scrambled into some kind of battle order. Grizz ran back up with a pirate flag and six men. The cold-heart delegation approached and ground to a halt.

The most powerful baron in Ontario and the pirate king of the Lakes regarded each other. They knew each other only by reputation. A flesh-headed mutant flanked Mace Henning along with some mini-Mace of a bastard son. Thorpe noted the silver *voyageur* the robed mutant wore. Mace's offspring wore one, too, and everyone in Ontario knew what that meant. Thorpe regarded Mace Henning noncommittally. "Mace."

"Thorpe," Mace replied. He looked around at the shattered locks and the smoke rising into the sky. "Bad day?"

"Had better," Thorpe admitted. He looked up at his adversary. Mace Henning looked every inch a powerful baron. Thorpe knew he didn't look like much up close. It was guts, determination and brains that had gotten him where he was. He scanned the line of motorcycles and offroad wags. "You don't have the men to take me, Mace. Not even on a day like today."

"Mebbe, mebbe not, but win or lose it'll eat up every bit of what you got left." Mace acted as though it was a matter of little import. "You'll be finished regardless."

Thorpe knew the truth when he heard it. "Well, me and you could talk a walk down to the shore, Mace. Settle it personal like."

Mace threw back his head and laughed. "Fire, thunder and fallout! I always heard you had sand!"

Mace Henning was right. Thorpe had sand, and he was also correct that Thorpe was having a bad day. "What do you want, Mace?"

The baron loomed over Thorpe, but he winked in a conspiratorial fashion. "I want a coal-black ear, a man's right eye and a redheaded slut I heard tell about. I want Captain McKenzie and the *Queen* under my thumb. I want those iron wags. I want the entire convoy. I want Cyrielle Toulalan tamed and preggers. I want Yoann Toulalan dyin' slow in my fire. I want Baron Luc Toulalan to die from the grief of it all, and I want Val-d'Or."

"There's no end to wanting things, Mace," Thorpe observed.

"True enough," Mace agreed. "So what I need is a partner."

"Never heard you were the partnering kind."

"Well, now, that's true enough, but I been thinking. Heard of some megabarons down in the Deathlands. Never comes to no good. Their power only extends as far as they can send their sec men, and here in the north the good weather is too short to send sec men far or get anything real done. I'm thinking it's going to take a confederation of industrious, farsighted men to run things. Men like you and me."

Thorpe chewed the word over. "Confederation."

"I'm the most powerful baron in Ontario. You're the pirate king of the Lakes. That's a good start. Smart men will flock to that. Practical men bend to it. The Soo Locks is wealth. Soo Locks is power. But you're gonna need help to rebuild that great big gate of yours, and help to hold on to it."

"And you want…?" Thorpe prompted.

"The *Queen* ran your locks, Thorpe."

The pirate's face tightened. "Noticed."

"The *Queen* ran your locks late summer. With a convoy aboard. Heading west. A convoy all the way from Val-d'Or, French territory, with genuine predark armored wags and more shiny new blasters than the shore has sand. Where'd they get those, do you think?"

"Dunno."

"Where do you think they're headed so late in the season?"

"Dunno."

"What do you think they're after, risking so much?"

"Dunno."

"Doesn't that make you a mite curious?"

"A mite," Thorpe admitted.

"Well, I'm curious, too. So I think I'm just going to go west and have me a boo. Take whatever they're after along with everything they already got."

"And you want my help."

Mace shrugged. "Be mighty neighborly, as a fellow confederate."

"Confederation," Thorpe repeated. "With you as First Man?"

"First among equals," Thorpe corrected. "But you get your locks rebuilt, I'll send men to help and see you get supplies to last the winter. Then you'll have me as an ally come spring. The day you don't like the arrangement, we can always take that walk down to the shore you were talking about."

Thorpe trusted Mace Henning about as far as he could drop him from the top of the lock. He had absolute trust in Henning's cunning and ambition. "What happens I refuse?"

"What happens?" Mace put his hands to his chest in mock hurt. "Why, nothing. I got no beef with you. Me? I'm a busy man. I got places to go and things to do before the freeze. I'll just be waggin' on my way and wish you luck." Mace's eyes went hard, and he leaned in close so that only the two of them could hear. "Good luck next spring, Thorpe. Good luck with

Jon Hard-knife, the Nations, McKenzie, Poncet, and every other ville on the Lakes that wants to settle your hash once and for all for making them pay the toll."

Mace turned back to his assembled horde and cut a circle overhead with his hand. "Rev 'em up boys! We're out of here!"

Thorpe spoke through clenched teeth. "What do you need, Mace?"

Mace leaned in again. "Well, now, I need every wag you got and every man you can put on them. I need every canoe you got. A lot of my bikes can ride double. I'll want your men riding, and I want every last drop of fuel you got. It's gonna be a long, hard haul to catch the *Queen*. Wouldn't mind you coming along, yourself, frankly. You got a sense of tactics."

"You gonna chase 'em? This late in the season?" Thorpe couldn't figure it. "Mace, you don't know where they're headed. You don't even know where they're gonna make landfall. We could end up at the Lake of the Woods, a thousand klicks from home and nothing to show for it but our dangles in our hands, and them shriveling fast in the freeze."

Mace Henning laughed again. "Never knew you were a poet, Thorpe."

The pirate wasn't amused. "Mebbe you best ride on, Mace."

Mace ignored the suggestion. "Tag, show our kingly confederate."

The robed mutant came forward and opened a green metal case.

Thorpe peered at the contents. It was a radio. Thorpe couldn't read, so the word "Diefenbunker," among others printed on the components meant nothing to him, but he recognized the Maple Leaf and the dark green color. The radio was military issue, predark, and looked absolutely cherry. Kind of like the LAVs that had shattered his locks.

The enormity of it struck Thorpe like a hammer. "Fire, thunder and fallout..."

Baron Mace Henning spoke very quietly. "Tell you what I know, Thorpe. I know that Yoann Toulalan is in bad shape and his sister gave command of the whole shebang to a one-eyed Deathlander named Ryan. I know some, particularly Six and some of his closest, ain't happy with the arrangement. I know every wag they got and their blasters by heart. By tonight I'll know the condition of the *Queen* and her casualties. And I guarantee it, I'll know exactly where they intend to make landfall, long before they make it." Mace smiled sweetly. It was a travesty on his face. "What else do you need to see things my way, Thorpe? A blow job?"

Thorpe turned his head and stared westward toward the Superior. Rage slowly kindled within him for the *Queen* and everyone on it. "Nah, Mace. Revenge'll do for now."

Chapter Nineteen

Ryan eased his blaster out of its holster. They'd had four days of smooth sailing, and it had become his habit to rise just before dawn, walk the decks and take in the clean air over the lakes and watch the sun rise. The chunk-chunk of the *Queen's* boilers vibrated through the soles of his boots. Ryan stood silent in the crepuscular gloom of the lower deck and stared at his LAV. The engine compartment was open. Seriah had been working on it. It didn't need much in the way of work, but she insisted on checking the LAVs daily. Her beloved lot in life was to keep ancient, endlessly rebuilt combustion engines running. For a wrench the pristine diesels of the two LAVs were Holy Grails. She couldn't keep her hands off them, when she wasn't busy putting her hands on Jak.

Ryan could hear a voice coming out of the engine compartment.

Not actually from the engine compartment itself, but with the engine hatches open Ryan could dimly hear a voice inside the LAV's crew cabin. He recognized Six's baritone. The big man was inside and he was speaking French. Ryan grabbed an outer storage cleat and soundlessly climbed to the top of the LAV. He waited a moment and listened, but Six kept right on speaking French. The Deathlands warrior grabbed the handle of the commander's hatch and flung it open. "Help you, Six?"

"Merde!" Six just about jumped out the commander's seat. He was wearing the com headset and his hands leaped off the

console. One hand went beneath his coat but stopped as he sagged with recognition. "*Sacre Bleu,* Ryan! If I had hair, it would be white!"

Ryan's eye didn't blink. His SIG-Sauer wasn't quite pointing down the hatch. "What are you doing in my wag, Six?"

"What do you mean, your wag?" Six blustered. "You're part of the convoy! You don't—"

"It's mine. Me and my friends. We own it," Ryan reiterated. "What are you doing in it without my say-so?"

Six regained his stony cool. "I feared the radio in the engineering wag might be damaged."

"Damaged how?"

Six regained his usual scowl. "I'm not sure I like your tone, Ryan."

"Not sure I give a glowing night shit what you like or don't like, Six, but I asked you a question."

"Very well." Six's voice was scathing. "In my experience, most electrical devices don't respond well to being splashed with boiling soap. We were having some malfunctions."

Ryan had to give him that one. "Yeah?"

"The keyboard of the engineering LAV's onboard computer was damaged," Six continued. "We replaced it with a spare we took from the Diefenbunker. Much of the radio's console was splattered, as well, and, as you know, your vehicle has become the central hub of all of our tactical radio communications."

"Little late for it."

Six's scowl was ferocious even for him. "I have many responsibilities. After the battle my responsibilities were to see to my people. Now that we approach land I must make sure of the convoy. I checked to see that the engineering LAV's radio can still send. It seems fine. Now I am seeing if it can receive as well as still act as a relay hub, as this LAV does. If it didn't, I would replace it with the spare we took from the Diefenbunker."

"And?" Ryan asked.

"It functions flawlessly."

"Good to know."

Six flicked the radio switches off and slammed the button for the LAV's ramp with his palm. "Good night, Ryan." Six unfolded his great frame from the commander's seat and stalked out of the LAV to disappear in the darkness between the lines of convoy wags.

"Good morning," Ryan muttered after him.

The one-eyed man slid down the hatch. The radio didn't appear to have been tampered with. He ran a quick check, everything seemed to be in place. Ryan buttoned up the LAV and went to the wheelhouse. McKenzie and Doc sat drinking hawberry-brandy with a chessboard between them on the chart table. Doc appeared to be winning handily. Mr. Smythe stood behind the wheel. McKenzie looked up with a smile. "Ryan, you're just in time! We passed Isle Royale a quarter of an hour ago. The sun rises soon. The entrance to Thunder Bay is guarded by the cliff wall of Cape Thunder on the mainland and Pie Island. They are something to see."

"You say Thunder Bay got hit?"

"Someone dropped fire on it, not bad like the rads that rained on the Michigan villes, but bad enough that no one much goes there." The captain smiled craftily. "I dropped a few hints in a few places that if I made the Soo Locks I would make landfall in Nipigon Bay. The baron of Red Rock is less of a bastard than some I know. He'll be disappointed when I don't show. But if Mace Henning is there waiting, you'll be about a 120 klicks west of him with a good head start. Plus, fifty klicks out of Thunder Bay, the Trans-Canada splits in two again for another four hundred. Even if Mace gets wind you leap-frogged him, he's going to have to choose one or the other. Even if he chooses right, you run hard for Manitoba and I'm betting he never catches you."

"And the rads?" Ryan asked.

"Bad enough that no one lives there, but I won't be at port any longer than it takes you to roll off, and you're just passing through. Keep your wags buttoned up and don't stop for anything until you've left Mount McKay and the Thunderbirds in your dust."

"Thunderbirds?"

"Keep your wags buttoned up," McKenzie repeated. "Once you've left Mace and Mount McKay behind you, far as I know there ain't no one or nothing with the juice to take on a convoy as big or powerful as yours. Our problems are all behind us."

"Behind us!" The door to the bridge flung open and Mr. Timms's giant frame filled the door. "Behind us! Behind us!"

The *Queen* was a roll-on/roll-off as Mildred had explained. It had a ramp on both ends and thus had a bridge at both ends, as well. Both bridges had a crow's nest constructed atop them each with a machine blaster. The stern nest had failed to inform them of any peril behind. McKenzie heaved his bulk up the iron ladder to the revetment above. Ryan and everyone else on the bridge swarmed up after him and looked aft.

Dozens of war canoes were paddling furiously toward the *Queen*.

McKenzie swore a blue streak. "Bastards! They must have been waiting off Isle Royale!" He reached out and began slamming the alarm bell as he roared. "Blasters and pikes! Prepare to repel borders!"

Everyone piled back down the ladder. "Mr. Smythe! Hard to starboard! Bring the LAV's cannon to bear!"

"Yes, Captain!" Mr. Smythe spun the wheel hard over.

Ryan hit his com unit. "J.B!"

J.B. was already on it. Ryan watched as J.B. flew up the stairs to the promenade favoring his wounded leg. He waved his hat at the bridge and disappeared up the ramp into the LAV. Blasterfire began to crack on the rear promenade and the back rails. The *Queen* slowly turned to bring her heavy weapons to bear. Ryan knew they weren't going to make it. The convoy's machine blasters had been taken from the *Queen* and remounted on the vehicles in preparation for debarking. Canoes sliced through the water. Men who weren't paddling were returning fire. As they closed, Ryan could make out the vests and scalp locks of pirates. It looked as though Thorpe was hitting them with every man he had left. Other men in the canoes wore the riding leathers of Mace's coldhearts. They were nearly on top of the *Queen,* and she was presenting herself broadside to the attack.

The battle was going to go hand to hand.

Ryan unslung his Scout and stalked to the door of the wheelhouse. McKenzie barked his ugly laugh. "Stick around, Ryan. You'll want to watch this. Mr. Smythe!"

The first mate went to a heavy iron switch box with a pair of levers made of brass and wood. He took a pair of cables that fed through the floor of the wheelhouse and connected them to the leads and tightened them down with brass wing nuts. Mr. Smythe threw one lever and the box hummed. "Power to the switch, Captain."

McKenzie strode to the starboard window. The canoes were less than a few dozen yards away. "Wait for it…"

"On your order, Captain," Smythe replied.

Ryan saw it. "The storm fencing, slung from the rails."

Mr. Smythe grinned ferociously. "Captain's got ten thousand volts of juice straight from the boilers to the fencing. There's things bigger than the lampreys in these lakes, and they need occasional discouragement."

Doc drew his LeMat. "They are upon us."

Canoes bumped the side of the *Queen,* and pirate and cold-heart hands and bare feet clawed into the fencing.

McKenzie had his short sword in hand and he slashed it down decisively. "Now, Mr. Smythe!"

The first mate clacked the lever over and a spark shot off the switch box leads. The boarders kept climbing. McKenzie roared in indignation. "Rad-blast your eyes, Mr. Smythe! Now!"

Smythe slammed the lever back and forth like a man priming a pump. "We don't have juice!"

"The boilers are on full!"

Smythe shook his head at the sparking switch box. "We have juice to the switch, but it's not going to the fence! We've lost the connection."

Ryan walked to the door. The storm fencing was no longer a deterrent. In fact it was a ready-made boarding ladder encircling the entire ship. The LAVs couldn't help them. The catapults were useless at this range. The ships electric fence had failed. Ryan hung his Scout longblaster on a peg and put a SIG-Sauer in his left hand and his panga in his right. He heard Doc unsheath his blade and fall into step behind him.

"At my back, Doc."

"Indeed, my dear friend."

Two dozen stickie men were already on the promenade. The great wag ramp at the prow was a blind spot for blaster-fire, and the stickie men had gone straight up it with ease. They had brought ropes, and pirates were scaling up behind them. Ryan had noticed the relative scarcity of blasters and ammo in Canada. Most he had seen were home-rolled or predark hunting weapons. It had left Canadians with a predilection for firing their blasters dry and then going for their hatchets and war clubs in a way that would have been no stranger to Canada's original settlers and aboriginals nearly four hundred years previous.

It also meant that nearly any battle in Canada almost instantly turned into a brawl.

Thorpe's stickie men had hair and wore clothes, but they shared many traits with their purebred brethren. They didn't seem to feel wounds, their thick rubbery skin made wounding them difficult in the first place and they were unnaturally strong. Worst of all they were beyond fearless. They had the gift of emptiness.

A stickie had a crewman's head vised in its suckered hands and was smashing it against the side of the LAV, ignoring two crewmen chopping and stabbing into its back with hatchets and knives. The easiest way to chill a stickie was to shoot it in the head.

They fought barehanded, and appeared to prefer suckering people's throats and ripping them out or firmly attaching themselves and repeatedly smashing their opponents into things between bites.

Ryan dropped the hammer on his SIG and popped the stickie man's head like a cyst. The crewman slid down the side of the LAV with his head crushed like an egg. Several stickies turned their empty black eyes on Ryan. "One-eye! One-eye!" they hooted.

Someone had given the stickie men a preferred target list. Several came charging in.

Boo Blacktree wasn't having it. "Nope!"

He'd sensed his bow wasn't going to help. He burst into the brawl with his three feet of paddle-shaped club and swung it like an ax. He sheared off a stickie man's jaw with a single blow. He also stepped into Ryan's line of fire. The forward promenade was a swirling, eddying mass of combat.

"Fireblast..." Ryan holstered his SIG, relying on his panga and slaughtering knife.

"My friend!" Doc shouted. "I am with you!"

Ryan waded in.

He chopped his panga into the neck of a stickie man. The hybrid turned, hooting and thrusting out its suckered hands. Ryan dropped beneath its clutches and ripped his slaughtering knife across its hamstrings. It flopped down and immediately did a sit-up. A sucking hand slapped for Ryan's head and mostly caught hair.

Doc's point pierced the stickie man's shark-black left eye and slid into its brain. "Up! Up! Up!" Doc urged.

Ryan took an extra heartbeat. He left his panga in the stickie man's neck for later retrieval and his hand closed around the hard wood handle of a war club shaped like a snake with an apple in its mouth. Right where the stem would be someone had inset a heavy pyramid of sharpened steel. He rolled up to one knee. A hooting stickie man came in clutching and scrabbling with is puckered paws. The one-eyed man cracked his club across its kneecaps. The stickie man tumbled legs-reversed to the deck. Ryan stood and his new war club rose over his head. The ironwood crunched into stickie man's skull. Bone splintered as Ryan ripped his weapon free. Stickie men charged.

It was ideal for Doc, and he deftly skewered one offender and then another each through the left eye. Despite their inhuman toughness and love of fire and explosions, stickies, whole or hybrid had no defense against forcibly being lobotomized.

Ryan took the war club in both hands and stepped in shoulder to shoulder with Doc. He was reminded of what he had learned of samurai swords by the Keepers of the Sun. The right hand pushed. The left hand pulled, and you let the weight of the weapon do the work. Ryan swung his club. It had a lot of end weight to work with. The spike punched through a stickie man's left eye but rather than skewering, the club mass tore away temple and socket. Pulped eye and spilled brain spattered.

The LAV was under attack.

A stickie man was halfway down the commander's hatch and a pirate was crouched on top of the turret trying to figure out the machine blaster. Ryan ran forward. He put one foot on the rear tire, grabbed a cleat in one hand and vaulted to the top deck of the LAV. The pirate took up his empty blaster and swung it like a club. Ryan was faster. His own club blurred in breaking the bones of both hands the man had wrapped around the barrel. He dropped the empty blaster, screaming. Ryan swung his club into the side of the pirate's head. The spike pierced the man's eardrum and the club ball followed halfway through his head. Ryan shoved the corpse aside. The stickie man's suckered feet were anchored onto the turret top as it shoved its torso down the hatch. Ryan swung his club twice and broke both of its feet. He grabbed it by its pirate vest and hauled it up out of the hatch.

The stickie man came up hooting and screeching, holding J.B.'s hat in one hand and his Uzi in the other. Ryan gave it the ball-headed club right between the legs. It dropped J.B.'s favorite accessories and fell vomiting and clutching itself. Ryan swung his club like a polo mallet and sent the stickie man tumbling off the top of the LAV.

"J.B.!" Ryan shouted. "J.B.!"

The Armorer's head popped up with his glasses askew and blood on his face. Ryan jammed J.B.'s fedora back on his dome. "Keep this on your head! Keep your head on underneath it!"

J.B. nodded as Ryan shoved the Uzi back into his hands. "Right, I— Ryan!"

Ryan spun and looked to where J.B. was staring.

The stickie men were in the wheelhouse.

One's feet disappeared as it snaked through the ripped-open armored shutters on one of the windows. Three more were tearing their way through. Ryan pulled the pin holding the LAV's machine blaster in its mount and snapped out the left bipod leg. He held the machine blaster on his and began hosing down the armored sides of the wheelhouse. Ryan cut down one stickie man and then another with head shots. He shouted over his own thunder, "Smythe! Blacktree! The bridge!"

The first mate and the scout broke from the battle and ran up the stairs. Ryan cut aside a third stickie man and set down the smoking autoblaster. "Keep her hot, J.B.!"

Ryan jumped down, club in hand as J.B. slapped in a fresh belt of ammo. The one-eyed man ripped his panga free and flew up the blood-spattered steel stairs to the upper deck. Pirates rushed screaming toward him along the starboard gangway waving tomahawks and cleavers. Ryan dropped the bludgeon and blade and pulled his SIG. He dropped to a knee and took the blaster in both hands and began chilling pirates. The gangway became a slaughter chute. There was no retreat. The pirates knew victory was their only option. Ryan fired his blaster dry. He rose and slapped a fresh mag into his smoking, empty SIG and released the slide on a fresh round. Leaving the gangway littered with the dead, he went through the broken door to the bridge, blaster and club in hand.

The wheelhouse was a slaughterhouse. Blood was everywhere. Mr. Smythe clutched his face and neck. He was a bloody mess but nothing was spurting. Three stickie men lay dead on the deck. Boo Blacktree was putting the finishing touches on a twitching fourth with repeated club blows.

McKenzie lay in front of the wheel of his ship with his throat torn open to the sky. Ryan picked up the captain's fallen sword and pressed it into the first mate's bloody hand. "Smythe."

The man blinked.

"Captain," Ryan tried again, "your ship is adrift. You're being boarded."

Smythe blinked past the blood curtaining down his face.

"Captain Smythe! The *Queen!*" Ryan shouted.

Smythe blinked again, but this time he was blinking away the fog of battle and shock. "The *Queen.*" He stared at the bloody blade in his hand. "Right you are, Mr. Cawdor. The *Queen.*"

Doc appeared in the doorway. "Is all… Oh no…"

"Captain! Steer your ship! Keep us off the rocks! Doc!" Ryan pointed his club at the shattered shutter in front of the wheel. "No one comes through the window! Blacktree! No one comes through that door except me!"

Captain Smythe took the wheel; Doc took station to defend him; Blacktree formed the new door to the bridge. Ryan went back out into battle. The forward promenade was clear, but the men defending it had been decimated. He stepped over his blasted dead on the gangway and moved toward the catapult deck. He encountered Hunk Poncet. The baron's son carried a rifleman's hawk with a hatchet bit on one side and a hammer peen on the other. Kagan, Kosha and Quinn each savaged the limb of a fallen stickie man while Hunk pounded the hybrid like a nail.

"Hunk! With me!"

"Ryan!" Hunk and his poodles snapped to bloodthirsty attention.

"Reload."

"What? Oh!" Hunk reached into leather pouch on his belt and began stuffing loose rounds into the single mag of his iron Glock on the fly. The last pirates on the catapult promenade were dead or screaming as they were butchered. Ryan shouted as he took the stairs down to the vehicle deck four at a time.

The tide of the battle had turned. The pirates had overwhelming numbers and nearly achieved complete surprise. LAVs, electric fences and siege engines had been of no avail and the stickie men had almost taken the bridge, but the *Queen* still had an advantage. Yoann Toulalan was hording his tech, but he passed out Diefenbunker blasters like party favors. The pirates had boarded the *Queen* in the teeth of massed full autofire from all sides. Pirates and coldhearts were desperately defending themselves in scattered pockets in the narrow lanes among the convoy vehicles, and it was going very badly for them. Convoy and crew were taking the time to reload and blast the invaders down. The dead, dying and mutilated lay everywhere. The deck was an ocean of gore that rivaled the worm attack. Ryan watched as a screaming pirate was hoisted into the air, impaled on three pikes and dumped into the lake. The water around the *Queen* was a churning red froth of blood, bodies and lampreys.

Hunk and the men from up top whooped and hurled themselves into the fray.

Ryan clicked his tactical radio and rounded the horn. "Krysty."

"I'm with Mildred, Cyrielle and Yoann. We're fine."

"Doc."

"The bridge is secure, my dear Ryan," Doc came back. "Captain Smythe stands before the wheel."

"J.B."

"Forward promenade secure. Few pirates getting back in their canoes." Ryan heard the LAV's machine blaster rattle off a burst. "Ain't going nowhere," the Armorer concluded.

"Jak."

"Vehicle deck. Aft. Mopping up."

His people were safe for the moment. Ryan allowed himself the luxury of a few long deep breaths. He considered the bloody, ball-headed war club in his hand. He wasn't about

Chapter Twenty

Mission Island

Thorpe lowered his spyglass. "Well that coulda gone better." The *Queen* was steaming toward the channel between the two islands, and she was leaving a carpet of drifting pirate canoes like dead leaves in her wake.

Mace lowered his own ancient binoculars. "Coulda been worse, and we whittled 'em down some."

"Whittled 'em down some?" Thorpe was incredulous. "The canoes got annihilated! And most of the men on 'em were mine! I'd say we've lost nearly half our forces!"

"Could be worse." Mace smiled his ugly smile as thunder rolled in the dark clouds advancing over Mount McKay. "Could be raining."

Thorpe just shook his head. He knew with great certainty that once again Mace knew something he didn't.

Tag was watching another direction. A pair of motorcycles were zipping across the rusting span of the Mission Bridge from the mainland. Thorpe frowned as the riders came in. Tag had recruited Grizz and Shorty for a job without telling Thorpe about it, and Grizz apparently because despite his woolly, mountain-man appearance he could read and write. They'd been gone about an hour and were just rolling back in now.

Thorpe scowled as they came to halt and turned their engines off. The two chillers were grinning like idiots. The violent giant and the violent runt seemed to be getting along famously. The pirate and the sec man's hands and clothing were spattered in red as if they had just got through slaughtering a hog. They were both grinning like schoolboys and stopping just short of slapping each other on the back.

"You make the Trans-Canada?" Tag asked.

"Oh yeah, Tag!" Shorty was delighted with his mission. "It weren't but a few klicks west!"

"How bad are the rads you figure?"

"Not bad, I'd say," Grizz said. "You got trees and sass growing. Nothing too twisted, but you can tell by the crater and the damage you probably wouldn't want to stay long or set down roots."

"You find a good spot on the road?"

"Oh yeah, Tag!" Shorty enthused. "They only got one route before the Trans-Can splits! They gotta see it!"

Tag nodded. "How's it look?"

Grizz was quite proud of his work. "Bigger'n life. Can't miss it."

"Shorty?"

"Aw, rads Tag!" Shorty grinned sheepishly. "I can't read and even I think it's good!"

Tag nodded in satisfaction and then at Mace. "Step one and two."

Mace nodded back.

Thorpe looked warily at the mutant. "Tag, what's goin' on?"

Tag pulled his hood over his stubbled head and covered his blaster as the first thin mists of rain began to drizzle down. "Just a little psychological warfare."

Thorpe struggled to control his anger. He was already tired of Tag and his two-loonie words. "Mace?"

"Yeah, Thorpe?"

"What's cycle-logical warfare?"

Mace smiled smugly and raised his optics again. Despite his reputation for brutality and terror tactics, Mace Henning was quite possibly the greatest psych-fighter in Canada, except maybe for Tag. Mace watched the *Queen* approach the pier. He happily muttered one of his favorite mantras of doom upon his enemies.

"Tension, apprehension and dissension have begun..."

THE BEAMS GIRDING the forward ramp hit the pier with a soggy thud. The capstans clanked as the ramp lowered. Crewmen leaped onto the raddled concrete pier with ropes to make the loading zone fast. They had wasted no time. Smythe had brought the *Queen* into Thunder Bay even while his men were dumping stripped pirate and coldheart bodies over the side, piling captured weapons and gear, and the dead and dying were attended to. No one questioned Smythe's battle-field ascendancy to captain. No one questioned his choice of Mr. Timms as first mate. Half of the convoy vehicles were painted with blood, but they had been prepped and ready to go before the attack. Ryan peered at the rad counter pinned to his coat. The needle wasn't spiking, but it was getting a bit twitchy.

Captain Smythe eased himself down the steps. His neck and half his face was swathed in bloody bandages. He wore McKenzie's hat. The former captain's ancient, abbreviated officer's sword hung from his belt.

Everyone in the convoy was making ready to go. Ryan leaned against the rail with his arm around Krysty and drank what he knew would be his last sleeve of spruce beer for a while. He spoke softly to Smythe. "Mace and Thorpe knew exactly where to intercept us."

Smythe glared at Ryan with his unbandaged eye. Ryan had more practice at it and won the stare down easily. Smythe looked away toward the overgrown, fallen skeleton of Thunder Bay. "I know it."

Six walked up and nodded at the captain. "The convoy is ready, Captain. Yoann has been made comfortable in the med wag. At the loadmaster's signal we will debark. Yoann says he looks forward to seeing you in the spring."

Captain Smythe clearly never expected to see Yoann Toulalan in this life again. Nevertheless he managed a defiant smile through his bandages. "You just tell that rad-blasted son of a gaudy slut I'll be looking for him on the Ottawa come spring, and he had better not keep me waiting."

One corner of Six's mouth twitched upward. "I will give him your fondest affections."

Ryan's right hand rested on his SIG. "Where were you, Six?"

"What?"

Ryan's eye narrowed. He didn't like repeating himself. "Asked where you were during the fight."

Six cocked his head incredulously. "Why do you ask! I was in the boiler room! I saw stickie men going for it! I went for them!"

Smythe flinched involuntarily. His engineers took a lot of training and were hard to replace. "And? Mr. Guilfoyle? Mr. Bryan?"

"Dead."

Smythe took it like a blow. "Miss Tamara!"

Tamara jerked to attention. "Dead, Captain! Mr. Timms had me put Jake and Bors on it."

"Why didn't you tell me!"

"I— Mr. Timms just told me to take care of it!"

Smythe closed his good eye and put his hand on a bulkhead to feel the throb of his boilers.

Ryan's voice was chilling cold. "What were you doing in my wag on my radio last night, Six?"

Six literally swelled with outrage. "I already told you."

Smythe's gaze snapped back and forth between the stare down. "What are you talking about?"

Ryan kept his eye on Six. "Guilfoyle and Bryan, chilled how, Tamara?"

Tamara frowned. "Skulls bashed in."

"And Six's three stickie men?"

The markswoman suddenly gave Six a baleful eye. "Weren't no stickie men in the boiler room. Just Bryan and Guilfoyle with stepped-on walnuts for heads."

Ryan slapped leather. It was so fast it caught even Six by surprise. "Lose the blaster, Six, and the hatchet and the blade." Six's huge hands creaked into fists and then opened loose and ready. Ryan's spare SIG appeared in his other hand like a magic trick. "Put your right hand on top of your head. Lose your gear with your left, use two fingers."

For a moment Ryan thought Six would snap. Instead the big man slowly shrugged his longblaster off his shoulder. It fell to the deck with a clank. With his thumb and forefinger he removed his tomahawk and bowie and blaster.

"And the hideout."

Six's eyes went to slits. Then he produced a large-caliber derringer and dropped it on the pile.

"Where are the stickie men you chilled?" Ryan asked.

Six cocked his head. "With permission?"

"Do it slow."

Six reached into his sheepskins. He pulled out three scalp locks and dropped them to the deck. Each had a bloody bit of milk-white scalp attached to it.

Ryan eyed them without commitment. "Where's the rest of them?"

"Mutant filth." Six spit. "I threw their carcasses in the boilers."

Krysty tensed at Ryan's side. His weapons never wavered.

It was just the sort of thing Ryan would expect Six to do. By the same token it was a very convenient explanation. They were all on a very hard timetable. Smythe would never turn off his boilers, let his fireboxes grow cold and send someone wading through cubic yards of ash and cinders looking for bone fragments.

Smythe turned a confused and hostile eye on Six. "Ryan, what do you mean, he was in your wag last night?"

"He was in our LAV. On the radio. Speaking French. Said he was using it to check the radio in the engineering LAV."

Shocked silence met this information.

A dozen sailors pointed their blasters at Six like a firing squad. Convoymen fingered their weapons and looked around nervously, shocked but uncertain about what to do.

"Who were you talking to?" Ryan asked Six.

"Myself."

Smythe sneered. "Yourself?"

"Given the current company, Captain, it is one of the few opportunities I have for intelligent conversation."

Smythe slowly pulled his sword. "You just don't do yourself any favors, do you?"

Tamara spoke the words on everyone's mind first. "Traitor."

The word was angrily murmured all over the deck.

Six turned his head and spit in the woman's face.

The murmurs turned to roars. Tamara rammed the butt of her blaster into Six's solar plexus. Six tensed slightly with the blow and smiled. "Go ahead. Do that once more. I dare you."

Tamara reversed her rifle and made ready her bayonet. "My pleasure."

"Hold!" Smythe looked at Six wearily. The burden of command was already like a stone around his neck. "Miss Tamara, clap Mr. Six in irons." He looked at the old captain's sword in his hand and pointed it out toward the dark waters of Thunder Bay. "Put him over the side."

Mildred exploded from the crowd. "You son of a bitch! You're just going to let the lampreys have him? Without any proof?"

It seemed mercy was as rare a commodity in Canada as it was in the Deathlands. Smythe stared at Mildred for long moments. "Fine, fill his pockets with rocks. Send him down quick."

Doc's sword rasped from its sheath as he stepped forward. "I would like to state categorically, publicly and for the record, that I trust Monsieur Six implicitly."

Six stared in shock. So did just about everyone else on deck.

"Doc…" Ryan warned.

"Furthermore, I do not believe a man of his moral courage and conviction could be complicit in such a heinous betrayal. I would like to further say it was he who pulled me forth from the jaws of the parasite-infected pigs in Borden, and for that I will be forever in his debt, and for whatever it is worth, he shall always have my fondest regards and friendship."

Six grinned delightedly.

The mob began muttering angrily.

Ryan kept one SIG on Six. The blaster in his left hand turned to cover Doc from the mob. "Doc…"

"And, perhaps first and foremost," Doc continued, "I shall not allow him to be lynched without further inquiry into the matter."

Smythe pointed his sword at Doc furiously. "I will send you down right next to him!"

"I will consider it an honor," Six declared.

Doc pulled himself up to his full height and cocked his left fist jauntily on his hip. He held his blade in front of him in a way that was just short of a low guard. He exposed his oddly perfect white teeth at Smythe. "Why, Captain, is that a sword I see in your hand?"

Smythe looked at his own blade and purpled. Everyone had seen Doc skewering stickie man, coldheart and pirate with impunity during the battle.

A voice rasped from the landing above. "The good doctor has asked for an inquiry, Smythe. I am afraid I demand one." Yoann Toulalan stood at the top of the steps. He looked like he should be on the last train west but he couldn't afford the ticket. Whatever was in his blood had eaten him down to skin and bones. All he wore was a blanket and a Diefenbunker Heckler & Koch MP-5 submachine gun. The day was calm. He swayed like a tree in a high breeze. His fevered eyes, his voice and his blaster were strangely steady. He rested the blaster across the spotted bandages covering his stump. Cyrielle Toulalan stood beside him. Her Diefenbunker C-7 carbine was shouldered and pointed straight at Smythe.

Smythe stared up their guns unflinchingly. "That's Captain Smythe to you, you half-chilled frog."

Crew, convoy and Islanders all looked around one another gripping their weapons, waiting for the fight to erupt and not exactly sure who they would have to chill first. More and more were looking toward Ryan.

The one-eyed man stepped up. "Captain, this is your ship, but I was the one asking the questions. I'd like to finish."

Smythe's knuckles were white around his blade of office. He was a sailing man, and it was clear he didn't intend to start his first day as a captain being told what to do. It was Seriah of all people who broke the standoff. She stepped away from Jak's side. "Ryan, we never enabled the computer on your LAV."

"Noticed," Ryan said coldly.

"The computer in the engineering LAV is up. If Six was

checking the com-link hub, our computer should have a log of it."

Ryan looked in Smythe's eyes and thought he had a good read on the man. He lowered his pistols. "With your permission?"

Smythe slammed his sword back in its sheath. "Do it."

Thunder Bay

CLOUDS ENSHROUDED the thousand-foot humped table of Mount McKay. Thunder rolled within them. The overcast day was turning raw as the convoy began to roll off the *Queen*. The computer had proved that Six had been checking the communications hub, but that was all it proved. Other than Yoann, Seriah and Doc no one in the convoy trusted Six. He had been relegated to a sec wag while a convoyman named Sebastien drove the engineering LAV. The losses during the attack had been bad. The *Queen* was down to a skeleton crew. The convoy had lost twelve, but Hunk and his nineteen surviving men of Manitoulin helped make up the difference. Despite being short-handed, Captain Smythe was sending Tamara and four crewmen to help insure the *Queen*'s interests.

The engineering LAV led the way off the pier. Her dozer blade scraped away saplings and undergrowth and pushed rubble out of the way. The wags were all buttoned up. The only men exposed were the men on the trucks manning the machine blasters and the men on cycles. They wore gloves and goggles and had scarves wrapped around their faces. Ryan shoved the big rig into gear and rolled off the ramp. Crewmen waved and cheered. Ryan gave them a honk of the air horn. The *Queen*'s steam whistles shrieked in return and the ramp started to rise as the last wag rolled off.

Krysty leaned her head against the window and sighed

wistfully as rain began misting the windshield. "Weather's turning."

"Cyrielle says it's the first storm of late summer, right on schedule." Ryan followed the path the LAV slowly cut through the downtown area. The needle of his rad counter was twitching ever upward into the yellow. He could see the crater of the missile hit through the shattered overgrown hulks of building near the downtown ahead. Sebastien had a Diefenbunker city map, and he was already swinging south toward the suburbs to avoid it. "Rain'll keep the dust down. It's in our favor."

Six's chicken-armored sec wag bounced by, riding outlier on its huge offroad tires. Six was driving and he wasn't alone. He still had two supporters. One was a woman named Camille manning the machine blaster in the back. She could have been Krysty's sister except that she was black-haired and yellow-skinned where Krysty was redheaded and fair. Riding shotgun was a horse of a woman named Marie-Laure. It was clear the two women were together. Rumor had it that one of their signing bonuses for convoy duty had been that when the convoy returned to Val-d'Or, Six had promised to give them both babies. Krysty sat up as the wag passed. She was taking her riding shotgun seriously and had a Diefenbunker MP-5 in her lap with a pair of mags banana-clipped together. "Ryan?"

"Yeah?"

"You think Six did it?"

It was something Ryan had been giving a lot of thought to. "Someone radioed Mace and Thorpe where we'd be. Someone cut the 'lectric fencing on the *Queen*. Six has the know-how and the motivation."

"So he did it."

"If I was sure I'd have chilled him already." The truck lurched over a bad patch. Ryan checked his mirror and saw the LAV behind them. "Hate to say it, but I can't help but think about what Doc said about him. Hard to imagine Doc's wrong on this one."

"And?"

"And if Six didn't do it, then sure as shit we need him."

Rain began sheeting down out of the sky. The Northern Lights pulsed through the bruised clouds, making the entire sky look like some kind of mutated, diseased digestive system hemorrhaging rain. The pounding on the cab seemed to be pushing Krysty down in her seat. "C'mon," Ryan tried. "You love the rain."

Krysty just shook her head and cringed at a sudden lightning flash over the mountain. Her prehensile red hair was laying flat against her head to match her mood. She shivered and hugged herself as thunder rolled. Her hair tightened and hugged her head. "Not this one."

Lightning cracked across the sky in forked bolts, and it seemed to dance around the thousand-foot peak of the mountain in the distance. Lightning cracked again and again and the thunder vibrated through the cab. Ryan hunched over the wheel and stared upward. Krysty sat up again.

"What?"

"Don't know."

Ryan loosened his SIG in its thigh holster and put his spare on the dash. He began counting seconds between lightning flash and thunder roll. "One...two..." Lightning split the sky and slammed into the exposed girders of a sagging building. Concrete and vegetation exploded with the hit, but that wasn't what Ryan was watching for.

"Gaia..." Krysty gasped.

"You saw it?"

"I saw it."

The lightning illuminated huge shapes wheeling and swooping in the clouds. To the big rig's left another offroad wag bounced over the raddled urban terrain. As scout, Donnie Goosekiller was crouched by the machine blaster man in the back. Ryan got on the radio. "Goose!"

"I saw it!" Goose said over the link. "The thunderbirds! Boo said he saw 'em once, but I never believed him!"

Six snarled over the radio. "You heard McKenzie! It is not just the rads that keep people away from this part of the Superior!"

Goose rattled on in fear and religious awe. "They say they sleep all winter in caves in the mountain. During spring and summer they take the big fish over the lakes by night. But when summer ends, they say they come out during the day to take the herds running before the freeze. But no one lives in Thunder Bay so—"

Donnie Goosekiller's transmission ended in a scream.

Ryan scooped up the blaster on the dash. "Fireblast!"

The one-eyed man had seen bald eagles before. He'd fought and killed screamwings. This was something else entirely—bigger, faster, and with an agenda in mind. Like all raptors it hit like a thunderbolt and from behind. Ryan saw giant wings, a glittering head and Donnie Goosekiller was plucked from the back of the wag like a rabbit in the talons of a hawk. The machine blaster man screamed and pumped rounds impotently into the sky as the thunderbird banked between two broken buildings and disappeared. Ryan watched as the giant eagle beat its way back up between the buildings and bore Donnie Goosekiller into the thunderstorm.

Shouts of alarm in French and English began clogging the link as the convoy became aware of the dark shapes circling above. Blasterfire popped and crackled into the heavens. Both Ryan and Krysty lurched back against their seats as something struck the front of the semi and the cab went dark. Ryan heard metal scream and he hit the dome light of the cab. The gray light outside suddenly flooded the cab.

A thunderbird sat perched on the hood. It was huge. Its wings and chest had occluded the cab windows on landing, but now it pulled back. It was like a bald eagle, but where a bald eagle's head plumage was white, quicksilver scales overlapped the thunderbird's head like the blades of knives. The scales ran down its chest like an armored vest and across its shoulders in a line out to the wingtips.

Its body was bigger than the semi's cab, and it looked big enough to fly off with a buffalo.

Huge talons crunched into the hood of the semi. The steel crumpled as the claws contracted to get a good grip. The thunderbird's amber eyes never left Ryan's single orb as it pulled back its head and then slammed its silver scimitar beak forward. The windshield radiated cracks from the impact point like a blaster shot.

Ryan knew with absolute certainty the thunderbird had cracked a wag before.

"Take the wheel!" Ryan rolled out of the driver's seat and lunged back into the sleeper cabin. The giant eagle shook its head in a spray of rain and pulled back to strike again. Ryan popped the gunner's hatch in the cab and ripped the waxed canvas off the machine blaster's action. "Hey!"

The thunderbird eyed the half-exposed human and flapped its wings and lunged forward. Ryan cut loose, burning his belt straight into the giant bird's center body mass. It didn't exactly throw sparks, but Ryan was appalled to note that he could see lead spalling and bits of broken lead ruffling black feathers as his 5.56 mm bullets failed to penetrate the thunderbird's body scales. The mutant avian recoiled slightly under the one-hundred-round high-velocity beating.

Ryan burned his belt dry and snarled as he clawed for his SIG to shoot for the eyes. Krysty hit the air-horn, but the giant bird didn't seem particularly intimidated. One set of

talons crunched into the top of the cab. The other set opened
for Ryan like a flower.

Six's voice matched the storm thunder for thunder.
"Come!"

The thunderbird craned around to peer at this new devel-
opment. Camille was gone, and Six had jumped out of his
sec wag. He stood exposed to the elements and any avian that
wanted to scoop him up.

His guide blaster spun in his hand and the .45-70 thudded
like a mortar round. A scale in the chest of the raptor burst.
The thunderbird's scream nearly burst Ryan's eardrums, and
it thrashed brokenly for altitude. Six flicked his lever and
fired again. "Come to Six!" A second scale burst next to the
first, right over the thunderbird's heart. The creature's head
and neck flopped like a dying snake and it fell backward,
bouncing off the hood to the mud of the road.

Ryan grabbed the sides of the hatch as the semi bucked,
and Krysty crushed the thunderbird beneath her wheels.

Six stared skyward into the rain as he pushed fresh shells
into his gleaming blaster.

Ryan slid down and slammed the hatch shut. He scooped
up his Scout. Krysty cried out in alarm. "Lover! No!"

The machine blasters couldn't be traversed to vertical, and
the Diefenbunker blasters wouldn't serve to pierce the thunderbirds' armored plumage. Ryan went out the door. Six was
drawing a bead on a thunderbird circling high over the engineering LAV. Behind him another thunderbird was silently
plummeting out of the sky for him with its wings folded like
a huge black fist.

"Six! Behind you!" Ryan snapped the Scout to shoulder
and fired, flicked the bolt and fired again. It seemed Canadian military full-metal-jacketed 7.62 mm rounds were up to
the task. The thunderbird nosed over from the two head shots

and dropped earthward out of control. Six leaped aside as the giant eagle hit the ground in a geyser of mud.

"The trailer!" Ryan shouted. Six scanned the skies while Ryan jumped onto the semi's trailer bed and climbed to the top of a pyramid of tarped and palletted goods. Ryan swung his muzzle skyward. "Go!"

Six ran for the trailer and clambered up next to him. The two men stood back to back. The thunderbirds had seen two of their number taken and now wheeled high above in the clouds, looking for any sign of weakness. Ryan kicked the back of the cab. "Krysty! Go!"

Krysty hit the air-horn short and sharp three times to signal the convoy to moved forward. Six clicked his com unit. *"Allez! Allez! Allez!"*

The convoy ground forward in the sheeting rain. Above, the thunderbirds wheeled and danced in thunder and lightning. The engineering LAV carved a path through the overgrown streets of Thunder Bay. It was slow going but the convoy moved forward. Six and Ryan watched the skies. The big sec man was speaking rapid French as the convoy turned onto an ancient highway.

"This is the 61!" Six shouted. "Cyrielle says we take it north for about five kilometers! It will take us to the Trans-Canada!"

Ryan and Six maintained their sodden vigil. The 61 turned into the Trans-Canada. Since the hard freeze killed almost all plants except the trees, nothing had been able to take root and rip up the highway. The roadway was cracked and raddled. A few rusted-out hulks of ancient wags blocked the road here and there, but mostly the lanes of the highway were wide and clear.

Ryan nearly went flying as Krysty slammed on the brakes. Six slipped down the side of the tarped pallet and sat hard on the trailer bed. *"Merde!* What's wrong, lover!"

Ryan stared.

The ancient road sign sagged on its one remaining support. The green paint and white lettering had long ago faded. New lettering had been painted on it in letters three feet tall. A sentence ran from edge to edge in bright red that was running like blood in the rain: RYANS WOMAN IS A MUTIE.

Chapter Twenty-One

Engineering LAV

Seriah spoke quietly after the lovemaking. "Is it true?"

Jak tensed. "Krysty?"

"Yeah."

"Yeah." Jak's ruby-red eyes burned into Seriah's brown ones in the light of the single candle. His voice turned ice cold. "Problem?"

Seriah flinched. "No. I...I ain't got no problem with muties, but a lot of people do. Val-d'Or prides itself on being rad free, mutie free ..." The little wrench's voice dropped to a whisper. "Clean."

Jak stared up at the steel ceiling. He had a congenital condition rather than a Deathlands-induced mutation, but he suspected he wouldn't have seen five minutes of life if he had been born in Val-d'Or.

The rain hadn't stopped. The convoy was circled in the parking lot of a ruined mall, which had turned into a field. Krysty hadn't left the sleeper cab of the semi. No one in the convoy had dared broach the subject to Ryan. The one-eyed man had silently taken his and Krysty's supper from the chuck wagon and joined her. Jak was pretty sure Ryan considered the matter closed until someone was stupe enough to bring it up to his face. But both Ryan and the semi were getting a lot of long hard looks. The rainy weather hadn't done Yoann any favors, and he had slumped back into fevered unconsciousness. Cyrielle hadn't left his side. Six had taken de facto command to get the camp established. His orders had been obeyed, but he received sullen looks and muttered insults behind his back that no one would have ever dared before. Jak had been giving the big man some thought. "Six?"

Seriah giggled, glad for the change of subject. She shifted her body in the two zipped-together sleeping bags to snuggle in closer. "Jak, I swear you talk less than Boo Blacktree."

"Like him," Jak acknowledged. Blacktree had been as silent as a stone since the eagles had carried away Donnie Goosekiller.

Seriah nuzzled the long line of an ancient knife wound that raddled Jak's ribs and changed the subject. "You have a lot of scars."

"Some have more," Jak said finally.

"Bet they do," Seriah admitted. "But I like kissing yours."

Jak's muscles tightened involuntarily as Seriah began tracing battle lines old and new that crisscrossed Jak's body with her tongue. He forced out the name at hand again. "Six?"

Seriah stopped and was quiet for several moments. Her hand strayed south and gave Jak a squeeze. "You know I like you?"

"Can tell," Jak groaned.

Seriah's voice went deadly serious. "I'll tell you. Old Vinny is about as bad as they come. He'd give you a nasty run for your jack. Your one-eyed, chilling friend Ryan don't want to meet up with Six on a dark night in the woods. Mace Henning's been offering shiny silver coins for one of Vincent's ears to any and all for years now. Six ain't nice but he'll get you through. He was a wandering sec man like Mace Henning back in the day. But the day Baron Toulalan hired on Six, Val-d'Or just kept getting stronger and better organized, and Six found a home. Swore his allegiance. Six loves that old man, and that old man loves him."

"And betrayed him? His son? Convoy?" Jak asked.

Seriah was quiet again. "I can't imagine it."

"Someone did."

Seriah shuddered. "I know."

All Jak could do was hug her closer.

"I'm scared," she said.

"Six wants Cyrielle."

"Everyone knows it."

"Wants Mildred."

"He wants Mildred because he can't have Cyrielle, and he ain't seen nothing that dark and pleasing in Canada in quite some time."

"He want you?" Jak asked.

Seriah tensed slightly. "He made it known, a while back."

"And?"

"He coulda took it. No one would've stopped him."

"And?"

"I was saving it for someone special. He let me alone."

"Your special," Jak asked. "Chilled?"

"Yeah, during a raid. Few months back at the start of the thaw."

Jak slid a hand across Seriah's belly. "Now you're pregnant."

She flinched beneath the blankets. "You can't tell anyone!"

Jak shrugged. "No secret soon."

"Promise!"

Jak pulled Seriah closer and breathed in her hair. "Promise." He cradled her head closer to look at his chron. "My watch."

Seriah gave Jak another squeeze down low. "Stay."

Jak clicked his com. "Ryan."

Ryan came back instantly. By his tone of voice he wasn't happy and hadn't been sleeping. "Jak."

"Switch watches?"

Seriah squeezed a little lower and elicited another groan out of Jak. Ryan made an amused noise. "No problem."

Jak clicked off. "Four hours."

Seriah kneeled up out of the sleeping bags and presented her hindquarters to the young warrior. "Make 'em count, Jak."

Jak rose and cracked his knuckles. Seriah giggled.

RYAN APPROACHED SIX through the rain. The sec man was wearing a poncho against the downpour. He occasionally brought up a pair of the precious few night-vision goggles they had and examined the terrain around them. Ryan wore his long coat, and his scarf was draped over his head to form a voluminous hood. "Six."

The man didn't turn. "Ryan."

The Deathlands warrior got to the point. "Do I have a problem?"

Six tossed off a shrug. "You have brought mutie filth among us."

Ryan just managed to keep his panga in its sheath. "And?"

Six shrugged again. "You are our war chief, upon the water and upon the land. All have seen your prowess in battle and know your wisdom." Six sighed philosophically. "It will take a disaster or two more before the convoy starts to turn on you, and her. I would keep her out of sight."

"I won't do that."

Six looked at Ryan for long moments and shrugged again.

Ryan's eye narrowed. "What're you thinking?"

"There is a creek on Cyrielle's map, not far from here. It leads back to the Superior." Six pointed north. "I think it would be best if I took a canoe and left."

Ryan felt the cold in the evening breeze and rain. "Doubt you could make Val-d'Or before winter without a wag."

"I could winter on Manitoulin. Baron Poncet is always

looking for good men." Six slowly shook his head. "Perhaps I would stay on come the spring."

"Stay here. Your people need you."

The massive shoulders sagged. Six's voice almost broke. "I'm not trusted anymore."

"Well—" Ryan tossed a shrug of his own "—Doc trusts you."

Six almost smiled. "Yes." He sighed and looked at Ryan frankly. "Is he truly mad?"

"It comes and goes, less often in days gone by, but I wouldn't call him crazy."

"Oh, and what would you call him?"

"Loyal," Ryan replied.

Six turned his gaze back upon the darkness and slowly nodded. "Yes, indeed."

"But if you're looking to hang a word on it, I'd call him damaged."

Six nodded and went back to staring out into the dark, wet night.

"Who do you think betrayed us?" Ryan asked.

"You do not think it was me?" Six countered.

Ryan had considered his answer. "I'm betting it wasn't you."

Six was silent for long moments. "Someone knew the *Queen*'s defenses and had the skill to sabotage them. That same person has been giving away our positions, and dispositions. I suspect they left a Diefenbunker radio for Mace to find with a secret frequency to use."

"Who do you think did it?"

"I do not believe it was Yoann or Cyrielle. If they wished to cut a deal with Mace, they would just do it. If it were myself, I would simply give him the location of our prize, leave the convoy, receive the reward and take service with him. I'll tell you that I have eliminated you and your friends as suspects. I don't suspect young Hunk or any of his islanders."

"Anyone high on your list?"

Six glowered balefully into the dark. "Sebastien is high on my list. As a sec man he is rash and quick to trigger. He resents the fact that I haven't promoted or rewarded him as he thinks he deserves. I chose him for the convoy and put him on LAV duty because he is a good wag driver."

"Anyone else?"

Six's voice went low as if now he thought someone might be listening. "Boo Blacktree."

Ryan had to admit he was surprised. "Really?"

"He and Goosekiller were issued a radio unit. He is a free-scout. I was a free-blaster once. Scouts and sec men need to find a home before they die alone in the cold. Goosekiller hadn't a devious bone in his body. Blacktree is deep."

"He fought hard on the *Queen*."

"He killed stickie men, mutant filth, and rewards require risk. Listen, Ryan, whoever is betraying us doesn't yet know our final destination or the prize. If they did, Mace would have jumped ahead of us for it, or the final battle would have been joined."

"Anyone else you want to point your finger at?"

"Tamara."

"She fought awful hard at the Soo Locks."

"She has the requisite skills, and Mace needed Thorpe humbled before he could recruit him as an ally. Besides she was born in Mace's territory, and why be the armorer of a ship when you can be an armorer for the baron of all of Canada."

"You don't trust much, do you?"

"I trust you, Ryan, to do whatever you have to for your people. Even if it means your life. I respect that, but it doesn't mean I trust you to do what is in Val-d'Or's best interest."

"And I trust you to do what is best for Val-d'Or, not necessarily what's best for me and my people."

"Then we understand each other, Ryan." Six shrugged. "However, if it makes you feel any better, I trust Doc implicitly."

Ryan smiled slightly. "You and me both."

"Go AWAY, Doc!" Krysty's snarl from inside the sleeper cab was low and full of menace. Doc stood outside in the morning rain feeling foolish. He waved the trencher board he held at the tinted glass of the sleeper cab's porthole.

"It is the last of the pancakes. I have covered them with my kerchief, but if you do not open your door they will be cold and sodden in but moments."

No response came back.

"Young Hunk Poncet has sent along a pot of hawberry jam with his compliments."

"That's because he's young, dumb and wants a piece of scarlet pussy."

Doc recoiled. He had seen and experienced more degradation than he cared to think about in this new world he found himself in. Women using uncultured language still shocked him. He sought about his mind for a response. "Well, who does not?"

Doc blushed furiously, then was horrorstruck at the comment. Dread silence met his remark. He was surprised to see the passenger door open. Krysty had a smile that could light up an entire ville when it was genuine, and she favored Doc with one now. "Doc, that may be the nicest thing you've ever said to me."

"Even in these perilous times I think it best to let the truth be known though the heavens fall." This elicited a smirk out of Krysty. Doc held up the steaming, kerchief-covered platter of food. "Please accept these pancakes in the spirit of love, respect and affection with which they are presented."

"I'll accept your pancakes, Doc. With love, respect and affection."

"I am immensely gratified."

"Gratitude is all mine, Doc. Thanks."

Doc basked in happiness as Krysty took the food.

"Doc?"

"Yes, Krysty?"

"You're standing in the rain."

"Oh, well, yes, so it seems," Doc blustered. "Thank you."

"Doc, get out of the rain or put on a poncho."

"Right you are! Bless you!" Doc spun on his heel and strode toward the tent in the middle of the wag circle. He followed the smell of coffee. That the Diefenbunker coffee bags were growing low and limp was of great concern to the whole convoy. Despite coffee's lack of nutritional value, no one was in any hurry to go back to pine needle tea.

Ryan, Six, Cyrielle, Hunk, J.B., Jak and Boo Blacktree were having a strategy session. Doc craned over the crouching council.

Cyrielle didn't like what she was hearing. "It sounds like suicide."

Ryan was adamant. "It has to be done."

"We have only two motorcycles left," Six said.

Jak had to agree. "Cycle noisy. Land open. Hard creep. Sentries'll see."

"Then we go on foot," Ryan said. "We've got to shake them off before we get to where we're going. If we take their fuel, I bet Thorpe will call it quits. Even most of Mace's men won't want to keep heading west with no juice. They'll head back for the Lakes on fumes and paddle back for the locks to beat the freeze."

"You and Six taught them to keep a loose tail," J.B. cautioned. "On foot? What if you miss them? For that matter, how are you extracting without getting ridden down?"

There was only one choice as far as Ryan could see. "Steal one of their wags, or cycles."

Six scowled at the map. "Many ifs."

Hunk shook his head. "Don't like it."

"You need horses," Doc suggested.

Everyone around the council circle was silent.

"Not many people keep horses," Cyrielle said.

"Mostly people just eat 'em," Hunk added.

"They are very expensive to keep during the winter," Six agreed. "Most keep dogsleds, skates and skis for the freeze, using the waters during the summer.

Doc peered around. "There are horses in Canada, I gather?"

"Mostly wild herds."

Doc raised a quizzical eyebrow. "None are domesticated? Not even in the western prairies? Say Alberta, Saskatchewan, pray, perhaps even Manitoba in which we are about to enter?"

Everyone looked at Boo Blacktree. He'd been farther west in the country than anyone else. The huge scout slowly nodded. "There's horse barons, out on the plains. Don't have villes as such. Nomads. They take their herds north in spring. Fatten 'em up on green grass, clean water and have 'em breed where there's no rads. Then they head south come the cold. On the way they trade with villes. Horse-powered labor for ville folk to get things done before the freeze and horseflesh for them to smoke and winter on. Do that till they get back to their winter pastures in the Deathlands." Boo looked up into the rain. "They'll be headin' south now. We head west, we gotta run into them."

Everyone stared. It was more words than Boo had spoken the whole trip.

Ryan nodded. "Good thinkin', Doc."

"Oh, well, it is nothing. I am sure any one of you would have intuited it."

"I need four for the war party," Ryan said. "Who here besides my people can ride?"

Six smiled as Fate continued to rain on him. "It has been a long time, but in my youth, I was a sec man for a trio of allied villes. They were wag poor, and each kept a small herd for postal riders and to be able to send out 'dragoons,' as Doc has mentioned."

Ryan didn't envy the horse that had to carry Six. "Blacktree?"

"Nope." Boo shook his head. It was the first time Ryan had seen the big man look leery. "Been kicked by one, though."

"I believe by now I am an accomplished equestrian," Doc said. "It was not so once."

"We'll take Jak," Ryan said.

Doc deflated.

"I was chattin' up Tamara…" Hunk said.

Ryan cocked his head at the young man. "Oh?"

"Well, she mostly prefers you," Hunk admitted, "but she was braggin' that no man could outshoot her, outpaddle her, or outride her. Not sure what kind of ridin' she meant. Not really quite sure what kind of paddling neither, but—"

"I'll talk to her," Ryan said.

Six nodded. "This is something Mace won't suspect."

Ryan rose. "I want to keep it that way. Cyrielle, you're going to collect every com unit. J.B., I want you to disable every radio except the one in our LAV. From now on it's mirrors, hand signals and smoke till I say different."

Chapter Twenty-Two

The Canadian prairie opened up in front of the convoy. The giant grass grew taller than the wags. The stalks had turned yellow with the late summer. The mutated grass sent forth its seeds like dandelions, and the air was full of floating white seed parachutes the size of grens. It was like being in a snowstorm in the middle of summer. Ryan tried to point out the beauty of what nature had wrought in Canada, but Krysty wasn't having it. She spent her time angrily lurking in the sleeper cab and spelling Ryan behind the wheel. He could see the beauty of it, but by all rumors death lurked in the long grass. Whatever form death took on the prairie, so far it seemed unwilling to take a crack at so many armed and armored wags.

This section of the Trans-Canada was remarkably well preserved. The giant grass couldn't seem to gain any purchase where the asphalt had once been. A smaller, greener variety pushed its way up through the concrete instead, forming a "green highway" that was easy to follow. Where the green grass started to rise in wag-threatening prominence or belts of giant grass had intruded, the dozer blade of the engineering LAV sheared the stalks and ground them beneath the wheels like an angry harvester.

Nevertheless it was fairly slow-going and met with occasional brutal encounters with rusted-out wag hulks that appeared out of the grass. Ryan and Krysty switched stints standing in the machine-gun nest over the cab, watching the road from the tallest position in the convoy. Ryan looked back with a frown for the hundredth time as they left the Lake of the Woods in their wake. Even where the convoy had been forced to leave the Trans for a stretch, they left an almost perfectly manicured path for Mace and Thorpe to follow.

Something was going to have to be done about that.

That something came along as they crossed into Manitoba.

Boo Blacktree knelt with one palm on the cracked asphalt of the Trans-Canada. He looked northward. "They're coming."

"Better not be another heard of goddamn pigs," Mildred muttered.

Blacktree said he had seen signs of the horse barons on this patch of land before. Between Winnipeg and Lake of the Woods, it formed a two-hundred-klick choke point where they were likely to meet one of the easternmost migrations.

Ryan turned his eye on a pothole the morning rain had turned into a puddle. The muddy water was very slightly but very distinctly shaking. The curtains of grass taller than a man had been trampled and shorn by the vast herds bison, elk, deer and wild mustangs that were migrating south. Clumps of giant grass that the herds had missed in their haste formed forlorn islands dotting the landscape.

"These horse barons," Ryan asked. "Are they First Nations?"

"First Nations, Canuck, Deathlander, all mixed. Say the first ones were the French who fled St. Boniface when the Peg got hit. Say they even take muties as long as…" Blacktree trailed off uncomfortably under Ryan's gaze.

"As long as they're useful and not too deformed," Ryan finished. He'd heard it all too often.

"Yup."

"They friendly?"

"Like anybody else." Blacktree had become downright

chatty since Goosekiller had left him to vocally fend for himself. "See an opportunity, they'll take it. You weak, they raid. You in a strong place, or stronger, they'll trade or go around."

Ryan raised his Navy longeye and looked out at the northern horizon. The rain kept down the dust, but there was a wavy line appearing right at the edge of sight. The line slowly resolved. It was horses. Hundreds of them. Ryan watched the line resolve into a sea of churning hooves and bobbing heads. They were already growing shaggy, corded winter coats that would allow them to survive the northern winter and the Deathlands harsh ultraviolet radiation. The riders were as wild and woolly as their mounts. They were mostly dressed in breechclouts, leggings and deerskin shirts like a horde of mountain man Mongols. Most carried black-smithed muzzle-loading muskets or longblasters. A few had more modern equipment. Some few had bows and lances but not many, and the lances mostly seemed to be used for carrying banners.

Ryan looked at J.B. where he stood in the LAV's commander hatch. "Flare."

J.B. raised the flare blaster and sent a burning red star into the blue skies over the prairie. Thirty riders detached from the horde and galloped toward the convoy. J.B. trained the LAV's turret on them. The horsemen came to a halt. The banner man carried a lance bearing a black pennant emblazoned with a white skull with a broken jaw.

Ryan stepped forward and gazed up at the leader.

He was a big man, tall and rangy. He had a strong, pointed chin that he took the time to shave. A wolfskin was draped over his shoulders, with the taxidermied head forming a hood. Wire-rimmed glasses hung incongruously on his nose and gave him the look of an intellectual savage. A long, flat, fish-shaped club hung from a thong on his wrist. A heavy-caliber, double-barrel, predark hunting blaster rested across his thighs.

Ryan slowly raised a canteen and took a sip. He capped it and tossed it to the horse lord. The man caught it and took a huge swallow. He gasped as the hawberry brandy burned like sweet gasoline down his throat. "What rad crater did you brew this in?" He capped it and made to toss it back.

Ryan gestured for him to keep it. "Compliments of the Lakes."

The man nodded and shoved the canteen in his saddlebag. "Compliments back."

"Baron...?" Ryan asked.

"Sternzon," the baron replied.

"I'm Ryan Cawdor, commander of this convoy."

Baron Sternzon took in the convoy. The iron wags were giving him serious pause. "Never heard of you."

"I am an ally of Baron Luc Toulalan of Val-d'Or."

"Heard of him. He's a long ways east." Sternzon leaned on his saddle horn casually. "Saw your signal. What do you want?"

Ryan shrugged. "Horses."

Sternzon rolled his eyes in amusement. "Got those. How many you want?"

"Eight."

"Eight?" Baron Sternzon sighed. The convoy was rich beyond the dreams of avarice in goods. Eight horses was going to get Baron Sternzon precious little of it.

"Eight."

J.B. spoke from the turret. "And blasters."

Baron Sternzon stared at the convoy bristling with out-of-the-box Diefenbunker specials. "You want blasters? From me?"

"Eight." J.B. nodded. He pointed at the baron's banner man

and his home-rolled bison blaster. "Like his .54 caliber. Or bigger."

Sternzon warmed to haggling. "Now my brother Todd has counted on that old horse-leg for some serious killing."

J.B. held up a C-8 carbine with the bayonet attached. "Count more with this."

Todd just about jumped out of his saddle. "Good trade!"

"Two for eight," J.B. insisted. "Spare mag each, all mags filled."

It was still a ridiculous trade. Todd passed his open hand over his fist in the age-old gesture. "Done!"

Baron Sternzon shifted in his saddle. This was too good to be true. "Horses?"

Ryan nodded. "Two for eight, spare mag each, all mags filled."

Sternzon passed his hand over his fist warily. "Done."

"You pick out the horses, best you got that no one's riding."

Sternzon nodded slowly. It was a compliment and a dare to cheat them. "Done." He struggled to keep his poker face. It was clear to him that these people were insane. They also happened to be insanely wealthy, and if they let primo blasters flow through their hands like water, they might as well flow to him and his band. "Good trade."

Ryan cocked his head judiciously. "Now you got some men blasterless."

Sternzon snorted. "We'll manage."

"Want more?"

Sternzon stopped just short of drooling. "Might."

"Got Mace Henning after us."

"Heard of him." Sternzon's face went flat. "And?"

"Want you to wait a day, meet up with him right here, same way you met with us. Tell him we went south."

"Don't think Mace is gonna thank me for that."

Cyrielle raised her little chin imperiously. "You will have the thanks of Baron Luc Toulalan."

"You know, lady, I respect you," Sternzon said, "but I just don't get across the Ottawa much."

Hunk thumped his chest. "You'll have the thanks of Baron Poncet of Manitoulin."

Sternzon peered down his nose at Hunk. "We get to Hawberry Island even less."

His men laughed. Hunk flushed. Ryan put a restraining hand on Hunk's shoulder. Boo Blacktree took a step forward. "You'll have the thanks of Jon Hard-knife and the First Nations."

Baron Sternzon chewed that one over. "Well, now, all this thanks is something, but thanks just don't fill any mags for me."

Cyrielle gestured at the weapon Todd was happily fondling. "Five more just like it."

"Ten."

"Done."

Sternzon scowled the scowl of a horse trader who knew he'd under bid.

"When you see Mace," Ryan said, "tell him during the trading one of your men heard something about a bunker and that we were asking about the Rat River."

"All right." Sternzon looked back at his herd. "Tell you what. I'll send about half south now. That'll cover any tracks you were supposed to have laid."

"Appreciate that. We'll take four more horses for meat, but tonight I invite you to join us at our fires. We got food like you ain't ever seen."

"You got everything like I ain't never seen. I'm bringing ten of my best, and your convoy will be surrounded."

"Bring twenty," Ryan said.

"Well, you're generous, I give you that."

"That's because I got a favor to ask."

Sternzon stiffened. "What kind of favor?"

Ryan made a dismissive gesture. "I'll ask after you've tried the poutine."

DIEFENBUNKER FRIES and cheese curds smothered in gravy had put Baron Sternzon in a very reasonable mood. Ryan mounted up. It had been several weeks since he'd sat on a horse, and he knew he was going to be sore the following day. Sternzon had picked him out an excellent pair of muscular, piebald mares with the creative names of Bullet and Blaster. Part of Ryan was relishing the chance to be on a good horse and let it stretch out in open country. Six and his horse regarded each other with great wariness as he clambered into the saddle. The mare had already thrown him twice, but Six was a "get back on the horse" kind of man. Jak sat astride a dreadlocked pinto gelding like he didn't have a care in the world. Tamara was feeding her roan a steady diet of baby talk and dried fruit slices, and the love affair between them was growing deeper by the second. Ryan clicked at his horse and the war party trotted over to the fighting LAV.

J.B. sat with his bound leg lying along the loading ramp as he examined what he had wrought. Ryan glanced at the weapons J.B. had traded for. They were all of a type, muzzle-loading, fairly short-barreled percussion cap rifles firing black powder. J.B. raised a .60-caliber weapon and checked the action a last time. "What're you thinking, J.B.?"

"Mace is burning alcohol. Doubt he has a semi like ours dragging it. I'm thinking he'll have two or three small trucks. Diesel doesn't burn or explode easy. Alcohol burns just fine. Figure mebbe it'd be easier to put a few holes in those tanks at range rather than trying to sneak up and fix a bomb to them."

"Range is good."

"Took some red phosphorous from one of the LAV grens. Wanted to add a little burn to the bullets. You each got two shots. Each blaster is sighted in for approximately two hundred yards."

Mildred handed up a pair of longblasters to each party member and they stuck them in the saddle scabbards. Ryan leaned down as she paused by him. "Yeah?"

Mildred spoke low. "Get back quick."

"I will."

"Listen, Yoann still can't stand up for more than ten seconds without fainting and J.B.'s got a bum leg. Half the people in the convoy are back to believing that Jak is a mutie, and they don't like it. You and Six are the two civilizing authority figures around here. I've heard grumbling while I've been tending wounds. Some around here might just take it in mind to do something stupid. That Sebastien talks real nasty when he's got some liquor in him and thinks no one important is listening. I'm gonna bunk with Krysty until you get back."

Ryan had heard the grumblings, as well. "I spoke to Hunk. He's going to keep an eye out for you."

Mildred smirked. "Well, now, I have love in my heart for that little beanpole, baron-in-the-making." She grew serious again. "Just get your ass back quick."

Jak reached back and checked a pair of bulging, jingling saddlebags on his horse. While J.B. had spent the day hand-loading and gunsmithing, Jak had spent the day with the engineering LAV's welder. Even the poorest ville's blacksmith could make a nail, but boxes of ready-made, galvanized nails traded about equal to bullets and the Diefenbunker outfitters had included both for use by staff and as trade goods. Jak had literally bent them to a use the Diefenbunker Table of Organization people had never intended.

"Thanks, Jak." Ryan looked at his war party. They were traveling light. Besides blasters and tools of the trade, they were carrying little besides a few cakes of pemmican and a waterskin each. The job at hand would get done quick or it wouldn't get done at all.

"Well," Ryan said. "Let's go join the horde."

RYAN WATCHED as Mace Henning consulted with Baron Sternzon.

A mob of horsemen confronted a mob of men on motorcycles. Ryan wasn't worried about being spotted. He was just one more mounted man in the Hunlike horde milling on the plain. Jak and Six were pulled well back out of sight. Ryan hunched beneath his buffalo robe and watched the proceedings. Sternzon and Henning spoke out in the open beneath white pennants of peace with a few sec men by their side. Both barons knew they couldn't take the other easily in an open fight, so the meeting was fairly cordial. They passed a skin of fermented mare's milk as they talked. Sternzon point south toward the Rat River, and Ryan watched Mace's face as he considered this bit of news. Baron Sternzon's script was simple, and he seemed to be sticking to it. The convoy had gone south. Sternzon was on a tight schedule to get to his winter pasturage and wanted no part of a battle between eastern barons, pirate kings and Deathlanders. He thought the convoy was insane to be so far from home this late in the season but they had too many blasters to argue with, much less attack. Sternzon, himself, would be happy to sell Mace as many horses as he wanted.

Ryan watched Mace closely but so was every member of Sternzon's horde who didn't have something better to do. Tamara sat her horse beside Ryan. She was wearing skins, her hair was braided and with her face painted she looked nothing at all like the *Queen of the Lakes* armorer's mate. "What do ya think?"

Ryan watched Mace think. "He's going to have to send reinforced scouting parties both south and west to try and reestablish contact with the convoy, and that suits me just fine."

Baron Sternzon had been good enough to send out portions of his heard west, as well, to help cover the convoy's tracks. The horde on the whole thought this was a very amusing trick. Tamara's joy was open as she smelled the big, fat kill. "And?"

"And I think he's going to stop right here. Probably buy some horses from Sternzon for fresh meat, and feed and rest his men until the scouts come back."

"And?"

Ryan read Mace's brutal face. The man looked south and west. He was no fool, and he was looking for the rub, the angle or the trap. That was in Ryan's favor. All too often in the century they lived in the rub was that things just sucked and there was no getting around it. Mace Henning just wasn't expecting Mildred's reverse *Road Warrior* attack on his tankers.

"And I think he's going to pull up his tankers, circle his cycles and ask for it from all eight of our barrels."

Tamara grinned delightedly. "You are one sexy, one-eyed son of a gaudy slut, I'll give you that."

The red mist of anger started to fill his mind, but Ryan reined in his temper. "Son of a baron's lady."

"Even better." Tamara leaned over in the saddle. "You sure you don't want none of this? It ain't flame-colored, but it's wet for you."

Ryan half successfully kept a smile off his face. He could forgive a crack blaster-shot almost anything. "You blow me a tanker, we'll talk."

"Blow anything you want, Ryan."

Mace and Sternzon nodded at each other respectfully and rode back to their men. Horsemen blew bison horns in long, lowing calls to get the herd moving. Ryan and Tamara slipped into the swirling mass of men and beasts. "We go with the herd, three miles mebbe, then we double back wide from the east. Any luck, and we hit Mace tonight."

Chapter Twenty-Three

Mace stood in the dark and wet. He didn't like being stationary in what could only be considered enemy territory without a ville's walls around him. Like most pirates Thorpe and his men got downright skittish being more than a day's ride from open water. It was raining again. Sternzon's herd and horde had torn up the ground for klicks in all directions, and now the trail was turning into a morass. Mace looked back at his forces. Except for the pickets, all the men on watch were hunched over fires. The other half off watch hung from the sagging hammock poles like sodden sausages. The pirates slept on their blankets even more miserably in the mud.

Mace glanced at his pride and joy, and the key to the whole venture.

There were actually two pride and joys and one weak sister, but they had done yeoman's work. He gazed upon a pair of gleaming white MD 950 sanitation service trucks. Mace had found them in one of the northernmost abandoned villes. They had been abandoned during the first great southern exodus out of Canada during skydark and the nuclear winter. To Mace's great amusement, Tag had explained that in predark times people paid to have their shit sucked up and wagged away. To Mace's even greater amusement Tag told him they had been called "honey trucks." It pleased Mace immensely that the rad-blasted bastards who had cracked the world had a sense of humor. The Ford F550 Super Duty trucks were four-wheel drive with 3,600-liter tanks in their beds. The men who had abandoned them had put them up on blocks to spare their tires, and there were spare tires in the warehouse, as well. They had to have thought after the world died there would be a renewed need for shit haulers.

They were Mace's honey wags now.

He had forced his men to boil the tanks clean and now rather than shit or honey they were filled with 106 octane, double-distilled alcohol from beet sugar he demanded as tribute from one of the southernmost villes in his sphere. Men, women and children had broken their backs from spring to fall and starved in the snow after harvest to fill his tanks with go juice.

The weak sister was a battered panel van with a smaller 1,500-liter tank from the same ancient warehouse bolted into the interior. It was having a hard time keeping up and had broken down numerous times, but the van and its crew kept arriving. Sometimes days late. In a strange sense Mace didn't like seeing his tankers. He liked them on back roads rather than in camp with the firelight playing on them. On the other hand they gave him a sense of security. Even with Thorpe's pirates festooning every wag his force was lean and tight. He had enough juice to follow Yoann Toulalan as well as Six and that one-eyed chiller from Deathlands. He would follow them to the Cific if need be. He would follow them until skydark came along again. In the end. He would have them. He'd have a black ear, a cold blue eye, Cyrielle Toulalan and Val-d'Or. Everyone else of use would swear fealty. Anyone who didn't would burn in his fires while his men danced jigs and reels till dawn. Mace played his future victories in his mind over and over in ever glowing detail.

He heard squelching in the mud and knew Tag was deliberately making noise so that he wouldn't get blasted by mistake. "Any word on the radio?"

"No, Mace. They know they have traitors among them.

If I had to bet, One-Eye has collected all the com units and given them out only to people he trusts."

Mace smiled grimly in the dark. "And how many do you think he can trust?"

Mace could almost hear Tag smiling back. The mutie loved strategy the same way Shorty loved violence. "Precious few, Mace. You've seen to that."

"Think it's enough?"

Tag considered the cards they had played. "Yoann is worm-bit, and by all accounts a step away from being worm food. No one trusts Six. One-Eye is a mutie-lover. The French love Cyrielle, but not as a war leader. One more nudge and they'll break apart."

"So, let's say you're One-Eye," Mace posed. "What would you do?"

"Easy answer is to head for that bunker. Burrow in like a tick. We back off or end up freezing."

"But he knows he's got a traitors among 'em. He knows someone might just open a door or a hatch one dark night for us."

"True enough."

"And I didn't ask what the easy answer was, Tag. I asked you what you'd do."

Tag had a ready answer. "Something desperate, something dangerous, something unexpected."

"You'd counterattack." Mace nodded. "It's what he would do, as well."

"Would if I could, Mace, but we got pickets and scouts out klicks in all directions, and we got reinforced scouting parties having a look both west and south. No way they can sneak one of those big iron battle wags past us, even if they did, we got Nolan on the recoilless to answer."

"They're nightcreeping us," Mace said. "I feel it."

"Don't see how—"

Both men started at the sound of the blaster shot. Mace recognized the sound of a black-powder blaster report. Mace dropped to a knee and slapped out the folding stock on his blaster. "Who fired? Who fired?"

"Mace!" One of the twins, Butch or Heath, he couldn't tell by the firelight, was waving his arms and screaming hysterically. "Mace!" The other twin was hopping up and down like a castrated ape and pointing. "Mace!"

Mace looked.

One of his honey wags had sprung a leak and was squirting an alarming stream of octane out of a blackened hole in its side. The stream was splashing and puddling dangerously near the campfire. "Move the wag! Move the wag!" A second blaster shot rang out, and Mace saw a strange flash of orange fire almost like an explosion against the tank much lower down. A second stream flowed beneath the first and the stream suddenly seemed to catch fire from behind and lit its predecessor. Mace's stomach dropped. "Get out there!"

The honey wag went up in a rupturing, uncoiling pulse of fire and took one of the twins and several pirates with it.

"Bastards! I'll—" Mace swung his blaster around as he caught a bit of spark and muzzle-flash out in the rain two hundred yards away. A red line streaked across the night and slammed into his second honey wag. Mace burned a mag in the shooter's general direction and roared at his men. "There! There! There! On the knoll!"

TAMARA TOSSED her blaster and dropped flat as bullets cracked by overhead. "Oh, he's mad!" She clapped her hands, as happy as a girl. "Give me another!" Jak passed her another rifle. Ryan aimed. He was tempted to go for Mace or Tag. In the gray-green world of his night-vision goggles, the baron and his right-hand man had been but two more hunched figures out in the rain and dark in oilskins, but they were run-

ning targets at night in the rain at over two hundred yards.
Ryan kept his eye on the objective. Hitting a fuel tank at two
hundred yards was child's play. He took up the slack in the
trigger and squeezed.

Cap and ball blasters weren't as bad as flintlocks for fire
and smoke, but they were bad enough. The cap sparked and
black powder was black powder. Regular powder burned very
fast to release its expanding propellant gas. Black powder exploded. Ryan's hammer slammed a cap cut from an ancient
Canadian nickel and black powder detonated in the .64-cal-
iber buffalo blaster. J.B.'s high-explosive ball flew like a
tiny meteor low into the bowels of the second tank and fuel
spurted. Ryan dropped the spent blaster. "Jak." The albino
teen passed Ryan a third rifle from the pile.

Tamara took a bead on the bleeding fuel tank.

"Aim low," Ryan advised.

"Yeah, yeah, yeah, whatever, sex machine." Nevertheless
Tamara lowered her sights a hair and her bullet slammed with
a bright flash into the side of the tank in line with Ryan's. The
campsite was bedlam. Men ran for wags and bikes. Some of
those with more sense were obeying Mace's orders and began
to lay blasterfire on the knoll.

Jak passed Ryan another longblaster. Six stood below holding the horses. The knoll was barely a ripple in the landscape
and he and the horse's head nearly topped it from below. Out
in the darkness around them the pickets were shouting in
alarm. Motorcycle engines snarled into life in camp and out
beyond them.

"It is starting to get hot…." Six commented

"About to get hotter." Ryan squeezed his trigger and the
longblaster bucked against his shoulder. The second tanker
made a deep thump noise and went sky-high. Tamara yowled
like a victorious puma. Ryan tossed aside the spent, smoking
blaster. "We're out of here."

He vaulted onto the back of his horse. Six and Jak were already in the saddle. Tamara hauled herself up. She wasn't the equestrian she had claimed, but she could make a horse stop, go and move right or left. She also had the advantage that her horse appeared to love her. "Don't wait on me!"

"Give Six your goggles." Tamara passed them over and Ryan nodded as Six turned his bug-eyed gaze upon him. "You lead."

Six took the lead line in hand and led the horses into a plunging charge through the dark. Ryan took the tail end of the war party. Men in camp were plunging torches into the fires and mounting up. The pickets had lit their own torches and were converging. Mace's voice boomed in godlike fury. "The Trans! They're headed for the Trans!"

Mace was right. They were well out of worm territory and they had made friends with a horse lord, but the story was that a person didn't want to get caught out in the long grass, particularly at night. They flew for the clean path of the Trans-Canada. Just as easily as they had penetrated Mace's widespread perimeter they galloped out of it, but the roar of engines followed them and a torch-lit line of cold-hearts formed a swiftly closing fire worm in the dark behind them. Ryan felt his horse's hooves hit the ancient highway. He reached back for the rip cords Mildred had sewn into his jingling saddlebags. A bullet cracked by Ryan's ear, but he waited until he knew his enemies could see him. He heard the whoops of bloodlust as his enemies caught sight of him.

Ryan pulled his rip cord.

A stream of nails poured out behind him. Jak had bent and welded the ten-penny trade nails together in formations of three so that no matter how they dropped one pointed end stood upright. Ryan waited a few seconds and pulled his second rip cord. Caltrops fell jingling down in the war party's wake; but they went unheard beneath the roar of the motorcycles and gray and unseen by torchlight.

A motorcycle tire blew like a blaster shot and the rider skidded out in the mud. The rider screamed as the coldheart behind him couldn't stop and ran him over. Another rider went wide around the pileup. He crashed as both tires popped as he hit Ryan's minefield of sharpened iron. The one-eyed man threw a quick glance back at the sound of three quick blaster shots. The coldheart called Shorty had stopped his ride in front of the wreckage and called a halt to the chase. A few riders overshot and a few more tires blew. Ryan rode on. They would drop the remaining two bags of caltrops at one-mile intervals they had marked on the map. They would be a pain in the ass to clean up on the return trip, but Mace would have to leave the Trans or slow his convoy to a crawl to sweep the path clean before them.

Ryan rode to the front to take lead, and he and his war party galloped hard for home.

MACE STOOD on the knoll and surveyed the chaos. Something dangerous, something desperate, something unexpected. That's what Tag had said, and it had come as though he'd whistled it out of the rain. The one bright spot was that their attackers had failed to recognize the van as a tanker. Mace had enough juice to make a careful decision or two rather than a desperate retreat back to the Lakes discarding motorcycles, wags and men on the way. He handled one of the discarded blasters. "Tracers?"

"Explosive," Tag said, "and incendiary. Word is they got a crackerjack armorer."

Shorty rode up on his motorcycle. He stuck his torch in the ground and held out his hand, revealing the wicked caltrops. "Scattered these behind 'em. Tire-killers."

"Caltrops," Tag corrected.

Mace took one and pricked his thumb against a hand-sharpened point. This was One-Eye's work. He'd bet his balls on it. "Vinny and One-Eye?"

Shorty cocked his head. "Yeah, Baron?"

"Don't know which one I hate more."

Shorty pondered this declaration for long moments. You could almost hear the gears grinding. "Both need chilling," he finally replied.

"That they do! We gotta step up our game plan."

Chapter Twenty-Four

Mildred stared down at Sebastien. His two usual accomplices, Michel and Roland, slouched behind him in their ponchos. Mildred had bound up the bullet crease on Sebastien's arm, but she remembered just enough of her high-school French to have had a gutful of the trash he'd been talking about Krysty and the state of her DNA. Mildred went clinical. "Your arm hurting?"

Sebastien lifted his arm with a shrug. "No, it is good, Mildred. *Merci, merci beaucoup.*"

Mildred wasn't having it. She gave Sebastien the evil eye. "What do you want?"

Sebastien scowled back. "I have traded watches with Hunk. He wanted me to ask of Miss Krysty. I did not wish to, but I owe him my life after the Soo Locks. She is—" the lean, wolflike, Quebecer sought for a word "—in better spirits? And if so…" The man looked down at his muddy boots. "Perhaps I should apologize."

Mildred made a noise at the contrite Canadian but looked back at Krysty. Krysty had dealt with the combination of Ryan's absence and her untouchable status by drinking more hawberry brandy than was good for her and passing out in the sleeper cab beneath a bearskin. "She's all right. You can tell her tomorrow at dawn, but you might want to wait until she's had breakfast, she's— Oh you motherfucker." Mildred found herself staring down the barrel of nickel-plated, single-action .44 missing most of its nickel. A thick, moist wad of cotton was wrapped around its muzzle and cylinder to muffle its report. "Step down, please."

"You aren't going to shoot me."

Sebastien lowered his aim. "You can still stitch up a wound without knees."

"Listen, you—"

Sebastien seized Mildred's wrist and yanked her out of the cab. Michel and Roland laughed as Mildred fell face-first in a splash and ate mud. "Her, too!" Michel rasped avidly. "I say we do both of them!"

"No," Sebastien said. "Leave the black. Six is fond of her. The mutie? He does not care so much about."

Sebastien climbed up into the cab for Krysty. Mildred did a push up out of the mud with one hand and reached for her revolver with the other. It was bad. Krysty had deliberately parked a bit away from the main convoy, and the ugly event that was transpiring was facing out into the night. Jak was out scouting the perimeter and J.B. was in the LAV in the center of camp. "Sons of—"

Roland put his boot between Mildred's shoulder blades and shoved her back down. He stripped away her revolver and her knife. He leaned in to his compatriot and whispered harsh and low in French. "Michel, when Sebastien closes the door and is pleasuring the red? We take the black." Roland slammed a fist across Mildred's kidney that left her paralyzed and sucking mud.

"Oui." Michel had been shaking with the wet and cold, now lust shook and warmed him. "Her black ass is—"

"Cretinous sons of Cupid!" Doc's swordstick was a blur in the rain. Michel screamed as it cut across his mouth and sent teeth flying in a spray of blood. "You besmirch Miss Wroth's genetics while at the same time shake and slobber like dogs in your concupiscence for what those very genes produced!" Roland raised his blaster and dropped it as he took a brutal thrust to the bladder that dropped him to his knees. Doc was a vengeful tower of moral outrage.

"Dear Mildred has salved a hundred wounds for you and yours, and this is how you repay her?" Doc gave Roland a lash across the kidneys for good measure that left him vomiting in the mud. "Your loins betray you!"

Sebastien swung out of the cab. He leaned out hanging on by one hand while his .44 made a click-click-clack as he thumbed back the hammer. "You should have a blaster in your hand if you want to beat on my friends, whitehair."

"I shall beat you like a rug, you cur!"

"Gaia...Earth Mother, aid me in my time of need." Krysty's voice spoke quietly from the sleeper cab. "Give me all the power...let me strive for life..."

Sebastien's blaster never wavered, but he looked back into the cab. "Mutie bitch! What are you babbling about— *Mon Dieu!*"

Krysty's hand shot forth and grabbed Sebastien's wrist in a viselike grip. He screamed as she squeezed. His scream cut off in a sharp yelp as he was bodily yanked back into the cab. Doc started at an unmistakable, wet tearing sound. Sebastien's screaming and yelping turned into a keening shriek like a rabbit being killed. Doc considered the young man's advice and drew his LeMat.

"My dear Mildred!" He helped her to her feet, raising his revolver as Sebastien reappeared in the door. In the yellow glare of the cab's dome light his face was ghostly pale. His jaws worked but no sound came out. His left arm was missing at the socket. Sebastien gasped and fell out of the cab.

Krysty appeared in the door, her power upon her.

Her beautifully turned form was bathed in Sebastien's arterial blood. Her titian tresses writhed and snapped around her head in snakelike tendrils. The look on her face was one of a rage that had nearly transformed itself into serenity.

Doc felt it had to be a trick of the light and the rain, but it was almost as if she levitated down out of the cab. Krysty's mother had taught her the ways of Gaia, the Earth Mother, and at times of need, the red-haired woman could call upon the Earth Mother for help, and was given immense physical power. Doc didn't believe in gods; he believed Gaia was something she clothed her power with, her focus for channeling it, but looking at her Doc realized that while Gaia was believed to be the Earth Mother and the source of life, she also had her terrible aspect of wind and fire, the shaking torn earth and the tidal wave. Carnivorous feeding, territoriality, and lust were also her purviews, and if she existed, Doc firmly believed she was as angry, wrathful goddess who when it came to vengeance could put the Old Testament of his upbringing to shame.

Krysty held Sebastien's avulsed arm in her hand and began beating Michel and Roland to death with it while Sebastien bled out into the mud and rain. Doc and Mildred both knew not to get in her way. Doc turned his head away; Mildred watched with clinical horror.

Krysty abruptly went boneless and Doc just caught her as she fell. "Mildred, take Krysty into the cab and lock the door. I'll go get J.B. and have him radio Ryan."

"You'd better rouse out Hunk and his islanders. This could get ugly."

Doc looked eastward and silently urged Ryan to greater speed. It was already far too ugly for his liking.

Ryan arrived with the dawn. The storm had stopped. It looked as though a new one was brewing. The convoy had turned into a lopsided pair of armed, angry and clearly delineated camps. The big rig and the fighting LAV formed the smaller camp. The two wags were surrounded by Hunk and his island sec men. J.B. sat in the LAV's turret top, and the autocannon was pointed at the rest of the convoy. The rest of the convoy was circled up. More than a few men with blasters had their eye on the LAV and the semi. Ryan smelled coffee and bacon coming from the convoy. Hunk and his men were eating, chewing cold pemmican and glaring across the fifty yards of no-man's-land between the two camps. Ryan noted not all of Hunk's men were present.

The Deathland warrior's voice was as cold as the oncoming Canadian winter. "Six, take command of your people."

Ryan rode to his own companions, followed by Jak and Tamara.

Mildred walked out of the back of the LAV to meet him. Ryan didn't dismount and his Scout was out of its scabbard. "How is she?"

"She's all right. Sleeping. She and Doc were the ones who did all the damage."

Ryan eyed Mildred. She looked exhausted. J.B. hadn't elaborated over the radio, but Ryan gathered she'd had a hard night. "What happened?"

"You and Six were gone, Yoann was fevered up. J.B. was working in the LAV and Jak was out in the dark on patrol. Sebastien and his asshole buddies Michel and Roland showed up in the night with bad intentions."

"And?"

Mildred shook her head. "I'm afraid I didn't handle it too well. They got the jump on me. Luckily, Doc stepped in and started handing out some beat down. Sebastien was about to blow his head off when Krysty went all Gaia on them."

Ryan knew how that usually turned out. "How bad is it?"

"She killed Sebastien and beat Roland stupid. Definitely brain damaged. I stabilized him, but if I had to bet, he's going to be a vegetable for the rest of his life."

"What about Michel?"

"Multiple broken bones and contusions. I took care of him.

The son of a bitch is over there lying his ass off and preaching death to muties and anyone who loves them."

"Not good."

"Get's worse. Yoann died in the night. You know that big guy, Patrice?"

Everyone in Canada seemed to be big, but Ryan knew the blond, bearded blaster man. "The driver of Six's sec wag?"

"Yeah, him. He says he's leader of the convoy now."

"What about Cyrielle?"

"She's in bad shape. Hasn't left Yoann's camper, and hasn't said word one about the situation." Mildred squinted up at Ryan. "So, what are you going to do?"

Ryan took a long breath. "Guess I'll ride over there."

Hunk charged up with Kagan, Kosha and Quinn at his heels. "Ryan! I—"

"You'll stay here."

Ryan rode over to the convoy. Most of the convoy had formed a mob behind Patrice. Only the big woman who had lost her lover to the thunderbirds, Marie-Laure, stood with Six. Patrice was speaking French, but Ryan could tell Patrice was giving his former boss a genuine ass-ripping. The thickly accented word *mutant* figured early and often in the conversation. Michel lay on the med-wag's gurney cheerleading and posing as Exhibit A. Despite the desperation of the situation, Ryan almost had to smile. It would have been far better for Patrice if Six had been roaring in rage and brandishing his big blaster. Instead the sec leader took in Patrice's increasingly inflammatory tirade like a man gazing at a very small dog that was barking and lunging at him. Patrice seemed hopped up on his new position of power and mob mentality and blissfully unaware of his impending mortality.

The mob's muttering and Patrice's oratory ceased as Ryan rode up. "I'm in command of this convoy until Cyrielle says different."

Patrice's head stopped just short of exploding. "You? You are a mutie lover! Yoann is dead! Six is a traitor and—" Patrice's head stopped just short of flying off his shoulders as Six hit him. His eyes rolled back in his head as he rubber-necked and fell unconscious. The mob stared mutely at their fallen spokesman. Six spoke conversationally to the closest man to him. "Lenard?"

Lenard backed up a step and bumped into the man behind him. "Uh...*oui?*"

"I need every man, so when Patrice wakes up, tell him I'll forgive his impertinence, this once. Next time I take his hair."

"Uh...*oui,* Six."

Michel began caterwauling from his gurney in apoplectic French. Six walked over and examined his sec man. He judiciously peered at Michel's splinted left forearm. Six reached down, grabbed the thumb sticking out of the splint and snapped it. Michel's face went white with shock. Six's voice was almost fatherly. "Best for you to be quiet now."

Six whirled on the mob, and his fury poured forth like thunder. "Now! I am in command of every Québécois in this convoy! Hunk is in command of his Islanders! Ryan commands his Deathlanders, and Ryan commands us all as long as one wag still has wheels! Who disputes this?"

The mob recoiled before Six's wrath. They stared warily at Ryan as he sat his horse like the Fourth Rider of the Apocalypse.

No one disputed it.

Ryan spoke quietly. "We're heading on for the last bunker. Anyone who wants to leave can take your blaster and all the food and ammo you can carry. The wags stay with the convoy." Ryan glanced back over his shoulder as he spun his mount. "Anyone who wants a horse can apply."

No one applied. No one left, either, but fear and suspicion were tearing the convoy apart, and only force of personality was holding it together. Ryan held a sitdown with his companions. Mildred had just returned from setting Michel's thumb and checking Patrice for concussion. She gave Krysty a long look. The beautiful redhead had never looked so miserable. Mildred knew part of it was that using her Earth power left her drained, and part of it was a hawberry brandy hangover.

The council was mostly quiet. The question was to stay or go.

Neither option held much appeal.

Six walked up and joined them. He looked at Ryan and smiled to reveal his gold and silver teeth. "*Bonjour,* Ryan."

"Well, *bonjour* to you, too, brother-man," Mildred quipped. "And just who the hell is minding the convoy?"

Six shrugged. "Patrice."

"Patrice! How the hell can you trust him?"

"Patrice will do exactly what I tell him to."

"And how do you know that?"

"Because, Mildred—" the ugly smile widened "—Patrice knows what's best."

Vincent Six was big, black, bad, brutal, bald and ugly, and Mildred had to admit he was growing on her. "I suppose he does."

"Forgive my temerity, Ryan," Six continued, "but if you still lead us, I think we must move. Our fuel runs short, our time shorter. We must reach the next bunker."

Ryan looked at Krysty. She rose without a word. Everyone in the group had a say in what they did, but they would follow her lead on this one. If she broke for the LAV, they were heading south. If she went to the semi, they were still heading west. Krysty turned on her heel, clambered up into the big rig's cab and slammed the door.

"Headin' west, eh?" Hunk grinned.

"Yeah," Ryan replied. "Six, how is Cyrielle?"

"Crushed."

"What's the mood in the convoy?"

"Distraught. Yoann was much loved. His father, the baron, is old. Val-d'Or does not accept a female baron. There is no heir. When we return, there will very likely be a fight over the succession. It will tear the ville apart. Many want to go home now, and, in my heart, I'm one of them. I should be beside my baron. He told me to protect his son. He made me promise." Six stared bitterly into the middle distance. "I've failed."

"But you've decided to go on."

"I must. We must seize the prize. Returning with the reactors will give me the power to enforce the baron's will, and have a say in which faction takes power." Six's face darkened. "And who takes Cyrielle's hand and the ville."

Chapter Twenty-Five

Manitoba

The convoy pressed on across the Canadian prairie. Compared to the Deathlands, Canada had gotten off fairly lightly when it the sky had fallen in fire, but several of her provincial capitals had been lit up. The needle of the rad counter pinned to Ryan's coat began to move out of the safe zone as they approached the quadruple craters that had been Winnipeg. Here the going got very hard. The overpasses had fallen, and erosion had taken its toll on the on- and off-ramps. This close to the capital was by the thousands had been abandoned on the roadways, some with the skeletons of their original passengers still strapped into their rotting seats, killed during the initial millisecond of the radiation wave during detonation.

Alain, Sebastien and édouard were dead, which left Six the only convoy man who could handle a LAV. Ryan and J.B. switched over to the engineering-recovery LAV and with winch, dozer blade and crane they cleared the path. It was slow, ponderous work, working wreck by wreck, roadblock by roadblock. Outside Transcona they met with heartbreak. The hulks of Canadian Land Force Leopard tanks blocked the Trans-Canada and the surrounding roads. They had long ago been stripped of their machine blasters and anything of use, but their rusted turrets pointed west toward Winnipeg. Beyond them makeshift roadblocks, poured concrete fighting positions and the rusted girder tripods of tank barriers formed more obstacles. That told Ryan that despite a direct nuke hit, something within the blasted city had required containment. Whether the Canadian Military had succeeded or failed was ancient news. The iron fact confronting them was that the Engineering LAV couldn't move a tank.

And it got worse.

The prairie ended abruptly to form dark formations of thick, radiation-twisted trees with black bark that bled white, weeping sap. They crowded and choked everything that wasn't covered in pavement in all directions. The trees were as thick as oaks, and their purple leaves were jagged like cannabis. Doc had no idea what their original species might once have been. The tall grass refused to grow within two hundred yards of the forest, forming a strange, sere, no-plants-land leading up to the ancient tank formations. From the top of the semi Ryan's Navy longeye showed the black forest forming a ring around the craters of Winnipeg like a walled city.

Ryan stood atop the semi with Six and a Diefenbunker map, eating creamed corn out of the can. Rations were running low. If they didn't reach the next bunker soon, they would be down to hunting and pemmican. The one-eyed man looked southward, and not without some longing, toward Deathlands. "It's clearer to the south. We can backtrack, swing wide and come up around the other side on Highway 2, mebbe back road it up to meet up with the Trans again."

Six shook his head. "No, our path lies north. There is no time for detours."

"North?" At every pause, around every campfire, all talk in the convoy revolved around how late it was in the season and how the hard freeze would be descending upon them like an avalanche from the north. No one made it sound pleasant. "No one's going to like that announcement."

Six shrugged. "We can't push past those tanks. Going south will cost us days with no way of reaching the 6 north except by looping all the way around Lake Manitoba and Lake Winnipegosis. That could cost us weeks."

Ryan looked at the map and gazed hard at the bridge of land between the long, Canadian lakes and Highway 6 that ran right up the middle. Getting to it meant cutting through the dark wood. "So we go through the trees." Ryan frowned. "No one's going to like that announcement, either."

"I know, but a klick or less of forest is the short way. The long loop around the lakes will take close to nine hundred." Six gave Ryan a wry look. "And they will do it if you tell them to."

Ryan was swiftly transforming from a leader who was respected and admired to one who was obeyed out of fear. It was his least favorite method of leadership. "Thanks."

"De rien." Six shrugged.

Ryan received no thanks for it but he gave the order, and the convoy went to work. Short of grabbing men in their branches and crushing them, the trees fought back. Their roots coiled around center dividers and when their branches weren't intertwining with one another, they wove their way through the hidden hulks of abandoned wags and any other wreckage they could find. People instantly found out that the white sap burned and stung the skin. The leaves were sharp enough to cut bare skin and cotton, and hooked into thicker garments with the tenacity of nettles. The men wore gloves, makeshift hoods, their winter leggings, leather shirts and Diefenbunker goggles and bandannas across their faces as armor.

When a tree finally gave in and fell, it released its sap like a dead man releasing his bowels, and the stench was twice as horrid. Beneath the canopy the humidity was horrific. The coffee-dark duff of the forest floor was the consistency of rotting flesh, and the spurting lakes of white sap churned it into the consistency of plasma. In places, men sank in knee-deep. It was a slogging, slow-motion war between plant and animal.

The animals fought back. Many of the men of Val-d'Or were miners, and they all knew what to do with a pick and a shovel. The men of Manitoulin were sailors from birth and understood ropes and tackles; and for that matter there wasn't a man alive in Canada who didn't know which end of a felling ax was which. The double-bitted blades rose and fell in grim determination.

Sap spurted. The twisted trees fell.

It was backbreaking and sickening work. Winching the LAV atop the promenade of the *Queen* had been simple in comparison. Human muscle alone would have sickened and failed long before any path to the northbound Highway 7 could have been cleared, but the men of the convoy had one advantage. As they carved their way into the dark forest yard by poisonous yard, they slowly made room for the engineering LAV to move. In Ryan and J.B.'s hands, Winnipeg's dark garden of evil found itself invaded by a voracious, nonlocal pest it had no answer for. The LAV craned away fallen timbers, winched out stumps and the dozer blade simply sheared away the smaller saplings at ground level.

Once they were within the forest Ryan didn't want to stop. By night they worked on by wag lights and torches. Men worked until they collapsed or were relieved. Ryan, Six, J.B. and Jak were like a captain and his officers on a ship at storm. For them there was no rest. One advantage they had was that no man or woman in the convoy wanted to stop during the day or night in the eerily silent, bleeding, palpably hostile forest.

The ball-busting ceaseless work provided a side benefit. It gave the convoy members no time for grumbling or internal division. It also gave them common purpose and a common enemy. Mildred was kept busy but it wasn't bad. The brutal, dangerous nature of the day and night work produced mostly bruises, strains and some broken bones. Nearly everyone had first- and some had second-degree chemical burns from the sap, and that put a dent in the med wag's topical ointments. There were only two causalities. The first morning the mess-wag driver, a woman named Betts, had disappeared without a trace. In the med wag someone left Michel unattended for a few moments to go and relieve himself and returned to find his gurney empty. Blacktree had scouted for them, but found no footprints, no sign of any disturbance and no trail.

After that anyone not employed road blazing was on top of a wag with a blaster ready, and anyone sleeping was in a wag that was buttoned up. Ryan instituted random recce by blasterfire into the forest as well as the random firing of flares ahead. Whatever lived in the forest, whatever Winnipeg's radioactive death throes had birthed, found itself unwilling to lock horns with the convoy directly.

On the third morning they broke through to the north. They found the no-plants-land, and they found Highway 7 stretching north. It was congested with the wag hulks of those who had fled south back in the day and either abandoned their wags or had fallen to Winnipeg's glowing craters, but it was free of armored vehicles. Despite the pressing need to move on, Six quietly requested a day of rest for the convoy and Ryan granted a halt and a day of light duty. People bathed their wounds in the clean water of the southern-flowing Red River and ate their first hot meal in days. The forest sap ate fabric and leather, and people sewed, patched and mended. The sap and mulch mix of the forest floor had done the wags' tires much like it had human skin. Nearly all the convoy's wags were festooned with spares, but they went through more of them than Ryan would have liked.

The next day the convoy pressed north up the corridor between the lakes and caught Highway 6.

Every mile north they went the land grew more open, hard and severe. The Northern Lights grew more lurid until the sun was an obscured lamp behind bleeding sky murals. The wind began to blow cold and straight from the north. Here the giant grass was already withering. No breed of tree survived this far north other than wind-twisted and cold-cramped stands of pines that the hard freeze had bent into phantasmagorical shapes.

They came to a headland, and Ryan could see Lake Winnipeg to the east and Cedar Lake to the west. Route 6 came to a dead end and the convoy came to a halt at the Saskatchewan River. Ryan clicked his CB. "Six, where are we?"

"Grand Rapids."

Ryan glanced at his map. "Grand Rapids is across the river."

"Yes."

Ryan looked up at the fallen expanse of the Grand Rapids Bridge. "Bridge is out." The hydroelectric plant was the only modern edifice still standing, and it was a cracked and raddled lump falling in upon itself as the Saskatchewan River's rapids fell past its clogged sluices and silent dynamos. People began debarking wags, staring disconsolately at the river in front of them, the expanses of lake to either side and the sadly twisted trees.

Hunk looked around blankly. "Where is it?"

There was little to see except scrubby trees; nothing to hear but the rushing of the river. There was no parking lot, not telltale sign of anything at all. Ryan looked at the map again. X marked the spot. The spot was a fallen bridge.

"Lady Cyrielle!" Six knocked at the camper wag's door. "Lady Cyrielle! You must come!" Six opened the door and went in.

Hunk wasn't happy, and he spoke for most of the people in the convoy. "Blasters! Food! Fuel! Tech! You said it was all here!" Hunk raised his arms and slowly spun in a disappointed circle. "Where?"

Lady Cyrielle emerged. She was wearing the same shift she had slept in for three days. Six had draped a parka around her and shoved boots onto her feet. Her eyes were red with weeping and dark-circled with exhaustion. With the death of her brother, she had seen the fall of the Toulalan dynasty in Val-d'Or. When her father died, she would end up the spoils of whatever faction came out on top. Unless Mace Henning took her first. She clutched a Diefenbunker laptop comp. Six gave the dazed, grief-racked lady gentle directions, and she opened the laptop, adjusted a plug-in antenna and hesitantly typed some keys.

Nothing happened.

Six nodded to her. "Again."

Lady Cyrielle typed the keys and nothing happened.

"Again."

Faces fell as Cyrielle typed the command code again with shaking hands. The anticlimax was agonizing. After everything they had been through, all the pain, all the loss, the payoff was an empty plain and a fallen bridge. Angry murmurs moved up and down the convoy. The wild dream of unlimited electrical power and the new society was dead. Ryan's eye narrowed. Of much more immediate concern was that they had been depending on the food and fuel the bunker was sure to have contained. Very soon they would be as bad off as Baron Henning and hundreds of miles farther north and west. The LAVs, the semi and the command camper wag were pigs for fuel. It would be a hell run to reach Val-d'Or through hostile territory, abandoning wags and gear every step of the way.

Tamara kicked a rock and muttered beneath her breath. "This is what happens when you sign up with landlubbers..." Six caught Cyrielle as she buckled. Her brother's death had been in vain. People silently began remounting their wags without being ordered, and blue smoke belched into the air.

Ryan's head snapped up. "Cut the engines!" The convoy drivers looked at him as though he was insane. The look on his face brooked no disobedience. The wag engines died. The one-eyed man knelt and put his fingers on the cracked concrete of the road. It was vibrating. He unslung his Scout and walked up the road toward the river. He stopped in front of the Grand Rapids Bridge on-ramp. Dust and dead grass was sifting off it. A slow smile spread across Ryan's face.

Pavement cracked like gunshots. The on-ramp split open down the middle, and the giant clamshell doors butterflied open. A ramp led downward, and it was wide and tall enough to accept the semi. Ryan knew it ran beneath the river and probably led to the highly modified basement of the hydro-electric plant. Ancient lights began snapping on along the length of the ceiling. Ryan stepped inside the giant doors and slid a finger along one gleaming hydraulic shaft. He felt the dry lubricant's oil on glass slickness. This wasn't one of Mildred's "retro" Diefenbunkers. This place was predark state-of-the-art.

Ryan glanced back at the convoy. The LAV would fit down the tunnel, but it wouldn't be able to turn in an emergency, and he wanted it up top defending the convoy in case someone or something came wandering along. "Six, we'll take your sec wag. Bring Lady Cyrielle and the laptop."

Six nodded. "Marie-Laure, you're driving. Tamara, would you care to accompany us and look after the *Queen*'s interests?"

"Rad-yes!" The markswoman beamed.

"Hunk?"

"Fuckin' eh!" the young man replied.

Ryan looked at J.B. "Circle the wags. You're in command. We'll take a com unit."

J.B. kept the disappointment off his face. He lived for discovering caches of predark blasters and tech, but duty was duty, and he knew more about defending convoys than even experienced Deathlands travelers had forgotten. "Right."

"Jak?"

The albino teen leaped into the back of the wag. He was always ready to roll.

"Mildred, this stuff is your era," Ryan said. "I want you along."

The physician checked the loads in her ZKR target pistol and slung her med kit. "On it like Blue Bonnet!"

Ryan was pretty sure that meant yes. He nodded at his recce team. "Let's do it."

Chapter Twenty-Six

The thunder of the sec wag's rebuilt V-8 engine echoed down the long tunnel beneath the rapids of the Saskatchewan River. Marie-Laure drove. The passenger-side chicken-armor slats had been raised to let Hunk man the hood-mounted squad automatic blaster. Cyrielle and Mildred were ensconced on the bench backseat. In the truck bed Six stood behind the post-mounted twin autoblasters. Ryan, Jak and Tamara each dropped to a knee around him with their weapons ready. Kagan and Kosha snuffed the ancient air of the redoubt.

A little seepage streaked the walls of the tunnel, and a few of the evenly spaced overhead lights had shorted out and left occasional pools of darkness, but otherwise the tunnel was remarkably well preserved. It ended in a huge wag circle with cranes inset in the walls. The blast doors hissed open instantly at Cyrielle's comp command. Ryan smiled at what he saw within. It was classic Deathlands redoubt architecture. In the midst of revamping their Diefenbunkers, Canada had built one last stronghold to spec.

His smile died when he saw its former occupants.

The ancient dead lay strewed around in the redoubt's deployment foyer. By their attitude some had died clawing at the doors to get out. "Mildred?"

Mildred hopped out and warily approached an air-cured corpse in a blue coverall. The dead man's paper-thin skin was raddled with coin-size lesions of various denominations. With no fluids left in his body the holes opened onto yellowed bone. "Something biological got in here. Looks like whoever was in command put the place in lockdown."

"We safe?" Ryan called.

"It's been a hundred years since it had a living host, so bugs should be dead by now." Or dormant Mildred mentally corrected herself. "But we don't have any safety protocols we can exercise except to not touch anything, and we came here expressly to pillage. It's your call."

"I'm willing to go in," Ryan stated. "The rest can stay here."

"I'm willing to accompany you," Six affirmed.

"We're the recce team." Tamara grinned. "We're all volunteers."

Hunk slammed a fist into his palm. "Let's kick this pig!"

Mildred looked for a piece of wood to knock on and couldn't find one among the stark metal and concrete of the redoubt. "Don't say pig. Just don't."

Marie-Laure rumbled the sec wag into the redoubt, and the rest of the team dismounted. Ryan took point, and Tamara immediately fixed her bayonet and moved to his back. Marie-Laure immediately took up the same position on Six. Cyrielle attached herself to Six's fire team and Mildred to Ryan's. Hunk took rear guard.

It was the first postmodern facility Hunk had ever laid eyes on. "Sure built fancy back then!" the young man observed.

Ryan pushed the button on a door and it hissed open.

"Rads, thunder and fallout!" Hunk was close to hopping up and down with delight. Like the last bunker the armory was right next to the door for quick deployment. This armory was untouched. Canadian hand-, long- and machine blasters of every description were racked and ready to go along with crates of ammo. Not a single weapon was out of place.

Tamara unracked a long green tube with folding grips and sights and read the top line of the instructions. "Antitank!"

Ryan went to a rack of four Scout longblasters and took some spare magazines and another accessory kit. "We strip it clean later. Right now we find the reactors."

The recce team moved through the redoubt and found occasional chilled corpses in various states of rigor mortis. The staff of the bunker had died hard. Whatever the disease was, it had raddled their flesh, and they had died where they had fallen, probably of dehydration. They found the cafeteria and kitchen. The cryo-freeze units were three-quarters full of food. The fuel bunker was just about full. The inhabitants had died of disease before they could ever deploy into the brave new world. The medical facilities and the dormitories were strangely devoid of corpses, as if the staff had decided to die at their stations or trying to escape.

Ryan kept the hesitation off his face as they entered a mat-trans control room. Cyrielle went to the door to the chamber and pressed the lever to open it with obvious experience. The walls of the chamber were the ocean blue of a tropical lagoon. Cyrielle frowned at the interior. "There was a chamber like this in the Val-d'Or Diefenbunker, and the one in Borden. We couldn't figure out their purpose. Their comps aren't linked to the rest of the bunker, and we couldn't access them." She looked at Ryan.

Ryan shrugged. "We were more interested in the food and the LAV."

Cyrielle closed the door to the chamber once more. The recce party moved on. Ryan figured they had gone about a thousand yards and were right below the hydroelectric plant when they found the mother lode. They walked into another storage chamber and stopped in their tracks.

"Behold," Cyrielle said, "my brother's dream."

"Wow, atomic outhouses." Mildred put her hands on her hips. "Wonders never cease."

It wasn't a bad description. Four eight-feet tall, sky-blue cuboids with rounded edges and a discernable, man-size door or hatch occupied the middle of the chamber. Each had the universal three-spoked radiation-warning sign and the Canadian flag emblazoned on the hatch. Ryan picked up a binder emblazoned with the Diefenbunker logo and read the title, "Endymion Industries Cartridge Reactor." Ryan was the son of a baron, and had been raised with the closest equivalent to a classical education that the Deathlands could manage. The dense text swiftly turned to a blur technical gobbledygook. "Mildred?"

Mildred took the binder. She was a physician, but she had spent years reading technical textbooks. "J.B. could make a lot more out of this, but it's written so that basic level electrical technicians could operate them. From what I can gather, they are self-contained units, though it says they can be linked and there are diagrams on how to do it. I know there is more to it, but basically you hook them up, add a water source and pull the rods." Mildred looked over at the pyramid of large military crates. "Those contain couplings and adapters for various applications, and there are specs in here on how to build basic steam turbines. As far as I can tell, standing before us is eighty-one megawatts of power looking for a job."

"We did it," Cyrielle said. Her voice gained strength with victory. "My brother did it."

Ryan clicked his com unit. "J.B., it's all here, food, fuel, an armory full of blasters, loads of supplies and gear, the reactors, everything. Tell Krysty to bring in the big rig. There's a wag circle at the end of the tunnel where she can turn it around. We'll bring the rest of the wags inside in relays and load them up with everything we can carry."

"If I may object?" Lady Cyrielle said.

"Yeah?"

"I suggest we bring all the wags in. We have hot showers, beds, central heating and the ovens. I think we might spend the night here. It is probably the securest place in Canada, and we would all benefit from the rest. We have been pushing hard, and the push home will be even harder."

"J.B., you catch that?"

"Yeah," the Armorer confirmed. Ryan knew J.B.'s leg was killing him, and that he was dying to take a look around inside. "Not a bad idea, and I ain't just saying it. Homeward bound is going to be a hell run."

"Six?" Ryan asked.

"I'm anxious to press on, but…" The big man raised a scarred eyebrow. "We bring in all the wags, fuel them, load them up. Get everything ready, then who knows what delights the kitchen freeze units hold, perhaps even beer. We sleep warm and safe behind blast doors, and leave tomorrow before noon."

"J.B.?" Ryan said.

"Yeah?"

"Bring everybody in, the big rig first."

RYAN YAWNED and stretched as the credits on the vid rolled. He had some problems with coldhearts who wore shoulder pads and loincloths in the desert but other than that Mildred had been right. *The Road Warrior* was a pretty good flick. The recce room was mostly deserted. The convoy had feasted and feasted well, except for those who had pulled guard duty. Most of the members of the convoy were passed out in bloated food comas. Between the infirmary and the dormitory there were enough beds to go around. Ryan and Krysty had claimed one of the couches in the recce room.

Ryan could have spent a week drinking beer and perusing the collection of flicks. It was extensive.

Krysty had stuffed her backpack with CDs for the player in the semi.

Six appeared and put his finger to his lips and jerked his head for Ryan to follow. The one-eyed man disentangled himself from Krysty and walked across the recce room as silent as Six had entered, following the big Québécois into the hall. "What?"

Six led him to the bunker's security suite. Marie-Laure was watching the screens looking very unhappy. Six pointed at the feed from three of the sec cams. "These are pointed north."

On clear nights the Canadian sky was a magic show of light curtains and acres of crystal-clear stars. In the distance the Northern Lights and the stars were reflected off a mass of white like an earthbound cloud bank. "What is it?"

"The freeze," Six replied. "It is early." The sec room had a shining chrome periscope, and Six slapped down the handles and invited Ryan to watch.

He peered. He clicked the thumb adjustment, and each time the magnification of the periscope jumped. It was a cloud bank, but as he upped the magnification he could see that it was a vast swirling mass, spinning in a westerly rotation like a revolving wall and trees and debris were swept ahead of it. It was a cyclone, thousands of feet tall and filling the horizon. It was a superstorm, and an arctic one. It was moving toward them at incredible speed. Ryan suddenly had to dial back his magnification as the storm jumped his view and whited out his lens. Ryan dialed back and dialed back again as the superstorm kept jumping his magnification. Even the Deathlands at its worst didn't have storms this big or so fast. "How does anything survive?"

"Below the 50th parallel the storms lose much of their

force. Some say it is the combination of the Rockies to the west and the updraft of the Great Lakes." Six gazed steadily at the suite of security monitors. "It's on us."

Ryan was at zero magnification as the storm hit. The Diefenbunker shuddered down to its foundations and the lens was enveloped in a maelstrom of white and gray. "How long do they last?"

"Not long, but they come marching one after the other, the sweep of a scythe from east to west."

Marie-Laure gazed at the gleaming shaft of the periscope. "Let me look!"

"Not much to see," Ryan said, stepping away, "except whiteout."

Marie-Laure took the handles and peered. "Oh no! It is clear!" She turned in a circle. "You can see the entire funnel from within!"

"The eye of the storm," Ryan said.

"*Oui,* it is…" Marie-Laure's breath misted like smoke and she suddenly jerked away from the periscope. Part of her cheek came off on the eyepiece. Her left hand stuck on the handle. "*Merde!* It burns!" She yanked her hand away and her left ring and little finger snapped off like a breaking stick. She staggered back in shock and Ryan caught her. The temperature in the room had plummeted. Cold radiated from the steel shaft of the periscope in a searing wave.

"Out!" Ryan roared. They piled out of the room and Ryan kicked the metal door shut. The toe of boot scraped frost. The walls of the redoubt clicked and hummed as the generators and internal heating tried to adjust to a cold it had never been designed for. The other side of the funnel hit and the walls rumbled and vibrated again as the storm shook the hydro-electric facility above. Ryan clicked his com as Marie-Laure sagged. "Mildred! I need you now!"

"I'VE HEARD OF IT," Mildred said to Ryan. She bandaged Marie-Laure's hand while Krysty held it. Marie-Laure's ring and little finger were back in the sec room. Her middle finger had required amputation, and the palm of her hand was the equivalent of a full thickness burn. Luckily the med facility's supply of cryogenically frozen drugs was still tip-top, and the facility itself was designed to deal with small-unit action level casualties. Mildred mentally fretted about the nerves to Marie-Laure's forefinger and thumb. Mildred had already sutured up her face. Marie-Laure hadn't been a good-looking woman by anyone's standards before, and the loss of flesh beneath her left eye was a freeze avulsion. The flesh had frozen to her cheekbone and snapped off. It was going to leave some very nasty scarring.

Mildred talked as she worked. "They called it supercooling back in my day. It was in a lot of end-of-the-world scenarios. Conduction, convection, I don't know the science, but somehow the eye of the storm gets colder than it was previously ever thought possible on Earth. It explains all this talk about a killing hard freeze."

Six strode into the med facility. "We have a window. This storm system has passed." He looked down at Marie-Laure on the gurney. "How are you?"

Marie-Laure looked at Six, looked at her crippled hand and bit her lip to stifle a sob. She was a big woman, and ugly. She had compensated for it by becoming sec. She and her lover had bargained with Six to give them children so that other men would leave them alone. She knew the beautiful Camille had been the bait. Now her lover was dead, and she was a sec woman with only one good hand. Tears burned unbidden down her cheeks as she looked at Six and her future in despair. "Six, I am…mutilated. Camille is…dead… I am… You do not have to honor your commitment. You may…"

"Marie-Laure—" it was the first time Ryan had ever seen

Six smile with genuine warmth "—you are my number one
sec girl." He nodded toward her left hand. "It takes but two
fingers to steady a long blaster, and that hand will do most
elegantly to hold the hand of my son, when you teach him to
walk."

Marie-Laure sobbed. So did Mildred and Krysty. Six took
Marie-Laure into his arms and held her as she cried and murmured to her in French.

"Six, how soon do you want to mount up?" Ryan asked.

Six gave Marie-Laure a squeeze. "We'll be ready to leave
in half an hour."

Chapter Twenty-Seven

The convoy cautiously crawled out into the Canadian winter. Many of the stunted pines had exploded, but many more had miraculously lived through the supercooling of the giant superstorm's cyclonic center. The supercooling in the eye allowed water to remain in a liquid state despite being below freezing. The second the eye passed, the rain and snow instantly solidified into crystalline structures of startling geometry and size like snowflakes blown to gigantic proportions.

A minority of the convoy had changed into the available Diefenbunker-issue arctic clothing. Most had exchanged moccasins for fur-lined mukluks and leggings and wore blanket-cut capotes. Ryan wore his buffalo robe, his scarf wound around his head like a turban, and was tolerably warm. Krysty looked the perfect ice princess in her bear coat, ushanka and muff.

The semi rolled out with its precious cargo tied down and tarped over in the bed.

Ryan was worried about the crystalline sculptures cutting tires, but they were ephemeral and shattered apart easily at the engineering LAV's dozer blade. The morning was bright and blissfully calm and clear after the superstorm. It was too clear, and it was still far too cold for Ryan's liking. He was very worried about what any wind-chill factor at all would do the wags' fuel lines, much less human flesh. They had rolled out of a nice warm bunker with the vehicles all primed. They had jumper cables, the mighty batteries of the LAVs, and

warming units but Ryan still feared that many of the wags
would never start again once stopped.

The ice sheathing Highway 6 was as slick as glass and despite the engineering LAV crunching the path, sliding was
a problem and the convoy's speed was dangerously reduced.
The good news was the land was tolerably flat, they had already blazed their path through the wreckage, and any vehicle
that slid off course and even off the road was easily winched
back in line by the LAV. Everyone constantly threw wary
glances backward. There was never just one storm. They
swept across Canada in a brutal, marching succession. They
were best survived behind thick walls or underground with
roaring fires in every hearth.

The convoy rolled south. They didn't stop. Refueling was
done on the move.

It was noon when the 84 mm recoilless rifle round
punched through the engineering LAV's dozer blade. The
high-explosive–antitank shaped-charged warhead sent a lance
of superheated gas and molten metal shrieking through the
engine compartment. The driver had no time to scream as
his body was incinerated except for his head sticking up out
of the driver's hatch, and it rolled smoking down the side
armor. Six's leather leggings were smoking as he leaped from
the commander's hatch, jumping from the burning armored
vehicle as it slewed off the road. Half the convoy slammed
on the brakes and slid perilously on the ice in all directions.
Ryan downshifted, and sparks flew off both fenders as he
swerved and threaded between two hulks rather than crushing the wag in front of him. "J.B.! Return fire!"

"I see him!" the Armorer replied. The fighting LAV's
turret turned toward a stand of the giant, twisted bonsai trees.
Smoke from the recoiless's back blast rose into the frigid
air. The 25 mm blaster slammed on slow autofire. Whatever
mutation allowed them to survive the supercooling failed

as high-explosive incendiary rounds burst their trunks and leveled them. Two motorcycles burst from the grove, their nailed snow tires hurling rainbow prisming arcs of ice crystals behind them as their riders clawed for purchase and raced for the easy ice of the highway. J.B. slowly traversed the turret like the iron hand of fate. The 25 mm blaster popped once, and one motorcycle and its rider were blown to pieces. He kept traversing and suddenly the coax blaster snarled off a burst and sent the other bike and rider slewing sideways into a violent sleigh ride into the next copse of trees.

Six was up and shoved one of his riders off his bike and headed for the fallen. Tamara was on a bike and right behind him. The man rose and Ryan saw his flaming hair as he tried to push himself along with his arms alone. It was Red. Hunk shouted from the back of a wag. "Kagan! Kosha! Quinn! Man fetch!"

The giant poodles coursed across the intervening ground as Red tried to pull himself into some kind of cover among the trees.

Ryan turned to Krysty. "Take the wheel." The one-eyed man slid out of the cab and started walking as the convoy slowly reassembled itself. He hurried to the ambush sight and found the broken bodies of the recoilless team. Their limbs were at unnatural angles, their wounds frozen over and their faces smeared away into abstract art of blood, bone and glittering rime. The tube blaster was torn and bent. Ryan shrugged his buffalo robe up higher and walked on. The one he had heard described as Mace's number one sec man, Shorty, lay with his parts intermixed and steaming with the parts of his cycle.

Ryan snapped away his silver coin and walked on.

Red lay in the second copse of bent pines. His legs were as twisted as the trees. The giant dogs stood over him growling and snarling. Tamara and Six stood over him. Six nodded at

Ryan and turned his attention back to Red. "I see you wear the *voyageur, mon ami*." Red flinched as Six ripped it from around his neck. "Did you do your papa, proud?"

Red glared upward and said nothing.

"How did you earn it?" Six smiled without an ounce of warmth. "Worming the *Queen,* no?"

Red knew he was dead. There would be no mercy here. Between the dogs and Six, there was no happy ending. All that mattered now was how he met it. "Something like that."

"Now, you and I shall talk."

"I don't talk to Frenchmen." Red spit on the leg pinning him down. "Much less black ones."

Tamara removed her bayonet from her longblaster. "I'm gonna cut off his balls."

Six held up a restraining hand. "I would never send a man to his grave without his balls." Six bent, flipped Red's broken body over with childlike ease and seized him by his flaming red locks. "But his hair…"

Red screamed as his scalp came off.

"Now," Six said, "you will talk to this black Frenchman."

Ryan had leaned hard upon man and mutie to get information required for the survival of his friends, but he wasn't a torturer. He could mostly get what he wanted through fear and intimidation. Red was as tough as they came, and Six would have to be brutal to get what he needed from his enemy. Ryan left the little frozen stand of pines and walked back to the semi. Krysty leaned out of the cab smiling, "Hey, lover, you catch—"

Red screamed as Six did something.

"Get back in the cab," Ryan advised.

"What's going on?"

Ryan clambered into the cab and turned on one of the CDs of country music Krysty had taken from the bunker recce room. Some predark woman named Emmylou Harris sang with heartbreaking sadness. "The Canadians are working things out among themselves."

The convoy sat motionless for about twenty minutes. In the end, Red gave up everything. In the end, beneath Six's and Tamara's knives just about all Red kept were his balls. The pair walked back to the convoy stone-faced, with spattered blood on their clothes. Six angrily boomed out orders in French.

Ryan opened his door and leaned out to Tamara. "What happened?"

Her M-16 snapped up to cover Ryan and Krysty in the cab. "You just stand down, sex machine." The convoy instantly turned on the Deathlanders.

Doc had heard the orders in French and was appalled. "What is the meaning of this! Why, I..." He was quite befuddled to find his arms pinned behind his back by Patrice. J.B. and Mildred found blasters pointed at their heads. Six marched on grimly to the fighting LAV. Jak leaned his head out at the commotion and found Marie-Laure pointing her blaster in his face with her good hand. "What—"

Six's right hand hit Jak like a thunderbolt and dropped the young man like a bad habit. The sec leader stepped inside the troop cabin and Seriah screamed. Tamara's muzzle never wavered from Ryan's face. "You just sit tight."

Six walked out carrying a flailing and crying Seriah by her hair and the back of her belt. He shoved her down the ramp. Seriah tumbled onto the ice-sheathed road, sobbing. Six raised his voice and spoke in English. "She is the traitor." He glanced down at the weeping wrench in the snow and ice without an ounce of pity. "It is she who has been giving Mace Henning our position since we crossed the Ottawa."

"No!" she cried.

Her denial was cut off by Six's brutal boot to her ribs. Jak was starting to push himself up, and Marie-Laure put a foot between his shoulder blades and pushed him back down. "Stay down, Jak." Six gave Seriah another brutal boot.

Tamara whooped. "Stomp a mudhole in her, Six! Walk it dry and…" Tamara didn't so much take her eyes off Ryan, as slightly divide her attention. It was enough to find herself staring in amazement at the 9 mm blaster that had appeared like sleight of hand in her face. "Um, Six?"

Jak spun beneath Marie-Laure's boot and slammed his arm into the back of her knees. The rolling chop block left the sec woman facedown in the permafrost with Jak's blade at her throat.

"Six?" Ryan inquired in the sudden silence. "What's going on?"

"Seriah is the traitor. Red told me everything. She left them a Diefenbunker radio in Borden. As chief mechanic, she had access to the radios in both LAVs day and night, the knowledge to erase their logs, and to turn the suspicion onto me. She has betrayed our every step." Six stood implacably over the little woman. "Tell them. Tell everyone why you betrayed us."

Seriah stared at the frozen ground. "I'm a mutie."

Angry muttering rippled through the convoy.

Seriah's voice was a dead whisper. "So is the baby inside me."

Patrice spit on Seriah. "She's a mutie. She's a traitor."

Cyrielle stepped beside Six and looked down coldly at the broken woman. "Chill her."

"No," Ryan said.

Six slowly slid out his bowie knife. "My lady is right. Seriah is a traitor to Val-d'Or. She deserves death."

"The only reason she's a traitor is because Val-d'Or would've turned her and her baby out in the snow, and look what that bought you."

Cyrielle's face was unreadable. Six spent several moments glowering over this. "You want mercy for her?"

"At the moment I want to know what Mace's plan is."

"It is simple enough. He plans roadblocks," Six replied. "With the engineering LAV destroyed, he will delay us at every turn. Felling trees, using black powder to bring down bridges and leave ramps impassable. All will have to be cleared by hand, and at each one snipers, booby-traps or ambush."

It would be a war of attrition that Mace could very well win. Ryan considered the frozen landscape they were passing through. "How did he survive the hard freeze?"

"There is only one way to survive the freeze in the open. One must dig pits, deep ones, cover them with branches and set roaring fires within. The earth insulates, and channels the heat upward against the cold. It is risky, often the roof catches fire, sometimes the fire isn't hot enough to hold off the freeze or the roof is ripped off by storm, sometimes men smother in the smoke, and Mace must make an attempt to preserve his vehicles in a similar fashion without destroying them."

It was an ugly gamble for both sides, a running battle as both sides ran south before the storms.

Lady Cyrielle ignored Seriah for the moment. "We can go back to the Diefenbunker, winter there. Come forth in spring."

Six scowled at Seriah ferociously. "*Oui,* but Mace now has the entry codes. He could winter in the ruins of the hydroelectric plant above and bid his time until he decides to break in. Or he could just use his blasting powder to seal the bunker doors against us, lock us in, and come back for us with a new army and dig us out come the thaw."

Ryan gazed north. He couldn't see the next storm, but he could feel it out in the distance. "Mace doesn't want to try and survive too many more storms. He doesn't want to winter here, and he doesn't want to seal us in and hope we're still here next year. He's going to try to win, now, while we're out in the open."

Six was of the same mind. He looked at Ryan hopefully. "You have a plan?"

"Yeah, but not a good one."

"What do you propose?"

"Am I still in command?"

Six looked at Lady Cyrielle. Her eyes narrowed, but she nodded minutely.

Ryan looked at Seriah. "I need her to make it work."

"No," Six said.

"Then I leave, and I take her with me. Good luck getting to the lakes without the LAV, and good luck making it back to Val-d'Or without a mechanic."

Cyrielle put a hand on Six's arm. "The lives of my people are more important than her death." Cyrielle lifted her chin. "What do you propose?"

"We're going to force Mace to make a choice." Ryan looked to the big rig and its cargo. "The convoy, or the reactors."

"Mace!" Tag skidded breathlessly to the edge of the uncovered fire pit. The baron sat below on his campstool roasting a sausage and toasting a chunk of hard biscuit over the embers of the bonfire that nearly singed off his beard and eyebrows but had saved his life when the eye of the storm had swept over.

"Yeah?"

"The mechanic. She's made contact."

"What'd the little mutie bitch have to say this time?"

"She confirmed the engineering LAV's been knocked out." Tag's voice lowered respectfully. "She also confirmed Red and Shorty are dead. The fighting LAV blasted their position apart. Six still took their hair, and their *voyageurs*. He wears them proudly."

Mace smeared bear grease onto his biscuit and chewed meditatively. Shorty was an old friend but he had never been smart; and while he had never shown it, Mace had been pleased with his bastard son Red. Of course he had dozens of bastards, and he intended to make more, starting with Cyrielle Toulalan and One-Eye's flame-haired mutie. Red and Shorty had volunteered to earn their silver, and they'd earned it the hard way. Losing the 84 mm Carl Gustav was a genuine fucking shame. "You didn't run here just to tell me that."

"The convoy has split up, Mace."

Mace rose. "What?"

"Word is One-Eye took the rig and the reactors east off the 6. The rest of the convoy is still on course heading south to pick up the Trans-Canada."

Mace wolfed down his sausage and bread and hauled himself out of the pit. He looked at the ancient, plastic-paged map of Canada that Tag held. "Well now, that is interesting."

Thorpe walked up with Grizz in tow. Camp was already buzzing. "Is it true?"

"Seems that way," Mace admitted.

Thorpe shook his head. "Gotta be some kind of sacrifice play."

"Nah," Mace countered. "He knows we can't afford to split our forces. He's making us make a choice, and I don't see One-Eye running without nowhere to go."

Thorpe peered at the map. "Heading west? He's taking old roads. He'll be going slow. His only choice is to try and pick up the 8 south at Riverton, but he's too far north. We'll intercept him long before he can reach it."

A slow smile spread across Mace's face. Men looked

around in alarm as the baron threw back his head and laughed. "You know, Thorpey? Your problem is you think like a landed pirate."

Thorpe considered this for long simmering moments, but he couldn't see where this was going. "The lakes are frozen over. I *am* a landed pirate."

"That's just it!" Mace roared. His green eyes twinkled with a piratical gleam of his own. "The lakes are frozen over! He ain't heading for the 8! He's heading straight for the Winnipeg! Give him a two hundred klick run, frozen over and flat as glass!"

"He's gonna wag the lake? In that rig? Fully loaded?" Thorpe goggled at the idea. "Will the ice hold?"

Mace shook his head and admired the gall of it. "Mebbe, mebbe not, but rads, thunder and fallout, that Cyclops son of a bitch is gonna try it! And that leaves us with a pretty choice. We're running low on juice. We either make our move on the convoy, and have a showdown with Six, that fighting LAV and every last person makin' his chilling last stand, and that without the Carl Gustav mind you, or we risk everything, and try to catch One-Eye on his ice run, take the reactors and worry about the convoy and Cyrielle's cherry later."

Thorpe considered the choices. "So what do we do?"

Mace gave Thorpe a disappointed look. "The reactors are everything. Imagine your locks with 'lectricity and steam. Imagine old Luc Toulalan without the reactors and without a son. We'll build a year to two, consolidate our confederacy, and meanwhile let the old bastard grieve himself into his grave. When the French start fighting over the barony, we make our play. Right now, we get on our bikes and we burn for the Winnipeg."

Chapter Twenty-Eight

Lake Winnipeg

Ryan rolled the rig toward the ice. It had taken them an hour to find a flat spot where the semi could mount the frozen lake. The truck bed with its heavy, tarped and tied-down payload rocked dangerously as he drove in low gear over the rocky scrap of beach. The snow-chains bit as Ryan eased onto the lake surface in low gear, and suddenly he was on the smoothest road he'd ever traveled on. Despite the cold, Six stood in the gunner's hatch and scanned southward with his binoculars in the morning light. The Northern Lights reflected off the frozen lake and turned it pink. Ryan turned south, but he stayed close to the shoreline where he knew the icepack was solid all the way to the bottom.

The weight of their predark cargo made him nervous. Ryan upshifted and slowly pressed his accelerator pedal. The rig's manual said the maximum recommended speed with chains was 45 mph. Ryan kept the big rig crunching along at 35 mph. The weather was clear, too clear for his liking. The needle of the semi's aneroid barometer just kept falling. Some very big weather was heading their way, and soon.

Six stayed topside as lookout as they rumbled along. Mace's coldhearts were burning alcohol, and alcohol burned clean. His mob of sec riders wouldn't send up much smoke nor were they going to raise much dust in the winter-bound countryside, but he had scores of men mounted and there would be no way to conceal the sound of his engines. Six's fist thumped the top of the cab in answer to Ryan's thought. "Here they come!"

Ryan looked past Six's tree-trunk legs to the shore. He spied bikers through the trees. They paralleled the semi on the road that girded the lake. A great deal of what had once been lakefront property was now overgrown, and the bikers were clearly scouting for a route to get Mace's wags out onto the ice. They whooped as they spotted the semi and waved their blasters around their heads. Ryan shifted gears, pushed the pedal down and the accelerator needle climbed to 45 mph.

Four motorcycles crashed through the underbrush and jumped a berm to mount the ice, their riders intent on winning their silver coin from Mace. One spun out and slid fifty feet across the ice. The other three roared up behind the big rig. They whooped as Six slid down the hatch and surged forward to assault the cab. The whooping stopped as Six kicked open his door, hung out by one hand, spun his guide gun around on its lever and shot the lead biker out of the saddle. The other two jinked left to avoid the big man's longblaster.

"Wheel," Ryan said. He hit cruise control as Six swung back in and grabbed the wheel. The one-eyed man threw open his door with a SIG in hand. He double tapped one rider into cartwheeling oblivion. His accomplice shot away Ryan's side mirror. The Deathlands warrior shot away his face with three quick rounds, and the biker slid away leaving a red trail across the ice. Ryan slid back behind the wheel.

"They come!" Six shouted.

Mace and his coldhearts spilled onto Lake Winnipeg down an old concrete boat ramp ahead of them. Ryan swerved the semi out toward the middle of the lake. Few shots cracked out and none hit the semi. Mace wanted the reactors, and he needed the semi to haul them away. Ryan stepped on the accelerator. Several snow chains shrieked and snapped away from his tires. Mace and his men came on. The semi was like an elephant beset by a pack of lions. Bikers came in whirling grapnels on ropes and chains. Men perched perilously on the hoods, roofs and in the trunks of Mace's offroad wags in boarding parties.

"Now?" Six asked.

Ryan nodded. "Now."

Six stood in the gunner's hatch and yanked the ropes tied to the top. Two fifty-liter bladders of precious Diefenbunker diesel suddenly found themselves devoid of their chalks and tipped off the back of the truck bed. They burst like balloons and stained the ice black. Bikers spun out and dropped their bikes. Wags slewed out of control and the boarding men crouching on the hoods tumbled onto the unforgiving ice at 50 mph.

Ryan stepped on the gas. His needle climbed to 55 mph. More of his snow chains popped like shrapnel and the wheel felt greasy, slick and disconnected beneath Ryan's hand as his traction on the ice became tenuous at best. He was in the middle of the lake, and he had more than a thousand yards of distance to work with before he slid into an unforgiving shoreline. On the other hand the semi was loaded to tolerance, and beneath the ice thirty-six yards of black winter water waited to swallow all comers.

The horde of riders and wags had reassembled after swerving around the oil slick, and they came on to close and board the big rig. Ryan was out of countermeasures. It was time to get down to fighting. He clicked his com. "Now, J.B."

The Armorer had set charges in the cleats that held the tarp down over the semi's cargo and rigged them with Diefenbunker Omega remote detonators. The charges snapped and the wind tore the tarp away. Mace's mixed force of coldhearts and pirates swerved and braked in alarm. The semi wasn't carrying four cartridge nuclear reactors on its truck bed.

It was carrying a Canadian Land Forces LAV III.

The enemy swarm broke into desperate evasive action. The turret traversed under J.B.'s steady hand. Motorcycles at this range were hard to track. Mace's offroad wags less so. J.B. went wag hunting. High-explosive incendiary rounds sent wags spinning out and burning across the ice. They slammed into bikers, and flesh was ground between flaming steel and unyielding ice.

It ended a little too quickly for Ryan's liking.

The Bushmaster 25 mm cannon clacked open on empty and J.B.'s voice came across the link. "I'm out."

Ryan stepped on the gas. They were out of cannon shells, and the autoblaster on top of the LAV and the coax had been dismounted. So had the machine blaster on top of the semi. If Mace hadn't taken the bait, the convoy would need every machine blaster that was to be had to defend itself with the LAV gone. But Mace had taken the bait, and he was in a fine rage.

"He's empty!" Mace bellowed. "Take him down!"

The bike-riding coldhearts swarmed around the big rig and fired their blasters into Ryan's tires. They were pre-dark run-flats, but lethal doses of lead shattered the snow chains and chewed the rubber composite right off the wheel. Mace's coldhearts didn't care about saving the semi anymore, and they sent torrents of lead into the cab. The convoy had stripped the chicken armor off two of the sec wags and lined the semi's cab and the doors with it. Nevertheless the fusillade shattered all the windows, and some of the bullets sparked and whined as they ricocheted around the cab. Other coldhearts poured fire into the engine cowling. The semi began to make a disturbing clanking sound as lead began to fill her mighty steel heart.

Six crouched below the level of the window, and Ryan was slumped so low in his seat he was driving by keeping the floating compass ball on the dash aimed due south. A stray bullet stripped the compass away in a spatter of plastic.

"Now?" Six suggested.

Ryan grimaced as he gripped the wheel and held the accelerator down. "Wait for it."

J.B.'s voice came across the radio. "Now?"

"Wait for it, J.B.," Ryan said.

The semi's engine screamed. The tachometer spiked into the red line as the dying engine revved out of control. "They're on the truck bed," J.B. said. "They're pounding on my hull. Some are working their way toward the cab."

"Now?" Six suggested a little more urgently.

Something inside the semi's engine broke away and the tachometer and the speedometer needles fell. Ryan spoke into the link over the solid roar of blasterfire. "Now, J.B."

Inside the LAV J.B. pumped his detonator box a second time. The bullet-size charges of C-4 he had put in the buckles of the cargo straps snapped and popped like a string of firecrackers. The straps flew away. Some of the men holding on to them flew away, as well. The LAV bounced and rocked dangerously on its road wheels free of restraints.

"LAV is free," J.B reported. He punched his ignition and the LAV's diesel rumbled into life. "LAV is hot."

"Hunk! Tamara!" Ryan ordered.

The commander and driver's hatch on the LAV slammed open. Hunk and Tamara popped up and popped caps into the coldhearts and pirates still crowding the truck bed. The semi was slowing by the second. Letting it come to a stop was suicide.

J.B.'s voice grim. "Now or never!"

"On my mark!" Ryan let go the wheel and ghost-rode his wag. Six surged up the shotgun rider's hatch, and Ryan followed him with a SIG in each hand. Six worked his lever and pumped lead into pirate and coldheart alike. He roared in triumph as his last round smashed Thorpe from the back of the truck bed and toppled him to be ground beneath the wheels of his men, leaving a red smear on the ice.

"Now!" Tamara shouted. Six leaped from the top of the cab to the top deck of the LAV. Tamara snaked down the hatch, and Six vaulted onto the turret top, his huge frame squeezing down the hatch. Hunk waved frantically at Ryan. "C'mon!" Hunk dropped down to leave the hatch clear.

Ryan emptied his Diefenbunker SIGs into the enemies swarming around the semi and leaped for the LAV.

Mace Henning's war club spun through the air and slammed into Ryan's chest like a sledgehammer. The one-eyed man's boots hit the nose of the LAV, but his knees buckled and he fell hard to the truck bed between the cab and the LAV. The semi was a ghost truck hurtling driverless across the frozen lake. Mace Henning scooped up his club and pulled his knife with his other hand. More of his men leaped from their cycles onto the truck. Ryan's Scout longblaster was slung and he would never live to bring it to bear. He wasn't going to live to reach the LAV. "Gonna have my way with you, Cyclops," Mace said, leering. He raised his voice to the dozens of motorcycles surrounding the runaway semi and it rang with hatred. "Bring it down! Bring it down! Bring it down!"

Ryan rose. He left his panga and his knife in their sheaths. He clicked his com in his last act of defiance. "You heard him, J.B. Bring it down."

Within the LAV, J.B. pumped his detonator box the third and final time. He had put tiny charges in the tarp cleats and the loading strap buckles. The Armorer had put vastly larger, shaped charges beneath the cab and the truck bed, and he had shaped them to blast downward. The charges detonated. The explosions rippled into the ice beneath the truck and shattered it. Ryan felt himself born aloft as a section of truck bed blew upward beneath his feet like a blast plate elevator. The truck continued on beneath him over the cracking ice, and the truck bed suddenly tipped backward and splashed into the expanding ice fissure. Pirates and coldhearts spun out as the ice shattered under their tires and they disappeared beneath the frigid black water. Ryan's trajectory hit its apex and the section of truck bed fell out beneath him. The truck bed sank into the fissure and pulled the cab back across the crumbling ice and dragged it down into the depths. The LAV was buttoned up and her wheels and aquatic propellers hot. As the semi sank, the LAV bobbed free on the still water.

The cold hit Ryan like a fist to the jaw as he plunged beneath the surface.

Beneath him he saw pirates, coldhearts and motorcycles sinking into the depths. Mace Henning clawed and screamed and blew bubbles below as he went down, down, down into the dark. In a country whose waters were swarming with giant lampreys and lake monsters, he, like many Canadians, considered learning to swim suicidal. But the giant, stiff, loglike lengths of lampreys watched the sinking swarm dully with eyes too stunned by hibernation beneath the ice to do anything about the feast falling into the depths all around them.

Ryan kicked upward as his limbs tried to contract with cold. His body went from burning to numb almost instantly. He broke the surface with an enfeebled dog paddle and knew there would be no going down for the second or third time. Hunk's voice shouted out a welcome refrain.

"Kagan! Kosha! Quinn! Man in the water! Lamprey! Lamprey! Lamprey!"

The giant, superinsulated canines leaped from the top deck of the LAV into the water. Ryan's limbs stopped obeying him and he started to sink, but teeth seized his blaster sling, belt and a huge mouthful of his hair to keep his head above the water. Ryan went from numb to a very dangerous feeling of being warm as he was towed toward the floating armored vehicle. J.B., Six, Hunk and Tamara were shouting and waving their arms in encouragement.

Ryan had his last coherent thought before he closed his eyes.

These dogs deserve steak....

Chapter Twenty-Nine

Ryan survived his hypothermia. It was a near thing. It had taken the LAV most of the day to crawl back across the breaking ice and reach shore, and another forty-eight hours at breakneck speed west to reach the Shilo Diefenbunker. Mildred's medicine had dealt with most of the damage the cold had done to Ryan. Krysty's red-hot ministrations had brought Ryan back to life. They were snug as superstorm after superstorm racked and supercooled the world above.

The Shilo Diefenbunker also had a mat-trans unit.

On the seventh day beneath the ground Ryan felt his old strength in his bones and quietly told his people to start packing up. He didn't want arguments, temptations, tearful goodbyes or festering recriminations. He and his companions were just going to pull a fade. Ryan lurked behind to make sure no one took notice. He walked into the warehouse room with his buffalo robe around his shoulders. Beyond the warehouse, stairs led down to the mat-trans. Six, Cyrielle and their people still had no idea what they represented. Ryan limped up to a cartridge reactor and ran his hand down its smooth steel side. It would have been something to wag the power supply south and present it to his nephew in Front Royal. But even with a LAV to pull it and defend it, it would be a suicide run, and his people had no desire to spend months in the bowels of the Manitoban Diefenbunker waiting for the thaw.

Ryan sensed Six behind him but waited for him to speak.

"So. You leave."

Ryan turned. "Yeah."

"I wish you were staying."

"I know."

"I wish you would come to Val-d'Or. It is something to see, and I could use you and your people during the fight for the succession."

"It doesn't have to come to that."

Six cocked his head. "What do you mean?"

Ryan looked at Six like he was a feeb. "Simple enough."

The huge brown eyes narrowed. "And how is that?"

"You become baron. You said the old man loves you. So did Cyrielle, Yoann and others. It makes perfect sense."

Six gave Ryan a very sad smile. "It is very kind of you to suggest it, but the laws of Val-d'Or are quite specific. To be the baron of Val-d'Or, you must have been born in Val-d'Or. I was a wanderer, a free blaster. Other than that it occurred in Canada, I do not know where I was born, nor do I know who my father was."

Ryan shrugged again. "Still seems simple enough."

Six's brief, uncharacteristic sadness returned to its more usual "storms a-brewin'" countenance. "And just what do you mean by that?"

"Marry the Lady Cyrielle."

Six's huge knuckles creaked into fists. For a moment Ryan thought there might be violence. "Fool! I told you! The baron of Val-d'Or must—"

Ryan took a big step forward and shouted the big man down. "Marry Cyrielle, and the baron of Val-d'Or, Luc Toulalan, declares you regent!"

Six actually backed up a step.

"Until *your* son, born in Val-d'Or and of the Lady Cyrielle, is old enough to become baron!"

It was the first time Ryan had ever seen Six dumbstruck.

"It isn't unheard of," Ryan relented. "You can have the LAV. Consider it a wedding present."

Six opened his mouth and closed it.

Ryan shrugged. "My advice? You got four reactors. Give a reactor to Mr. Smythe on the *Queen* as agreed, keep one for yourself and Val-d'Or, give one to Hunk and Manitoulin, and one to Jon Hard-knife and the First Nations. That'd be a good start on Yoann's dream of a new Canada. Oh, and make Blacktree your head sec man. You're going to be busy, and you're going to want someone who scares the shit out of people."

Six's fists fell open at his sides. "And you want nothing? You don't want to winter here? You don't claim a reactor? You give us the LAV?"

"My people don't want to stay holed up for months, and wagging a reactor south?" Ryan seized on a Doc-worthy word. "It's problematic. Our bags are packed and our mags are full. We're fine."

"Nothing?" Six protested.

"Something," Ryan answered.

"Name it."

Ryan's voice went cold. "Change your fucking mutie policy. It's brought you nothing but grief, and me and mine won't ever come to Val-d'Or until you do."

"That would grieve me sore, Ryan." Six nodded slowly. "If I am made regent, it will be done."

Ryan's voice stayed hard. "Seriah likes Jak, but she doesn't want to wander the Deathlands. She wants to go home. She wants to raise her kid and fix wags in Val-d'Or."

"Anyone who wishes to revenge themselves upon Seriah or her child—" Six pulled himself up to his full height "—will find that road long, hard, fraught with peril, and that it lies through me."

Ryan held out his hand. "You're a good man, Six."

Six's palm slammed into Ryan's. "As are you."

Ryan released Six's hand and turned to leave.

Six spoke warily. "The chamber of glass?"

Ryan saw no reason to lie to a fellow warrior. "Yeah."

Six shook his head. "What happens?"

"The day you don't care where you go or what happens, step inside and throw the lever to shut the door."

Six grinned to show his gold and silver teeth. "I must get Cyrielle and Marie-Laure pregnant, and I have a ville to preside over. I have no time for sight-seeing."

"Good thinking."

Six nodded. "Ryan, remember you have friends in the north."

"I will."

"Ryan?"

"What?"

Six regarded Ryan warily. "May I embrace you?"

Ryan considered the giant black warrior in front of him. "No fucking way."

Six threw back his head and laughed. *"Bon chance."*

Ryan turned to the stairs. Below his friends were sitting on the mat-trans pad waiting for him. "Good luck."

* * * * *

TAKE 'EM FREE
2 action-packed novels plus a mystery bonus

NO RISK
NO OBLIGATION TO BUY

James Axler
Outlanders®

DRAGON CITY

**A vengeful enemy plots
a horrifying new assault on humanity.**

A cruel alien race, the Annunaki, has been reborn in a new and more horrifying form. Enlil, cruelest of them all, is set to revive the sadistic pantheon that will rule the Earth. Based in his Dragon City, Enlil plans to create infinite gods—at the cost of humankind. With the Cerberus team at its lowest ebb, can they possibly stop his twisted plan?

Available May wherever books are sold.